*In*
# Firefly Valley

## Books by Amanda Cabot

### TEXAS DREAMS

*Paper Roses*

*Scattered Petals*

*Tomorrow's Garden*

### WESTWARD WINDS

*Summer of Promise*

*Waiting for Spring*

*With Autumn's Return*

### TEXAS CROSSROADS

*At Bluebonnet Lake*

*In Firefly Valley*

*Christmas Roses*

*One Little Word: A Sincerely Yours Novella*

# In Firefly Valley

A Novel

## Amanda Cabot

Revell

a division of Baker Publishing Group
Grand Rapids, Michigan

© 2015 by Amanda Cabot

Published by Revell
a division of Baker Publishing Group
P.O. Box 6287, Grand Rapids, MI 49516-6287
www.revellbooks.com

Printed in the United States of America

Library of Congress Cataloging-in-Publication Data
Cabot, Amanda, 1948–
    In Firefly Valley : a novel / Amanda Cabot.
        pages ; cm. — (Texas crossroads ; #2)
    ISBN 978-0-8007-3435-0 (softcover)
    1. Life change events—Fiction. 2. Mistaken identity—Fiction. 3. Resorts—Fiction. I. Title.
PS3603.A35I5  2015
813'.6—dc23                                                    2014044363

15  16  17  18  19  20  21        7  6  5  4  3  2  1

For Martha Long,
whose emails, Smileboxes,
and special snail mails
have brightened so many days.
Thank you!

# 1

It wasn't the homecoming of her dreams. When she'd pictured this moment, Marisa St. George had imagined herself riding in a shiny new Lexus. She'd be wearing a designer dress and sporting an impressive diamond on her left hand, while her tall, dark, and handsome husband smiled at her as if she were the most beautiful woman in the world. Instead she was driving an ordinary white sedan with more than its share of dents and a loud rattle that the previous owner had assured her wasn't serious. Her clothes were as ordinary as the car, and the diamond ring and doting husband were as much a figment of her imagination as the luxury car and expensive clothing.

The car clanked again, reminding Marisa she was no longer a rising star at a prestigious Atlanta accounting firm but was back in the town she'd been so eager to flee and headed for a job that was definitely not part of her career plan.

*Think of something positive*, she admonished herself. She glanced at the sign marking the entrance to town and nodded. It still said "Welcome to Dupree, the Heart of the Hills," reminding passing motorists that they were in Texas's famed Hill Country, but the sagging wooden post that had turned it into a Texas version of the Leaning Tower of Pisa had been replaced by two perfectly straight shiny metal poles. The sign itself was freshly painted, a nice improvement over the faded and peeling greeting Marisa had seen the last time she'd been here.

Maybe it wasn't just wishful thinking. Maybe Mom and Lauren were right when they said Dupree was changing. Marisa hoped that was the case. The town needed a boost, and so did her mother and her best friend. Being with them again was the one good thing to come out of all that had happened this year.

Marisa was smiling as she turned onto Hickory Street and pulled into the driveway of what had once felt like her second home. Her smile turned into a grin as a seven-year-old dynamo launched herself from the porch, her dark brown braids bouncing against her shoulders as she ran, and her socks—one purple, the other an unfortunate shade of puce—sagging around her ankles.

"Aunt Marisa, I thought you'd never get here," the young girl announced, throwing her arms around Marisa. "Mom baked brownies, and she wouldn't let me have any until you came. But now you're here, and we can eat. So, hurry up." Fiona turned, raced up the steps, and flung the front door open. "Come on. You've got to hurry."

Marisa rubbed her stomach, smiling at the girl who'd made her an honorary aunt. "It just so happens that I'm extra hungry. I might have to eat all the brownies," she teased.

"You wouldn't." A stomp accompanied Fiona's words, and her smile turned into a pout. That wasn't normal. The last time Marisa had video called Fiona, she'd seemed to enjoy a little teasing.

"Don't get her started," Lauren called from the doorway. "She threw a fit this morning and yelled so loudly I thought the neighbors might call Child Services."

"All because you wouldn't let her have a brownie?" Marisa asked as she hugged her friend, holding on a second longer than normal when she sensed that Lauren needed comfort.

The woman who'd been her best friend since grade school was the same height as Marisa—an inch over five and a half feet. When they were growing up, no one would have mistaken them for sisters, but thanks to L'Oreal, Marisa's once-blonde hair was now the same dark brown as Lauren's, and colored contacts had transformed her blue eyes to a shade of brown only slightly lighter than Lauren's chocolate brown. Now the most striking difference between the two women was that Lauren was thin enough to be called skinny, whereas Marisa's weight was well within the normal range.

"What's wrong?" Marisa asked.

Turning to her daughter, Lauren laid her hand on the child's head, giving her a loving pat. "Why don't you pour yourself some milk and get Aunt Marisa a glass of tea? We'll be there in a minute."

When Fiona scampered off to the kitchen, Lauren shrugged and gestured toward the stack of boxes that filled one corner of the living room. Like the rest of the house, this room had changed little since Lauren had lived here as a child. When she and Patrick had inherited it after her parents' deaths, they'd planned to renovate but had never had enough money to turn plans into reality, and so the house retained what Lauren called shabby chic décor.

"Fiona's upset because I'm cleaning out Patrick's belongings. She saw me folding clothes and started wailing."

"Oh, Lauren." Marisa gave her friend another hug. "You should have waited until I arrived. I could have distracted her."

"I didn't expect that reaction. She doesn't talk about Patrick very often anymore. Now she's focused on wanting a new daddy."

"I thought you'd resolved that. I saw her socks." Earlier that year, when Fiona had been playing matchmaker for her mother, they'd struck an agreement. Fiona could choose her own socks—even on Sunday—and she'd let her mother choose a man to replace Patrick.

Not that anyone could do that. From the day Patrick Ahrens had walked into Dupree High and set eyes on Lauren Manning, everyone had known they were meant for each other. They'd married the day after Lauren graduated and had lived what had appeared to be a fairy-tale marriage until Patrick was diagnosed with leukemia. Now Lauren was a young widow, trying to rebuild her life in a town where single mothers were uncommon.

Lauren's lips curved into a smile. "Those socks. You couldn't miss them, could you? Unfortunately, when we made our agreement, I didn't stipulate that she couldn't whine about how much she wants a new daddy."

Marisa couldn't help laughing. "That sounds like hairsplitting to me. Do you suppose you have a future lawyer on your hands?"

"Heaven forbid. Fiona already tries to outtalk me. Imagine if she were trained!" Lauren laid her hand on the back of Marisa's waist and pushed her toward the kitchen door. "I can't vouch for the brownies' safety if we don't get in there."

The brownies proved to be as delicious as they smelled. Once Fiona had devoured two, she regained her normal sweetness and announced that it was time to play with Alice. As if on cue, the doorbell rang.

"Alice has a baby brother," Fiona announced as she jumped up from the table, giving her mother a look that told Marisa this was another point of contention. Lauren merely sighed.

"So she wants siblings as well as a father?" Marisa asked when Fiona had left.

"And a dog. I think Alice is behind that one. Every time she's here, she tells me we're lucky to have a backyard."

"I gather that she doesn't."

Lauren shook her head. "The Kozinskis live in Hickory View," she said, referring to Dupree's only apartment complex. "No pets."

"So, is Fiona going to get a puppy for Christmas?"

Wrinkling her nose, Lauren broke off a piece of brownie. "I'm not sure. Of course, if you promise to clean up after it and do all the training . . ." She popped the brownie into her mouth.

"In your dreams."

"Some friend you are." When Marisa refused another brownie, Lauren's expression sobered. "I'm really sorry you lost your job and that Trent turned out to be such a scoundrel, but I'd be lying if I said I was sorry you're back home. I've missed you so much."

"And I've missed you." Seeing the moisture beginning to pool in Lauren's eyes, Marisa decided they both needed a change of subject.

She glanced at her watch. "Mom's not expecting me for an hour. Can I help you do some more sorting and packing?"

"Sure." Lauren sounded grateful, although Marisa wasn't certain whether it was for the change of subject or the offer of help. When they were back in the living room, Lauren pointed to one of a set of two matched bookcases. "That one's filled with Patrick's books. I know I won't read them, so I might as well find them a new home." She handed Marisa two empty boxes, then disappeared for a moment, returning with a pile of her late husband's clothing.

Marisa heard her friend's quick intake of breath. It couldn't be easy, disposing of a loved one's belongings. As far as Marisa knew, her mother hadn't given away her father's clothes, even though it had been more than eight years since anyone in Dupree had seen Eric St. George. Eight years, three months, and . . .

Marisa shook herself mentally. There was nothing to be gained by counting, just as nothing would be gained by continuing to search. She'd done everything she could to find her father, and she'd failed. It was time—well past time—to admit that she would never have the answers she sought.

"What can you tell me about my new employers?" Marisa asked, hoping to distract both herself and Lauren. This was the first time she had taken a job without an in-person interview. Although she was familiar with Rainbow's End, since her mother had been employed at the resort for over seven years, Marisa's only contact with the new owners had been by phone.

"Greg and Kate?"

Marisa nodded. "According to my mother, they practically walk on water. I wanted a less biased opinion."

Lauren turned a jeans pocket inside out, checking for anything Patrick might have left. "Greg and Kate are probably the best thing to happen to Dupree in this century. Kate's a former advertising whiz, and Greg made more money than I can even imagine with his software company."

As Marisa placed three more books in the first box, she heard the smile in Lauren's voice as she continued. "It had to be a God thing that they both came to Rainbow's End at the same time, fell in love, and decided to revive the resort. No one in Dupree wants to admit it, but you've been there, so you know I'm not exaggerating when I say the place was on its last legs. It wasn't helping the town much, but if it had closed, it would have been another blow to our economy."

Though she didn't say it, Marisa knew that the resort's closure would have impacted Lauren's livelihood.

"How is HCP doing?" Although officially named Hill Country Pieces, Lauren and Marisa always referred to the quilt shop by its initials.

"Better than I dreamed possible." Lauren's grin underscored her words. "I had my best Labor Day ever yesterday. That's why I was able to close this afternoon. Best of all, Kate has commissioned a quilt for every bed at Rainbow's End, and that's in addition to the ones she wants as wall hangings for the dining room."

"Fabulous." Marisa was thrilled that her friend was doing so well. If anyone deserved good fortune, Lauren did.

"It is fabulous," Lauren agreed. "I no longer have to worry about paying bills. Now my biggest worry is sidestepping the Matchers."

"The Matchers?" Marisa wasn't aware of anyone in town with that name.

Lauren chuckled. "That's my abbreviation for the matchmakers. You remember Amelia, Debra, and Edie," she said, naming three of the older women who attended her church. "They've made it their mission to ensure there are no single women in Dupree." Lauren folded another pair of jeans and laid them carefully in the box, then looked up at Marisa and grinned. "That's one of the reasons I'm so glad you're back in town: they'll have a new target."

"I hope they're prepared for failure." Though her dreams included a husband and children, Marisa knew she was not ready for either. She needed more time to heal. After plunking two more books into the box, she grabbed the cover, thankful that Lauren was using bankers' boxes with separate covers and cutouts for handles. That would make carrying the decidedly heavy boxes easier. "This is just a temporary stage—one year, no more." If she was very careful, she'd be able to replenish her bank account, and with some luck, the job market would improve.

"You might change your mind. Dupree's not so bad."

But working at a small resort in a small town was not what Marisa had in mind when she'd studied so hard for the CPA exam. She wanted big city lights and large corporate clients. Now was not the time to say that. Instead, she pulled a couple books from the next shelf and glanced at the first cover.

"Ken Blake," she said, not bothering to hide her disgust. "I'm surprised Patrick would buy books like that." Marisa had read one, curious about what had intrigued so many people. One was more than enough.

Lauren took a quick look at the book that was causing Marisa such distress. "Oh, those. Patrick said they kept his mind off the cancer."

"With a hero who's a heavy drinker and breaks just about every commandment? There had to have been a better diversion." Though Marisa wanted to toss the book into the wastebasket, she laid it in the box destined for the library's sale shelf.

"Don't you think you're overreacting just a bit?" Lauren said. "I understand where you're coming from, with your dad and all, but Patrick said the hero is like a modern Superman who always defeats the bad guys."

Marisa shook her head. She picked up another of Ken Blake's thrillers and pointed to the back cover. Instead of the typical photo of an author's smiling face, this one featured the back of a man wearing a Stetson and a khaki trench coat. He was turned in such a way that there wasn't even the slightest hint of a profile.

"If his characters are so good, why won't he show his face?"

———— ✳ ————

He had no idea why it had happened. Blake Kendall paced the office that bore his name along with the string of initials he'd acquired as a financial consultant. Door to window, window to door. It did no good. The muse that had served him so faithfully for close to a decade, the same muse that had propelled his books to the top of the national bestseller lists, spawned a series of blockbuster movies, and made his name—correction, his pseudonym—a household word, had vanished, leaving him with a seemingly incurable case of writer's block.

He poured himself another cup of coffee. Perhaps an infusion of caffeine would help. When he'd drained half the cup, Blake settled back in the chair whose superb ergonomics ensured that he never suffered from back pain or excessive fatigue and positioned his hands over the keyboard. Nothing. Not even a glimmer of an idea. Why had he expected anything different?

He hadn't worried the first day. After all, everyone had bad days. But as the days turned to weeks, Blake had begun to wonder whether he would ever be able to write again. The inspiration well that had once required only light priming was now bone dry. He emptied the coffee cup and rose. There had to be something he could do.

After taking three long strides, he stood next to the window with its million-dollar view of the Golden Gate Bridge and San Francisco Bay. The sight never failed to stir him, and it did not disappoint today. He could wax eloquent over the beauty of his adopted hometown. Perhaps he ought to begin writing tourist brochures, since it was clear that that was all he could do today. But tourist brochures were not what readers expected from Ken Blake. They wanted another thriller. They wanted to know what disaster Cliff Pearson would encounter, what clever way he would find to foil the evildoers. Unfortunately, Cliff Pearson's next adventure was nothing more than a blank sheet of paper, all because Blake's creativity was locked up tighter than Alcatraz's prisoners used to be.

Caffeine, walking, staring. Nothing was working. He had to find another stimulus. Blake sank into his chair and opened the file drawer on the right side of his desk. He didn't expect to find inspiration there. That drawer held the files of his few remaining investment clients. While those clients provided a modest but steady source of income, he knew nothing in the files would trigger ideas for a new book.

He fingered the folders, stopping when he reached the last one. Vange, Gregory. The image of his former college roommate flashed before him. Maybe Greg was the answer. A glance at his watch told Blake he had enough time to get to Greg's office before noon. Why not?

He picked up the phone. "Greg Vange, please," he said when the receptionist answered. With some luck, Greg would be free. If not, they could meet for an early dinner. Blake didn't delude himself into believing that his friend and client would have any ideas for the next foe Cliff would defeat, but perhaps all Blake needed was a change of scenery and a bit of friendly conversation.

"I'm sorry, sir. Mr. Vange is no longer with Sys=Simpl."

He blinked in surprise. Had the earth suddenly stopped rotating around the sun? Sys=Simpl was the company Greg had founded when they'd still been at Stanford. Surely nothing less than an earthshaking event would have caused him to leave.

"Are you certain?"

"Yes, sir."

Sensing that she would not provide details, Blake asked for Drew Carroll, Greg's former partner and another of Blake's college friends.

"Hey, Drew, it's Blake," he said when they were connected. "I was trying to get ahold of Greg. The woman who answered the phone said he doesn't work there anymore."

"It's true." The unexpected terseness in Drew's voice made Blake suspect there was much he wanted to say but couldn't. "We sold the company, and Greg left."

Without telling Blake. That was almost as odd as the fact that Greg had abandoned Sys=Simpl. Though they saw each other only a couple times a year, Blake and Greg usually talked every quarter when Greg asked for a review of his investments.

Blake pulled out the file and frowned. They'd missed their second quarter review. How had he not noticed that? His frown deepened as he realized that the MIA muse had affected more than his writing.

"Where is he now?"

"I'm not sure." This time there was no question. Drew was angry. "The last I knew, he was at the most pathetic excuse for a resort I've ever seen."

That didn't sound like Greg. As far as Blake knew, he'd never taken a vacation. But then, Blake wouldn't have predicted that Greg would sell his firm. It had been his brainchild and, at least from what Blake had seen, the most important part of his life.

"Is the resort on the coast?" If so, perhaps Blake still had time to find Greg today.

"Nope. He was in the Texas Hill Country, if you can believe that. I haven't heard from him since Easter, but I can give you his cell number if you don't have it." Blake heard a keyboard clacking and realized Drew was searching for the number. "I've got to warn you, though. There's no cell service there, so you'll probably get voice mail."

Greg Vange, the man who believed in being connected 24/7, living in a place with no cell service. The story became stranger by the minute. "Do you remember the name of the resort?" Presumably they'd have a landline.

"Rainbow something. Trust me, Blake, you don't want to go there."

But Blake wanted to talk to Greg. The urge he'd felt when he looked at the file had intensified. His friend had made a life-changing decision. Drew might not understand, but Blake wanted to find out what had happened and why.

Drew was right. The call to Greg's cell went to voice mail, but a quick Google search revealed a resort in the Texas Hill Country called Rainbow's End. It had to be the one.

"I'm trying to reach Greg Vange," Blake said when a teenager answered the phone. "Is he by any chance still a guest?"

"Not exactly." Blake heard a peal of laughter in the distance as the girl called out, "Greg! Phone for you."

A second later, a familiar voice said, "Greg Vange speaking. How can I help you?"

"Blake Kendall here." He matched his friend's formality, then chuckled, more relieved than he'd expected that he'd been able to reach Greg. "What on earth are you doing in Texas?"

"You won't believe it." Greg took a deep breath and exhaled slowly in a technique Blake had seen him use when he wanted to increase the suspense. "You'd better sit down for this. Ready?" When Blake assured him that he was prepared for whatever Greg was going to send his way, Greg said, "I bought a resort, and I'm getting married in four days and three hours."

Though he'd been leaning back in his chair, Blake bolted upright. "You what?" He'd never thought Greg would leave his company, but to buy a run-down resort in the middle of Texas was even more incomprehensible. And then there was the almost casual announcement that he was getting married . . . this Saturday. To the best of Blake's knowledge, Greg had never dated seriously. He'd been too busy making Sys=Simpl one of the most successful companies of its kind to have time for dating and falling in love.

Though he felt like the world had indeed spun off its axis, Blake knew he owed his friend a response. "It seems congratulations are in order."

"Thanks, pal." If Greg heard the shock in Blake's voice, he gave no sign. "It all happened pretty fast. Now, what can I do for you?"

"I was hoping to buy you lunch, but I guess that won't happen unless . . ." The appeal of sitting down with Greg, even if it was only for a couple hours, to learn what had caused him to reinvent his life continued to grow. "You say you own a resort. Any chance you have a room for an old buddy?"

The hesitation, though only momentary, told Blake his question was unexpected. "We're in the middle of renovations. The grand opening is in a month."

"I can't wait a month." Seeing Greg wasn't guaranteed to break through his writer's block, but Blake had to try. And, though he hadn't thought it possible, he found himself excited by the prospect of visiting the Hill Country. It was supposed to be beautiful and very different from California. Perhaps that was what he needed to jump-start his imagination. "Can you recommend someplace else?"

Greg did not hesitate. "Carmen will probably kill me for this, but you can have my cabin starting Saturday. Kate and I'll be on our honeymoon for two weeks, and we're moving into the owners' suite when we return." Greg chuckled. "In case you were wondering, Carmen's our cook, and Kate is the wonderful woman who agreed to take a chance on me." The happiness radiating from his voice left no doubt that whatever had happened to Greg at Rainbow's End, it had been good.

"Are you sure?"

"Yeah. Something tells me you need Rainbow's End right now."

Blake did indeed. After he'd gotten directions to Greg's new home and made his plane reservations, he called Drew.

"Why didn't you tell me?" he demanded when Drew answered.

"Tell you what?"

"That Greg's getting married. I thought he was a confirmed bachelor like me." Drew had always been one step from the altar, but Greg and Blake had, for different reasons, steered clear of matrimony.

"So he's really doing it. This is something I've got to see."

"Me too."

2

Mom was right. The place had changed. Marisa braked to make the right turn into Rainbow's End. The last time she'd been here, everything from the sign on the front gate to the cabins had been dilapidated. Now the wrought iron was freshly painted, and the gate boasted a new sign. Like the old one, it featured a rainbow with Noah's ark replacing the fabled pot of gold at its end, but now, instead of animals peering from the windows, the ark bore a heart with a cross in its center. It had new lettering too, the crisp font proclaiming that this was Rainbow's End, the Heart and Soul of the Hill Country.

Marisa smiled at what had to have been Kate's work. Mom had described her as a hotshot advertising exec. Though Marisa had no idea what other work Kate had done, this was inspired. Marisa admired the choice of a tagline that linked the resort to Dupree, which proclaimed itself the Heart of the Hills, at the same time that it left no doubt of Rainbow's End's Christian focus. With a single image and a few words, Kate had captured the essence of the resort. If the entrance was any indication, Rainbow's End had indeed changed and for the better now that Kate Sherwood and Greg Vange were running it.

Marisa's smile broadened as she drove toward the resort's office, noting that her car no longer bumped and jolted as it had on previous visits. Perhaps being back here wouldn't be as bad as she'd expected. The road was now smooth and surfaced with gravel. Not ordinary gravel, either, but costly multicolored stones. It appeared that Kate and Greg were taking the rainbow theme seriously.

Though the oaks and cypresses that lined the entrance road hadn't changed, the Tyrolean-style building that housed the office sported new paint, and the live plants in its window boxes were a definite improvement over the faded plastic ones the last owners had chosen. The source of all the changes was readily evident in the number of trucks parked near the office and the bevy of workers practically swarming the grounds. It appeared that when Greg and Kate did something, they spared no expense. Her own salary was proof of that. While less than she'd earned in Atlanta, it was more than generous for the work she was expected to perform here. As Kate had said when she'd hired her, Marisa was overqualified for the position. Overqualified and, although Marisa would never admit it to Kate, desperate.

"I'm glad you're here," Olivia, the teenager who was manning the front desk, said when she greeted Marisa. She made a face at the computer screen. "We need all the help we can get, especially with this dinosaur."

"I'm sure you're doing fine."

Olivia's lip curled in disgust. "That makes one of us. This reservation system is impossible. People tell me they've been here before, and they want the same cabin they had the last time, but I can't find the records. I don't want to disappoint anyone, but what can I do? I can't manufacture something that's not there."

Marisa tried not to frown. From all accounts, Greg was a software genius. Surely he could have found a better system for Rainbow's End. "I'll see what I can do." Part of her agreement with him and Kate had been that as business manager, Marisa would handle the computer systems. It sounded as if that was going to be more of a challenge than she'd expected. But perhaps that was good.

There was nothing worse than boredom. She'd had a lifetime's worth of that during the past four months.

"I'd better see my mom," she told Olivia, filing a mental note to spend some time experimenting with the reservation system.

"Yes, you'd better. If she finds out that I waylaid you here, she will cut me off from dessert tonight." With a faux shudder, Olivia grinned. "That's a fate worse than death."

It was only a mild exaggeration. Carmen St. George's meals were the one thing about Rainbow's End that everyone agreed needed no improvement. Growing up, Marisa hadn't realized how fortunate she was to have superbly cooked meals and had never dreamt that her mother's culinary skills would finance her college education, but for the past seven and a half years, feeding Rainbow's End's guests had provided Mom's only source of income. And though Mom had earned only a modest wage, she'd done everything she could to ensure that Marisa did not need a college loan. Between Mom's contribution, two scholarships, and her own part-time jobs, Marisa had come out of college debt-free.

She entered the well-appointed industrial kitchen and called out to her mother, who was busily chopping parsley. From this perspective, Mom looked the same as she had when Marisa had spent Christmas with her. Her dark brown hair, pulled back into a severe bun, revealed no threads of gray. Since Mom was only fifty-three, that sign of aging should be a few years away yet, but Marisa had long suspected that the trials her mother had endured would result in premature graying. It was a relief to see that it hadn't occurred yet. Today Mom was clad in the Rainbow's End uniform of navy polo and khaki pants, with a blue gingham apron added in deference to her role.

"Marisa, *mi hija*!" She spun around, a huge smile and open arms accompanying her greeting. Marisa returned the smile as she ran into her mother's arms, knowing that Mom lapsed into her native language only when she was excited. Marisa might not be thrilled by her return to Dupree, but there was no doubt that her mother was.

"I'm so glad you're here." Mom used the same words Olivia had, only with far more intensity. After another quick hug, she held Marisa at arm's length and studied her. "Look at you. You haven't been eating well." That, too, was a familiar refrain. Just because Marisa wasn't short and plump like her mother didn't mean she was on the verge of starvation. She'd been short of funds in Atlanta, but never to the extent of not eating.

"I'm perfectly healthy." Marisa performed her own inspection. The lines that had bracketed Mom's mouth for as long as Marisa could recall had deepened, but her brown eyes were filled with happiness.

Her mother shook her head and drew herself up to her full five feet two inches, the precursor to another pronouncement. "You need more padding on those bones."

"Mom! I'm here to work, not get fat." And if she'd been able to find a job anywhere else, she wouldn't even be here.

"I know. I know." Mom gave Marisa another hug. "It's just that having you here is the answer to prayer. Now, let's get you settled in the cabin. Then I'll introduce you to Kate and Greg. You couldn't ask for nicer bosses. They're wonderful."

Marisa had thought her last bosses were wonderful too, until the day they announced the elimination of both her job and the bonus she'd been counting on to pay off her debts. She hoped Kate and Greg treated their employees better than that, especially since both she and Mom depended on them.

Recognizing the futility of arguing that she could do it herself, Marisa led her mother to her car and grabbed the largest suitcase from the trunk.

"This is all you brought?" Mom frowned. "I thought you'd have a rental truck."

Marisa shook her head. "I sold the furniture."

It hadn't been worth much anyway. Other than the expensive suits that she'd needed to impress clients, Marisa had lived frugally, saving her money for the search for her father. And then she'd lost it all to a sweet-talking con man named Trent, who'd assured her that he had sources the other investigators she'd hired did not. A month after Trent had disappeared with Marisa's savings, she'd lost her job. The rest was history.

"I never liked that furniture anyway," Mom said as she led the way up the three steps to the fieldstone cabin that had been her home for as long as she'd worked at Rainbow's End. Though the other cabins were arranged in clusters, this one sat alone and was closer to the road than the others. Marisa had always wondered whether the solitary location was the reason the former owners had offered it to her mother, but Mom liked it and pointed out that as the only cabin with a kitchen, it was the one best suited for a permanent residence. "That chrome and leather might be stylish, but it's not your style, any more than that dark hair is."

There was nothing to be gained by telling Mom that the furniture had been vinyl—not leather—and that its primary appeal had been the low price. Marisa didn't want to talk about furniture any more than she did about her hair color. That had been a point of contention since the day she had first dyed it. Mom didn't approve, and she probably never would.

Wordlessly, Marisa deposited her suitcase in the smaller of the bedrooms, then returned to the car to retrieve one of the three cartons of books she'd thought she might need at Rainbow's End. There was room for little more than that, because the cabin Marisa would share with her mother consisted of two bedrooms, a tiny living/dining room combination, and an even smaller kitchen.

Marisa gave the trunk a second slam, trying not to wince at the realization that a Lexus would not have needed to be slammed. The dream of a Lexus was gone, along with the rest of her former life. This was the new reality.

"I could have helped with that," Mom said as Marisa deposited the carton in one corner of her bedroom.

"I'm fine." Mom had already done enough; she didn't need to be hauling heavy boxes. One of the reasons Marisa had hesitated before she accepted Kate and Greg's offer was that she had feared her being here would create more work for her mother, but there had been no alternative.

When she'd heard that Marisa was returning to Dupree, Lauren had invited her to stay with her and Fiona, but Marisa had refused, claiming she hadn't wanted to intrude on Lauren's privacy. The truth was, until she'd collected a few paychecks and started to make a dent in her credit card debt, Marisa couldn't afford to pay Lauren even her share of food and utilities. At Rainbow's End, both food and lodging were included. That made staying here an offer Marisa literally couldn't afford to refuse.

Living with Mom would have its difficult moments. Marisa knew that as surely as she knew that she would never again set foot in the house on Live Oak where she'd grown up. At least this place held no painful memories.

As she opened the closet door to hang her garment bag, she glanced at the floor. Of course there were no empty bottles in brown bags hidden behind shoe boxes. That part of her life had ended on graduation day.

"I'll unpack later," Marisa said brusquely. It was an excuse. What she needed was to escape the memories that had followed her here. "Let's find Kate and Greg."

Mom nodded and led the way to the resort's dining room, where Kate was working.

"My guess is this isn't the most impressive office you've ever seen," Kate said, a smile lighting her face as she greeted Marisa. An inch or so shorter than Marisa, Kate Sherwood might not be a classic beauty, but the combination of her golden blonde hair and those striking brown eyes along with finely chiseled features and an almost palpable air of self-confidence made her a woman who attracted attention. She had commandeered one corner of the dining room and had blueprints, paint, and fabric swatches spread over three long folding tables, while file folders and reams of paper covered a fourth.

"If it works, that's all that matters."

When she'd made the official offer of employment, Kate had

assured Marisa that she would have her own office. Apparently, Greg had decided that the contents of the storage room should be moved to the toolshed and that what had been the storage room could be turned into an office for Marisa. "It's small, but it's right next to the front desk area," Kate had explained. "You'll be close to the action but still have privacy and quiet if you need that."

Marisa did. Unlike Kate, who appeared to be thriving in what she would have termed disarray, Marisa needed a highly organized work environment.

"I hope you'll be as happy here as Greg and I are," Kate continued.

"Did I hear my name?" The tall man with brown hair, green eyes, and a square chin grinned as he entered the room and extended his hand to Marisa. "Welcome to Rainbow's End. Kate and I are fortunate to have someone with your credentials as part of the team. Neither one of us could make much sense of the Sinclairs' records."

Marisa nodded. She had dealt with clients who kept their receipts in shoe boxes and others who kept no receipts at all, expecting their suppliers to provide them with year-end summaries. Surely whatever the previous owners had done couldn't be that bad. And if it was, Marisa was trained to deal with that. The software issue was different. While Marisa was comfortable using standard accounting software, she had no experience with hotel reservations.

"Olivia said the reservation system is confusing."

Kate shot Greg a look that said, *I told you so.* "That's a major understatement. We definitely need a new one."

At least they'd recognized the need.

"I've got a stack of brochures from systems that look promising, but the decision is yours," Greg told her.

"It's too bad the Sys=Simpl software won't work," Marisa said, referring to the system that had made Greg a billionaire. "I've read nothing but rave reviews of it."

His shrug surprised her. She had expected him to display pride of authorship. "It's designed for manufacturing companies, not the hospitality industry," he said.

"I suggested he design something for us," Kate interjected.

"And I told her I was out of that business. We need something already developed."

Marisa agreed with Greg. She'd seen the delays caused by one of her clients trying to develop their own software and didn't want to risk that.

"I've had experience selecting accounting packages, but this is new for me. I'd like to spend some time looking at the existing records and the system you're currently using before I make a recommendation."

Kate nodded. "That sounds like a plan. How long do you think that'll take?"

"Two or three weeks." Though Marisa knew she could muddle through with a second-rate system, she didn't want to leave her successor with something kludgy.

When Kate started to frown, Marisa amended her estimate. "I'll try to be finished by the time you get back from your honeymoon." She glanced from Kate to Greg and then back to Kate. "Where are you going, or is it a secret?"

"Europe, and it's no secret," Kate replied.

"Kate told me she dreamt about us walking under the Eiffel Tower and riding in a gondola in Venice."

"So Greg decided to make my dreams come true."

Marisa grinned. "My mouth is watering, thinking about French pastries and Italian gelato."

"You're definitely your mother's daughter," Kate said, rubbing her stomach as if she had just devoured a delicious treat. "She makes the most incredible meals I've ever eaten."

"Mom loves to cook. To tell you the truth, I'm surprised she's not catering your reception." Mom had mentioned that when she'd volunteered, Kate and Greg had refused her offer, claiming they couldn't impose on her.

Kate exchanged what appeared to be a guilty look with her fiancé. "Didn't Carmen tell you? She wouldn't take no for an answer, and when she knew you were going to be here, she said you'd help supervise the high school kids she's enlisted to do most of the work. It's an extra credit project for them."

Marisa sighed inwardly. That sounded like Mom: overextending herself to help someone else. If she had known about the catering, Marisa would have asked for an additional week to complete the software evaluation, but now that she'd committed, she didn't want to back down. She'd simply have to work extra hours after the wedding. "At least Rainbow's End won't have any guests," she said.

No doubt about it. Greg's expression was sheepish. "Actually, there will be one. One of my college buddies needs a place to stay for a couple weeks, so I told him he could use my cabin after Saturday."

"Oh, Greg, you didn't!" It was clear that Kate wasn't party to that agreement. "Marisa doesn't need anything else to do." And with Kate and Greg gone, she would be in charge of the resort.

There was only one possible response. "It won't be a problem." *I hope.*

———————— ✳ ————————

The people who'd claimed that the Texas Hill Country was one of the prettiest places on earth hadn't exaggerated, Blake reflected as he followed his GPS's directions. The rolling green hills, the trees so different from those he was accustomed to in California, and the deep blue sky were all magnificent. It might not be the Garden of Eden, as he'd heard one person call it, but it was definitely beautiful.

His flight had been uneventful, and since it was Saturday morning, traffic had been light. Once he'd left San Antonio, he'd found himself starting to relax.

Blake frowned. He didn't need relaxation. He needed ideas. When he'd called Jack Darlington to say he'd be out of town with only sporadic cell service for a few weeks, he'd carefully sidestepped his agent's questions about the new book. He didn't need anyone, including the man who lived quite well on his 15 percent commission, putting more pressure on him.

"Turn left," the surprisingly realistic mechanical voice directed.

Blake turned, his eyes registering the sign welcoming him to Dupree, the Heart of the Hills. It was a small, rather nondescript town—definitely not a place he'd send Cliff Pearson. His fictional hero's adventures took place in world capitals and glamorous resorts, not small towns in Texas, no matter how pretty the surroundings might be.

As the rental car reached the summit of the hill just west of Dupree, Blake smiled. This might not be a spot for Cliff Pearson, but the valley was spectacular. On the right side of the road, trees in more shades of green than Blake had ever seen provided welcome shade during the late summer heat, while the left side appeared to be a meadow with only an occasional tree breaking the velvety green expanse. If this was Firefly Valley, and he suspected it must be, it was no wonder Greg had decided to stay.

Blake looked down the road, nodding when he saw the road's abrupt ending and the sun glinting off a handful of metal roofs that ringed one edge of a sparkling lake. Rainbow's End. Though he hadn't expected it, a sense of anticipation bubbled up inside him.

He gave the car more gas, suddenly in a hurry to see the place Greg Vange now called home. The gates were a nice touch, seeming to welcome guests rather than exclude them. And, while the rainbow logo could appear juvenile or amateur, it didn't. Instead, it only increased Blake's belief that this was where he was supposed to be. This was where he'd rediscover his muse.

After parking in front of the small Tyrolean-style building whose sign identified the office, Blake hurried through the door. If this building and the charming gazebo were any indication, Rainbow's End was an eclectic collection of cabins that seemed to be unified only by their metal roofs.

"Hello." He blinked as his eyes adjusted to the relative darkness of the office. No one answered. Blake looked around. Though this was clearly the place where guests would check in and out, there were no employees behind the counter. He spotted an old-fashioned bell and tapped it. No answer. Another tap. Still no answer. He turned to leave the building, but then he heard footsteps on the tile floor.

"May I help you?"

Blake spun around at the sound of a melodic voice. That voice was attached to one of the prettiest female forms he'd ever seen. The woman, whom he guessed to be in her midtwenties, was an inch or two above average height. Her long dark hair was dusted with what appeared to be flour, and her left cheek held a smudge of what was undeniably chocolate frosting, but what caught his attention were her eyes. A warm tawny brown, they radiated both intelligence and exasperation. He hoped he wasn't the cause of the latter.

"I'm Blake Kendall," he said, wondering why it was suddenly so vital that this woman not be annoyed with him. He'd seen beautiful women before. He'd even dated a woman whose beauty rivaled a model's until he'd discovered how high maintenance she was. And then there was Ashley. But now was not the time to be thinking about Ashley and her temper. She was part of the past, and this woman was definitely the present. More importantly, this woman's appeal was more than physical. Blake felt as if they shared some deep connection. It was crazy. They'd just met and had exchanged only a few words. He had no reason to feel this way, and yet he did.

"Greg Vange is expecting me." To Blake's relief, his voice sounded normal.

"He is?" She appeared shocked. Was it because she'd felt that same inexplicable attraction, or was it simply that she hadn't been told of his arrival?

Blake nodded. "He said I could stay in his cabin."

A hint of something—confusion, perhaps—crossed her face, and she frowned. "There must have been a misunderstanding. We thought you were coming tomorrow."

The way her eyes flickered to the side combined with the evidence that she'd obviously been frosting a cake made Blake think this woman was overloaded with work, and he'd just made it worse.

"I'm sorry. I thought Greg said to come this morning." He was certain that was what his friend had said, but there was no reason to be emphatic about it, since the message had obviously been garbled at some point.

"Greg's getting married in three hours and seven minutes." The fact that she didn't have to look at a clock to make that announcement confirmed Blake's assumption that the lovely woman with hair the color of dark chocolate was scrambling to get things ready for the wedding. "I'm not sure where he is right now."

"Look, miss . . ."

"I'm sorry. I should have introduced myself. I'm Marisa St. George." She extended her hand in greeting.

It was only a handshake, Blake told himself. A simple touching of two palms. Nothing more than he'd done hundreds of times before. And yet this handshake was unlike any other. For the second or two that he held Marisa St. George's hand clasped in his, Blake knew he hadn't been mistaken. There was a connection between them, a fundamental magnetism that sent sparks shooting up his arm. And the glint in those lovely brown eyes told him she felt it too.

"I'm sorry for the confusion." Her voice bore only the slightest of tremors. "It's simply that my mother is catering the reception. We're a bit behind schedule, so I was helping."

"And I made it worse." She didn't have to say it. That was apparent. "The apologies are all mine. If you'll point me to the nearest motel, I'll stay there tonight, and we'll try this again tomorrow."

Marisa shook her head. "The nearest motel is more than twenty miles away." She walked behind the counter and opened a drawer. "Let me grab the key and some sheets and towels, and I'll show you to your cabin."

Her manner was 100 percent business, a sharp change from the harried woman who had greeted him. It was almost as if she'd donned a mask, determined to hide her thoughts. But why? Blake would have sworn she'd felt the same attraction he had, but now Marisa St. George was acting as if that had never happened.

It had. Blake knew that.

3

"What's wrong?"

It was clear that coming back to the kitchen had been a mistake. Though Marisa had expected it to be filled with teenagers putting the final touches on the food for Kate and Greg's reception, only Mom was there. The kids must be on one of the breaks Mom claimed were essential. That meant Marisa would have to face her mother's version of the Spanish Inquisition when what she wanted was a chance to make sense of what had just happened. If Mom hadn't needed her for the wedding preparations, Marisa would have taken a walk—a long walk—along the lake in an attempt to clear her mind. As it was, she couldn't desert her mother.

"What's wrong?" A touch of asperity colored Mom's voice as she repeated the question.

"Nothing." *Everything.* Marisa felt as if she'd been walking along a familiar path when the ground had suddenly shifted and she'd found herself free-falling into a chasm. In the blink of an eye, day had turned to a night filled with shooting stars and the brilliant undulating bands of the northern lights. Before she could register all the details, the scene had changed again, the darkness instantly transformed into the brightest day Marisa had ever experienced. It was almost like looking through a kaleidoscope, watching colors slide and shift as she turned the wheel, but there was no kaleidoscope. Whatever was happening was outside her control. The strangest part was that it had been exciting at the same time as it had been terrifying.

"You don't look like it's nothing. Sit down, Marisa." Mom accompanied her words with a gentle push on Marisa's shoulder. "I'll get you something to eat." Food was the Carmen St. George cure for everything.

"It's not low blood sugar," Marisa insisted. While it was true that she felt light-headed, lack of food was not the cause. The sensation that the world was spinning at three times its normal speed was due to Blake Kendall.

"Here, drink this." Knowing it was futile to protest, Marisa accepted the glass of sweet tea. "I told you you were overdoing it," Mom continued. "Just sit for a moment and take deep breaths."

She might not need the tea, but measured breathing was good advice. Maybe then her heartbeat would return to normal. Marisa had felt as if the wind had been knocked out of her when she'd entered the lobby and seen Blake standing there. The instant she spotted him standing by the door she felt as if they'd already met—and that was before he'd turned to face her. Something was so familiar, so very familiar, about him that she held her breath, waiting for him to turn.

When he did, disappointment stabbed her. The man was a stranger. She had never seen that face, and yet, though Marisa couldn't explain it, she couldn't ignore the sense that they shared a connection. She was a woman who dealt with facts, not feelings, but in that moment, nothing mattered except the way she felt.

Mom folded her arms as she always did when she was deep in thought, and her eyes narrowed as she studied Marisa. "You look better now," she announced. "There's more color in your face."

Though the color could have been due to the memory of the handsome stranger who hadn't seemed like a stranger, Marisa let her mother believe it was the result of the therapeutic effects of sweet tea. "I'll finish glazing the cakes," she said as she started to rise.

"And wind up face-first in one? No thanks. You just sit there." For a few seconds, the room was silent except for the squeak of a silicone spatula on glass. Then Mom spoke. "So, what does he look like?"

"Who?" Marisa wasn't ready to talk about him, not even to her mother. Perhaps if she played innocent, the conversation would die a natural death.

"Our new guest. Greg's friend." She should have known Mom wouldn't let her off the hook. "That's who was in the lobby, wasn't it?"

Innocence wasn't working. "Yes. Blake Kendall." Marisa hoped that her mother hadn't noticed the way her voice rose as she pronounced the man's name. It was as embarrassing as when she'd been a teenager with her first crush.

"What does he look like?"

*Breathtaking.* But she wouldn't say that. Instead, Marisa tried to steady her voice as she said, "About the same height as Greg. Light brown hair, hazel eyes." And a face she knew she'd never forget.

"Handsome?"

*Oh yes!* "Most women would say so." To Marisa's delight, she sounded far more nonchalant than she felt. Her mother would never guess what an impression Blake Kendall had made on her. She'd believe he was just another guest.

Mom stared at her for a second before she clapped her hands. "I knew it would happen." Her smile was the broadest Marisa had seen all day. "My little girl has met the man she's going to marry."

Feeling as if she'd been punched in the stomach, Marisa tried to smile. She should have realized that her mother would see through her pretense, but she didn't want to discuss Blake. Not until she'd had a chance to make sense of her reaction.

"That's ridiculous. I just met him." But when their hands had touched, excitement had shot through Marisa's veins, and her palms had tingled. It wasn't like an electrical shock—those were unpleasant, while this was a decidedly enjoyable experience—and yet it was just as unexpected and as powerful as the shock she'd gotten when she'd pulled out a plug with wet hands.

Her mother's smile widened. "You can deny it all you want, but I know what I see. You look exactly the way I did the day I met Eric."

And look how that had ended.

---

"Hey, man, good to see you. I'm just sorry I wasn't here to greet you."

Blake stared at the man standing in the cabin doorway. The cabin had been a pleasant surprise. After Drew's description, Blake had expected a ramshackle building complete with bare bulbs for light fixtures and a sagging mattress. Instead he'd found what could almost be called a bungalow. The cinder block walls promised winter warmth and summer coolness, while the front porch provided an excellent view of Bluebonnet Lake. Inside, he'd discovered a small but apparently fully functional bathroom, a separate bedroom, and a medium-sized living area complete with a table, sofa, and two comfortable chairs. Whoever had designed the cabin had meant it to be a place for extended stays.

The cabin was not what Blake had expected. Neither was Greg. The voice was the same, the features were the same, and yet Greg looked like a different man from the one Blake had known in California. His posture was more relaxed, the lines that had bracketed his mouth were gone, but the most dramatic change was in his eyes. They radiated happiness and something else, something Blake would have described as peace.

"I didn't expect to see you before the wedding," Blake said, his lips curving into a smile as he gave his friend a bear hug. "I suspect you have a few other things on your mind."

"One or two. I still can't believe this is happening." Greg glanced at his watch, as if calculating the minutes until he would be wed. "Wait until you meet Kate. She's one of a kind."

"As are you." Blake paused, wondering whether to continue. Curiosity trumped discretion. "I probably shouldn't say this, but you look different. It's not that I wouldn't recognize you, but something has changed, and it looks like it's important."

Greg nodded. "You're not mistaken. I feel different in many ways. Two years ago if anyone had told me I'd sell Sys=Simpl and buy a resort, I'd have laughed them out of the room. Now I know this is where I'm meant to be."

"Getting married." Blake was still reeling over that particular piece of news. The Greg he'd known had been the quintessential geek: a brilliant software designer but awkward around women. This Greg appeared both happy and self-assured.

Greg nodded again. "Kate's made a big difference in my life. And believe it or not, my dad's going to be my best man."

The news that Greg had moved to the Hill Country and was getting married had surprised Blake; this announcement shocked him. Though Greg had never shared details, Blake knew that his relationship with his father had been rocky. "You are different," he said softly.

"Thanks to God and a good woman, I am. It's an unbeatable combination. You ought to try it."

Blake was still thinking about Greg's words five minutes later when his friend left the cabin, saying he'd see him at the church. God and a good woman. No doubt about it, it was an unbeatable combination, at least for Greg. God was already a vital part of Blake's life. As for the second part of that equation, he was still waiting for the perfect woman to appear. When his father had had the father/son birds and bees discussion with him, he'd cautioned Blake not to be in a hurry to choose a wife. "Wait until you're sure she's the right one," Dad had advised. More than twenty years later, Blake was still waiting.

He walked to the picture window in the living area and stared into the distance, admiring the small lake that he'd seen from the hilltop before he'd descended into Firefly Valley. Although fully half of the cabins at Rainbow's End were nestled among the trees, the one that would be Blake's temporary home was lakefront property. When Marisa had shown it to him, he'd felt a surge of adrenaline. For reasons he could not explain, water had always fueled his creativity. That was one of the reasons he'd chosen an office with a view of the bay.

Bluebonnet Lake was different. Not only was it smaller, but unlike the ocean or even San Francisco Bay, the lake was calm, its smooth surface barely disturbed by ripples. Perhaps, like Greg, he would find that this was where he was meant to be, at least for a few weeks. The change of scenery and the tranquil setting might be just what he needed.

Blake closed his eyes for a second, and as he did, he pictured Marisa St. George and the smile that had sent his heartbeat into overdrive. Could she be the woman God had destined for him? He wouldn't deny the attraction he'd felt, but the timing was wrong. Totally wrong. All he needed right now was an idea for a new book, not a potential wife.

———————✦———————

Marisa slid into the last pew next to her mother. She hadn't planned to attend the ceremony, which was limited to immediate family, a few very close friends, and Rainbow's End employees, but once she'd met Kate and Greg, Marisa had realized that she wanted to witness their vows.

She looked at the people gathered to celebrate with them. The four young women with the same shade of hair as Greg must be his sisters. Directly behind them were two men. The first was Blake Kendall, the second . . . Marisa's heart thudded with dread. Surely that wasn't Hal Lundquist. The man was as blond as Hal, with shoulders as broad as the former football star's. His head was held at the same almost arrogant angle. It could be Hal, her teenage nemesis, the man who'd made her into the laughingstock of Dupree High School, and yet that made no sense. Hal was in the army, or so she'd heard. It was unlikely he'd met either Kate or Greg and even less likely that he would have been invited to their wedding.

The man shifted slightly, revealing his profile. Not Hal. Definitely not Hal. Marisa let out a sigh of relief. The blond-haired man must be one of Greg's friends.

She closed her eyes briefly, hoping that he wouldn't be another unplanned guest. She and Mom had enough on their plates without adding another guest into the mix. Mom was already committed to serving the workers both breakfast and a noon meal. While that involved no more cooking than if the resort were open, the timing made it more stressful for Marisa's mother. Now, with Blake in residence, she had to worry about his evening meal too.

As the music changed, Marisa joined others in watching a man whose resemblance to Greg left no doubt that this was his father escort his wife to her seat then walk closer to the altar to take his place next to Greg. It was the first time Marisa had heard of a father serving as his son's best man, but as Mom had told her, this was not a typical wedding party.

Next in the procession came Kate's grandmother, escorted down the aisle by her new husband. Marisa couldn't help smiling at the sight of Roy Gordon. Growing up, she hadn't known him well, because his children were considerably older than she, but he had a reputation as a good guy, and from all accounts, he'd been devastated when his wife had died. Marisa was thankful he was getting a second chance at love. If only Mom would, but she . . . Marisa bit the inside of her cheek and forced her thoughts back to Kate and Greg's wedding.

Though normally Roy would have taken a seat next to his wife, he returned to the back of the church. As soon as he reached it, a pretty woman with auburn hair began to walk slowly down the aisle. This must be Kate's childhood friend Gillian. Mom had said that she was going to be Kate's maid of honor.

And then came the moment everyone had been waiting for. As the familiar strains of "Here Comes the Bride" filled the church, everyone rose and watched as Roy escorted Kate to the man who would soon be her husband.

The ceremony was beautiful, so filled with loving promises that Marisa found herself dashing a tear from her eye as she said a silent prayer that Kate and Greg's marriage would be long and happy.

Once the final vows were made, Marisa and her mother slipped out. It was time to get to work. Though the ceremony had been small, there were six hundred people to feed, for the whole town of Dupree had been invited to the reception.

Half an hour later, the food Marisa, her mother, and the high school food science students had spent most of the week preparing was set out on long tables under a tent that provided respite from the sun as well as protection if it should rain. While Mom flitted from platter to platter, adjusting the position of the hot and cold hors d'oeuvres, Marisa watched with amusement. She doubted anyone would care that her mother's tamales were arranged just so. What mattered was that they were the best in the state, and that the fruit punch and sweet tea were cold.

"That's the most unusual cake I've ever seen."

Marisa turned, surprised to see Blake standing next to her. She had thought he might remain with the bridal couple while the photographs were being taken. Unlike Marisa, he was a guest and not part of the help. But instead he was pointing at the wedding cake.

"Kate saw a picture of one in an old magazine she found in the storeroom," Marisa explained. "According to my mother, once she saw it, Kate insisted that was what she wanted. It was a bit of a challenge, but Mom had fun creating it."

What made the cake unusual was that it was shaped like a church, complete with a bride and groom at the front door and stained glass windows on the sides. Those stained glass windows, made from special fondant so that everything on the cake itself was edible, had proven to be the most difficult part of the project.

"It sends a message, doesn't it?"

Marisa nodded. No one would doubt that God was an integral part of this marriage. "That's the cake they'll cut," she told Blake. "It's white cake with buttercream frosting, but if you prefer chocolate, we have dozens—literally—of chocolate pound cakes."

"With chocolate frosting?"

Cakes, no matter how creative the design, were hardly an earth-shaking subject, and yet Marisa could not deny that her pulse had accelerated the moment she'd heard Blake's voice.

"A glaze," she replied in a surprisingly normal voice. "Why do you ask?"

"Because you had what appeared to be chocolate frosting on your face when I met you this morning."

"Oh!" How embarrassing. "I guess you can tell that I'm not a chef."

As guests began to arrive to congratulate the bride and groom, who'd emerged from the church and were now greeting the townspeople, Marisa moved to the side. At this point, her only responsibility was replacing platters as they were emptied and hoping that not too many people would ask why she'd come back to Dupree and whether this was a permanent move. Perhaps if she were obviously engaged in a conversation with Blake, others would hesitate to interrupt.

There were dangers, though. Marisa had already spotted Amelia, Debra, and Edie, the women Lauren had nicknamed the Matchers, and had tried to deflect their questions about when she would be walking down the aisle. It didn't take a genius to imagine what they'd say if they saw her with Blake. But maybe seeing her with Blake wasn't all bad. He'd only be here for a week or so, and if they were speculating about her, perhaps Lauren would be off the hook for a while.

"So what do you do if you're not a chef?" he asked.

"I'm a CPA. I used to work for a firm in Atlanta, but now I'm the business manager for Rainbow's End. That's actually a fancy term for bookkeeper and gofer," Marisa said with a self-deprecating chuckle. Though she had no intention of mentioning that she'd been downsized and hadn't been able to find a similar position in Georgia, she saw no need to glorify her job. "How about you?"

As Blake looked into the distance for a moment, something about his expression made her think he was choosing his words. That was silly, of course. He had no reason to dissemble about something as straightforward as a career.

"I have a small financial planning firm in San Francisco." His matter-of-fact tone told Marisa she'd imagined his hesitation. "Although 'firm' is a bit of an overstatement. I'm the one and only employee."

Before Marisa could respond, one of her high school teachers spotted her and welcomed her back to town. "I always hoped you'd come back," Ms. Shackelford said. "You belong in Dupree."

Forcing her lips into a polite smile, Marisa gave the woman a noncommittal nod. When she'd left, Marisa turned back to Blake and sighed. "Is San Francisco as beautiful as everyone says?"

As Blake shrugged, the action highlighted his well-formed shoulders and sent a whiff of his aftershave toward Marisa. She wasn't sure which entranced her more; all she knew was that the attraction she'd tried so hard to deny was real. Something about this man appealed to her in ways no other man had. Mom was wrong, though. This wasn't love at first sight. It couldn't be, because Marisa and Blake weren't like her mother and father. Not at all.

"The whole Bay Area is definitely beautiful," Blake agreed, his words reminding Marisa that they were discussing California. Good. That subject was far less troublesome than the thought of love at first sight and the way it could turn into a living nightmare.

"But so is the Hill Country. I'm glad I have a chance to see it." Blake looked around, as if he were viewing Dupree's sole park for the first time. Though no more than a city block in size, it was large enough for a town with a population of just under six hundred. Trees lined the perimeter, but the center had been cleared to accommodate Dupree's holiday celebrations, when parades culminated in patriotic speeches and songs. At other times of the year, the park was the site of parties like this one.

"You've never been here before?" The sense of instant recognition had lingered, niggling at the back of Marisa's mind all the time she'd been glazing the cakes and stashing platters of food into Greg's SUV.

"No." Blake appeared surprised by the question. "Why do you ask?"

"Because you look familiar. I can't explain it, but when I first walked into the office, I thought I'd seen you before."

Though he'd met her gaze a second before, Blake looked away as he shook his head. "That's unlikely. You haven't been to San Francisco, I've never been to Atlanta, and this is my first day in Texas. I'm sure we haven't met." He raised his eyes and grinned. "Trust me. I'd remember if I'd met you."

The warm smile sent a flush to Marisa's cheeks, almost distracting her from her continuing sense of déjà vu. Everything Blake said made sense, and yet . . . Marisa brushed her doubts aside. There was only one logical explanation. "It must have been my imagination."

It was definitely her imagination that Blake seemed relieved.

# 4

At least she hadn't been invited to the wedding. Though she wished Kate and Greg every happiness, Lauren knew she wasn't ready to watch another couple exchange vows. "In sickness and in health." Simple but powerful words. Just the thought of them made her cry. *Oh, Patrick, I miss you so much.* He'd been her first love, her only love, and though she would not have wanted his suffering to continue, not a day went by that she didn't wish he were still with her. Lauren squeezed her eyes closed, trying to keep tears at bay.

"C'mon, Fiona. It's time to go," she called to her daughter as soon as she'd recovered her composure.

"It's going to be boring." Fiona stomped one foot, which for some reason was clad in a sock that matched the other. That was the first time matching socks had happened since Lauren and Fiona had made their agreement last spring. As for the foot stomping, Lauren knew better than to ask, but she couldn't help wondering whether Fiona had sensed her mood and was reacting.

"Alice will be there, and Aunt Carmen did all the cooking." Marisa's mother had been a godsend during Patrick's illness and the first month after his death when Lauren had felt as if she were walking through a fog. Without being asked, Carmen had provided her version of Meals on Wheels so that Lauren didn't have to worry whether her daughter was well fed.

The second announcement put a smile on Fiona's face. "Tamales?"

"I wouldn't be surprised. The only way to know is to go."

Locking the door behind her, Lauren turned to the right. With less than two blocks separating her house from the park, there was no point in driving. She extended her hand, planning to clasp Fiona's, but her daughter refused to walk next to her, seeming to prefer to remain two steps behind. It appeared that Fiona's normally sunny disposition had taken a leave of absence.

As they approached Pecan Street, the sound of hundreds of voices and a few barking dogs told Lauren she and Fiona would be among the last to arrive. It was no surprise that everyone in Dupree wanted to join in the celebration of Kate and Greg's wedding. After what they'd done for the town, and considering what the renovated Rainbow's End would mean to Dupree, Greg and Kate could win the Citizens of the Year award, if the town had one.

"Where's the food?" Fiona demanded as they entered the park.

"I imagine it's in the big tent." One of the large white tents that seemed to be a staple of outdoor celebrations filled the center of the park, while dozens of bistro-style tables and chairs were arranged around its perimeter to supplement the family-sized picnic tables clustered in the far corner. "We'll go there as soon as we talk to the bride and groom."

Fiona nodded as Lauren led them to the tail of the receiving line. "I like Mr. Greg. I wanted him to be my daddy."

"I know you did, but he loves Miss Kate." Perhaps the fact that Greg had married someone else was the reason for Fiona's disgruntled mood.

Tugging on Lauren's hand, Fiona waited until Lauren looked at her before she spoke. When she did, her voice was filled with urgency. "When are you going to find me another daddy?"

"I don't know, honey. We have to wait for God to send us one." She wouldn't tell Fiona that, though the Matchers claimed otherwise, she wasn't convinced that God intended her to marry again.

"I'm tired of waiting. Do you think you'll find one by Christmas?"

Though it was still a few weeks before the first anniversary of Patrick's death, Lauren knew that a year was a very long time for a child of seven, and the hole that Patrick had left in her life was huge. Lauren wished there were something she could say to comfort her daughter, but the only words Fiona wanted to hear would have been a lie. Lauren could not promise that a second daddy would share Christmas with them.

To Lauren's relief, Alice Kozinski spotted Fiona and pushed her way through the crowd toward her. "My mom saved space for you and Fiona," the blonde-haired girl who was an inch shorter and three inches wider than Fiona told Lauren, pointing to the picnic tables at the north end of the park. "She said receiving lines weren't for kids."

"Can I go?" Fiona's question came out as a plea, and Lauren found herself nodding. Susan Kozinski had a point.

"I'll join you as soon as I can," she told her daughter. "You know the rules."

"Yes, Mom. Don't leave without telling you where we're going. Don't talk to strangers. And never, never cross the street without looking."

Lauren was smiling when she reached the end of the receiving line. Only a curmudgeon wouldn't smile at the sight of the new Mr. and Mrs. Vange, whose happiness was readily apparent to everyone. After she'd congratulated the bride and groom, she made her way to the food tent, not surprised when Carmen told her that Fiona had had no interest in anything other than tamales. According to Carmen, Alice and Fiona had been talking nonstop all the while Fiona loaded her plate with her favorite food. Lauren could feel herself relaxing at the realization that whatever had been bothering her daughter was forgotten.

She stepped outside the tent, stopping for a second to let her eyes adjust to the sunshine.

"Lauren," a man called. "I was hoping to see you."

Her blinking had more to do with being startled than the sun's rays. What was *he* doing here? There was no mistaking the blond, blue-eyed man with the California tan who'd annoyed virtually everyone he'd met the last time he'd come to Dupree.

Lauren moved to the side, hoping Drew Carroll would disappear. He did not. And so she raised an eyebrow. "I didn't think anything would bring you back to Dupree," she said, keeping her voice as cool as the ice cubes that were even now melting in her glass. "I guess Greg's wedding was important enough for you to forget how much you disliked this—what was it you called it?—pathetic excuse for a town." Though Lauren knew Dupree had its shortcomings, she would not allow a man who hadn't bothered to look beneath the surface to denigrate it, especially a man like Drew Carroll.

He smiled, a white-toothed smile that appeared to radiate sincerity but only served to deepen Lauren's distrust. This was the man who'd ignored Rainbow's End's clearly posted no-alcohol rule, apparently believing that rules did not apply to multimillionaires.

"Did you ever consider that I might have come to see you?"

"Never. That would happen when not just pigs but elephants fly."

"Dumbo's an elephant, and he flies." As a small hand tugged on hers, Lauren looked down at her daughter and guessed she had been sent to escort her to the Kozinski table.

"You're right, sweetheart. I forgot about Dumbo," Lauren said, her smile fading when she returned her gaze to Drew. "Do you remember my daughter?"

"Of course I . . ." As she raised her eyebrow again, the lie died on his lips. "No, I don't."

Of course he didn't. The day they'd met, it had been apparent that Drew had no time for anyone under the age of twenty-five.

"This is Fiona," she said. Turning to her daughter, Lauren completed the introduction. "This is Mr. Carroll."

Fiona tugged on Lauren's hand again. "Our table's over there." She pointed to the last row, where Alice was seated with her parents and baby Liam. "Alice and me want to play on the swings. Her mom says it's okay."

"Alice and I," Lauren corrected automatically. "All right, but be careful." Fiona had a tendency to swing too high. "I'll be with you in a few minutes."

It wouldn't take longer than that to dismiss Drew. But she hadn't counted on his tenacity. He gestured toward the plate he held and an empty table for two. "Will you join me? If I thought it would work, I'd claim it was your civic duty, but since I doubt that would convince you, I'll resort to the truth: I'd enjoy your company."

Though she wanted to refuse, Lauren hesitated. The first time she'd met Drew Carroll, she'd formed an instant dislike for the brash Californian. This was the same man, and yet he seemed different. While no one would call him self-effacing, he appeared less arrogant, and though she might be misreading it, Lauren thought that was pain she saw in his eyes. If she understood one thing, it was pain and the way a friendly gesture could assuage it.

"All right. I'll be back in a minute." When she'd made her excuses to the Kozinskis and endured Susan's knowing smile at the sight of Drew, Lauren returned to the table he'd appropriated. Unrolling her napkin, she looked up at him. "I assume you attended the ceremony."

He appeared amused by the question. "You could say that. I crashed it."

"What?" It was not the response Lauren had anticipated. Even though the guest list was small, surely he would have been on it. "You're Greg's partner."

"Past tense. I haven't spoken to him since right after Easter." Drew took a bite of tamale, chewing carefully before he added, "After seeing them together last spring, I'm not surprised that he married Kate, but I am surprised by the secrecy. As far as I can tell, no one in California knows he was getting married. Even though he's no longer part of the company, Greg Vange's wedding is newsworthy."

46

Lauren sipped her tea, considering her response. She forced a smile when one of the Matchers walked by, eyeing Drew. The only good thing she could say about the woman's curiosity was that she'd buy at least one item when she came to HCP on Monday to learn whatever she could about Lauren's companion.

"I don't think they wanted media attention," she told Drew when the woman was out of earshot. "They want publicity for Rainbow's End, not their personal lives."

"I can't blame them for that. What surprises me is how much Greg has changed."

Lauren couldn't comment on that, because she hadn't known Greg before he'd sold his software company and come to Texas, and so she said only, "People do change."

After he'd washed down his tamale with a long slug of iced tea, Drew tipped his head to the side, as if evaluating her statement. "You think so?"

"I know so. I'm not the same person I was a year ago." Why had she said that? Half an hour ago she hadn't even liked this man, and now she was discussing her personal life with him. Drew was a virtual stranger, but when he nodded, encouraging her to continue, Lauren knew she had to explain.

"Everything changed when Patrick died. It wasn't just being a widow." Although that was bad enough. "Being a single parent is much harder than I realized."

"Especially since you've got your business to run."

Lauren was surprised by the astute comment. Few in Dupree realized how much of a drain HCP was on her energy. Some days just smiling at customers felt like a herculean task. But Drew knew. As part owner of Sys=Simpl, he understood the demands. Of course, his software firm was far larger than her quilt shop.

"There were some tough weeks," she admitted. "But I'm fortunate that I love what I do, because it's what puts food on the table." Patrick hadn't worked long enough to earn a pension, and uncovered medical expenses had exhausted their savings. "I don't imagine you've ever been worried about that." Lauren doubted that Drew's life was perfect—no one's was—but at least he had no financial concerns.

"Not recently," he agreed, "but there are other worries."

"Like what?"

"Like whether someone else will come up with a better product and we'll lose all our clients."

That was one worry Lauren didn't have. There were no other quilt shops in Dupree. "Is that likely?"

"If Greg were still part of the company, I'd say no. Now . . ." Drew paused, and his eyes grew somber. "I don't know." Shaking his head, he said, "That's much too gloomy a subject for today. Let's talk about you instead."

Lauren had already told him more than she'd intended. "I'd rather hear about life in California."

One subject led to another, and before Lauren knew it, they'd discussed everything from favorite movies to white-water rafting to red versus green chili. She stood up occasionally to look at the swings, and when it was apparent that Fiona was still having fun with Alice, she sat back down. But now, as the crowd began to thin, Lauren knew it was time to leave.

"I'd better get my daughter. She's on a sugar high, and I need to get her home before she crashes."

Drew rose and pulled out Lauren's chair for her, then walked with her toward the swings. The number of curious glances their progress elicited told Lauren that Monday would be a banner day at HCP. She wondered if Drew was finding being the center of attention as annoying as she was. Before she could say anything, he turned toward her. "Can I buy you dinner tonight?"

Though the thought was strangely appealing, coming as it did from a man she'd thought she disliked an hour ago, Lauren knew there was only one possible answer. "I'm afraid not. I've got to work tonight."

"It's Saturday," he pointed out.

"Believe me, I'm well aware of that, but I have less than a month to finish a dozen quilts. There are going to be a lot of late nights between now and then." That was why Lauren had brought one of her sewing machines home. While she couldn't do the actual quilting there, she could at least piece the tops.

They'd reached the swings. Drew thrust his hands into his pants pockets and stared at Lauren for a long moment. "Okay . . . well . . ." This was the first time he'd seemed tongue-tied, and she wondered at the cause. Finally he said, "It was nice seeing you again," and headed toward Kate and Greg, who were saying their good-byes.

Fiona ran up to Lauren. "You spent a lot of time with that man." Her tone left no doubt that she disapproved.

"Yes, I did." Lauren was the mother; she had no need to explain her actions to her daughter.

"I don't like him."

*But I do.* Though she hadn't expected to, Lauren had enjoyed the time they'd spent together. Somehow Drew had banished her melancholy thoughts, and somehow she'd managed to diminish the pain she'd seen in his eyes.

She wouldn't see him again, for he'd told her he was returning to California in the morning, but that was good. Drew was a complicated man, and complications were one thing Lauren did not need. Drew was also unlike anyone she'd ever met. That had to be the reason—the only reason—why Lauren found herself sketching his face that evening when she was supposed to be designing a quilt.

5

"Hello, Blake," Marisa said as she left the church the next morning and saw him standing at the foot of the steps. Her mother was still inside, chatting with friends, but Marisa had wanted to escape the endless refrains of "so glad you're back." Blake might provide the respite she needed.

Though she refused to accept her mother's theory of love at first sight, Marisa wouldn't deny that she enjoyed his company. For whatever reason, none of the men she'd met in Atlanta had affected her the way Blake Kendall did.

She smiled at him. "I thought your friend might be with you." Greg had said nothing about a second guest, but Marisa wouldn't have been surprised if the blond-haired man had shared Blake's cabin last night. The couches in the living area of each cabin opened into beds, providing accommodations for larger families or overnight guests.

"Drew?" Blake shook his head. "He was only here for the day. He had an early morning flight to California, so he stayed at a hotel near the airport."

Marisa felt her pulse racing. It seemed that every time she was with Blake, her heart beat faster, her cheeks flushed, and she felt as if every nerve ending was on alert. That had never, ever happened before.

Keeping her voice even, as if this were an ordinary conversation and not one that turned her world upside down, Marisa said, "It seems like a long way to come for such a short time." Of course, if Drew Carroll was as wealthy as her mother claimed, he could have chartered a plane. That would have made the trip less onerous.

Blake nodded his agreement. "It was a lot of travel time for him, but it was good to see Drew. It's been years since he and Greg and I were together."

"Was that at Stanford?" Mom had given Marisa an abbreviated history of Drew's first visit to Rainbow's End, one that included a few choice comments about the man's poor judgment. Apparently Drew had made a strong impression, albeit a negative one.

"We all shared an apartment our senior year," Blake explained. "After graduation, I moved into the city, while Greg and Drew stayed in Silicon Valley. I rarely talked to Drew after that and probably wouldn't have seen Greg if he hadn't been a client."

Marisa wasn't surprised. Though she and her college classmates had vowed to keep in touch, distance and the pressure of jobs and family had taken their toll on what she'd once thought would be lifelong friendships.

"So you wound up having a reunion in Dupree, Texas." It was more than a little ironic that three cosmopolitan men had found each other here.

"The Heart of the Hills."

Marisa chuckled. "You saw the sign."

"It was pretty hard to miss, but that's all I saw of the town. Could I convince you to give me a guided tour?"

Though he'd been standing only a couple feet from her, Blake took a step closer, and as he did, Marisa caught a whiff of his aftershave. It was spicy and musky and made her want to take a deep breath, simply to inhale it. Instead, she tipped her head to the side and asked, "Do you have five minutes to spare?"

Blake's smile showcased teeth so evenly spaced they had to be the result of orthodontia. "I just might. Maybe even ten."

"In that case, we'll walk." It was a beautiful morning, perfect weather for a stroll, especially a stroll with Blake.

"In those shoes?" He stared at the four-inch heels Marisa had worn to church.

"Sure. It's a small town." After she told her mother that Blake would take her back to Rainbow's End, Marisa rejoined him and pointed to the street in front of the church. "I don't know whether you noticed the sign, but this is Lone Star Trail. When the town was founded early in the twentieth century, it was called Main Street, but for a while after Sinclair Lewis's book of that name was published, people didn't want any connection to Main Street. The mayor proposed Lone Star Trail, and it's been called that ever since."

Marisa paused for a second, trying to judge Blake's reaction. When he appeared genuinely interested, she added, "The other east-west streets are all avenues. Avenue A, Avenue B—you get the idea. And, sorry to disappoint you, but I don't know why the town fathers decided to use the alphabet rather than calling them First and Second Street." When Blake merely nodded, Marisa laughed. "You really do want to learn about Dupree, don't you?"

Blake held up both hands in surrender. "Guilty as charged. Besides, only a crazy man would pass up the chance for a walk with a pretty girl."

As flirtations went, it was mild, and yet Marisa felt blood heating her cheeks. "Flattery will get you . . ." She paused, trying to think of something outrageous to say while she waited for her pulse to stop racing. "An all-expenses-paid trip to the east side of Dupree."

"Which is where we were heading anyway."

"Exactly." They walked slowly, passing the bank, the town hall, and the supermarket that did double duty as a newsstand. When they reached the movie theater, Marisa paused. "You'll notice that it's called the Bijou, like hundreds of other cinemas in the country, and that it has only one screen. The films are tenth run."

"You're exaggerating."

She shrugged, gazing at the building where she and Lauren had watched so many movies. It was old enough now that instead of appearing old-fashioned, it seemed classic. "I may be exaggerating a little, but all the shows are at least six months old. One week each month, the features are what the owner calls classics."

"Like *Star Wars?*"

"Think older. Much older. Think *Casablanca* and *Whatever Happened to Baby Jane?*"

Blake's chuckle warmed Marisa's heart. "Sounds like my grand-parents' generation's movies."

"Exactly. If Mr. Benton could find them, I wouldn't be surprised to see silent films on the list." The owner had grown up in the fifties and had what Mom described as a terminal case of nostalgia. Unfortunately, Dupree's younger generation wasn't particularly enamored with film stars whose careers had ended decades earlier, and attendance was low during nostalgia weeks.

Blake looked down the street to the business establishment that fronted the main highway. "Let me guess. That's the only gas station in town."

"A shrewd guess."

"Is there a soft drink machine in front?"

"Of course. As you've already discovered, Dupree is the quintessential American small town. But if you were looking for Coke or Pepsi, you might be disappointed. This is Texas, so we offer Dr Pepper." While the gas station's sign had been updated over the years, some things hadn't changed, including the owner's loyalty to the soft drink that had its origin not too far from Dupree.

Marisa frowned as she thought of the many paydays Mom had given her money to buy a Dr Pepper if she would wait for her father and walk home with him as soon as his shift ended. It was only as she grew older that she realized Mom was trying to keep him from stopping at the liquor store or the town's sole bar and drinking half of his paycheck but didn't want to humiliate him by coming to the station herself. Marisa forced her lips into a smile. Nothing would be gained by dredging up painful memories.

"Is that all of Dupree?" Marisa wondered if Blake had sensed her melancholy mood, because he gave her shoulders a quick squeeze when he spoke, as if seeking to comfort her.

"Oh no," she responded. "There are more shops on Pecan, and of course there are houses. Mostly single family homes, but the south end of town has an apartment building for lower-income families."

"Is it nice?"

"Not very. I'd say it's kind of dilapidated now." How odd. She'd grown up with Hickory View and never gave it a second thought until Blake asked about it. "It didn't start out that way. According to my mother, it was once an attractive building, but the owner got tired of the constant repairs and let some maintenance slip. Now everything's so old that anyone who can afford to live elsewhere does."

"That's sad."

Though his responses were terse, they continued to reveal new facets to Blake. He, a stranger who was only passing through Dupree, seemed more concerned about Hickory View than most of the town's permanent residents.

"It is sad," Marisa agreed, "especially when you know that the owner is the town's former mayor. He doesn't live here any longer, but from all accounts, he could afford to renovate it."

Blake nodded again. "I've heard similar stories about absentee landlords." He gave Marisa's shoulder another squeeze. "We can't solve the world's problems this morning, so I propose that we try to enjoy the beautiful day. I wouldn't mind seeing more of the town." He winked and added, "Lead on, Macduff."

As Blake let his arm drop, Marisa felt a sense of loss. It was probably silly, but the combination of his sympathetic words and his arm around her shoulders had made her feel more than comforted; she had felt connected. The sense that they shared something special had filled her heart, but with the physical connection severed, she'd been jolted back to the reality that they were virtual strangers.

Marisa shook her head, determined to regain the camaraderie that had made the walk so pleasant. "My English teacher would tell you that Shakespeare wrote, 'Lay on, Macduff,' not 'lead on.' She claimed that's one of the Bard's most frequently misquoted phrases."

Blake's laugh was light and carefree, telling Marisa she'd succeeded in changing the mood along with the subject. "We must have had the same English teacher. Mine said the same thing but told us that it's been misquoted for more than a century. According to her, in something like 1898, a London drunk named Joseph Callaway is reported to have shouted 'Lead on, Macduff' when he was being arrested for disorderly conduct. So I'm in good or, rather, dubious, company."

Blake chuckled. Though Marisa guessed she was supposed to laugh, she couldn't when the word *drunk* kept reverberating through her brain.

*"Your dad's the town drunk."*

*"How's it feel, living with a drunk?"*

*"Your old man's nothing but a drunk."*

It had been years since she'd heard the cruel taunts, but the memories lingered, ready to ambush her when she least expected it. It wasn't Blake's fault. He had no way of knowing that his story would touch a sensitive chord. Marisa took a deep breath, trying to regain her equilibrium.

"Are you sure you can stand the excitement?" she asked, forcing a lilt to her voice.

Blake nodded. "If your feet can survive it, so can I."

They began to retrace their footsteps. When they reached Live Oak, Marisa turned south. She wouldn't even venture a glance in the opposite direction, for she had no desire to see the house that held so many memories. Lauren claimed that it was vacant now but that the last tenants had taken good care of the yard, nurturing Mom's flowers.

Marisa didn't care if they'd turned it into the Taj Mahal. It was still the house where dreams had died. She would not revisit it. Instead, she put on her tour guide persona and proceeded to tell Blake that the north-south streets were named for trees, pointing out the live oaks that had given this street its name. Four blocks later, they turned on Avenue H and headed to Pecan.

Marisa wondered whether Blake would comment on the number of empty storefronts. Although Lauren had said that the mayor and town council believed the changes to Rainbow's End would attract new businesses to Dupree, it was too soon to see if their predictions would come true, and so a full third of the shops on Pecan remained vacant.

Blake said nothing, although Marisa saw the assessing looks he gave the first two shops. One was boarded up with plywood, while the other had a now-dusty plate glass window that had once been filled with toys. Fortunately, the next one practically shouted prosperity.

"This is my friend Lauren's shop," Marisa said as she paused in front of Hill Country Pieces. The storefront boasted a new blue awning and a polished oak door, but what drew the passersby's attention was the red, white, and blue quilt with the Texas flag as its central design hanging in the front window.

Blake gave a low whistle. "I don't know much about quilts, but that's impressive."

In less talented hands, it might have been gaudy, but Lauren had chosen lighter shades of blue to contrast with the vivid blue of the flag, and the only red she'd used besides the flag itself was for the outer border and the backing.

"She's very good. So is Samantha." Marisa led the way across the street to Sam's Bootery, the family-owned enterprise that was gaining nationwide recognition, thanks to Kate and her suggestions for Samantha's website.

Blake studied the assortment of footwear. The boots ranged from child size to adult and from relatively simple to intricate designs, but what they shared was meticulous tooling.

"Looking at those is almost enough to convince me to buy a pair."

"I can assure you that they're the most comfortable footwear in town." Which was more than she could say for what she was currently wearing. Though she wouldn't admit it to Blake, Marisa's feet were beginning to ache. The shoes that had seemed comfortable for brief walks in Atlanta hadn't been the best choice for a stroll through Dupree.

"Because this is the only store?"

"Exactly. But Sam's boots are remarkably comfortable. My college friends couldn't believe it when they tried mine."

Gesturing to the other side of the street, Marisa pointed out the Sit 'n' Sip. "This is the best—and only—place to eat in Dupree. The coffee's not the world's finest, but Russ Walker makes a mean omelet, and the muffins are almost as good as my mom's."

When Blake nodded, Marisa continued to the intersection. "And here we are, back on Lone Star. There's a sporting goods store two blocks north on Cherry, and the school's at the end. You've already seen the park, so that concludes our grand tour."

Blake looked up and down Lone Star, as if imprinting the locations on his brain. "You've got almost everything people need, with one exception. I didn't see a bookstore."

Marisa nodded. "You're right. We don't have one, although we have a pretty good library." That had been one of Marisa's childhood haunts, because although she loved to read, her family could not afford to buy many books. "The supermarket carries a few paperback bestsellers. For anything else, folks go to San Antonio or shop online. Were you looking for something specific?"

While Blake had displayed a knowledge of *Macbeth*, Marisa doubted he read Shakespeare on a daily basis, and she wondered what books would appeal to him. Had he read classics as a child? It was unlikely he'd ever opened the covers of her favorite, the Anne of Green Gables series, but he must have read something.

"Nothing specific," he said, disappointing her. "I'm just curious."

"Are you one of those who agrees with Thomas Jefferson when he said, 'I cannot live without books'?"

An ironic smile lit Blake's face. "You could say that."

6

"Are you sure this is all I can do to help?" Blake asked as he took the pan of lasagna from Carmen. Though he'd insisted that she did not need to provide supper for him, Carmen had dismissed his protests, pointing out that she was already cooking for herself and Marisa and that it was no trouble to set another place at the table.

It hadn't taken much to persuade him. The truth was, Blake welcomed the opportunity to learn more about Marisa. For all that she appeared open and friendly, he sensed depths to her that she let few see. He hadn't missed the way she'd avoided looking north on Live Oak, and it hadn't been his imagination that something about the Macduff conversation had bothered her. Watching the interaction between Marisa and her mother might reveal new clues to the mystery of the beautiful woman with the pain-filled eyes.

Carmen grabbed a bowl of tossed salad with one hand and a covered basket whose distinctive aroma told Blake it contained garlic bread with the other. "You're saving me a trip; that's all the help I need." As she switched off the lights in Rainbow's End's industrial-sized kitchen, Marisa's mother shrugged. "We have a kitchen in the cabin, but it can't compare to this, so I do all my cooking here."

Though Blake had no aspirations of becoming a chef, he also had no trouble understanding why this was Carmen's preferred work space. She was in her element here, just as he'd once been in his element in his office, surrounded by all the tools he needed to make Cliff Pearson's adventures come to life. Unfortunately, writer's block had ended that.

As they walked toward the front of the building, Carmen knocked on the next door before opening it. "Dinner will be ready in fifteen minutes," she called to her daughter.

Marisa looked up from her desk, the furrows between her eyes telling Blake she had been trying to concentrate. "Thanks," she said, sounding more than a little distracted. "I have one more thing to check."

"There's spumoni in the freezer. Bring it when you come." When Marisa nodded and returned her attention to the papers that covered the desk, Carmen shook her head. "She'll forget. When she starts working, she forgets the rest of the world exists."

It had always been like that for Blake when he was writing. Though he doubted anyone who wasn't a writer would understand, he had felt as if he were transported to another world. He'd forget to eat and drink. He'd forget everything except the story that was taking shape in his mind. While his fingers flew across the keyboard, it was almost as if he became Cliff Pearson.

But Blake would not tell Carmen that. Other than Greg and now Kate, no one at Rainbow's End knew that he was Ken Blake, and he intended to keep it that way. Instead he said, "I can't speak for Kate, but at least when he owned his software company, Greg was a workaholic. He'll appreciate Marisa's work ethic."

As Blake held the outside door open for Carmen, she scowled. "He'd better not take advantage of her the way her last bosses did."

Blake knew he shouldn't pry, but Carmen had given him an opening. "What happened?"

Carmen's scowl deepened. "They were happy enough when she worked night and day to get hundreds of tax returns done, but then they laid her off on April 16. They didn't even give her her bonus." Carmen muttered a few Spanish phrases that left Blake no doubt of her anger and that if Marisa's former bosses were within earshot, she would give them a piece of her mind.

"That doesn't seem fair," he said, wondering if the abrupt and apparently unpleasant end of Marisa's job was the reason for the occasional flashes of pain he'd seen.

As Carmen led the way up the steps to her cabin, she nodded. "It wasn't, but one good thing came out of it. I got my daughter back."

She switched on lights, then put the lasagna and garlic bread into the oven to keep them warm. "It probably seems silly, carrying everything over here when we have a table in the kitchen and a perfectly good dining room right next to it."

Blake thought he understood Carmen's motives. "This is your home. You're comfortable here."

She nodded vigorously. "You understand."

As Carmen pulled place mats and silverware from a drawer, Blake offered to set the table. Though she shook her head, Carmen smiled. "You have good manners, Blake. Your mother taught you well."

"The credit goes to my dad. My mother died when I was two—complications from measles, if you can believe it."

"And your father never remarried." She made it a statement rather than a question. When Blake shook his head, Carmen continued. "It must have been hard for him, raising you alone." Her words reminded him that she was a single parent too.

"Dad had help." If you could call it that. Blake tried not to frown at the memory of his grandfather's stern and often disapproving face and the sound of his angry shouts. Grandfather was gone, his tyranny ended. Keeping his voice as even as he could, Blake said, "Dad's father lived with us."

Carmen smiled as she arranged the place mats. "So you had both a father's and a grandfather's love. You were a lucky boy."

*Lucky* wasn't the way Blake would have described it. Though he'd come to accept that his grandfather had loved him as best he could, he had spent the majority of his adolescence wishing the man lived on another planet or at least on the opposite side of the continent.

Eager to change the subject, Blake looked at the two photos on the end table. One showed a very young Marisa standing in what Blake guessed was her backyard. Holding what appeared to be a mason jar, she was the picture of happiness. The second picture showed a far more serious young woman in a cap and gown.

He might not have paid too much attention to the pictures had it not been for the fact that the Marisa in both of them was a blue-eyed blonde. Blake knew women who bleached their hair and wore colored contacts to transform themselves into the stereotypical California blonde, but this was the first time he'd seen anyone disguise such glorious natural color.

"Wow! I didn't realize Marisa was a blonde. She's even more beautiful that way."

"That's what I told her." Carmen placed three glasses on the table and stood back, narrowing her eyes as if verifying that she had forgotten nothing. "She was the spitting image of Eric, her father."

Though he was curious about the reason for such a dramatic change of appearance, Blake didn't want to squander the opportunity to learn more about Marisa's father. The fact that Carmen still wore a wedding ring made him believe she was a widow. What he didn't know was how long Eric St. George had been gone and how he had died. "When did your husband—"

Before Blake could finish the sentence, Marisa rushed into the cabin, a large towel-wrapped container in her hand, her expression so carefree that Blake knew he'd do nothing to destroy the mood. His opportunity had evaporated.

"I remembered the spumoni."

Carmen chuckled. "There's hope for you yet."

---- ✳ ----

There was no hope for this system. Marisa glared at the computer screen, as if that would change the display. The fancy sales brochure promised that it was user-friendly. Reality was far different. It was true that the optimistically named Acme Premier Hospitality System would generate a general ledger, but doing that required too many steps and far too much time.

And that was the least of its flaws. One of Marisa's requirements for the system was that anyone could enter a reservation without special training. Acme Premier failed that test. Rainbow's End needed—and deserved—better than this.

Fortunately, she had one more system on her short list of likely packages. If that one proved to have substance behind the marketing hype, she'd be able to deliver on her promise to have software selection completed before Kate and Greg returned from their honeymoon. Then she could begin to develop an operating budget.

Kate had admitted that she and Greg hadn't worried about how much they were spending on renovations—one of the advantages of being a billionaire—but they both realized they needed a budget and the accountability that came with it.

And then . . . Marisa sighed, unsure how she would fill her days. There had never been a shortage of work at Haslett Associates. To the contrary, she had often felt as if she could be in the office 24/7 and still not complete everything. But working here was far different from being an employee of a firm with hundreds of clients.

"Am I interrupting?"

Marisa smiled as Blake poked his head into her office two hours later. It had taken her that long to get the final software package loaded and configured on her computer. Now she was ready to begin the evaluation.

"You are interrupting," she told him, "but it's welcome." She rose from behind her desk and flexed her shoulders, trying to work out the kinks. It had been a long morning, and though Mom had protested, Marisa had refused to take a normal lunch break. Instead, she'd remained at her desk, a sandwich in one hand as she clicked her way through the installation instructions. "I can use a break."

Blake grinned and handed her a can of soda. "I thought you

might need this. I can't count the number of midafternoon caffeine breaks I've taken."

"Perfect timing. Now I'll have the energy to finish this." She gestured toward the computer. "This is my last hope. If it doesn't work, I'll have to resort to the B list, and I don't want to do that." When Blake raised an eyebrow, Marisa explained that she'd categorized more than a dozen software packages based on the features they provided. The A list had everything she wanted; the Bs were lacking in one or more aspects.

"How long will it take before you know?"

"If I'm lucky, five or six hours."

"And you plan to work through dinner again."

Marisa nodded. Though she'd enjoyed the meal Blake had shared with her and Mom, she had worked through dinner last night, determined to make progress on the software selection.

Wrinkling his nose in apparent disapproval, Blake said, "I was hoping I could convince you to play hooky. I have one of those offers you can't refuse."

As tempting as time with him sounded, Marisa couldn't forget the promises she had made to Kate and Greg. "I've got a lot of work."

"It's only one night." Blake gave her his most persuasive smile. "Think of it as a public service. You can tell your workaholic side that you'll be saving this guest from terminal boredom."

Marisa knew that was an exaggeration. Blake had plenty of ways to pass the time. He'd gotten a stack of books from the library this morning, and her mother had issued a standing challenge to a game of checkers. Still, spending an evening with Blake was undeniably appealing.

"What was that offer I can't refuse?"

As if sensing that she was on the verge of agreeing, Blake's smile widened. "The Bijou is having double feature week. Tonight's *An Affair to Remember* and *Sleepless in Seattle*. I haven't seen either of them." He made that sound as if it were a grave personal deficiency.

"I'm not surprised. They're chick flicks. From what I've heard, men only go to movies like those on dates." And, by even the most conservative definition, this would be a date. Marisa couldn't deny the rush of pleasure that thought gave her.

"According to Mr. Benton, my life will not be complete unless I see those particular movies." Blake forced his face into a parody of despair.

Marisa couldn't help it. She laughed. "Now I understand. This would be more than a public service. It would be humanitarian aid."

When Blake nodded, obviously struggling to keep his expression solemn, Marisa chuckled. This light banter was just what she needed, and though it might mean working extra late tomorrow, she wouldn't pass up the opportunity Blake offered.

"Now that I understand everything that's at stake, I can see that I have no alternative. I couldn't let your life be incomplete." She paused for dramatic effect before adding, "Or mine, either. Believe it or not, even though every other woman in the country has seen them at least twice, tonight will be my first time."

"Then it's a date."

———————— ✦ ————————

"Wear the green dress," Marisa's mother advised four hours later when Marisa stood in front of her closet with an expression she suspected was reminiscent of a deer in the headlights. "It's pretty but not too fancy."

Even though her wardrobe was only a fraction of the size it had been in Atlanta, Marisa had spent far too much time trying to decide what to wear. She had eaten only half of her dinner, telling Mom she had to get ready. Almost as if he'd realized that she would need time alone, Blake had refused Mom's dinner invitation, claiming he'd brought a sandwich home from the Sit 'n' Sip. That gave Marisa time to obsess over her wardrobe selection.

First dates were special, and even if it was nothing more than an evening at Dupree's aging theater, she wanted to wear something more than jeans and a sweater. The green dress was one she'd worn to the office on days when she had dinner meetings scheduled. As Mom said, it was flattering without being overly dressy.

"Would it be crass to whistle?" Blake asked as he entered the cabin, his gaze moving from the top of Marisa's head to her peep-toe pumps.

"Yes," Marisa said at the same time as her mother shook her head and declared, "No."

Not bothering to hide his amusement, Blake looked at Mom. "I'm sorry, Carmen, but in this case, she overrules you." He turned to Marisa. "If I can't whistle, I hope I'm not out of bounds by saying you look beautiful, because you do."

He wasn't out of bounds. To the contrary, his obviously genuine compliment filled Marisa with pleasure. It had been a long time since a man had gazed at her with such approval.

"You look pretty good yourself." Dressed in an open-collared shirt, navy slacks, and loafers, Blake could have been an advertisement for men's casual clothing.

"Thanks." He put his hand on the small of Marisa's back and guided her toward the door. "Don't wait up for us," he called to Mom. "Your daughter and I are going to have a wild night on the town."

Laughter was Mom's only response. There were few opportunities for wild nights in Dupree, and even if there were, Marisa St. George was unlikely to indulge.

The Bijou was more crowded than Marisa had expected. Either it was a slow night in Dupree, or Mr. Benton had convinced more than just Blake that this was a pair of movies they absolutely had to see. The only seats Marisa and Blake could find were farther forward than she would have liked, and she found herself craning her neck to see the screen. It was going to be a long and possibly painful evening.

The discomfort lasted only a few seconds. Though Marisa said nothing and knew she hadn't even groaned, Blake recognized what was happening and slid his arm behind her neck. In the space of an instant, discomfort turned to pure pleasure, leaving Marisa tempted to close her eyes and simply savor the sensation of being so close to Blake. But as the opening credits for *An Affair to Remember* rolled across the screen, she found herself drawn into the story.

Two hours later, she smiled as the theater lights came on.

"Not bad."

"Not bad?" Marisa stared at the man who'd made the movie so enjoyable. "It was wonderful."

Blake grinned. "I was talking about the popcorn. It was just the right amount." He turned the cardboard container upside down to demonstrate its emptiness. "Do you want more for *Sleepless*?"

As Marisa looked at the line of patrons now filling the aisles, she shook her head. "You'd wait forever."

"This way there'll be more room for ice cream."

"Ice cream?" Perhaps that was Blake's idea of a wild night on the town. It certainly beat the teenagers' version that involved fast cars, loud radios, and the occasional controlled substance.

He flashed her a mischievous grin. "Sure. It's not a real movie date without a sundae afterward. Russ Walker assured me he makes the best in town."

"I hope you didn't point out that he makes the only sundaes in town."

"Of course not." Blake faked a grimace. "Do I look stupid?"

He looked handsome. Handsome and kind and wonderful.

"Only a stupid woman would answer that question with anything other than a resounding no," she said, "and I'd like to think that neither of us is stupid. I'm glad you met Russ. He and the Sit 'n' Sip are one of our local institutions."

The conversation turned to Dupree's downtown and Russ's claim that it was on the verge of renewal. Before Blake had finished listing all the reasons he'd been given, the lights dimmed, and it was time for another rendezvous at the Empire State Building. When the movie ended, Marisa sighed.

"Does that mean you didn't like it?" Though she no longer needed his arm as a neck rest, Blake did not remove it. Instead, he lowered it to circle her shoulders.

Marisa shook her head. "That was a sigh of pleasure. And please don't ask which I liked better. I can't decide."

"I can't either," he admitted. "I'm saving my decision-making brain cells for sundae flavors."

"Hot fudge, butterscotch, or strawberry. Those are the choices. Of course, Russ has been known to put all three on one scoop of ice cream for people who can't make a decision."

"A man after my own heart. I knew I liked Dupree for a reason."

Both Blake and Marisa were laughing as they started to make their way toward the exit now that the first rush was over and the theater had begun to empty. They were halfway to the back when Marisa glanced to the right and blinked. Why was Lauren here? She had claimed that she had no desire to watch a movie after Patrick became too ill to accompany her.

Marisa stepped into the row. "Are you all right?" The question was rhetorical, for her friend's eyes were red-rimmed, and her nose rivaled Santa's favorite reindeer's.

Lauren rose and approached Marisa. "I was an idiot," she said, her voice still thick with tears. "I thought I could do this. I thought I was ready, but all I could think about was how Patrick and I used to come here together."

Marisa put her arm around her friend's waist and gave her a quick hug. Though she doubted Lauren was in any mood to meet new people, Marisa couldn't ignore Blake's presence. He had followed her into the row and stood right behind her. "I don't think you've met Blake Kendall," Marisa said. "He's a guest at Rainbow's End. Blake, this is Lauren Ahrens, my best friend in the whole world."

Though Lauren's eyes brightened slightly at the introduction, she said nothing.

"I'm pleased to meet you, Lauren." Blake looked at her for a second, and Marisa suspected he was seeing the same vulnerability she had. "Marisa and I were going to the Sit 'n' Sip for sundaes. I hope you'll join us."

Lauren shook her head. "I can't." Her expression contradicted her words. Lauren might not want to admit it, but she craved adult company, particularly tonight when her emotions had been abraded by being alone in a place where she'd come so often as part of a couple.

"The babysitter won't mind an extra hour's pay," Marisa said, hoping that would be all the encouragement Lauren needed.

"That's not an issue. Fiona's staying with Alice tonight."

Blake gave Lauren one of his most engaging smiles. "Then the only reason for refusing would be that you've taken an instant dislike to me." He turned to Marisa, feigning the expression of a woebegone puppy. "Surely you can convince your friend that I'm not an axe murderer or a shady politician hoping that a dish of ice cream and a spoonful of hot fudge sauce will convince her to vote for me."

Struggling to keep her face solemn, Marisa looked at Lauren. "As far as I know, Blake's not an axe murderer or a politician of any kind. If you need more references, Mom's been feeding him dinner every night."

"That's not saying much." Lauren's lips curved into a smile, and Marisa saw the hint of laughter in her eyes. "She feeds everyone at Rainbow's End."

"But Blake's the only one invited to our cabin."

Her eyes widening with surprise at the announcement, Lauren started to nod. "If you're sure . . ."

"We are." Blake didn't wait for Marisa to respond.

And so the three of them spent an hour at the Sit 'n' Sip, talking about everything and nothing. It wasn't Marisa's imagination that Lauren's smiles grew more frequent and her laughter more genuine. Like Marisa, she seemed to be falling under the spell of Blake's charm. Lauren's eyes lost their haunted expression, and though her nose was still faintly pink, she no longer looked like a woman who'd spent hours weeping.

When they'd devoured the last bite of ice cream and assured Russ Walker that he hadn't exaggerated the quality of his sundaes, Blake rose. "Ladies, your chariot awaits," he said as he offered each of them an arm. And though Lauren protested that she was perfectly capable of walking, Blake insisted on driving her home.

"You forgot to read the fine print," he told her. "When you agreed to the sundae, you also agreed to door-to-door chauffeur service. It's a package deal."

Lauren looked as if she wanted to argue but capitulated with a smile. "Thank you," she said, repeating the words when they reached her home. Though Marisa suspected she would shed a few more tears when she was inside the empty house, the worst was over. Thanks to Blake.

"She's a nice person," Blake said as he drove away.

Marisa reached across the console and laid her hand on his arm. "So are you, Blake. So are you."

7

Blake slowed his pace as he climbed the hill. Greg had assured him that jogging up Ranger Hill was far better exercise than running on a treadmill. Of course, the fact that neither Rainbow's End nor the town of Dupree boasted a gym meant that jogging was virtually the only form of weight-bearing exercise available. And so here he was, struggling to make it to the top of what looked like Mount Everest.

Funny how it hadn't seemed so steep when he'd driven it. Then he'd thought it quaint that the summit of Lone Star Trail was called Ranger Hill. The residents of Dupree were fiercely proud of their Texas heritage, and Blake couldn't blame them. The state had a rich and colorful history. Right now, though, he was more concerned with putting one foot in front of the other than with Lone Star lore.

The hill wasn't the real problem, and Blake knew it. His muscles were fine, all except for the one called a brain. That was the one that was failing him. The empty well, the dried-up pond, the blank screen. No matter what cliché he used, it was still writer's block, and it didn't appear to be diminishing.

Blake took another step, his pace now little more than walking.

He could make it to the top of the hill; he *would* make it to the top. He wasn't going to admit defeat, not with jogging nor with his book.

He'd tried everything he knew to stimulate the muse yesterday. First he'd stared at Bluebonnet Lake for what felt like hours, even though his watch said a mere ten minutes had passed before he'd realized that the only thing that lake watching did was cause him to nod off. Next he'd tried rowing. All that had accomplished was leaving him with arms that felt as if they were going to fall out of their sockets. In desperation, he'd walked around Dupree, talking to everyone he met. They were friendly enough, but nothing they said or did sparked a single idea.

When that hadn't accomplished anything other than confirming Marisa's statement that Dupree was a small-with-a-capital-*S* town, he'd borrowed her mother's library card and checked out a dozen books he would never have considered reading, everything from Lorena McCourtney's cozy mysteries to Ann Gabhart's historical fiction, hoping something might inspire him.

He'd even discovered a book on overcoming writer's block. He hadn't checked that out, of course. That might have triggered questions Blake didn't want to answer. Instead, he'd tucked it inside an oversized encyclopedia and had read it at one of the library tables.

For a moment, he'd felt as if he were back in high school, pretending to be studying when he'd actually been reading comic books. Though Dad had said nothing at the time, Blake suspected he knew what was going on, but as long as Grandfather didn't, the house had been peaceful. Unfortunately, the book Blake had read so surreptitiously hadn't helped any more than his other efforts had.

His lungs burned, and his legs felt as if they'd turned to rubber, but when he reached the top of the hill, elation rushed through him. Though he was tempted to pump his fists as if he were Rocky sprinting up the steps to the Philadelphia Museum of Art, he simply jogged in place as he savored the triumph of cresting Ranger

Hill. He could do this. Now, if only he could find an idea for Cliff Pearson's next adventure.

The muse was silent. The change of scenery that he'd hoped would bring it back to life had accomplished nothing. Blake shook his head and began to jog back down the hill. That wasn't true. If he hadn't come to Rainbow's End, he would not have met Marisa. And that would have been a shame. He liked her. Blake shook his head again. He was a man who made his living with words. *Liked* didn't come close to describing what he felt for Marisa. He was attracted to her, deeply attracted.

He'd thought the instant magnetism he'd felt the first time he met her had been a figment of his imagination, but it wasn't. He felt the same way each time he saw her, as if they were meant to be together.

Blake liked her sense of humor; he liked the fact that they could discuss everything from *Anna Karenina* to what made Dr Pepper different from other colas; he even liked the way she'd tried to hide the tears that had slipped down her cheeks while they'd watched those silly, sentimental movies at the Bijou.

He liked the way her perfume lingered in his memory and the ripples of pleasure he'd felt when she'd settled her head against his arm. He liked her obvious love for her mother and the protective air she had when she was with Lauren. The fact was, Blake liked everything about Marisa, but that wasn't bringing the muse back.

He needed something else, something more than a change of scenery, if he was going to have any chance of making his deadline. For the briefest of instants, he'd considered telling Marisa about his alter ego Ken Blake and the dilemma he was facing. It might have been a flight of fancy, but he'd thought she might say something that would somehow break the logjam inside his brain and get the ideas flowing.

The words were on the tip of his tongue when he'd stopped himself. Only four people knew that Blake Kendall was also Ken Blake: his editor, his agent, Greg, and now Kate. It would be sheer foolishness to add another person to the circle, even if she was the most intriguing woman he'd ever met.

There had to be another way to reenergize his muse.

———————— ✳ ————————

"Nice office."

Lauren stepped inside and looked around, giving Marisa a chance to study her. Though her friend had deep circles under her eyes as if she'd spent a sleepless night, Marisa saw no sign of tears, and her smile was infectious. This was the Lauren who'd always been able to boost Marisa's spirits.

"As closets go, it's not a bad office," Marisa conceded. "Greg said this used to be the storage room, but he figured I needed a space of my own." And he'd done his best to provide all the normal office accoutrements, including an ergonomic chair that made the long hours Marisa spent here comfortable. Though the room was not large, it was big enough to accommodate a desk, two tall filing cabinets, and a printer stand, plus two visitors' chairs.

As she rose to hug her friend, Marisa gestured to the back wall. "A window would be nice, but with everything I have on my plate, I wouldn't have much time to look outside anyway." Her office in Atlanta had boasted floor-to-ceiling windows with breathtaking views, but other than checking the weather, Marisa had had little time to enjoy them.

Though she might regret the absence of a window in a couple months, she had been too busy to think about much more than the software she was evaluating. And Blake. It had been more difficult than Marisa had expected to focus on the chart of accounts structure when her mind kept replaying the hours she'd been with him.

Lauren fingered the large tote bag she'd slung over her shoulder. "I know you're busy, so I won't stay long, but I come bearing gifts and an apology. Which do you want first?"

Marisa could imagine no reason for either. It wasn't her birthday or any other special occasion, and Lauren had done nothing to warrant an apology. "I don't know why you think you owe me an apology."

"How about the fact that I spoiled your date with one of the best-looking men to set foot in Dupree? Friends shouldn't do things like that."

Marisa shook her head at the woman who'd been her best friend for more than two decades. "You didn't spoil anything. You may have noticed that Blake invited you to join us. It wasn't your suggestion, and you weren't intruding. Besides, it isn't like the Sit 'n' Sip is the world's most romantic spot." Last night it had been filled with teenagers talking so loudly that Marisa had felt as if she were shouting to be heard.

"That's true, but it was still nice of you two to invite me. By the time I got home, I felt better than I have in a long time. Thanks, Marisa."

"That's what friends are for." Even when her life had centered on Patrick and the excitement of first love, Lauren had done everything she could to comfort Marisa when Hal and then her father had disappointed her.

It had been Lauren who'd declared that she would stay home and that Patrick would be Marisa's date for the prom the day Marisa's dream of being the football star's date had turned into a nightmare.

"It was all a joke," Hal had said when Marisa called to ask why he was so late in picking her up. "You didn't really think I'd take the town drunk's daughter anywhere, did you?"

But Marisa had. She'd believed Hal was serious when he said he'd broken up with Tiffany and that he wanted Marisa to be his date for the prom. That was why she'd worked every job she could find to pay for her gown and all the accessories that were part of prom night. And then she'd been stood up. Instead of arriving on the arm of the most popular boy in her class, Marisa had spent the night at home, crying as if her heart had broken.

Less than a month later, she had learned the true meaning of heartbreak when Eric disappeared. And through it all, Lauren had tried to comfort Marisa. Inviting her for a sundae was the least Marisa could do.

"You're the best," Lauren said, "but Blake's pretty good too. Any chance he'll stay in Dupree and you two will become what my mom used to call 'an item'? The Matchers would be thrilled."

Marisa shook her head. This was moving way too fast for comfort. While it was true that she felt an undeniable attraction to Blake, that didn't mean they were on their way to being a couple.

"Time out." Marisa formed a *T* with her hands. "Blake's only going to be here a few weeks. This is like a shipboard romance, only there's no ship and it's not a romance. We're just friends."

Lauren's look left no doubt that she did not believe Marisa. "So you say. Friends."

Her eyes narrowed as she looked at the bare walls, and Marisa suspected she was trying to decide what kind of artwork they needed. If she were planning to be here permanently, Marisa would have chosen a couple prints, but as it was, the stark room met her needs.

"Speaking of friends, I'm surprised at how different Greg's friends are." Lauren had apparently decided not to comment on the spartan décor. "Blake is nothing like Drew, but they're both charming in their own way."

If she'd been a dog, Marisa knew her ears would have perked up at the change she'd heard in Lauren's voice. She studied her friend's face. It wasn't her imagination. Though her expression was calm, Lauren's eyes held a hint of excitement. Interesting. "You know Drew Carroll?"

Nodding, Lauren said, "I met him when he was here last April, and we spent some time together at the reception. He's an intriguing guy."

There was no doubt about it. Lauren had more than a casual interest in Drew Carroll. For her friend's sake, Marisa hoped that wasn't a mistake. "Intriguing is not the way my mother described him. I got an earful about Drew after she saw him at the wedding. She said he was as arrogant as sin and that they found an empty whiskey bottle in his cabin when he stayed here. You can imagine how Mom reacted to that." If there was one thing that roused her mother's hackles, it was excessive drinking. She had firsthand experience of how destructive that could be.

"I think Drew's changed." Lauren's voice rang with emotion, telling Marisa this was no casual observation but something she'd spent time considering. "I don't know what happened, but he doesn't seem like the same man I met last spring."

That was Lauren being Pollyanna. Marisa knew better. "I don't believe people change. They may put on different masks, but fundamentally, they're the same." It was a lesson she'd learned from her father, and one Hal had reinforced.

Raising her hands in the universal sign of surrender, Lauren nodded. "Okay, okay. I'm not going to argue with you. It's time for the second part of this visit—the gift."

She reached into her tote bag and withdrew a tissue-wrapped item whose shape told Marisa it was one of Lauren's handmade quilted pillows. Unwrapping it, Marisa gasped.

"Oh, Lauren, it's exquisite." Made of half a dozen shades of red and yellow, the quilted border was an intricate pattern that Lauren had developed and turned into her trademark, but what drew Marisa's attention was the center design. The Mason jar filled with fireflies brought back a host of memories. As young children, she and Lauren had searched for fireflies in her backyard. Later they'd moved the search to the park, and still later they'd ventured all the way to Firefly Valley, hoping to find even more of the fascinating insects there.

"Oh, Lauren, I love it." Marisa gave her friend a warm hug. "There were fireflies near Atlanta—one woman told me I should call them lightning bugs—but it wasn't the same." Marisa traced the quilted image. "Remember how much fun we used to have trying to catch them?"

Lauren nodded. "The season's over now, but maybe next year you can help me teach Fiona the way your father taught us."

"My father chased fireflies?" Marisa's hand stilled, and she gripped the edge of the pillow. The only thing her father had chased was oblivion at the bottom of a bottle.

"Sure. Don't you remember?" It was clear that Lauren had no idea of the direction Marisa's memories had taken. "He poked all those holes in the lids. Then he showed us how to swing the jars so that the fireflies would come inside. My mom said she'd never seen anyone catch as many as you and I did, and it was all because of your dad." Lauren gave Marisa a quizzical look. "Don't you remember?"

Marisa did not.

8

It was Saturday morning, one week since Kate and Greg's wedding, and the weather was just as beautiful as it had been then. Though Marisa had heard some of the townspeople muttering about drought and its impact on everything from lawns to cattle prices, she was enjoying the sunshine, or she would have been if she weren't cooped up in a windowless office.

Marisa sighed as she stared at the mound of paperwork on her desk. Perhaps it was just as well that she couldn't see outside. She was distracted enough as it was. What she remembered most about last Saturday wasn't the wedding, even though it had been a beautiful one. What made the day special was that she'd met Blake Kendall, the man who continued to occupy far too many of her thoughts. She was supposed to be overseeing the renovations during Kate and Greg's absence in addition to trying to make sense of the accounting records, not daydreaming about the handsome brown-haired man who was Rainbow's End's sole guest.

Fortunately, the last of Marisa's A list software packages had proven to be a winner. Though the marketing brochure had been the least impressive, the system had all the functionality she needed. With the software selection complete, her next challenge was to determine how much the building renovations would cost and what a reasonable revenue stream might be so that she could establish a budget.

Marisa had no time to waste, and yet she found herself distracted, glancing at her watch and wondering what Blake was doing. She knew he jogged each morning and joined the workers for the midday meal. He ate supper with her and Mom and sometimes stayed to play a game of checkers with Mom while Marisa came back here to work, but other than those basics, she didn't know how he spent his days. What she did know was that he wasn't a typical resort guest.

Blake might have come here to relax, but he seemed tense. Eric would have said he was wound up tighter than a cheap watch. Marisa clenched her fists. She didn't want to think about Eric. He'd made his choices, and apparently one of those choices was that he did not want to be found. The disaster with Trent had been the final wake-up call, forcing Marisa to admit that she would never be able to get the closure she and Mom deserved, but oh, how she wished it were otherwise!

Marisa closed her eyes, willing the tears not to fall. When she opened them, the numbers still swam on the page. She was accomplishing nothing sitting here. Somehow, she had to clear her head.

After switching off her computer monitor, Marisa grabbed her sunglasses and headed outside. A quick walk along the lakeshore might be the break she needed. She moved briskly, hoping the exercise would banish the demons that whirled inside her head, but her pace slowed when she saw she was not alone. Blake stood at the edge of the lake, and judging from his posture, his morning was going even worse than hers. His head was bowed, his shoulders slumped. If Marisa had been asked to paint a picture of dejection, it would be Blake at this moment.

"What's wrong?" It wasn't much of a greeting, but the words slipped out.

Blake turned, his obviously forced smile doing nothing to reassure her. "Nothing."

Though he was lying, Marisa wouldn't challenge him. "I imagine it gets pretty boring here. There's not a lot to do with no other guests around." She kept walking at a slow but steady pace, hoping Blake would come with her. Anything had to be better than standing there looking and feeling miserable.

"I'm used to being alone," he said. "I do my best work alone." The words were almost defiant, but at least he had joined her and was matching her pace. Though she wanted to wrap her arms around him and comfort him the way she would have Fiona, Marisa hesitated. Blake was not a child. He was a man who might misunderstand if she hugged him.

"You're not working here," she said softly. Perhaps that was the problem. Perhaps he was a workaholic who felt lost if he had too much unscheduled time.

Blake's head jerked as if he'd been punched, and he shot her a look that combined surprise with something else, something Marisa couldn't identify. "That's true," he said shortly. "I'm not."

Somehow, she'd hit a sensitive chord, deepening whatever was bothering Blake, when she had hoped to do the exact opposite. It was time to try a different tactic.

"I'm the one who's supposed to be working, but now I feel like playing hooky again. Can I convince you to be my partner in crime?" When a hint of amusement touched Blake's expression, Marisa knew she was on the right track. It didn't matter that she'd have to work tonight if she could help Blake by taking a long break now.

"What did you have in mind?" he asked. "I doubt you're planning to rob the bank."

Marisa shook her head. "I was thinking about running away from home, at least for a few hours. Lauren has a tandem that's been gathering dust ever since Patrick got sick. I know she'd let us borrow it. Say yes, Blake. The weather's great and Mom will pack us a lunch." Marisa felt like a carousel barker, reciting a patter designed to convince reluctant riders.

"A tandem as in bicycle?" Blake focused on one part of her invitation, his expression as skeptical as if she'd proposed skydiving without a parachute.

"Exactly. You know how to ride a bike, don't you?"

Though he shrugged, Marisa took comfort in the fact that he'd straightened his shoulders, his morose mood apparently dissipating. "It's been years."

"Me too. We can test the theory that you never forget."

Blake appeared dubious, but he didn't refuse. Instead, he shrugged again. "Don't blame me if we tip over."

They didn't. Lauren closed her store briefly to haul the tandem from the back of the garage and give them what she called the Tandem Riders 101 course. Once the picnic basket was strapped on the rear rack, Blake, as the captain, got onto the bike and held it upright while stoker Marisa climbed on behind him. When she had both feet in the toe clips, Blake pushed off.

Although it felt awkward for a few minutes, they soon discovered their rhythm, finding a cadence that was comfortable for both of them and learning to lean in the same direction as they turned. Sooner than she'd thought possible, Marisa felt as if she and Blake had been riding together for years.

"Where next?" he asked as they reached the end of Hickory and turned east on Avenue C, passing the Hickory View apartments. Fiona, who was spending the day with her friend Alice, waved as they rode by, proudly telling Alice that that was her mom's bike.

"Let's take one more circuit of the town. Then we'll see." Until she was confident they had mastered the basics, Marisa was not going to suggest they venture out of Dupree.

"This is fun," Blake said as he increased their pace.

Though he couldn't see her, Marisa nodded. "That's what Lauren always said. She used to claim the tandem was the secret to her happy marriage. Once she and Patrick learned to pedal together, the rest was easy, or so she said."

Blake swiveled his head to glance at Marisa. "What happened to her husband?"

"Cancer. By the time he was diagnosed, it was inoperable." Like many men, Patrick had been reluctant to visit a doctor, claiming that everyone had minor aches and pains. His had turned out to be not so minor.

When they reached Lone Star Trail, Marisa agreed that they were ready to try the "big road," as she called the highway. They zipped past the gas station that held more than its share of memories, then turned south onto the highway.

"Lauren may remarry." Blake was obviously thinking about the tandem's owner. Though Lauren's story was not a happy one, at least Blake was no longer dwelling on whatever had depressed him earlier this morning. Tandem therapy appeared to be working.

"I don't know. Fiona's been pretty outspoken about wanting a new daddy, but Lauren's leery." Other than her unexpected comments about Drew Carroll, Lauren had not so much as mentioned another man.

"Is she afraid she'll never find someone who can hold a candle to Patrick?"

"Either that, or she's afraid of losing another person she loves."

———— ✦ ————

Blake was still pondering Marisa's comment as they pedaled up a hill. It was a beautiful day, and the exercise was starting to clear his mind, but now the clouds were rolling in—figuratively—because of what Marisa had said.

Perhaps it was the writer in him, but ever since he'd seen those photos and realized that she had taken drastic action to mute her resemblance to her father, Blake had been spinning stories in his head, trying to understand why. The only answer that made sense to him was that Marisa had been so devastated by her father's death that she did not want to be reminded of him every time she looked in a mirror. Her comment about the fear of losing loved ones seemed to confirm that. Though she'd attributed it to Lauren, the sadness in Marisa's eyes when she said it made Blake believe she was the one who harbored that particular fear. He wouldn't pry—not overtly, at any rate—but he had every intention of learning whether his assumption was correct.

When they reached the summit of the small hill, he turned to look at Marisa. "Whatever your mother put in that basket," he said, tipping his head toward the rack on the back of the bike, "it smells delicious. Let's find a place to eat before I faint from hunger." He'd been so angry with himself when he'd wakened this morning without a single idea for Cliff Pearson's next adventure that he'd skipped breakfast.

"Good idea." Marisa reached in front of him and pointed to the bottom of the hill. "See the white gate on the right? We can stop there. I know the owner, and he won't mind if we picnic on his land."

"Sounds like a plan to me." Blake leaned forward, enjoying the speed with which they descended the hill. Lauren hadn't exaggerated when she'd told them that tandems gained speed rapidly on downhill stretches.

When they reached the gate, Blake steered the bike off the road, holding it steady until Marisa had dismounted. Within minutes they had the tandem propped against the fence and had spread a small tarp under one of the live oaks. To Blake's amusement, Marisa had picked up a few acorns and tossed them aside before they laid the tarp.

"Trust me. You don't want to sit on one."

She was right, he realized a few seconds later when he discovered an acorn digging into his thigh.

When they were settled, Marisa opened the basket and handed Blake a sandwich carefully wrapped in waxed paper. "Mom sent her new favorite sandwich: roast beef, ham, and coleslaw on pumpernickel."

"Sounds good." After Marisa pulled two insulated bottles from the basket and laid them on the tarp, Blake bowed his head and gave thanks for the food. Seconds after saying amen, he had unwrapped the sandwich and taken a bite. "Your mom's a genius. This tastes even better than it smells." It wasn't simply hunger talking. The combination of flavors was unexpected but delicious. "I've got to tell my dad about this. He's always looking for a good sandwich."

"Does he live in California too?" Marisa sat with her back against the tree trunk, her legs stretched out in front of her. Like Blake, she wore shorts and a T-shirt, but on her the ordinary clothes looked extraordinary. With her hair pulled back in a ponytail, she looked nothing like a stodgy accountant.

Blake shook his head, as much at the thought of Marisa being stodgy as in response to her question. "Dad lives in Bethlehem, Pennsylvania. Have you ever been there?"

When Marisa shook her head, Blake continued. "Things have changed, but Bethlehem Steel used to be one of the best-known names in the country. It's their steel that's in the Golden Gate Bridge." That was one of the reasons Blake had insisted on an office with a view of the bridge. In his mind, the famous landmark was a tie between him and his father. "My dad was a steelworker like his father."

Marisa chewed slowly, as if she were ruminating on his words. "He must be proud of you, having a college degree and your own firm. It's the American dream, isn't it, that each generation surpasses the previous one?"

Though Blake didn't know how Dad would feel if he knew how Blake earned most of his money, he'd seen his father's reaction to his education and his work as a financial planner. When Grandfather had warned him about the dangers of pride the day he'd announced that he had been accepted at Stanford, Dad had patted him on the back. Once he'd graduated, Dad had insisted that he wanted Blake to be the one to invest his savings. "There's no one I trust more," he had said the day he transferred the funds to Blake.

Smiling at the memory, Blake nodded. "Dad's a man of few words, but I think he's pleased."

Blake was pleased that he'd managed to steer the conversation to fathers. "What about your father? Would he have been proud of you?" Blake hoped that Marisa hadn't been as young as Fiona when her father had died. Though Fiona was old enough to retain some memories of her dad, they would fade as new memories took their place. If Marisa had had her father with her through her teenage years, she would have more enduring memories.

There were several seconds of silence before Marisa crumpled her waxed paper and tossed it into the basket, her face flushed with unexpected anger. "That's one subject that's off-limits," she said tersely. "I don't talk about Eric St. George."

---

Marisa bit the inside of her lip, trying to hold back the bitter words that threatened to erupt. She should have said something innocuous like "I hope so." If she had, Blake would have dropped the subject. Instead, she'd obviously aroused his interest. Her goal had been to lighten Blake's mood, not subject him to her temper, and she definitely did not want him asking more questions about Eric. Though the townspeople appeared to have been silent on the subject, undoubtedly because Blake was an outsider, there was no telling what Mom might say if Blake asked direct questions. The best thing was to attempt to deflect them.

"I'm sorry," Marisa said as she repacked the basket. "My father is a painful subject for my mother and me." With some luck, that would keep Blake from interrogating Mom.

He nodded shortly, his expression telling Marisa that while he might not understand, he respected her wishes. "Are you ready to head back?"

She was indeed.

An hour later, Marisa was in the cabin she shared with her mother, wishing it had a bathtub instead of a shower. Her muscles could use a long soak, but since that wasn't possible, she took a quick shower and headed for her office.

"I'm so glad you're here." Brandi, the teenager who'd been

manning the front desk, wore a harried expression. "We didn't know how to reach you."

Marisa frowned at the realization that she hadn't taken her cell phone. She'd become so accustomed to Rainbow's End being out of cell range that she often forgot to carry it when she left the valley.

"What's wrong?"

"You'll see." Brandi led the way to the kitchen. "It's Carmen."

"I can't believe I did this." Marisa's mother gestured toward her visibly swollen right ankle. She was seated next to the table, her foot propped on a second chair. "All I did was turn around, and the next thing I knew, I was on the floor."

Fortunately, Brandi had heard her cries and had helped her into the chair, putting a bag of ice on the ankle, then calling Dupree's sole physician.

"Doc Santos said to bring you right in," Brandi said. "A couple X-rays, and he'll know the extent of the damage."

With one arm wrapped around Marisa's waist and the other around Brandi, Mom managed to hobble to the car, all the while complaining that she didn't need the doctor, that a few more minutes with the ice pack would cure whatever was wrong. It was vintage Mom.

Marisa ignored the complaints along with the protests that erupted when she insisted that Mom sit in the back where she could keep her ankle elevated. "I know it's only three miles," Marisa told her, "but you need to take care of that ankle."

Mom grumbled as she settled into the backseat, and the grumbling continued as Marisa headed up Ranger Hill. "What's that rattling?" her mother demanded when the car began its familiar *clank, clank*.

The last thing Marisa wanted to worry about was the rattle in the car's suspension. She was far more concerned with whether Mom's ankle was broken. "It's nothing serious," she assured her mother. "It's been like that since I bought it."

"You shouldn't ignore a rattle. You know that." Mom winced

as they hit a bump. "If your father were here, he'd know what's wrong just from listening to it."

Why did everyone want to talk about Eric St. George today? "But he's not here. He's been gone for more than eight years."

"He'll come back."

Marisa took a deep breath, trying not to frown as she looked at her mother in the rearview mirror. "You're deluding yourself, Mom." Part of her wanted to shout the words, but she kept her voice low and even. Though this wasn't the time or place she would have chosen, the discussion was long overdue.

"I know you don't want to hear this, but you need to accept the fact that you've been deserted. Divorce him or declare him dead, but don't go on in this limbo. It's not fair."

The quick intake of breath told Marisa her salvo had hit its target. "Fair for whom?" her mother demanded.

"You, of course. You need to be free to start the next phase of your life." Mom had been delighted when Kate's grandmother had discovered a second chance for love at Rainbow's End. It was time Mom looked for one for herself. If she didn't, she'd be facing decades of loneliness.

"What if I don't want to be free? Did that ever occur to you?" Mom thumped the back of Marisa's seat to get her attention. "I love your father. I'll never forget the man I married."

That was the reason Marisa had hired so many investigators. Until she knew what had happened to Eric, Mom would continue to cling to the fantasy that he'd return. She needed—and, truth be told, Marisa needed—to know whether the man was still alive. But none of the investigators—not even the legitimate ones—had been able to locate Eric. And Trent . . . Dozens of women including Marisa had fallen for his line, only to discover that once the money was deposited in his account, Trent and his promises disappeared.

"The man you married no longer exists. He may even be dead."

In the rearview mirror, Marisa saw Mom shake her head. "Eric's alive. Deep in my heart, I know that." To add emphasis to her words, she laid her hand over her heart. "I love you, Marisa, and I want you to be happy, but it doesn't matter what you say. I won't divorce him. I won't throw away the love we shared."

Mom took a deep breath, exhaling slowly. "When I said my wedding vows, I meant them. 'For richer, for poorer, in sickness and in health.' Eric is sick. I hate what he's done to you, but I can't abandon him any more than you would abandon me just because I hurt my ankle."

Marisa blinked, astonished by the direction the conversation had taken. "That's different. Totally different. He chose to drink. He chose to leave us. He doesn't deserve our love."

Mom shook her head again. "I don't believe that, and neither do you."

9

**P**oor Carmen." Lauren looked up as she finished a seam. When Marisa had realized that she would get no work done tonight, she'd headed for Dupree and Lauren. Fiona had already gone to bed, so Marisa's friend offered her a cup of coffee and ushered her into the spare bedroom that had been turned into a sewing workshop.

Marisa stirred a teaspoon of honey into the herb tea she'd chosen. Unlike Lauren, she didn't want to be awake all night, especially after the day she'd had. "Lucky Carmen. It's only a strain. Doc wrapped her ankle and said all she needs to do is rest it for a couple weeks."

"And she agreed?" Lauren had no trouble making her skepticism heard over the sewing machine's whirring.

"Of course not. I think Doc was testing her. When she refused, he pulled out the ugliest boot I've ever seen and told Mom she'd have to wear that. You could have knocked me over when she said it was a brilliant idea and put it on. And, as if that wasn't enough, she let me cook supper."

After snipping the threads, Lauren laid the quilt strip aside and picked up the first two pieces for the next row. "Are you sure your mom didn't hit her head? I thought she claimed you need adult supervision in a kitchen."

"That hasn't changed." Marisa sipped the tea, enjoying the delicate flavor of chamomile and honey. "I told her I was the queen of freezer cuisine, but she wouldn't listen. She sat on a stool and watched as I thawed some of her vegetarian chili. Then we made cornbread. Yes, we. Of course she didn't have any boxed mixes, so she directed every single step. Do you have any idea how annoying it can be to have someone tell you that the quarter teaspoon is smaller than the half teaspoon? Even I know that."

Lauren chuckled. "No wonder you wanted a break."

"I love my mom. You know I do, but she's not the easiest person to live with." She'd been crankier than normal today, undoubtedly the result of pain and frustration. It hadn't helped when Blake had declared the cornbread the best he'd ever eaten. Mom had taken that as a personal affront, even though it was her recipe with her secret ingredients.

"You're always welcome to stay here." Lauren looked around. "It wouldn't take more than an hour to shovel out enough fabric so that you could find your way to the bed." Right now the bed was covered with bolts of fabric, with more draped over the dresser. The only clear surface in the room was the bedside chest that Lauren had cleared to serve as a table for Marisa's tea.

"Fiona and I would love the company," Lauren continued as she fed another piece of fabric under the presser foot. "I get lonely sometimes."

As she set her cup back on the table, Marisa gazed at her friend. "How do you do it?" she asked. "How do you get through each day knowing . . ." She broke off, angry with herself for introducing such a sensitive topic. She had hated it when Blake and Mom wanted to talk about Eric, and now she was subjecting her best friend to even worse pain.

Lauren looked up from her sewing, her eyes solemn as they met Marisa's gaze. "How do I deal with knowing that Patrick won't be walking through the door? Is that what you were going to ask?"

Marisa nodded. "I'm sorry. The last thing you need is someone reminding you of that. With friends like me, you sure don't need any enemies."

"Don't apologize." Lauren looked at the pieces of cotton she'd stacked on the floor next to her sewing machine. "It's a valid question," she said as she selected two. "Some days I ask myself the same thing. But don't worry. It's not like it was when your father left."

Marisa tried not to cringe at the memory of the days and weeks following Eric's disappearance. At first she'd woken each day, certain it would be the day he'd return. But he hadn't. And as days turned to weeks, certainty had turned to worry that he had been killed.

Though Lauren had been a newlywed, caught up in the magic of her love for Patrick and the thrill of their first home, she had helped Marisa through that horrible summer. She had dried Marisa's tears, held her hand, and tried to convince her that Eric St. George's absence was only temporary. Eight years later, though she'd endured almost unspeakable loss, Lauren was once again trying to help her friend.

"There's grief but no uncertainty," Lauren told Marisa. "It's true that I won't see Patrick again on this earth, but I know we'll be reunited in heaven. That's what keeps me going. That and the belief that God has a plan for me. I know something good will come from this."

Marisa took another sip of tea as she tried to formulate her response. She had always known that Lauren's faith was stronger than hers. As teenagers, Marisa had believed it was because her friend had never been tested, but she could say that no longer. Lauren had survived far more serious problems than Marisa had.

"I wish I could be as certain as you," Marisa told her friend. "This year feels like pretty much a fiasco. The mess with Trent was all my fault, but I don't understand why I had to lose my job too."

Lauren looked up from her sewing, her brown eyes filled with sympathy. "Maybe it was to get you back here. I'm glad you're home, and so is your mom."

Biting back the retort that Dupree wasn't her home, Marisa said only, "Yes, but—"

Lauren wouldn't let her finish her sentence. "And then there's Blake. A person would have to be blind to miss the sparks between you. Admit it, Marisa. You're attracted to him."

Though she wanted to deny it, Marisa didn't. "I am," she admitted, "but I'm scared too. You've got to admit that my record with men is pretty bad. Sometimes I feel as if I must be the most gullible person on the planet the way I trust all the wrong men. First my dad, then Hal, then Trent. What if Blake's like them?"

Lauren shook her head as she pulled the fabric from the sewing machine and held it up, admiring the combination of colors. "Hal was a jerk, and somehow I don't think his years in the army changed that. As for Trent, you said you were just the latest in a string of cons. He was obviously a pro at duping women."

"That's what the cops said. They told me he had a history of joining support groups like the one I was in for the sole purpose of finding vulnerable women." Marisa took another sip of tea in a vain attempt to soothe her nerves. "I should have been a better judge of character. I should have known that if a story sounded too good to be true, it was. Instead, I fell for his line."

Shrugging as if the deception had been of little importance, Lauren kept her gaze fixed on Marisa. "Has Blake been handing you a line?"

That was the critical question. "I don't want to think so, but how would I know? It isn't as if he'd wear a sign saying, 'Trust me, even though I'm a con man.'" Marisa smiled at the image. "Blake seems like a nice guy, but he might be . . ."

"A serial killer? I doubt it. You've got to have a little faith in yourself. You're not a poor judge of character." Lauren rose and stretched. "After all, you picked me for your best friend. I'd say that shows sterling judgment."

"You would."

They both laughed.

---

He couldn't put it off any longer. When he'd left church yesterday, Blake had felt as if his spirit had been renewed, and he'd returned to Rainbow's End believing that a breakthrough was close. When he'd made his weekly call to his father, he'd been encouraged by the obvious happiness in Dad's voice when he mentioned that he was seeing—Dad's term—a woman named Hilary. When he'd helped Marisa serve supper, Blake had taken heart from the fact that she hadn't flinched when Carmen had announced that the chicken and dumplings were her husband's favorite Sunday meal. The day of rest had gone well, leading Blake to believe that he would wake on Monday with his brain teeming with ideas. It hadn't happened.

As he approached the newly installed phone booth, Blake managed a mirthless smile. It was ridiculous to feel as if he were a prisoner going to his execution. He was simply an author delivering some unwelcome news to his agent.

"Blake, where on earth are you?" Jack Darlington asked after Blake identified himself.

"Still in Texas." Even though the trip hadn't accomplished what he sought, nothing was drawing him back to California. He wouldn't leave before Greg returned, and even then—depending on how his relationship with Marisa progressed—he might stay. If he wasn't able to write, he might as well be here.

"Tell me that's good news and that you're half done with the book." Jack's innate optimism was one of the things Blake liked about him. Unfortunately, today it was misplaced.

"You know I don't want to lie. The truth is, I don't have an inkling of what Cliff's next adventure should be. I haven't written a single word. That's why I'm calling."

Blake heard a rapid intake of breath as his agent absorbed the news. It was only seconds later that Jack asked, "Have you considered . . . ?" He started rattling off cities that Cliff Pearson had not visited, crimes he had not solved. The ideas were solid. In another author's hands, they could be turned into good books. But not one of them piqued Blake's imagination. Sadly, not one made him want to turn on his computer and start writing.

"It's not working, Jack. Nothing's working. I've tried everything I can think of, but the result is the same. Nothing."

Like the old metal phone booths that Blake remembered from his childhood, the new one at Rainbow's End boasted a window. Someone—probably Kate—had aligned it with an exterior window so that callers could look outside while they were seated in the unusually spacious cabinet. Looking through the two windows, Blake saw workers scurrying toward one of the cabins. They knew what they had to do, and so did he.

"I think we need to buy back the contract."

"Ouch!" Jack's reaction was immediate. "Your publisher's not going to be any happier than I am about this. You're a major name for them. Their bottom line depends on your books coming out every year."

Blake refused to take the guilt trip. "I don't like this any more than you do, but I can't write unless I'm excited about the story. Nothing you've suggested and nothing I've come up with is exciting." And oh, how it hurt to admit that. Blake prided himself on being a reliable author, one who delivered good, clean manuscripts on schedule. He wasn't only disappointing Jack and his publisher. He was disappointing himself.

Jack was silent for a moment, during which Blake pictured the wheels churning in his agent's brain. "I'm sure this is just a temporary glitch," Jack said, his voice as smooth as if he were convincing an editor to double Blake's advance. "In the meantime, we've got to do something to boost sales of your backlist. I think it's time."

There was something ominous about the way he said that. "Time for what?"

"To reveal Ken Blake. To put a face to the name. Once the media hears you're going public, there'll be a bidding war to see which talk show gets you first. Blake, this is just what we need. I can see it now. There'll be new dust jackets with your photo, maybe even new cover designs. This could be huge."

"No."

"What do you mean, no? We could probably get a year's extension on the deadline if you agree to do the talk shows."

Another author might have jumped at the opportunity. Blake was not another author. "No means no. I won't do it. You knew that when I signed with you. That's why I've got that ironclad nondisclosure clause in our contract."

Grandfather was no longer alive to make Dad's life miserable if it became public knowledge that Blake was a bestselling author, but that didn't change Blake's determination to remain anonymous. He'd seen the problems fame could bring, and he wanted no part of them. It felt good to walk through an airport or into a restaurant and not be mobbed by fans wanting his autograph or his photo. It felt good, never having to answer questions about how much of himself he put into Cliff Pearson. Most of all, it felt good that when people talked to him, they saw him, not their idea of a celebrity.

"I'm sorry, Jack, but that's nonnegotiable. No one, and I mean no one, is to know that Blake Kendall is Ken Blake."

"But, Blake . . ."

"No buts."

---

"Are you sure you'll be all right?" Marisa frowned as she watched her mother prop her leg on a footstool. Mom had said nothing during supper other than expressing regret that Blake had not joined them, but now her brow was furrowed, telling Marisa the pain must be more intense than she had admitted.

"I still think I should stay with you."

Mom shook her head. "Stop worrying, Marisa. It's just a strain. It'll heal. You should be worrying about Fiona. She needs her cheering section."

Though Marisa had volunteered to cancel her evening plans,

Mom was adamant that one of them needed to attend Fiona's dance recital. "It's bad enough that I can't go. We can't disappoint the child."

Marisa knew her mother was right. She was overreacting, but this was the first time Mom had admitted that she couldn't do everything.

"Can I get you anything before I go?" It was a perfunctory question, but Marisa asked anyway. To her surprise, Mom nodded.

"I've almost finished the book I'm reading. Will you bring me another? I think there are some mysteries in the lodge."

"Sure." Though she had not had a chance to explore them, Marisa had noticed the well-stocked bookshelves lining one wall of the lodge. She hurried across the driveway, flipping on the lights when she entered the resort's main gathering room. With its soaring ceiling, exposed beams, and two walls with large windows overlooking the lake, it encouraged guests to linger. There would be no lingering tonight. Marisa went directly to the books. A quick look at the shelves revealed that they were organized by genre. Romance, suspense . . . where were the mysteries?

As she scanned the spines, Marisa's gaze was caught by the row of Ken Blake thrillers. What were they doing here? Stories with a hero who acted as if heavy drinking every evening was normal were an odd choice for a resort that prided itself on being a Christian family destination. They must be a mistake, some books that were left from the years the Sinclairs owned Rainbow's End. Perhaps they'd even been donated by a guest.

Marisa pulled the first book off the shelf. When Greg and Kate returned, she'd suggest they remove all of them. Tonight she stared at the cover with its deceptively simple lettering. If readers didn't know better, they might not realize they were buying the story of a man who was never far from a glass of whiskey. Her lip curling in disgust, she flipped open the cover and blinked.

Property of Greg Vange.

# 10

"Don't let my mother see you," Marisa warned Kate as she settled into a chair in front of Marisa's desk. The lovely blonde was wearing her favorite uniform of jeans, a Rainbow's End polo shirt, and a huge grin. This was her third day back at Rainbow's End, and not once had Marisa seen Kate without a smile. It had faltered slightly when Marisa had told Greg she didn't believe Ken Blake thrillers were appropriate reading material for their guests, but when Greg had merely saluted and said "Aye, aye, Ledger Lady" as he scooped the books into his arms, Kate's smile resumed its full wattage.

Surely it was only Marisa's imagination that Kate and Greg had exchanged a guarded look when she'd begun her argument for removing the books from the lodge. Perhaps Greg, like Patrick, hadn't considered what a poor role model Cliff Pearson was and was embarrassed that Marisa had had to point it out to him. That wasn't important. What was important was that the books were gone and neither Kate nor Greg seemed to think Marisa had overstepped her authority.

She gave Kate an arch smile. "Be careful. Mom would tell you your face is going to crack."

Though Marisa hadn't thought it possible, Kate's smile broadened. "I can't help it," she admitted. "All I want to do is smile. I feel like every one of my dreams has come true. I'm married to the most wonderful man in the world; we had a honeymoon straight out of a fairy tale; we're ten days away from our grand reopening and—thanks to you—everything is on schedule. Why shouldn't I smile?"

Her happiness was contagious. It was good to see Kate and Greg looking so—Marisa's thoughts stumbled as she searched for the correct word—blissful. Even better, their happiness seemed to have a ripple effect. Thanks to them, Lauren was looking more relaxed. Knowing that she had no financial worries for the foreseeable future more than compensated for the long hours Marisa's friend had been working and had erased the lines that had begun to furrow her forehead.

Mom was happier too, and though this wasn't Marisa's dream job, she had to admit that it felt surprisingly good to be back in Dupree. Contrary to her fears, not a single person had mentioned either Hal or her father. It appeared that Lauren was correct. Either the townspeople had short memories or their innate sense of courtesy kept them from saying something that might embarrass Marisa.

Now if only the Matchers would stop asking about Blake. The three women had cornered her after church, broadly hinting that she was the reason Blake was still in Dupree. But that wasn't Kate's fault.

"You have every reason to smile," Marisa told her. "You've got a lot to be proud of. Rainbow's End is the talk of the town."

Kate took a sip of coffee from the mug she'd brought with her. "I hope it'll be the talk of a lot more than that. *Philharmonic* magazine is planning a feature article, and *American Pianist* has promised me a spread. They're both intrigued by the fact that Gillian Hodge, pianist extraordinaire, is coming to a small resort in the Hill Country." Kate chuckled. "I didn't tell them she's my best friend."

That was one of the things Marisa had wanted to discuss with Kate. Though she agreed that entertainment would make the grand opening more special, she had reservations about Gillian. "You're the marketing expert, so you'd know, but are you sure she's the right person? It seems to me that guests will be expecting country rather than classical music."

"Johnny Cash instead of Frederic Chopin?"

"Exactly." Marisa had lived in Dupree for her first eighteen years, and the only time she'd heard classical music had been at children's piano recitals. Even more to the point, Gillian Hodge's expertise with Beethoven sonatas didn't mesh with Rainbow's End's image. It was a down-to-earth resort that hoped to offer families a chance to recharge their spirits as well as their bodies. While classical music could be soothing, Marisa did not believe it would appeal to the majority of the guests.

As if she'd heard Marisa's thoughts, Kate gave her another smile, this one tinged with amusement. "You might be surprised at how highbrow some of our guests are." She paused to drain her coffee cup. "Don't look so skeptical, Marisa. I'm not going to risk Rainbow's End's reputation on this. Gillian's going to play country music. That's part of what interested *American Pianist*." She glanced at her watch. "If everything's on schedule, she should be leaving the recording studio right about now. We're going to sell her CDs in our gift shop."

It was a morning for surprises. "Gift shop? Did I miss something?" When Marisa had reviewed the construction budget, there had been nothing about a gift shop.

Kate nodded. "That's one of the things I wanted to discuss this morning. Greg and I started talking about a gift shop when Gillian agreed to do a recording. We figured this was the perfect place to sell her music, especially since she's promised us autographed jewel case liners. And if we were going to sell that, why not carry other things that our guests might want to take home with them?"

Gesturing to the blank wall behind Marisa, Kate continued. "Greg decided we should build it between the dining room and the lodge, possibly with a covered walkway connecting the three buildings. Unfortunately, since it's right behind your office, you'll probably hear a lot of construction noise, but it'll be temporary."

Marisa's brain began to whirl. "Do you expect to have it finished before the opening?" Money could expedite many things, but it couldn't work miracles.

Shaking her head, Kate explained that they were hoping it would be ready by Thanksgiving. "In addition to the music, we thought we'd sell some of Lauren's smaller pieces, and Samantha's already planning to expand her leather line to include wallets and key chains—things that don't require fitting and are a bit easier on the pocketbook than her boots."

Though Marisa hated to dilute Kate's enthusiasm, she owed it to her bosses to express her reservations. "The CDs are a good idea, but what about all the people who want an MP3 version?" She couldn't recall the last time she'd bought a CD.

"Greg's working on that. He's even considering putting the music out on vinyl for those who like retro." Kate tipped her head to one side, fixing her gaze on Marisa. "So, what do you think about the whole idea of a gift shop?"

Marisa chose her words carefully, hoping she wouldn't appear pushy. "I think it's brilliant, but I also think you're missing an opportunity."

"And what would that be?"

"A cookbook. Everyone asks for Mom's recipes. Why not sell them?"

Kate's eyes lit as she considered the idea. "Do you think she'd agree?"

"I can't imagine why she wouldn't, but let's ask her."

A minute later, the two women were inside the kitchen, pitching the idea. To Marisa's surprise, her mother was sitting on a stool as she peeled vegetables, obviously taking seriously the doctor's advice to rest her ankle whenever she could. Mom's face flushed with pleasure as Kate praised her cooking.

"You wouldn't have to include your special dishes—things like chocolate pound cake and vegetarian chili," Marisa said. "We can call those Rainbow's End exclusives."

Mom shook her head, saying she was willing to share everything, and encouraged Kate to continue.

"You mean you'd pay me every time someone buys a cookbook?" Mom asked, her skepticism evident when Kate finished her explanation.

"Yes. That's called royalties."

"And even if I retire, I would still get paid?" The skepticism started to fade, replaced by a spark of excitement. Marisa knew her mother well enough to know how appealing that prospect was. Rainbow's End had never offered a pension plan, nor had it paid enough for her mother to accumulate more than minimal savings. While that might change under Kate and Greg's ownership, the income from cookbooks would be a nice bonus.

"Definitely," Kate confirmed, "but I don't want to hear any more talk of retirement. That's not allowed for the next"—she paused, pretending to consider the issue—"oh, let's say the next fifty years." When Mom's eyes widened, Kate grinned. "So, what do you think?"

Before Mom could reply, the phone rang. Marisa reached over the counter and picked up the receiver. "Sure, she's right here." Covering the receiver with her hand, Marisa nodded toward Kate. "It's a woman, and she sounds upset."

Kate took the phone. "Kate Vange speaking. How can I help you?" Though the greeting was businesslike, within seconds the blood had drained from Kate's face, and she gripped the edge of the counter as if to balance herself.

"Where are you? What happened? Oh no!" The pain reflecting from Kate's eyes left no doubt that the caller had delivered tragic news. "I'll get there as soon as I can." Her frown deepened as the woman on the other end said something. "All right. Call me when you know more."

Kate hung up the phone and sank onto a chair. "That was Gillian," she said, her voice trembling. "She was hit by a motorcycle outside the recording studio."

No wonder she had sounded so distraught. Marisa's heart went out to Kate as well as to the woman she'd met only briefly at the wedding. From what Kate had said, she and Gillian had a relationship similar to hers with Lauren, which meant that Kate was sharing her friend's pain. She was clenching and unclenching her right hand, staring at the fingers as if she'd never before seen them.

"What happened?" Marisa asked.

Kate looked up, her eyes filled with anguish. "Gillian's not quite sure how it happened, but she fell and somehow the motorcycle crushed her right hand. She's at the hospital now." Kate's voice choked, and tears began to slide down her cheeks. "The surgeons are afraid she'll never regain full use of her hand."

"Oh, Kate." Marisa wrapped her arms around the woman who'd become her friend as well as her boss. "I don't know what to say." The loss of mobility in a hand would be terrible for anyone, but it was disastrous for a pianist. Gillian's whole future might have been destroyed in a second.

Mom slid down from the stool and moved to Kate's side. Laying her hand on Kate's, she said, "You need to trust God. I know it looks bleak now, but he'll find a way to turn this into good."

Though Marisa had started to seethe, she said nothing. Kate was silent for a few seconds before she nodded. "I hope so." Kate rose, her newlywed smile gone. "I need to tell Greg."

When she'd left the room and Marisa was sure she was out of earshot, she turned toward her mother. "How could you do that?" she demanded. "How could you hold out false hope? From what Kate said, it would take a miracle for Gillian to play again. The poor woman is less than thirty and her career is over."

Though Mom flinched at the anger in Marisa's voice, she merely shook her head. "You don't know that. God's in the miracle business. Even if he doesn't heal Gillian's hand, he'll bring her something good. He always does."

It was the story Marisa had heard countless times over the years. When she'd been a child, she'd believed it, but like Santa Claus and the Tooth Fairy, it had proven to be a myth. Though Kate had appeared to be comforted by the idea, Marisa knew it for what it was: an empty platitude.

"Sure thing, Mom. You're living in a fantasy land. If God always brings good, tell me what good he brought us when Eric left."

Her demand was met with silence. "You can't answer that, can you? There was no good. Don't pretend otherwise." Marisa strode toward the door. "I need to work."

---

Blake didn't intend to eavesdrop. Though he couldn't distinguish the words, no one could mistake Marisa's anger, and his heart wrenched at the pain in her voice. "Slow down, Marisa," he said, following her as she headed toward her office. "There's no race." He might as well have been speaking to an empty room for all the response he received.

Another man might have surrendered, but Blake wouldn't give up in defeat, not when Marisa was so upset. "Please, Marisa." He grabbed her hand, hoping to somehow calm her, but she tugged it away.

"Just leave me alone!" The pain he'd heard before had intensified, mingling with anger and annoyance.

Marisa stormed into her office and closed the door behind her. At least she hadn't slammed it. Though she might think she wanted to be alone, Blake knew anger like hers could fester. Dad had claimed it was suppressed anger that had made Grandfather so cantankerous. Blake wouldn't let that happen to Marisa. He opened the door and walked inside.

Marisa glared at him, her eyes colder than he'd ever seen them. "I asked for one simple thing: to be left alone. Can't you do that?"

Blake shook his head. "Not when you're so upset."

"I don't want to talk, and I definitely do not want to listen. All I get are platitudes."

Though she looked nothing like Blake's grandfather, at the moment the firm line of Marisa's lips reminded him of times when Grandfather was getting ready to launch a tirade.

"I wasn't planning to be the one talking. You look like you need to vent." Maybe venting would defuse the situation.

"What I need is for everyone to leave me alone."

Recognizing that he was getting nowhere, Blake nodded. "All right, but the offer is open. You know where to find me if you need me."

Marisa simply glared.

As he passed the kitchen, Blake saw Carmen, her head bent as if she were praying. Though he hated to interrupt her, his instincts told him not to miss this opportunity. She was the only other person who could explain why Marisa was so angry and in such pain.

Blake cleared his throat and walked in.

"Marisa seems pretty upset," he said, not bothering with polite preliminaries. "Can you tell me what that's all about?"

Carmen's reluctance was evident in the way she twisted a towel between her hands, and for a moment Blake thought she might refuse to answer. Instead, she moved from the stool to settle on a chair.

When he was seated across the table from her, she said, "My daughter has a hard time asking for help. She's always the first one there to help me or one of her friends, but she thinks it's a sign of weakness to admit she needs help."

That sounded like Marisa. Blake had seen how she shouldered everyone else's problems as if they were hers, and she'd certainly refused his bungling attempt at comfort. "We all need help at times."

"Of course we do." Carmen nodded. "The problem is, Marisa's afraid to trust anyone, even God. She wasn't always that way, but ever since Eric's been gone, she's had a hard time."

Perhaps something good had come from Marisa and Carmen's

argument, for it had given Blake a chance to learn more about Marisa's father. "When did your husband die?"

Carmen shook her head, sadness radiating from her dark eyes, and for a moment Blake thought she might not answer. When she did, her words surprised him. "Eric didn't die. He left Dupree the day of Marisa's graduation. Neither of us has heard from him since."

Blake blinked as he absorbed the significance of Carmen's revelation. Marisa's father wasn't dead. For some reason, he'd abandoned his family. No wonder Marisa had so much pain bottled up inside her; no wonder she didn't want to see blonde hair and blue eyes when she looked in the mirror. "That's horrible."

"Yes, it is," Carmen agreed. "It's bad enough not knowing where Eric is and whether he's well, but what it's done to Marisa is worse." Carmen lowered her eyes and clutched the towel as if it were a lifeline. "She's bitter and angry at both her earthly and her heavenly father."

Carmen looked up, her eyes swimming with tears. "I want my daughter to be happy, but I don't know what to do. I've tried everything I could think of, and nothing has helped. It's in God's hands now."

Poor Marisa, Blake thought half an hour later as he pounded the pavement, hoping a second run up Ranger Hill would clear his thoughts. It was no wonder she was so afraid of losing someone. As a writer, Blake had a vivid imagination, but he couldn't imagine what her life must have been like. It would have been difficult to have a father disappear at any time, but having it happen on graduation day was even worse.

Graduation was a day to be surrounded by family. Blake panted as he forced himself to increase his pace. His school hadn't had a formal grade-school graduation, but he had happy memories of his high school and college commencement ceremonies. Both Grandfather and Dad had attended them, and though Grandfather had been his normal disapproving self, Blake had caught a hint of pride in his expression. His father's reaction had been far different. Dad had been openly thrilled by his son's diplomas, telling everyone Blake was going to have a better life than he had.

Blake took a swig of water when he reached the top of the hill. His life might not be better than his father's—after all, Dad got a lot of satisfaction out of his work, and right now Blake was having a terrible time with his chosen career—but it was definitely easier.

He had been fortunate, and once this dry spell ended, he would be fortunate again. Marisa was not so lucky. Blake would say that she bore scars from her father's disappearance, but that was not accurate. Scars implied healing, and from what he'd heard, there had been none of that. Marisa was still enduring open wounds.

There had to be a way to comfort her. If only he could find it.

## 11

"Kate looks better." Though it wasn't Kate he'd come to see, Blake was glad that Greg's wife no longer wore the stricken expression he'd seen when she'd left the kitchen this morning. He only wished Marisa had recovered as well, but when he'd seen Carmen soon after lunch, she'd reported that Marisa had not emerged from her office. That was why Blake was here: in hopes Greg would have at least one suggestion of how he could break through Marisa's anger.

"I think she is better." Greg led Blake back out of the dining room that Kate had turned into her makeshift office. "I reminded her that Gillian doesn't want her with her now and that she'll be heavily sedated. In my not-so-humble opinion, the best thing Kate can do is make our opening a success. When she called Gillian back, all her friend would talk about was how sorry she was that she had to cancel so close to our opening. The woman's sustained what could be a life-changing injury, and she's worried that we won't be able to find a replacement."

"Maybe worrying about that keeps her from thinking about the fact that her hand was crushed," Blake suggested.

Greg nodded. "You're probably right. At times like this, people aren't completely rational."

"You can say that again. Irrational behavior is what I wanted to talk to you about. I just learned that Marisa's father disappeared on her graduation day. All I was trying to do was help, but she brushed me off." She'd done more than that. She'd practically ordered him out of her office. "Now that you've been a married man for over two weeks, I thought you might have some insights."

Jogging up Ranger Hill hadn't helped. Neither had the hot shower or the large cup of coffee he'd consumed. Though Blake's brain was whirling, the thoughts were chaotic rather than coherent.

"Women!" Greg opened the door and stepped outside, taking a deep breath of the cool fall air. "I doubt I'll ever understand how their minds work. What did you do?"

While Blake explained, Greg stared into the distance, his eyes focused on the island at the other side of Bluebonnet Lake. When Blake finished, Greg turned to face him. "I make no guarantees, but you might want to try a different approach."

At this point, Blake was willing to try almost anything. "What do you suggest?" He listened, intrigued by Greg's story of the day he had proposed to Kate. "That just might work." With a few changes, that is.

———— ✦ ————

"Put me down!" Marisa couldn't believe it. She'd been standing at one of the tall file cabinets, looking for an invoice, when the next thing she knew, she was swept up into Blake's arms. What on earth was going on? She'd told the man the only thing she wanted was to be left alone, and now he appeared determined to play Rhett Butler in the famous staircase scene from *Gone with the Wind*.

Marisa wasn't certain what was more embarrassing, the fact that Blake was carrying her or that she had wrapped her arms around his neck and leaned closer. This wasn't supposed to be happening. When she'd realized that she was unlikely to accomplish anything productive and that in her current state her mind was not creative enough to devise entertainment for the opening weekend now that

Gillian Hodge would be unable to perform, Marisa had assigned herself the most tedious task on her to-do list in an effort to vanquish the anger that had overtaken her this morning.

Neither Mom nor Blake deserved her fit of temper. Marisa knew that, just as she knew she owed them both an apology. The problem was, she was still struggling with her anger, or she had been until Blake barged into her office and began his alpha male routine. Now she felt herself relaxing, her senses tantalized by the clean scent of his aftershave and the faint prickle of his hair against her cheek.

"Put me down." Marisa repeated the demand, keeping her voice as low as she could. If Mom saw them like this, Marisa would never hear the end of it, and if the Matchers caught wind of it, the Dupree gossip line would be buzzing within seconds.

"Not until we get where we're going." Blake strode out of her office and across the hallway to the exterior door that someone had propped open. As he stepped outside, Marisa realized two things: this had been carefully planned, and it felt surprisingly good to be held in his arms.

"What's going on?" she asked, trying to maintain the fiction that she was annoyed. The truth was, her anger had vanished, dissolving as quickly as sugar in hot coffee.

Blake chuckled, and his breath tickled her face. "I thought it was obvious. You're being kidnapped."

This was as outrageous as being cradled in his arms. Though she was tempted to laugh at the sheer audacity of his statement, Marisa feigned indignation. "Isn't kidnapping a federal offense?"

Blake turned, his face so close to hers that Marisa could count the pores on his cheeks. "Only if someone reports it."

"And you don't think I will?" It was becoming increasingly difficult to pretend she was annoyed, when all she wanted to do was grin. Never before had Marisa been the victim of a faux kidnapping; never before had she been held in a man's arms as if she were a cherished prize; never before had she enjoyed sparring with someone this way. The day that had begun so poorly had been transformed, leaving Marisa feeling as if the sun had emerged after weeks of hiding behind thick clouds.

"Nope." Blake's lips curved into the sweetest of smiles as he continued walking. "I'm predicting that by nightfall you'll wish you could do this every day."

She already did, but rather than admit that he was right, Marisa forced a mocking tone to her voice. "You're pretty sure of yourself, aren't you?"

Blake shrugged, the action drawing her closer to him. "It has been suggested that I have an inflated ego. But now let's get you into this boat."

To Marisa's surprise, they'd reached the dock, and one of the newly painted rowboats was tied to it.

"I don't want to drop you into the boat, but I'm afraid that if we both get in at once, it might tip over." Though Blake's grin said he wasn't convinced that would be a tragedy, Marisa had no desire to test the water's temperature. "I'm going to put you down," Blake continued, "and ask you to climb in on your own. Will you do that, or are you going to try to escape?"

Escape from the most fun she could remember having? Not likely. "I think Stockholm syndrome is settling in, because I don't want to leave," she admitted as she climbed into the boat. The truth was, Blake's silly antics had swept her blues away. Anger had turned to anticipation and depression to delight at the sheer pleasure of being held in his arms. "What I don't understand is why you'd want to kidnap me after the way I acted this morning. I'm sorry I was in such a snit."

Blake shrugged. "We all have bad days. That's where friends come into play. I'm hoping this day will end better than it began."

"You can count on that." Marisa gave him the warmest smile she could produce. "Thanks, Blake."

She settled onto the rear seat and watched as he climbed in as gracefully as if he did this daily. He'd said that he jogged each day, but there had been no mention of rowing. Perhaps he rowed in California.

"Where are we going?" Marisa asked when Blake had pushed the boat away from the dock. Oddly, she'd felt bereft when he'd placed her back on the ground. It had felt amazingly good to be carried, to be so close to Blake that she could see the pulse beating in his throat and hear each breath he took. Now that they were separated, Marisa missed the temporary intimacy they'd shared.

"Our options are somewhat limited," he said. "There are no exotic destinations, but Greg told me the island is a good place for a picnic." Blake looked down at the picnic basket in the front of the boat. "Judging from its weight, your mother gave us enough food for a week."

Marisa's first impression had been accurate. Blake had done a lot of planning for the pretend kidnapping. "That's Mom for you." She had always provided Marisa with comfort food, including a bedtime snack of milk and cookies. Marisa couldn't recall when that had started, but if she'd had to guess, she would have said that it was when Eric had started drinking so heavily that he'd spent most evenings passed out in the master bedroom. Marisa brushed those thoughts aside.

"Everyone in Dupree knows that if you want good home cooking, you call Carmen St. George. Most times folks didn't even need to call. Whenever Mom heard that someone was going through a rough time, she'd take them a basket of food."

At the time, Marisa hadn't considered the effect that extra food must have had on the family's budget, but her perspective had changed. The reality of unemployment and dwindling savings made her wonder how Mom had managed to do all she had when Eric drank half his pay.

"I doubt Mom ever dreamt she'd wind up being paid to cook, but being a chef is the perfect job for her."

Blake nodded. "I've never met anyone who loves cooking the way she does." He nodded again, this time toward the pile of beach towels next to the picnic basket. "She sent more than food. There's a bottle of sunblock there. You'd better slather some on. She gave me your sunbonnet too."

"Sunbonnet?" Marisa raised an eyebrow at the sight of a floppy-brimmed straw hat that had to be ten years old. Marisa had never worn it, but she could recall her mother plunking it on her head when she worked in the garden. "Sunbonnet makes me sound like a pioneer woman."

Blake continued the rhythmic rowing that was propelling them across the lake. "What would you call it?"

"A hat. A broad-brimmed hat." Marisa adjusted the brim. Mom was right. Though the sun was not at its zenith, the reflection from the water was enough to burn skin quickly. Fortunately, she had worn a long-sleeved shirt and slacks today. White slacks might not be practical for a picnic, but Marisa didn't care. She knew the fit flattered her, and right now that was more important than grass stains.

She narrowed her eyes as she looked at Blake. "You'd better use some of that sunblock yourself." While the gray T-shirt highlighted his muscles and was more attractive than such an ordinary piece of clothing ought to be, the short sleeves left his arms exposed to the sun. "You ought to get a different hat too. That ratty ball cap you're wearing doesn't protect your neck." Though it might have been blue once, it was now faded to a dingy gray.

"I'll have you know that I like this hat. My dad gave it to me."

Marisa sighed as a memory assailed her. She had been perhaps five or six years old the summer her parents had taken her to the county fair. When she'd seen a pink sunbonnet for sale at one of the countless vendor stalls lining the perimeter, she'd known that she had to have it. Eric had bought it, even though Mom insisted Marisa didn't need another hat.

That sunbonnet had become her most prized possession. She'd worn it every day that summer, and when she'd outgrown it, she'd hung it on a hook in her bedroom as a reminder of what had seemed like a perfect day. But then, two days after graduation, she'd tossed it into the trash along with everything else her father had given her.

"You're looking sad," Blake said. "That's not allowed on this cruise ship."

"Sorry. I was thinking about a hat I once had. I wish I'd kept it and given it to Fiona."

"The girl with the mismatched socks?"

"The one and only."

Marisa and Blake spoke about inconsequential things as he rowed them across the lake. When they reached Paintbrush Island, although there was a good spot to dock the boat on the edge closest to Rainbow's End, Blake continued to the opposite side, telling Marisa that Greg claimed the best spot was out of sight of the resort.

"This looks like it," Blake said, slowing as they approached a part of the island where the trees came closer to the shore but still left enough room for beaching the boat. "He said we might appreciate the shade."

Though the day was relatively cool, Marisa couldn't fault the logic. Besides, the trees, though not as tall as the ones that surrounded Rainbow's End itself, were lovely. "It's beautiful," she said, admiring the way the ground rose from the lake edge to a small hill covered with hickory and mesquite. In the spring there would be wildflowers, including the Indian paintbrush that had given the island its name. A recent rain, though brief, had been enough to make the formerly dry grass lush. Together the grass and the varying greens of the trees provided a pleasing contrast to the deep blue sky with its puffy cumulus clouds. It was a beautiful spot for a picnic, made all the more special by the fact that Marisa would be sharing it with Blake.

"I always wondered what this side of the island looked like," she said softly. "It's even prettier than I'd expected."

"You mean you haven't been here before?" Blake asked as he hopped into the water and began to drag the boat onto the shore.

"When Greg told me how private it was, I figured it would have been a teenage hangout."

Marisa stepped out of the boat. "Like Lover's Lane?" She shook her head. "If kids came here, I never heard about it. Of course, I didn't date much in high school." Why had she told him that? It was like painting "loser" on her forehead. The next thing you knew, she'd be telling him about Hal and how he'd stood her up for the prom.

With the boat secured on dry land, Blake turned to Marisa, his eyes reflecting his surprise. "That's hard to believe. I had you and Lauren pegged as cheerleaders."

Marisa shook her head. He couldn't have been further from the truth. "I was too busy working, and Lauren spent every spare hour with Patrick."

"So, where did you work?"

Breathing a sigh of relief that Blake hadn't questioned her lack of dates, Marisa held up one hand and started folding down fingers as she enumerated her part-time jobs. "The supermarket, the hardware store, the library—any place I could get a few hours' pay. I even sold popcorn at the movie theater." She tipped her head to one side. "Why do you ask?"

He shrugged. "Just curious. I wondered if life was different for teenagers here than it was in Bethlehem."

"And is it?"

"Nope. What you described sounds like my teenage years, if you add in flipping burgers at fast-food restaurants and clerking at the mall."

"Dupree, as you may have noticed, has no Golden Arches and no mall." And, for the past few years, it had an ever-dwindling number of stores on Lone Star Trail and Pecan Street.

"But it has this beautiful lake and island. Someone with a romantic bent must have chosen the names. My guess is it was a woman."

Marisa raised a questioning eyebrow. "You don't think a man would call places Firefly Valley, Bluebonnet Lake, and Paintbrush

Island?" When Blake shook his head, she smiled. "You're right. It was the first mayor's wife. She claimed the area was too pretty to have ordinary names."

"I agree." Blake gestured toward the faint trail that led to the center of the island. "Do you want to explore or eat first?"

As if in response, Marisa's stomach grumbled. "Let's eat. I skipped lunch."

"No wonder Carmen sent so much food."

Marisa reached into the boat and pulled out the tarp, spreading it on the ground like a tablecloth, while Blake hoisted the picnic basket, feigning strain as he lifted it.

"Let's see what Mom gave us." Marisa smiled as she opened the lid of the cooler that filled two-thirds of the basket and counted half a dozen sandwiches, a platter of deviled eggs, and a bowl of coleslaw. The rest of the basket was filled with plates and utensils, thermoses of sweet tea and lemonade, and a container of peanut butter cookies for dessert. Mom had indeed provided more than enough food.

When he'd given thanks, Marisa handed Blake a plate, cup, and silverware. "Ham, roast beef, or tuna?" she asked, seeing the codes Mom had put on each of the sandwiches.

"Yes."

Marisa raised a brow. "What does that mean?"

"It means I'll try one of each. I wouldn't want to disappoint your mother." And she would be disappointed if they didn't eat the majority of what she'd sent.

Marisa reached for a tuna sandwich, then smiled as a bird flew out of the trees and squawked as if expecting her to offer it some food.

"Sorry, bird, but this is for the humans."

"Ouch!"

That was not the response she'd expected. Marisa looked at Blake, who was unwrapping the first of his sandwiches. "What happened?"

He shook his head. "Nothing serious. Just a paper cut." But the paper Mom had used to wrap the sandwiches was thicker than normal waxed paper.

"Let me see it." Marisa reached over and took Blake's hand, inspecting the wound. Grabbing a clean napkin, she wiped away the tiny drops of blood, then raised his hand to her lips and pressed a kiss on the injured finger. "Mom always says a kiss will make it better," she explained as she laid Blake's hand back on his thigh.

He grinned. "Funny. My dad never said anything like that."

"It's probably a mom thing."

"That and the fact that my grandfather would have considered it a case of spoiling the child."

Though she would never meet him, Marisa already disliked Blake's grandfather. "A little comfort and a bit of whimsy isn't spoiling."

"I know, but Grandfather was set in his ways. Dad and I learned not to make waves." Blake took a bite of sandwich. "I heard your mother is going to write a cookbook," he said, his change of subject telling Marisa more clearly than words that he did not want to discuss his grandfather any more than she wanted to talk about Eric.

"That's the plan. It seemed like a good idea when I suggested it to Kate, but I wonder if I've bitten off more than I should have. Mom'll write the recipes, but I'm the one who needs to learn about the publishing business."

Blake nodded slowly as he reached for a deviled egg. "I might be able to help you with that. Not today, though. Let's just relax now."

They did. Blake apparently had no trouble eating three sandwiches, and Marisa surprised herself by consuming one and a half while he regaled her with stories of the sea lions that had become a major tourist attraction on San Francisco's wharves. By the time they'd finished their meal, she felt happier and more relaxed than she had in months, all because of Blake.

When she'd repacked the basket, Blake rose and tugged Marisa to her feet. "Let's see what this island has to offer before the sun sets. A moonlight row might be romantic, but tripping over a tree root would not." A mischievous grin tilted the corners of his mouth upward. "Or maybe it would."

"I can't imagine how."

The grin widened. "You might feel compelled to kiss me again." Blake's eyes dipped, and he stared at her lips.

Marisa felt herself blushing. Had he guessed that she'd thought of little else since she'd touched her lips to his finger? It had been an impulsive gesture, something she would have done for Fiona. But Blake was not Fiona. He was the most attractive man she'd ever met, and the brief kiss combined with the memory of how good it had felt to be in his arms had sent Marisa's senses into overdrive.

"I draw the line at smelly feet," she said, hoping he hadn't noticed the way blood had flooded her face.

To Marisa's surprise, Blake shook his head. "That wasn't exactly what I had in mind."

"What was?"

"This."

Slowly, deliberately, he took one step, then another, until only inches separated them. Slowly, deliberately, he wrapped his arms around her. Slowly, deliberately, he lowered his lips to hers.

It was not the first time Marisa had been kissed. It was not the first time she'd stood enfolded in a man's arms. But it was the first time a kiss had set every nerve ending in her body on edge. Blake's kiss was sweeter than any she'd ever experienced, his lips firm and strong at the same time that they were tender. Marisa could feel her blood coursing faster while his lips caressed hers, and as his hands moved slowly across her back, the circular motion sent waves of delight up and down her spine.

She closed her eyes, wanting nothing to distract her from the sheer delight of Blake's first kiss. It was bliss, pure bliss, the perfect ending to the day.

*12*

$\mathcal{L}$auren kept her eyes focused on the pieces of fabric she was feeding through her sewing machine. Perhaps if she tried very, very hard, she would be able to lose herself in the joy of creating a new design. So far it wasn't working.

She had known today would be a bad day. Fortunately, Fiona was too young to remember dates, and so she hadn't realized that today was the anniversary of Patrick's death. Lauren wasn't so fortunate, and sorrow weighed more heavily than it had in months. One year. Twelve months since Patrick had taken his last breath. Three hundred and sixty-five days without his love and laughter.

"Oh, Patrick, I miss you so much." Lauren brushed the tears from her cheeks and forced a smile onto her face. Crying accomplished nothing other than giving her red-rimmed eyes and blotchy cheeks. She couldn't afford either while the store was open. Customers didn't want to see their normally cheerful shopkeeper in the doldrums.

As if on cue, the front doorbell tinkled.

"I come bearing gifts."

Lauren's smile became genuine when she saw that the visitor was her best friend. Clad in the quilted vest that Lauren had given her last Christmas, Marisa was just what Lauren needed to chase away her sorrow. Perhaps she had more Blake stories to recount. Marisa had been beaming, her expression happier than Lauren had ever seen it, the day after she and Blake had picnicked on Paintbrush Island. Marisa might deny it, but she was giving a very good impression of being head-over-heels in love.

Today, though she smiled, Marisa's eyes reflected concern. Concern over Lauren. Placing a basket of what smelled like cinnamon rolls on the counter, Marisa stretched out her arms. "I thought you might need a hug."

It was all the invitation Lauren needed. She walked into Marisa's embrace and wrapped her arms around her friend.

"How are you?" Marisa asked softly.

"Holding up as well as can be expected." Though she had thought she was over tears, Lauren was wrong. To her dismay, they came out in a torrent, accompanied by deep, wracking sobs. She hadn't cried like this even at Patrick's funeral. For a few days afterward, she'd been numb. When feeling had returned, though she'd wept, it hadn't been this intense.

"I'm sorry, Marisa," Lauren said when the last tear was shed. She moved away and sank onto a chair. "I guess I'm not doing as well as I thought." Her legs felt as weak as a newborn lamb's.

Marisa handed her a box of tissues. "It's all right to cry." She reached for the basket and pulled out a cinnamon roll, placing it on one of the plates her mother had sent along with the fragrant pastry. "It's also all right to eat this. You know Mom thinks food's the remedy for everything that ails us."

Lauren wiped her eyes, blew her nose, then looked at the cinnamon roll. As she broke off a piece, she kept her eyes on the plate lest the sight of Marisa's sympathy provoke another spate of tears. "It seems I ought to be past crying now."

Marisa laid a hand on her shoulder. "Anniversaries are difficult. I remember counting—one day, one week, one month. The end of the first year was worse than I'd expected. I think that's when I gave up hope that he'd come back."

Though Marisa's voice was matter-of-fact, Lauren felt the faint trembling in her hand and knew that, no matter what her friend said, she had not accepted the possibility of never seeing her father again. That was why she'd spent so much money trying to find him. Though Marisa claimed she was doing it for her mother, Lauren knew that was only part of the reason. The truth was, Marisa's life was incomplete without her dad, and not knowing where he was or whether he was still alive left her in limbo.

"At least I knew what was happening, and Patrick and I had a chance to say good-bye." Even at the time, Lauren had realized how fortunate they were to be able to prepare for their separation. "It's just that some days I'm so lonely. I miss Patrick, and I miss being married." She took another bite of the roll, trying to savor the gooey sweetness. Carmen was right. Sugar helped.

Without bidding, Marisa refilled Lauren's coffee cup as she said, "Of course you do. It's only natural. But I know Patrick would not want you to spend the rest of your life mourning him."

"That's true." Lauren sipped the coffee. "He told me he hoped I'd find another man to love. He said he wanted both Fiona and me to be surrounded by love." Lauren closed her eyes, trying not to weep as she thought of the day her husband had held her hand and begged her to promise him that she wouldn't waste her life in regret.

"Patrick was a very special man."

Lauren nodded. "That's why it's so hard. I know Fiona wants a new daddy, and I wish I could give her one, but . . ." Lauren's lips curved into a smile as she looked at Marisa. "I didn't tell you before, but Rob asked me to marry him."

As she'd expected, Marisa's eyes widened in surprise. "Rob Anderson? The most-married and most-divorced man in our class?"

"That's the one."

Marisa shook her head as if trying to clear her thoughts. "I hope you set him straight."

"I did. I told him I wasn't willing to take the chance that our marriage would be as short-lived as his first three. What I wanted to say was that I wasn't so desperate that I'd consider risking my daughter's happiness with a man like him. If I marry again, it will be someone who loves us both."

"Rob Anderson loves no one but himself."

"Those were my thoughts too."

The bell tinkled again, signaling the entrance of another customer and prompting Marisa to look at her watch. Declaring that she was late for work, she gave Lauren a quick hug and left after extracting Lauren's promise to call if she needed another shoulder to cry on.

But Lauren did not call. The rest of the day was unexpectedly busy, as if the residents of Dupree knew she needed company, and by the time she returned home, she felt tired, drained, but oddly at peace. Perhaps the healing had begun.

That night after Fiona was asleep, Lauren knelt beside her bed and bowed her head. "Dear God, I know you have a plan for me, and I know it's a good one. You know I'm not very patient, though, so if it includes a second husband, would you send me a sign?"

As she drifted off to sleep, the image of Drew Carroll's smiling face drifted across her consciousness.

---

Blake frowned as he stared out the window at the steady rain. It had been falling since last night, and although it meant that the worries of drought would subside, he hoped it would stop by noon. Today was the official opening of the new Rainbow's End, with guests starting to arrive this afternoon. Today was the reason he'd seen little of Marisa for the past week, other than the meals they shared. The woman who'd been hired to make sense of the resort's finances had been totally consumed with plans for its reopening.

Tonight would be low-key, with nothing scheduled after Carmen's tamale and flan dinner. Marisa claimed that would give the guests a chance to settle in and meet each other. The festivities would take place tomorrow night. Carmen was serving a barbecue, complete with three kinds of chili, including the vegetarian one that Blake, a confirmed carnivore, found particularly tasty.

But the meal was only the prelude to what promised to be the highlight of the weekend: the entertainment Marisa had planned. She'd admitted that she'd been obsessed with the idea of providing a replacement for Gillian. Since it had been too late to hire another musician, Marisa had had to improvise, and from what Blake could tell, she was going to succeed in giving the guests an unforgettable evening. He was looking forward to it. At least for the hour or so that he was watching her production, he'd be able to forget . . .

A knock on the cabin door interrupted Blake's thoughts.

"Hey, man," Greg said as he entered, shaking raindrops from his slicker. "What's with the scowl? You can't tell me that you find a little bit of liquid sunshine depressing."

"It's not that."

Greg took another step inside, closing the door behind him, his eyes narrowing as he looked at Blake. "Then what is it? Is Cliff Pearson giving you trouble?"

"You could say that." Greg had known about Ken Blake from the day he'd arrived early for a meeting and had seen page proofs spread over Blake's desk. "The manuscript's due November 15, and I don't have a clue what's going to be in it."

"Writer's block?"

"Yeah." It was surprising how reluctant he was to admit it. Even with his agent, Blake hadn't used those words, but Greg would not be judgmental. "It's never happened before, and I don't know what to do. That's the reason I came here. I was hoping a change of scenery would trigger ideas."

"And it hasn't?" For some reason, Greg looked almost relieved.

"No. Don't get me wrong. This is a great place. I didn't see it before you and Kate took over, but from everything I've heard, the changes you made are just short of miraculous. The problem is, it doesn't seem to matter where I am. I can't come up with any ideas." Blake thrust his hands into his jeans pockets to stop himself from clenching them. "I don't understand it. Ideas used to flow like Niagara Falls, and now there's not even a trickle."

"So Cliff isn't going to deal with murder and mayhem at a Hill Country resort." This time there was no doubt about it. Greg was relieved. "When you first came, I wondered if you were doing on-site research."

When they'd brainstormed ideas, that had been one of the things Jack had suggested, but it had been a nonstarter. Not only could Blake not imagine his hero in a place like Rainbow's End, but he wouldn't have abused his friend's hospitality that way.

"And if I was?"

Greg leaned against the door frame. Though he looked relaxed, Blake knew he was crafting his response. "I wouldn't have stopped you," Greg admitted, "but I would have asked you to make sure your resort had no resemblance to Rainbow's End. Kate and I want publicity, but we don't need guests fearing terrorist attacks or mob hits while they're here."

"My thoughts exactly. I wouldn't do that to you two." Or to Marisa or Carmen. While Greg had enough money that he never needed to work again, Marisa and Carmen and the rest of the staff depended on Rainbow's End for their livelihood. Blake shook his head slowly. "I just wish I knew why I can't come up with a concept."

It was frustrating, and not for the reasons most people might imagine. Although Blake was not a billionaire like Greg, his books had sold well, and thanks to his background as a financial planner, he'd invested wisely. Even if he never wrote another story, Blake would be comfortable financially. Money wasn't the reason he wrote.

"Maybe you need more than a change of scenery," Greg suggested. "Maybe it's time for a change of direction. Maybe Cliff Pearson is played out."

Blake shook his head, not liking the direction the conversation had taken. That was one thought he didn't want to consider. "Cliff Pearson is my brand. He's what readers expect from Ken Blake."

Greg was silent for a moment, and Blake knew he was once again framing his response. "That may be true for Ken Blake, but what about Blake Kendall? What does he want to write?"

As rain sheeted down the window, Blake turned away to look at his friend. "That's easy: another book that hits the *Times* list." That would make his agent and his publisher happy. For his part, Blake wouldn't deny that he enjoyed the validation of knowing that tens of thousands of readers had chosen his story over the literally millions of other titles available to them.

"Is that why you write, to see your name on a bestseller list?" The frown that accompanied Greg's question made Blake wonder if he was remembering the day at Stanford when they'd talked about the future and Blake had claimed that everyone was put on Earth to make it better, even if only in the smallest of ways. Blake had helped his clients achieve financial security. His books served a different purpose.

"The lists are the result, not the reason for writing. I write to entertain people, to give them the thrill of vicarious adventure. If they're afraid to turn off the light after a chapter, I've done my job."

Greg's relief was obvious. "You definitely succeeded with Kate. She had one of your books on her e-reader for the flight to Europe, and she wasn't happy when the flight attendants dimmed the cabin lights so everyone else could sleep. She said the story was so scary she wanted bright lights everywhere."

The way Greg glanced at his watch told Blake he hadn't come here for casual conversation. "Speaking of my bride, she wondered if you had any seating preference for dinner. Guests are assigned to a table for the length of their stay. Since this weekend is special, some of the staff are joining the guests. Kate thought you might want to be at Marisa's table."

"Sounds like a plan to me."

Greg's smile made Blake wonder if his friend realized how attracted he was to Marisa. It wasn't something they'd ever discussed, and Blake had hoped that he wasn't being obvious, but . . .

When Greg headed back to the lodge, Blake settled into a chair. This was turning into a year for firsts. It was his first experience with writer's block. It was also the first time he couldn't get a woman out of his mind. It didn't matter whether he was jogging or shaving or drifting off to sleep. No matter where he was, thoughts of Marisa were never far away.

Blake closed his eyes, and as he did, her image popped into his mind. The long hair that refused to stay confined in a ponytail, the dimples that accompanied her smiles, the way she cupped her chin when she was thinking. Marisa was beautiful—at least in Blake's eyes—but that was only part of her appeal. There were unplumbed depths to her, starting with the reason she'd chosen to alter her appearance so dramatically. He considered that it might have been a knee-jerk reaction to her father's disappearance, but that didn't explain why she was still doing it eight years later. Surely the pain should have diminished.

Blake wished—oh, how he wished—he could do something to ease Marisa's pain, but he felt as clueless about that as he did about Cliff Pearson's next adventure.

The picnic on the island had been a good idea. Correction: it had been a great idea. Blake couldn't forget how relaxed and happy Marisa had looked when they'd wandered along the trail, exploring the small island. He couldn't forget how content she'd seemed when they'd rowed back to Rainbow's End with the sun setting behind them. He definitely couldn't forget their kiss. Even now, almost a week later, Blake couldn't forget how sweet Marisa's lips had tasted and how wonderful it had been to hold her in his arms.

Marisa St. George was the best thing that had happened to him in a long, long time. Now, if only he could break through his writer's block.

"You're brilliant," Kate told Marisa as she leaned back in her chair. "When Greg and I hired you for your accounting skills, we never dreamt you'd turn into a producer."

The two women were sitting in the back of the main lodge, watching the dress rehearsal for tomorrow's program.

"I knew you wanted entertainment," Marisa told her boss. "I thought this would accomplish that plus be a good way to promote Gillian's CD." The idea had popped into her brain while Blake rowed back from Paintbrush Island. Marisa wasn't certain how it had happened. One minute she'd been relaxing in the boat. The next her mind had been whirling with ideas.

"It's more than a good idea," Kate said, her face glowing with enthusiasm. "It's brilliant. I'm just annoyed that I didn't think of it myself. After all, I'm supposed to be the marketing expert."

"You're still dealing with Gillian's accident. You're too close to that to think about ways to use her music."

Since they weren't going to have Gillian Hodge in person, Marisa had enlisted the staff, including Kate and Greg, to perform comic skits with Gillian's recording of country songs as background music. Though Kate had been mildly skeptical when Marisa had proposed the concept, she'd agreed that it might work and had given Marisa the go-ahead. Kate had been in New York, spending a few days with Gillian after the surgery, so this was the first time she had seen anything other than her own part of the show.

"I have to say that it's turning out better than I expected," Marisa added. The staff's enthusiasm over the idea had transformed what could have been ordinary skits into ones that were bound to make the audience laugh. Even Mom, who had been dubious at first, seemed to enjoy her role as a beleaguered short-order cook with a defective stove and an ever-increasing number of orders, while the teenagers loved the idea that their ordinary tasks of cleaning guest rooms and doing laundry had been transformed into a melodrama complete with a sheet-stealing villain.

"It's what I told you before," Kate said, laying her hand on

Marisa's. "You're brilliant. Even Gillian agreed." Kate blinked as if to keep tears at bay. "I keep praying everything will turn out well for her. She tried to put a good face on it, but I'm really worried about her."

"And you wish you could take away her pain." It was Marisa's time to offer comfort. "I know. I feel that way about Lauren. I wonder if she'll wind up spending the rest of her life alone."

Kate nodded. "I want to believe Lauren will have a second chance at love just as Gillian will have a second chance at her career. It could happen."

Kate's eyes lost their glassy sheen as she focused on happier thoughts. "Look at my grandmother and Roy. Neither of them thought they'd remarry, but they're as happy as can be in their new life. And then there's Greg and me. We didn't think we'd have a first chance at love, but it came when we least expected it." Her lips curved upward. "I may have been married for only a couple weeks, but I know that happily-ever-after is real."

Sadly, it hadn't been that way for Mom and Lauren.

# 13

The guests were still raving about your skits at dinner. I expected it at breakfast, but after listening to the pastor's sermon, I thought that would have been the noontime topic of discussion," Blake said as he fitted the tire pressure gauge onto the front valve stem. Unlike the bicycle he'd ridden as a boy, the tandem had skinny tires under such high pressure that the only way to determine whether they were properly inflated was to use a gauge.

It had been a busy day: breakfast followed by church and the minister's provocative message of what "love your neighbor" really means, then Carmen's delicious Sunday dinner and the guests' departure. When everyone had left and Marisa had appeared a bit frazzled, Blake had suggested they borrow Lauren's tandem for another ride. To his relief, she had agreed, acting as if he'd presented the path to world peace.

Blake smiled as he recalled the previous evening's entertainment. He'd expected it to be good, but it had exceeded his expectations. "It was clever the way you managed to make each person's job seem funny."

"I wanted to show that Rainbow's End is a group effort. Everyone contributes, and we're all links in a chain." Marisa was so close that Blake could smell the light floral fragrance of her shampoo.

He stood up, reassured that the tires were fine. "The finale was great." The staff had worn costumes that looked like large gold links, and when they'd joined hands, they had formed a chain, dancing to Gillian's recorded rendition of "The Yellow Rose of Texas." Though the original lyrics had nothing to do with chains or teamwork, someone—probably Marisa—had rewritten them to describe the effort each person had contributed and the camaraderie they'd found, the clever verses interspersed with a chorus that even now echoed through Blake's head.

> It's the greatest little resort that Texas ever knew;
> The meals are mighty tasty, the staff is friendly too.
> You can talk about big city lights and sing of foreign
>     shores,
> But Rainbow's End's the place for me, now and ever
>     more.

Blake doubted he'd ever hear the song without thinking of the Rainbow's End staff mispronouncing "resort" as "ree-zort" so that it would fit the music, all the while grinning as if a slight mangling of the English language was of no account. And it wasn't. What mattered was that everyone was having fun.

Though the song was met with exuberant applause, the entertainment wasn't over. As the music ended, instead of taking curtain calls, Greg invited all the guests to join hands with the staff and sing one more chorus. One had turned into half a dozen, each one a bit louder than the previous.

When the singing had reached a level that Blake suspected could be heard in Dupree, Kate switched off the CD player and presented each of the guests with a key chain with the Rainbow's End logo, telling them they were now part of the Rainbow's End family. It had been an evening Blake knew he wouldn't forget, and the praise that had continued today told him the other guests had had the same reaction.

"I was happy with the way it turned out," Marisa admitted as she tied the cycling shoes she'd borrowed from Lauren, carefully tucking the ends of the laces in so they would not loosen or get caught in the chain. "It's nice to be working for a billionaire. When I told Greg I wanted special costumes, he didn't blink at the cost."

"Greg always did believe if something was worth doing, it was worth doing well." As Blake gave the bike a quick safety check, he glanced up at Marisa. "Which skit was the most difficult to write?"

"Mine." She answered without hesitation. "I had no idea how to make my job seem funny."

Blake wasn't surprised that she'd lacked the perspective to view her position the way she did the other staff members'. "But you did. Seeing you throw off the green eyeshades and pin-striped suit to turn into a hippy-looking director made everyone laugh."

"The credit goes to Kate. She told me she used a similar idea for one of her advertising campaigns. Not accountants, of course. She transformed a humble peanut into something special."

"I hope her ads worked as well as your skit did."

"Me too." Marisa's smile faded. "She said she was inspired by Ken Blake's books."

Blake tried not to let his surprise show. He couldn't imagine what connection Cliff Pearson's adventures had to a peanut. He'd have to ask Kate, but right now he was more concerned by Marisa's frown. "Is something wrong?"

She shrugged. "Just the thought of those books." She turned the words into an epithet.

"Ken Blake's thrillers? Have you read them?" Market research had told Blake that his readership spanned age, gender, and socioeconomic groups, but somehow he had never thought of Marisa being one of those readers.

"Just one." Her frown turned into a scowl. "I've always loved books. In fact, at one point I fantasized about opening a bookstore. That never happened, but I still try to sample everything that makes the bestseller list. I'm always curious about what others find appealing."

"And you didn't like what you found." Blake tried not to let that thought bother him. He had had his share of bad reviews and had learned that they were part of the business, but this was different. This was Marisa, the woman who dominated so many of his thoughts. She might be only one reader, but she was one whose opinion mattered.

"'Didn't like' is an understatement. Oh, I'll admit that they're well-written, but I hate the way Cliff Pearson makes heavy drinking seem perfectly acceptable."

It was the first time anyone had made that comment, and it stung. Blake forced himself to keep his voice noncommittal. After all, Marisa had no way of knowing that he was Ken Blake and that this was his book she was criticizing.

"It's fiction, Marisa. It's designed to entertain."

Her frown deepened. "Maybe so, but writers have such power. I believe they should use it for good."

Blake nodded. His instincts had been correct. He had been wise not to tell Marisa of his alter ego, although not for the reasons that had kept him silent initially. He'd feared she'd be star struck. Not once had he considered that she might disapprove of what he did.

Taking a deep breath, Blake exhaled slowly. There had to be a way to work around that problem. But right now his first priority was to learn more about Marisa's relationship with her father and help ease her pain. Somehow he'd find a way to steer their conversation toward fathers.

He grabbed his helmet and buckled the chin strap. "Ready to go?"

"You bet." Marisa's momentary unhappiness seemed to have passed. "Tandems are addictive. I can see why Lauren and Patrick enjoyed this one."

When they reached the highway, they headed north. The terrain was slightly hillier this direction, and Blake had to downshift several times as they climbed a hill. By the time they reached the summit, he could hear Marisa panting.

"Want to stop there?" he asked, pointing to what appeared to be a lemonade stand at the bottom of the hill.

"Sure. I always like to help out kids."

So did Blake. In what seemed like only seconds, they coasted to a stop in front of the oilcloth-covered table. Two identical twins whom he guessed to be no more than ten years old stood behind the table. Fortunately, their green shirts were embroidered with their names.

"Cool bike," Jim announced, while Jeff narrowed his eyes and asked, "Two cups, mister?"

Still straddling the bike, Blake shook his head slightly. "I'm pretty thirsty. You'd better make it three."

The boys' eyes lit with such enthusiasm that Blake wondered if this was their first sale of the day. "Sure thing," Jim said as he ladled the slightly orange liquid into three plastic cups.

"This is peach lemonade, you know," Jeff said. "The finest in the state." Jeff, Blake had already decided, was the more entrepreneurial twin.

"Did you grow the peaches?" Marisa asked as she accepted a cup and took a sip.

"Yeah." Jim amended his declaration. "Well, our dad did."

"But we help pick them," his brother explained.

"Ma makes the lemonade."

Blake took a long swallow and grinned. "It's good."

"Of course it is," Jeff said with a matching grin. "Best in the state. Ma's got the blue ribbon to prove it."

Jim eyed Blake. "Did your ma make lemonade when you were a kid?"

"Mine did," Marisa announced before Blake could tell the boys that he had no memories of his mother, "but she didn't put peaches in hers." She drained the cup and held it out to the boys.

"Another cup?" Blake asked Marisa.

"Not right now. Maybe on the way back."

Disappointment etched Jeff's face. "We might not be here."

"All right. Can you fill up my water bottle instead?" Marisa pulled the bottle from its cage and handed it to Jim.

"How do we charge for that?" Jim asked his brother. Jeff's expression told Blake he hadn't faced that question before.

Rather than pointing out that the boys could simply fill cups and count them as they poured the contents into the water bottle, Blake pretended to study the water bottle. "I'd say it holds six or eight cups." More like four, but the kids obviously wanted the sale. "I'll pay you for eight." High fives greeted his words.

"You made their day," Marisa said as they rode away. "I have a feeling they're going to be talking about this when they're supposed to be sleeping tonight. Eleven cups has to be one of their biggest sales."

She was acting as if he had done something important like curing world hunger, when all he'd done was give two boys a little extra money. "I remember what it was like at their age. Having spending money meant a lot."

"Which is why you and I both had after-school jobs."

"Exactly. Now, how far do you want to go?"

---

"I think we went too far," Marisa said half an hour later. Her thigh muscles ached, and once again she wished the cabin had a tub instead of a shower. It would be good to sit and soak the aches away.

"Don't say that," Blake cautioned as he steered them around the tree branch blocking part of their lane. "We still need to get back. You can't start feeling defeated now. Besides, whose idea was it to go up that last hill?"

Marisa pressed as hard as she could on the pedals, trying not to wince as her muscles protested. "I have no one to blame but myself. I know that, but it looked like it would be so much fun to coast down this hill."

"And it was," Blake reminded her. "All you need is a little rest and you'll get your second wind."

When they reached a level spot in the road, Blake stopped the bike and leaned it against a fence. Handing Marisa an energy bar, he sank to the ground next to her and stretched his legs before him.

"I never believed in second wind," Marisa said as she opened the foil wrapper.

"It's real," Blake insisted. "So is third and fourth wind. My dad claims that's what got him through days at the steel mill."

This was not the first time Blake had steered the conversation to his father. Perhaps it was coincidence, but Marisa suspected that he had his father on his mind for some reason.

"That must have been exhausting work." Occasionally Marisa's father had complained about his job as a mechanic at the gas station, but it wasn't the same constantly demanding work as a steel mill.

Blake nodded and took a swig from his water bottle. "It was hot and dirty, but Dad claims it built men. I don't know if that's the reason, but he's the strongest man I've ever met. Not just physically, either."

*Strong* was not an adjective Marisa would apply to her father. "What do you mean?" It was clear that Blake's father was far different from hers.

"I told you that Dad's dad lived with us. The man was incredibly demanding. He had his own way of doing things, and he expected everyone to follow it. Everything had to be done his way."

Blake looked into the distance for a moment, and the way his lips were pursed told Marisa his thoughts were unhappy. "Grandfather even demanded that the salt and pepper shakers be put in a specific place on the table. He'd become livid if they weren't in the right spot."

Though Eric had been irrational at times when he was under the influence of alcohol, he had never made demands like that. "Why would anyone care where the salt and pepper were so long as they were on the table?"

Blake shrugged. "I gave up trying to understand him years ago. The problem is, he got worse the older he became—even less reasonable. Then he started to become forgetful and would blame us if he couldn't find something. I'd have put him into assisted living, but Dad wouldn't hear of it. He said the Bible told him to honor his father, and that's what he was going to do."

"Your father sounds like a saint."

Wrinkling his nose, Blake shook his head. "Maybe not that, but definitely a better man than I'll ever be. Dad may have turned the other cheek, but I've learned to run the other way from angry people."

Marisa closed her eyes for a second, not wanting Blake to see the emotions his words had evoked.

"My dad wasn't like that," she said softly, realizing she envied Blake. Not for his difficult grandfather but for the love he and his father shared. It was obvious that Mr. Kendall was very different from her father. At one point, Eric might have been physically strong, but he'd lacked the strength to resist alcohol.

Years with support groups had helped Marisa accept that it wasn't her fault, but she still couldn't understand the lure alcohol held for him. And, no matter what her mother, her minister, or Colleen, the therapist who'd helped her deal with her anger, had urged, Marisa was unable to forgive Eric for the pain he'd caused Mom and her. The memories were still too vivid, memories of him staggering through the house, collapsing on the couch, and forgetting that he had promised to attend her . . .

Marisa paused, a rueful smile crossing her face. This was a fill-in-the-blanks exercise. School play, vacation Bible school closing day celebration, birthday party. It didn't matter what the occasion was. Eric wasn't there. There was no question about it. Eric St. George was not a strong man.

But Blake was. His inner strength translated into kindness toward others. Marisa had seen people feign kindness and concern, mostly when it would serve their interests, but Blake wasn't like that. He had been genuinely kind to the lemonade stand boys, and right now he was looking at her as if he would do anything to make her smile.

As if on cue, the corners of Marisa's mouth turned up in a real smile. Blake hadn't erased her painful memories—no one could do that—but he had shown her that not all men were like Eric or even Hal and Trent. Blake was a man she could trust, and that made him special. Very, very special.

———— ✶ ————

"This is wonderful!" Marisa scooped a handful of bubbles onto her hand and lifted them to her nose, inhaling the sweet scent of strawberry foam. She couldn't recall the last time she'd luxuriated in a tub filled with fragrant bubble bath.

"I didn't want to confuse your nose, so I brought strawberry tea," Lauren said as she entered the bathroom door bearing a tray with two mugs, a large teapot, and a plate of what appeared to be cookies.

"Did I ever tell you that you're my favorite person on Earth?" Marisa asked as she accepted the steaming mug.

"Just because I let you soak in my tub?"

Marisa shook her head. "That's only the tip of the iceberg. I feel like a princess with all these bubbles." When Lauren had seen Marisa hobbling as she got off the bike, she had insisted she had the perfect cure. Telling Blake she was kidnapping his date, Lauren promised she would call him when Marisa needed a ride back to Rainbow's End.

"You should pamper yourself occasionally," Lauren said, holding out the plate of thumbprint cookies. "That's one thing you're not very good at."

"Do I sense a lecture coming?" Marisa asked as she bit into the cookie and savored the strawberry jam in its center.

"It all depends."

"On what?"

"On whether you tell me what's going on in that head of yours.

When you rode in, you were smiling with what looked like pure happiness, but your eyes looked scared. What's happening?"

Marisa finished the cookie, chewing carefully to prolong the time before she had to respond. Though she was tempted to deny that anything was different, she knew better. This was Lauren, the woman who knew her almost as well as she knew herself.

"I didn't realize it was so obvious," Marisa said when she could find no excuse for further delays. "I'm confused, and—yes—I'm a little scared. I've never felt this way before."

"If that was meant to hook me, it did. What is it you're feeling?" Lauren dragged a chair into the bathroom and leaned back in it, looking as if she were prepared to remain there for however long it took Marisa to explain.

"I can't stop thinking about him. I dream about him every night, and when I'm awake, all I can think about is what he might be doing."

Lauren nodded slightly, encouraging Marisa to continue. When she'd taken another swallow of tea, she did. "He's not like anyone I've ever met."

Marisa closed her eyes for a second, trying to corral her thoughts. If they were so jumbled that they didn't make sense to her, she'd never be able to make Lauren understand. When she opened her eyes, Lauren was staring at her, her expression inscrutable.

"There are times when I think he needs me and other times when I know I need him. Mostly, though, I just want to be with him." Marisa shook her head as she thought about all she'd experienced. "I'm hot; I'm cold. I'm happy; I'm scared."

"You're in love." Lauren completed the sentence.

Marisa was silent for a moment as she considered her friend's announcement. It was what she had thought, what she had feared. "Are you sure?"

"As sure as I can be without being in your skin."

"Oh, Lauren, that's what I was afraid of."

Lauren blinked. "Afraid of love? It's the most wonderful thing in the world."

It was amazing that Lauren could say that when her own love was gone. "What if he doesn't love me?" Marisa demanded. "What if I give him my heart and he disappears the way my dad did? What will I do then?"

Though Marisa had told herself that she could trust Blake, part of her feared she was wrong, that no one could be as perfect as Blake appeared. Another part feared that even if Blake was everything he seemed to be, he'd realize that Marisa didn't deserve him. Most men weren't eager to take on a woman with as much baggage as she carried.

Lauren leaned forward and laid her hand on Marisa's head, ruffling her hair. "You've got to learn to trust. You need to trust Blake not to hurt you, and you have to trust yourself." Settling back in her chair, Lauren said, "I know it's not easy after what happened with your dad, but that's in the past. You can't change it, but you also can't let it control your future. Let it go, Marisa. Let yourself love."

"I want to. I can't tell you how much I want to. The problem is, I'm not sure I can."

# 14

October was supposed to bring cooler weather, but today felt more like August than autumn, Lauren reflected as she wiped a bead of perspiration from her forehead. Days like this made her wish she'd brought her car, but in a town as small as Dupree, it made more sense to walk unless she was carrying heavy packages. Or so she thought. Right now an air-conditioned vehicle sounded appealing. So did one of those frilly parasols her great-grandmother had carried whenever she set foot outside the house. Instead, Lauren was walking down Pecan without even a hat to block the sun. She should have known better.

It had been cold and rainy last October, matching her mood as she struggled with the reality of being a widow and a single parent. This year was different. The days were bright and sunny, and her heart was filled with hope. Part of the reason was the simple passage of time—it did lessen the intensity of pain—but part was the fact that Marisa was back in Dupree.

Lauren waved at Russ Walker as she walked by the Sit 'n' Sip. Business was typically slow at this time of the day, and he was taking advantage of a momentary lull to wash his front window. She should do the same, and she would, but first she needed to finish the quilts Kate had commissioned. And today she had to get to the school in time to watch her daughter's baton twirling practice.

Fortunately Susan Kozinski had promised to take Fiona back to her apartment with Alice and had reminded Lauren that Fiona had a standing invitation to spend the night with them. It was a generous offer, but Lauren always felt as if she were taking advantage of Susan's generosity. Though Susan did not work outside the home, she had many demands on her energy, including baby Liam, who was not yet sleeping through the night.

And then there were the financial considerations. While Fiona might not eat as much as a teenage boy, she had a healthy appetite, and that appetite could wreak havoc with a tight grocery budget. Lauren knew that, like almost everyone who lived in Hickory View, Susan and Bert were saving to buy a house. The rent might be low, but no one wanted to stay in apartments as poorly maintained as those.

Though she wouldn't let Fiona sleep over at Alice's, Lauren was considering asking Marisa if she'd babysit for a couple hours so Lauren could put the finishing touches on a quilt. Marisa. The very thought made Lauren smile as she crossed Lone Star. Just having her back in town was wonderful, but what made Lauren's heart sing was seeing her dearest friend in love. There was no doubt about it. Marisa glowed with happiness, and when she and Blake were together, that glow turned into a full-fledged fire. The best part was that he was as smitten with Marisa as she was with him.

Lauren's smile widened as she thought of the way they held hands when they walked, stopping occasionally to simply smile at each other, other times to steal a kiss when they thought no one was watching. It was so sweet that it made Lauren's eyes prickle with tears of joy.

She had expected the bubble bath to relax Marisa's muscles, but it appeared to have done more than that. Ever since that night, Marisa seemed to be breaking through the barriers she had erected around her heart, leaving her free to love. Perhaps now she could put the past and all the anger it provoked behind her.

As she approached the school yard where the second graders were practicing twirling, Lauren spotted her daughter trying to toss the baton into the air and catch it before it landed.

*Oh, Patrick, you would have loved this! She looks like you stretching to shoot a basket.* Lauren narrowed her eyes, studying her daughter. Why hadn't she realized that Fiona was a miniature feminine version of Patrick? She liked the same things Patrick did: being outdoors, playing sports, swinging as high as she could in an attempt to touch the sky. She had his smile and his zest for life. She even had his carefree attitude toward fashion. Lauren smiled. Patrick was gone, but she saw part of him in Fiona every day. As memories flooded through her, Lauren's smile broadened, and today for the first time sorrow took second place to joy.

"Mommy, you came!" Fiona shrieked, completely forgetting that she was supposed to be watching the baton, seemingly oblivious when it tumbled to the ground next to her. Patrick had been like that and had missed an easy shot when Lauren had unexpectedly arrived at the court. Afterward, they'd agreed that she would not surprise him and cause distractions during a game.

Lauren gave the teacher an apologetic glance as she crossed the yard to hug her daughter. "Of course I came. I promised, didn't I?"

"Yeah." Fiona looked up at Lauren, her expression serious. "But you promised me a new daddy too."

They were back to that.

———— ✳ ————

Marisa twirled in front of the mirror. The fringe on her vest swayed; the pearl buttons on her shirt gleamed; the jeans were neither too new nor too old; the hand-tooled boots provided an authentic western touch. Everything was just right. Marisa looked like a woman going to a rodeo, which was exactly what she was.

She plucked the white Stetson from the bed and tried it on. Not bad. Though she hadn't worn a western hat in years, Lauren had insisted on lending her hers, declaring that she couldn't attend a rodeo without proper headgear. Now she was ready, and not just for the rodeo. Marisa was ready for life.

"You look beautiful, *mi hija*," Mom said as she stepped into the living area.

"I feel beautiful." Marisa knew she wasn't, but Blake made her feel as if anything, even beauty, was possible. When he smiled at her, she felt as if she were Cinderella, Sleeping Beauty, Snow White—all those beautiful Disney heroines wrapped into one package. It was wonderful, simply wonderful, being with Blake.

Marisa smiled at her mother, knowing she'd smiled more in the last few weeks than she had in the rest of her life. She'd learned so much about Blake. They'd talked and talked, sharing stories of their past and their dreams for the future. She'd told Blake how she'd wanted to be a ballerina, only to be informed that she had no sense of rhythm. He admitted that he'd told his friends tall tales, delighting in scaring them with gory stories each Halloween. She'd confessed that her most fervent wish was to learn what had happened to her father. He admitted that, while he was glad that his father seemed romantically interested in a woman named Hilary, he couldn't help wondering how that would change his relationship with his dad.

Though Marisa knew there were aspects of Blake's life that he hadn't revealed, it no longer seemed to matter. How could she demand that he tell her everything when she was harboring her own secrets? She hadn't told Blake how both Hal and Trent had duped her. She hadn't told him the truth about Eric's drinking. Instead, Marisa had taken Lauren's advice and was trying to put the past behind her. It was working. For the first time, she was starting to believe in a bright and happy future.

"He's here!" Mom announced when she heard the clomp of boots on the front steps. She flung the door open and ushered Blake inside.

"Wow!" Blake let out a low whistle. "Annie Oakley never looked that good." His gaze moved from the top of Marisa's Stetson-clad head to her intricately tooled boots, as if he were inspecting each inch. "I'm not sure we ought to go. I don't want to spend the whole day fighting off cowboys."

It was a flattering thought, even if totally unrealistic. "Trust me. There's no need to worry."

Blake simply shook his head. "I have eyes in my head. I know what those cowboys will see."

Mom grinned as if the compliment had been directed at her, then wagged her finger at Blake. "You take good care of my daughter. Don't let her eat too much cotton candy."

"That's one thing you can count on, Carmen," Blake said with patently false solemnity. "I'll cut her off after four."

Marisa joined in the banter. "One's my limit."

"See, I told you you didn't have to worry."

Marisa couldn't let him get away with the last word. "All bets are off if they have funnel cakes."

They were still laughing as they approached Blake's car now parked next to the main entrance. As if they'd been waiting for them, Kate and Greg emerged from the Tyrolean-style building.

"You look like a real cowgirl," Kate said with an approving smile.

"I'm a native Texan. What did you expect?"

Greg laid a hand on Blake's shoulder. "You, my friend, are a sorry excuse for a cowboy. Where's your hat?"

"I've got a ball cap in the car."

"You want to be laughed out of the arena?" Greg opened the back of his SUV, pulled out a Stetson, and plopped it on Blake's head. "This is what you need. Now you've got to learn to swagger. Try it."

Marisa started to laugh at Blake's exaggerated swagger as he strode away from her, but the laughter died a second later. Shock mingled with disbelief. It couldn't be true. She wouldn't let it be true. But it was. As she stared at the back of a man wearing a large hat, Marisa knew why Blake had seemed so familiar the first time she met him. That day he'd had his back to her, and that had triggered memories she hadn't been able to place. Today she had no doubts. The angle of the shoulders was the same; so was the tilt of the head. The hat was the final confirmation.

As if that weren't enough, there was the similarity in names. Marisa had once read that when writers chose pseudonyms, they frequently kept their initials. Blake had done more than that. He'd kept his name.

"You're Ken Blake!" The words came out as more of an accusation than an exclamation.

Kate took one look at Marisa's face and grabbed her husband's hand. "That's our exit line," she said, dragging him back into the office.

Blake turned and stared at Marisa. It was the face she knew so well, the one that had starred in her dreams. And yet it wasn't the same, because now she knew his secret. She'd been wrong when she'd thought that secrets didn't matter. They did.

"Tell me I'm mistaken," Marisa begged. "Tell me it isn't true."

Blake came closer. Though his steps were steady, the swagger was gone. "I can't do that. This isn't the way I had planned to tell you, but—yes—I am Ken Blake, or at least I write books under that name."

He'd planned to tell her. That was something, but the fact was, he *hadn't* told her. This wasn't part of his past, the way Hal and Trent were part of hers. This was Blake's present and his future. This was who he was.

"When were you planning to tell me?"

Blake's silence told Marisa everything she needed to know, leaving her trying to tamp back the horrible sensation that the world would never be the same. She took a deep breath as she attempted to reconcile the knowledge that the man who'd captured her heart, the man who'd brought love and laughter into her life, was the one who'd also created that loathsome character, Cliff Pearson.

"How can you do it?" she demanded.

Blake's lips tightened, and she knew she'd hit a sensitive nerve.

"It's my job, just as filing tax returns and auditing clients' books is yours."

He was trying to justify it, but it wasn't working. Not for her. "It's not the same. You created Cliff Pearson, and you chose to make him a man who smokes, drinks, curses, and lusts after other men's wives." Blake's hero could have been an upstanding citizen, but he wasn't. He was a man who drank more than Eric, yet he never seemed drunk. How many readers thought they could do the same? How many families had been torn apart like hers, all because someone tried to emulate Cliff Pearson?

"He also saves lives. Sometimes he stops whole cities or small countries from being destroyed." The steel in Blake's voice left no doubt that he felt strongly about his character and that he saw nothing wrong with Cliff's flaws.

"And you think that justifies his other behavior?" Of course he did. Marisa's heart sank at the realization that this was the man who, even though they'd discussed Ken Blake's books, hadn't told her he was the author. He'd had the perfect opportunity, but he'd let it slip by. Marisa dismissed the memory of her critical comments about his books. Blake was the one who was in the wrong. Not her. In all likelihood, he never intended to tell her he was Ken Blake.

What a fool she'd been! Silly Marisa, gullible Marisa had trusted Blake the way she had trusted Hal and Trent. It seemed she'd never learn.

Blake shook his head, then removed the hat and held it in one hand. Though he looked more like himself and not the writer whose back was shown on so many book jackets, Marisa couldn't forget that they were the same man.

"It's not a case of justification," Blake said. "Cliff Pearson is a fictional character, but there are many men in the real world with the same habits you dislike so much. His behavior is true to life."

That didn't make it right. "I'm not denying that his flaws are common. What I don't understand is why you had to make them seem acceptable. You practically glorified them."

Blake took a step toward her, stopping when she glared at him. Marisa couldn't let him come too close. She knew she'd shatter if he touched her.

"I'm not glorifying them," Blake insisted. "I'm simply depicting a character with human frailties."

Either he didn't understand or he chose not to admit it. It was up to Marisa to make Blake see how wrong he was.

"It's more than that. You've made Cliff heroic. He does things ordinary people can only dream about. Sure, most readers know they'll never be able to foil a terrorist plot, but what about the impressionable teenager who reads your books or watches the movies? What if he tries to emulate everything Cliff Pearson does and winds up so drunk that he kills someone when he drives home? Do you want that on your conscience?"

Though Blake blanched at the image she'd presented, he refused to back down. "I think you're overreacting. People buy my books or go to the movies because they want to be entertained, not because they're looking for a guide to life."

That might be true, but . . . "People see a movie star eating a specific brand of cereal and they buy a box. Manufacturers pay to have that box of cereal sitting on the table. You're doing the same thing in your books. Fans know what kind of cigarettes Cliff Pearson smokes and the name of his favorite Scotch. Don't you think at least someone will want to see if those are as good as Cliff thinks?"

Blake shook his head. "I doubt it."

"You're naïve."

He shook his head again, more vehemently this time. "I'm not naïve. What I am is angry that you're attacking me because of the way I earn a living. I'm not an axe murderer."

"I never said you were." The truth was, he had the ability to affect far more people than a lone axe murderer.

"But you're acting as if I'm single-handedly destroying the moral fiber of this country. I write books, Marisa. Bestselling books. I'm not ashamed of that."

"Aren't you?" She didn't believe him. "If you're not ashamed, why do you use a pseudonym and why do you refuse to have your face on the dust jacket? Those are the actions of a man who knows what he's doing is wrong. Why are you hiding?"

Anger suffused Blake's face, and his voice seethed as he said, "I have my reasons, but since you're so sure you're right, since you're so sure you know everything that's in my mind, there's no need for me to tell you."

He took a step toward her, his expression menacing. "You act as if you're perfect, as if you're not hiding anything. If that's true, tell me why you dyed your hair and why you're wearing colored contacts?"

Before Marisa could answer, Blake spun on his heel and left.

# 15

I can't believe I was such a fool!" If it wouldn't have made her appear childish, Marisa might have pounded her fist on the counter. "I trusted him. What kind of an idiot does that make me? I should have known better."

When Blake had turned away, Marisa had known that she also needed a time-out. Mom wouldn't help. She thought the moon rose and set in Blake, all because the man complimented her cooking. There was only one place where Marisa could be assured of comfort, which was why she was now standing inside HCP, staring at her best friend.

Furrows appeared between Lauren's eyes as she rose from her perch behind the counter. "You're not making sense. Sit down," she said, gesturing toward the pair of chintz-covered chairs that flanked the front window, "and start from the beginning." After she locked the door and turned the sign to "closed," Lauren took the other chair. "Now, what did Blake do?"

Marisa explained, the words tumbling over each other as she related what she'd discovered. "He wouldn't even admit how wrong he was," she concluded.

Though she'd expected Lauren to murmur comforting words,

her friend simply gazed at her for a long moment before she said, "I know you're upset, but have you considered that you might be overreacting?"

"Not you too." Marisa felt as if she'd been betrayed twice in the space of less than an hour. "That's what he said. I might have expected it from him, but I thought you were my friend."

"I am your friend," Lauren insisted, "but that doesn't mean I agree with everything you do or say. It seems to me Blake made a valid point when he said writing was his job. And quite frankly, I think it's pretty cool that we have a celebrity in Dupree. Folks are going to be lining up to get his autograph."

Marisa blanched at the realization that she had opened Pandora's box. She was angry with Blake and deeply hurt, but that was no excuse for ignoring his desire for anonymity. He'd spent the better part of a decade keeping his two identities separate, and she had no right to change that.

"You can't tell anyone." Marisa leaned forward, hoping Lauren would realize how important this was. "Blake doesn't want anyone to know he's Ken Blake."

Lauren nodded slowly, and if she found it odd that the woman who'd been condemning Blake's choice of a profession was now defending him, she said nothing. "You know, Marisa," she said at last, "just because Blake writes about a man who does things you don't like doesn't mean he's that man."

"But Cliff Pearson drinks scotch the way you and I do iced tea." And that was only one of his many flaws.

"Have you ever seen Blake drink?"

"No, but . . ."

"But what?"

Marisa should have remembered that Lauren was nothing if not persistent. "He could be a closet drinker." That was how Eric had started. Literally. He'd hidden inside the master bedroom closet, sitting on the floor with his bottle in a brown bag. The first time Marisa had found him there, he claimed he was looking for a pair of shoes. She'd still been young enough to believe that daddies didn't tell lies, but as the years passed and the drinking became more open, she'd realized what was happening.

Lauren shook her head, making Marisa wonder if she had read her mind. "You don't believe that. You'd have heard if the cleaning staff found bottles in Blake's cabin, and I doubt the trunk of his car is stuffed with empties."

"Alcoholics are sneaky, Lauren. They know how to hide their tracks."

"And you know what to look for. The reason you haven't seen any signs of drinking is because Blake is not a drinker. He's just a writer."

That could be true, and Marisa hoped it was, but it didn't negate the fact that she felt betrayed. "Whether he drinks or not, he lied to me. He told me he was a financial planner."

Lauren rose and poured them each a cup of coffee before she responded. "Maybe he is."

"Sure." Lacing her words with sarcasm, Marisa shook her head at her friend. "All *New York Times* bestselling authors moonlight as financial planners." Though the coffee was delicious, one of the flavored blends that Lauren's customers preferred, it did nothing to diminish Marisa's anger.

"Blake wasn't always a bestselling author. Maybe he worked as a planner before his books sold."

That was possible, even likely, but it didn't exonerate him. "If that's the case, he should have used the past tense. He told me that's what he does now." And she'd been so naïve that she hadn't questioned how he could take so much time off from work.

"How do you know it's a lie?" When Marisa did not answer, Lauren walked behind the counter and pulled out her laptop. "Let's see what we can find. Where did he say his office was?"

"San Francisco with a view of the Golden Gate Bridge."

A few clicks and mere seconds later, Lauren gave Marisa a satisfied smile. "There it is. Blake Kendall, CFP and a bunch of other initials. I can't tell you how many clients he has, but he's a Certified Financial Planner and he's still open for business." She closed the laptop and returned to her seat across from Marisa. "I think you owe him an apology."

"Never." When Lauren raised an eyebrow, Marisa tried to soften her reaction with an explanation. "He's like Hal and Trent. He's good looking and charming, and I was foolish enough to believe he was honest and that he genuinely liked me."

Marisa pursed her lips, feeling as if she'd eaten a sour persimmon. "Silly me. I even thought he loved me. Now I know better. Three strikes. I've watched enough baseball to know what that means. I'm out of the game. No more men. No more trusting."

Lauren's eyes flashed with anger and something else, something that might have been sorrow. "What about second chances and turning the other cheek?"

Shaking her head, Marisa rose. "Save your sermon for someone else. I'm having a bad day." As she left Lauren's shop, Marisa told herself it couldn't get any worse.

She drove aimlessly for several hours, the radio blaring as she tried to drown out the car's rattle and the voices that echoed in her head. Lauren didn't understand. Though she'd been with Marisa for the prom night debacle, she hadn't met Trent. She hadn't watched him woo Marisa, talking about how they were two of a kind. She hadn't heard him claim that the reason he wanted to help Marisa find her father was that he understood how she felt. She hadn't been there the day the check had cleared and Trent had disappeared. She didn't know that Marisa had lost more than her savings that day; she'd lost a good measure of her self-esteem.

Marisa had thought Blake was different. In fact, during those magical days when she'd believed she was falling in love, she had told Blake they must be a case of opposites attracting because they were two very different people. She'd been convinced that that was good, that Blake had nothing in common with either Hal or Trent. She'd been wrong.

Marisa blinked at the sign advertising rodeo parking. No thank you. Somehow without her realizing it, she'd arrived at the place where she and Blake had been headed. There was no way she was going to enter the arena and watch the cowboys compete. That would be like pouring salt into her wounds. She made a quick U-turn and half an hour later found herself in Blytheville.

After parking on the main street, Marisa made her way to the small dress shop that Lauren had raved about. Retail therapy might be just what she needed. It didn't help. Though she looked at the artfully arranged clothing and even pulled a few blouses from the rack to see the details, nothing registered. Instead of neat pintucks and western embroidery, her mind pictured Blake, the man she had thought she loved, the one who'd conveniently neglected to tell her who he was.

Oh, he could say that writing was his job, but Marisa knew better. She'd read enough interviews with authors, each of whom made it clear that writing wasn't what they did; it was who they were. Though he might claim otherwise, Blake didn't love her. If he did, he wouldn't have hidden such an important part of his life.

And how dare he act as if coloring her hair was wrong? She had reasons—good reasons—for that. He had no idea what it had been like living with Eric.

Marisa clenched her fists and took a deep breath, trying to relinquish the anger that gripped her like a vise. Colleen had warned her that there would be times when anger would ambush her and that she'd need every technique in her arsenal to manage it, but never once during the sessions they'd had together had Marisa thought it would be like this. Colleen might be one of the best counselors in Atlanta, but she'd never been in this situation. She didn't know what it felt like to be betrayed. And that's what it felt like: betrayal.

With a sigh of disgust that she was accomplishing nothing here, Marisa returned to her car and headed back to Rainbow's End.

The sun was setting by the time she reached the resort, and her stomach was announcing its need for food. *Soon*, she told herself.

Soon she'd be inside the cabin, and even if Mom wouldn't provide comfort, there would be comfort food. That was one thing you could depend on from Carmen St. George.

Marisa pulled her car into the small parking area next to the cabin, noting that an unfamiliar vehicle had taken the remaining spot. How odd. She glanced at the car as she climbed out. The nondescript white sedan, probably five or six years old, was the kind of car the non-truck-driving residents of Dupree favored, but the Alabama plates made it unlikely that it belonged to one of the workers. Marisa frowned. Although guests came from all over the country, each of the other cabins had its own parking, giving them no reason to be here.

Brushing aside the question of who had left the car near her new home, Marisa registered the fact that the cabin lights were on. That meant Mom was inside. With her bag slung over her shoulder, Marisa climbed the three steps and pushed the door open.

"Something smells . . ." The words died as she entered the cabin. She felt blood drain from her head and grabbed the doorknob to keep from falling. A second later, heat suffused her face as she stared into the living area. There, seated on the couch as if he belonged there, was the man she had thought she would never see again.

"What are you doing here?" The words burst out before Marisa could stop them.

Eric St. George rose from the couch and started to open his arms. He looked like her father, and yet he didn't. The dad she remembered was far younger than this, with silver blond hair and vibrant blue eyes. This man's hair had faded and was streaked with gray, and his face bore more lines than many men twenty years his senior.

The years had not been kind to Marisa's father. He was thinner than she recalled, his shoulders slumped as if he'd carried a heavy burden for too long. The only part of him that hadn't changed was his eyes. They were still the same blue Marisa saw when she changed her contacts. Right now, those eyes were filled with hope and uncertainty as he took a step toward her, his arms ready to embrace her. Her expression must have warned him, because he let his arms fall to his sides.

"Manners, Marisa. No matter what he's done, he's still your father." Though Mom's voice was as filled with anger as Marisa's had been, there was no ignoring the change in her demeanor. She stood taller than she had this morning, and the lines that bracketed her mouth seemed to have lessened.

"What made you come now?" Marisa hadn't thought the day could get worse, but it had. There had been times during the years she'd searched for Eric that she had believed their reunion would be joyful. She'd pictured herself running into his arms and being whirled in the air as she had as a child. But as the years had passed, hope had been replaced by anger and bitterness. Today the sight of her father brought back memories of the nights she'd cried, the years she'd worried, and the money she'd spent trying to find him.

"It was time. I was ready." Eric spoke the words calmly, as if he hadn't realized how his sudden reappearance would affect them.

"What if we're not ready to have you here?" Marisa clenched her fists. Though she wanted nothing more than to pound something, she wouldn't give Eric the satisfaction of knowing how much he'd hurt her. Again. Instead, she glared at him.

"You left us without so much as a good-bye. I don't know what you've been doing, but in case you've lost track of time, you've been gone for more than eight years. That's eight years when Mom and I had no idea where you were or whether you were still alive. And now because *you're* ready, you've come back. It doesn't work that way, Eric."

He flinched at the name.

Mom grabbed Marisa's arm. "Sit down. Let's discuss this like civilized adults."

Mom and Eric took the same seats they'd had when Marisa had entered the cabin, Eric on the couch, Mom in one of the chairs. Marisa perched on the edge of the remaining chair. From there, she could watch Eric's expression and study his body language. If there was one thing she'd learned from her sessions with Colleen, it was to look for non-verbal cues. She wouldn't let Eric deceive her the way Hal and Trent and Blake had.

"Where have you been?" Somehow, her voice managed to sound almost conciliatory, as if the memories of those eight years of waiting and wondering weren't churning inside her stomach.

Eric shrugged, the motion highlighting the fact that he was no longer the burly man Marisa remembered. "A lot of places. Mostly Mexico."

No wonder she hadn't been able to find him. The investigators she'd hired had searched only the US. Even Trent, who claimed he knew tricks the other PIs did not, had not suggested looking outside the US. Of course, the only true investigation Trent had done had been of likely marks' bank accounts.

"I came back to the States about a year ago," Eric continued. "I've been working for a car dealer near Birmingham, but now that I'm on my feet again, I wanted to be here."

Though Mom said nothing, hope shone from her eyes. Marisa couldn't count the number of times her mother had insisted that Eric was still alive and that he would return. He had.

Though Marisa knew she should be happy or at least relieved to know that Eric was still alive, everything about his return felt wrong. Perhaps it was only because she'd been so distraught by Blake's revelation, but Marisa couldn't shake the feeling that this was a temporary reunion. If Eric left again, Mom's heart would be shattered. Marisa couldn't let that happen. She couldn't let Mom cling to false hopes.

"And how long will you stay this time?"

Eric flinched as if Marisa had hit him. "You've changed. You didn't use to be so cynical."

As if he'd remember what she had been like. His memories had to have been colored by the whiskey, gin, vodka—whatever kind of alcohol he was drinking that day.

"I grew up," she said shortly.

"And you changed your hair and eyes. All those years, I tried to imagine what you'd look like. I knew you would have matured, but I never thought you'd color your hair." He stared, as if memorizing her features. "It used to be like mine."

"I know." That had been the reason she'd colored it. Like the gifts she'd tossed out or given away, her blonde hair had been a reminder that had to be destroyed.

"I'm no longer the little girl who used to cry when her dad missed seeing her win the spelling bee," Marisa said, keeping her gaze fixed on him. When Eric's eyes darkened, she knew her words had met their mark. "I learned not to expect anything from you. That way I wasn't disappointed."

He closed his eyes for a second, making Marisa wonder whether he was praying. When he opened them, he said, "I've got a lot to make up to both of you."

Mom nodded slowly. "You do, but we'll give you a chance."

"Speak for yourself, Mom. I'm not sure he deserves another chance. I don't understand how he could abandon us that way. A man who loved us wouldn't have done that."

Marisa had read countless books; she'd heard numerous lectures; she'd spent hours discussing it with Colleen. All that had told her that alcoholism was a disease that became the most important part of a person's life, damaging families at the same time that it destroyed the drinker. Most of all, she'd been told that it wasn't her fault and that nothing she could have done or said would have changed Eric.

Until today, she had thought she believed that. Now, faced with the reality of Eric's return, Marisa knew the truth. Her brain understood, but her heart did not. No matter what she had claimed, the hurt, confused little girl who didn't understand why her daddy wasn't like the others was still inside her.

"I was wrong. I know that." Eric sounded sincere, and nothing in his posture gave lie to his words. "I can't undo the past, but I will do everything I can to make the future better."

Marisa closed her eyes, not wanting him to see the sheen of tears. Though she wanted to believe him—oh, how she wanted to—she couldn't dismiss the fear that he might hurt her mother and her again. It had taken years for her trust to be eroded; it would take more than a few minutes and a few promises to rebuild it. Right now Marisa wanted nothing more than to throw herself on her bed and try to put this day behind her.

She gave Eric a steely gaze. "Where are you planning to live? Lauren mentioned that our old house is up for rent."

"Why would he go there?" Mom looked surprised by Marisa's suggestion. "If we're going to rebuild our family, we need to be closer. Your father is staying in one of the other cabins."

No! Marisa wanted to shriek the denial. She wasn't ready, wasn't sure she'd ever be ready to share her life with a man who was practically a stranger. He'd been gone for eight years, almost a third of her life. He couldn't expect to walk back into it as if nothing had happened.

Mom might have accepted Eric's protestations of love and reform, but Marisa wasn't so gullible. He would have to prove that he'd changed, and that wouldn't occur overnight. In the meantime, he needed to keep his distance, and that meant more than a few hundred yards.

Marisa shook her head. "I'm not staying at Rainbow's End if he's here." He'd try to worm his way back into Mom's heart, and that was something Marisa couldn't bear to watch, not when she feared he'd leave the next time the desire for a bottle of whiskey grew too strong.

Before her mother could protest, Marisa rushed into the kitchen and picked up the phone. "Lauren," she said the instant her friend answered, "is the offer of your spare room still open?"

## 16

Ashamed? Blake shook his head as he placed another slice of
bacon next to the scrambled eggs on his plate. The internal
conversation that had started the previous afternoon continued. He
wasn't ashamed of his books, he told himself as he ladled maple
syrup over the pancakes. No, siree, or whatever it was Texans would
say. He wasn't ashamed. He was a writer, and if the critics were to
be believed, a good one. They'd described his writing as solid, his
plots innovative, his characters compelling. Judging from his sales
and the fan mail he'd received, readers agreed. That was cause for
pride, not shame.

This must be the morning lull that Carmen had mentioned at
supper one day, because the dining room was practically empty.
That suited Blake just fine. In his current mood, he wouldn't be
a congenial companion for anyone. He wasn't ashamed of what
he wrote, but he did regret the way he'd left Marisa. He should
have explained why he used a pseudonym. He'd told her about
his grandfather, so she already knew that the older man had been
deeply opinionated. When she learned how vehemently Grandfather felt about fiction, she would have understood.

She would also understand that when he had first started writing, Blake had depended on the income from his financial planning practice. He wasn't certain how his more conservative clients would have reacted to the knowledge that he had a second job, especially such a different one, and so anonymity had seemed the best course for multiple reasons.

Blake should have explained that to Marisa. But he hadn't. At the time he'd been so incensed by her accusations and alarmed by the anger that had reminded him all too forcefully of Grandfather on one of this tirades that the only thing he could do was walk away. Then, when he'd recovered from his initial anger enough to talk to Marisa, to try to understand her over-the-top reaction, she was gone, the absence of her car clearly indicating that she'd left Rainbow's End. Blake had looked for her again after supper, but her car was still missing, its spot taken by an unfamiliar vehicle with Alabama plates.

He hadn't wanted to appear like a lovelorn swain, constantly searching for the object of his affections, and so he'd waited a few hours before strolling by the stone cabin. The result had been the same: no Marisa. He'd checked again this morning, but there was still no sign of Marisa's car. Even stranger, one of the teenagers was replenishing the breakfast buffet, a job that Carmen usually reserved for herself. Something was going on.

Blake forced himself to chew slowly. He didn't need indigestion, even though the pancakes weren't as light as they'd been yesterday. The only reason he could imagine for that was that Carmen hadn't made them. She had a special touch with pancakes, as she did with almost everything she cooked, and these flapjacks lacked that touch. Perhaps she was ill, but that didn't explain the presence of the strange car and the absence of Marisa's.

There was only one way to learn what had happened. Blake swallowed the last bite of pancake, washed it down with a final slug of coffee, and rose. A quick glance at his watch told him it was after nine. Ever a creature of habit, Marisa ought to be in her office. She was. Though the door was closed, he saw light seeping under it.

"Come in," she called when he knocked. That was a good sign. At least she wasn't ignoring everyone, although her reaction to him remained to be seen.

Blake tried not to reveal his shock. She looked awful. Even carefully applied makeup couldn't disguise the dark circles under her eyes and the pallor of her complexion. That alone would have worried him, but the way her shoulders slumped was even more concerning. Surely her discovery that he was Ken Blake hadn't been enough to cause such a change.

"Oh, it's you." Her greeting left no doubt that he was not welcome. Blake wouldn't let that discourage him. If he had learned one lesson from his father, it was to take responsibility for his actions and apologize when they hurt others. And, though her reaction had been extreme, Blake couldn't ignore the fact that it had been triggered by something he had done.

"I came to explain about yesterday."

Marisa shook her head, dismissing him. "There's no need. You said everything there was to be said. Now, if you don't mind, I'd appreciate being left alone. I have a lot of work to do."

What had happened to the warm, caring woman, the woman he'd held in his arms and kissed, the woman who'd captured his heart? This woman was a stranger. More than that, she was a stranger he didn't particularly like, one who reminded him of Ashley in her worst moments. Still, he couldn't walk away without understanding what had caused the change.

"Marisa, I want to—"

"But I don't." She wouldn't even let him finish his sentence. "Please leave."

This time he did. Though he was tempted to slam it, Blake knew that anger solved nothing and so he closed the door softly behind him. Marisa needed time to recover from whatever was bothering her this morning, and he needed time to reassess their relationship.

It was clear that Marisa had more baggage than he'd realized. Perhaps it was time to walk away, both literally and figuratively.

The last thing Blake needed was another woman like Ashley in his life, and yet Marisa hadn't seemed the least bit like Ashley until yesterday afternoon. There had to be an explanation, a logical reason, for the change.

As he walked toward the front of the building, Blake heard the sound of singing in the kitchen and recognized Carmen's voice. Excellent. If anyone could give him a clue to Marisa, it was her mother. And judging from the joyful song, Carmen was having a better day than her daughter.

Blake poked his head through the open doorway. "Come on in," Carmen called when she spotted him. Though he'd never seen her in a foul mood, her smile was unusually bright this morning. As he entered the room, Blake revised his opinion. The smile looked almost artificial, making him wonder if it and the song were part of an attempt to project happiness.

"Maybe I should come back later." Blake had no desire to get himself involved in another difficult situation.

Carmen shook her head. "'There's no reason to do that. You're always welcome here." She gestured toward the plate of cinnamon rolls that sat on one corner of the counter. "Help yourself. I made extras for Eric." Her smile faltered as she added, "He came home yesterday."

Eric. Marisa's father. Blake inhaled deeply as the significance of Carmen's statement registered. It explained not just the unfamiliar car but also Marisa's mood. Though he wasn't trying to exonerate himself for the anger his revelation had provoked, Blake's supposition that he was not the primary cause of the pain he'd seen in Marisa's eyes was confirmed. A reunion ought to be joyous, and yet it was clear that this one had not been. At least not for Marisa.

Blake knew that her feelings for her father were complex and that the wounds inflicted by his disappearance had yet to heal. He also knew that Marisa was not a woman who liked surprises, at least not surprises of this magnitude. While he had no idea what she had said when she'd seen her dad, judging from the circles under Marisa's eyes, she had had a sleepless night, and morning had brought no resolution.

"That's good news, isn't it?"

"It is for me. Eric's return is the answer to eight years' worth of prayer. Now I'm praying that having him here will be a blessing for Marisa." Though a shadow crossed Carmen's face, she said nothing more, and Blake knew better than to pry. Carmen would tell him what she wanted him to know, but only in her time frame.

When she started to discuss the supper menu, he realized he'd learn nothing more from her today, but at least the detour had been worthwhile. He'd learned two things: Marisa hadn't told her mother that he was Ken Blake, and that discovery wasn't the only—probably not even the primary—reason Marisa was upset this morning.

He couldn't do anything about her father's return, but Blake could try to make amends for the way he'd left her yesterday. Marisa might not accept a verbal apology, but surely she wouldn't refuse a peace offering. And if she did, that would open the door to a discussion of exactly what had happened yesterday. If they were going to have any kind of a future together, he needed to know why she'd reacted the way she had.

Blake frowned as he recalled his visits to Dupree. With no florist or candy shop, he'd have a hard time finding the traditional apology gifts. It was possible, though, that the supermarket might have something. He'd try there, and if that didn't pan out, he'd go to Blytheville.

Fifteen minutes later, he was wandering through the supermarket aisles, searching for something that would say "I'm sorry" more eloquently than the words Marisa refused to hear. As he'd expected, the store's selection of flowers was limited, but the candy aisle held more promise. He was debating the merits of locally made goat milk fudge versus an assortment of chocolates when two teenagers entered the same aisle.

"Have you figured out how to get it yet?" the first one asked.

Blake gave the boys a quick glance. The one who'd spoken was tall, skinny, and dark-haired, while his companion was half a foot shorter with blond hair.

"I'm working on it," Blondie said. "I told my mom I'd heard that was the best brand of scotch and that's what she should buy for the party. She took the bait—hook, line, and sinker." He scuffed one shoe on the floor. "I won't be able to sneak out a whole bottle, but once she opens one, I can fill some jars for us." He slouched against a cookie display and fixed his gaze on his companion. "How about you? Did you get the cigarettes?"

Blake tried not to frown at these obviously underage boys scheming to smoke and drink. Though he was tempted to remind them that what they were planning was not only illegal but also dangerous to their health, he suspected they'd be even less inclined to listen to him than Marisa had been.

The dark-haired boy shook his head and stared at the floor as if the pockmarked linoleum would magically produce cigarettes. "Just my luck that my dad decided he was going to quit smoking this week. He threw a whole carton away before I knew what was going on."

"So, what now? We need them." Blondie's voice cracked as he spoke.

"Not to worry," his companion assured him. "I got a cousin in Blytheville who's coming to dinner this weekend. His dad smokes the right brand, so he's gonna bring me a pack or two."

Blondie grinned. "Cool. By this time next week, we'll be just like Cliff Pearson."

---

The time of reckoning had come. Marisa had known it was a matter of when—not whether—her mother would appear, and here she was, looking determined to have her say. Mom closed the door behind her and took a seat in front of Marisa's desk.

"I'm not going to leave until you listen to me."

"You said everything there was to say yesterday." It had been only half an hour since Marisa had told Blake the same thing. It appeared that that was the refrain of the day. She looked at her mother. Though Mom's expression was serious, the lines around her mouth seemed to have lessened. "You've gotten what you wanted. Eric is back." She would not, she absolutely would not, refer to him as Dad.

Mom inclined her head in agreement. "You're right. I wanted him to come back. He's my husband, and no matter what happened in the past, I never stopped loving him." She stared at Marisa, her expression slightly defiant. "Of course I'm happy that he's here, but I don't want to lose you." The defiance turned to pleading.

Marisa reached across the desk and grabbed her mother's hands. "You're not losing me. I'll always be your daughter."

"Then come back. Let us work on becoming a family again."

No matter what Mom thought, it wasn't that simple. "I can't. I see Eric, and all I can remember are the bad times. I think about how he was never there when I needed him and how much money I wasted trying to find him."

Mom tightened the grip on Marisa's hands. "Money? What are you saying?"

Though Marisa hadn't planned to tell her mother about the searches, the words had escaped before she could censor them. Now she had no choice but to admit what she'd done. "I knew how much you wanted him to come back. I thought I could find him, so I hired a few investigators over the years." Marisa frowned as she thought of the men who'd tried to help her. Other than Trent, they'd been honest but unsuccessful.

"It seems we were looking in the wrong place. I never thought Eric would leave the country. One of the few good memories I have is of Fourth of July celebrations and how proud he was to be an American." Though he'd marched in both the Christmas and the Independence Day parades, Eric had once told Marisa he believed Jesus's birthday was better celebrated in church. Parades and marching bands should be reserved for July Fourth.

"That's true. Eric loves this country." Mom gave Marisa one of those 'you'd better tell the truth, because I'll know if you're lying' stares as she asked, "Why didn't you tell me what you were doing?"

"I didn't want to get your hopes up when there were no guarantees." The first time Marisa had hired a PI had been her first year out of college when she was finally earning enough to pay the fees. After that, she'd waited two years and had tried a more expensive firm reported to have a high success rate. And then there had been Trent.

Tears filled Mom's eyes, and she squeezed Marisa's hands so tightly they hurt. "Oh, *mi hija*, thank you."

"I didn't accomplish anything other than wasting money." And she deserved neither thanks nor praise for that.

"You're wrong." A vehement shake of the head accompanied Mom's words. "What you did shows me that you still love him."

"I did it for you." And for herself. Marisa had wanted what Colleen called closure, what she simply referred to as answers. She wanted to see her father again to learn why he'd left and especially why he'd left on graduation day.

"That's the first step." Mom rose and made her way around the desk. "Thank you, Marisa," she said as she wrapped her arms around her. "I know it won't be easy, but I hope you will give him a second chance."

Second chance? It would be more like a fiftieth chance. Marisa shook her head, unwilling to raise false hopes. "I'm sorry, Mom, but I don't think I can do that."

————— ✳ —————

"I could get used to this." Lauren pulled out a chair and took her place at the kitchen table, smiling as Marisa poured pancake batter into a pan.

"It's the least I can do for someone who won't let me pay room and board." This was the second day Marisa had made breakfast. Yesterday's oatmeal muffins and yogurt parfait had been such a hit that she had decided to expand her repertoire and make banana buckwheat pancakes. While her culinary skills would never match her mother's, Marisa was a reasonably good cook, and preparing breakfast was something she could do to repay her friend.

Lauren shrugged as if her hospitality were insignificant. "The guest room was empty, and—"

"Empty? Is that how you describe a hundred pounds of fabric and thread?" It had taken the better part of an hour to clear enough space for Marisa and the few belongings she'd brought that first night.

"You know what I mean." Lauren accepted a cup of orange juice from Marisa and nodded when she poured another one for Fiona. Though the little girl was later than normal today, since it was Saturday and a no-school day, Lauren didn't seem to mind.

"I'm thankful for the adult companionship," Lauren continued, "and Fiona's so excited about having Aunt Marisa living here that she's forgotten to nag me about finding her a new daddy."

As the bubbles burst on the top of the pancakes, Marisa began to flip them. "Correct me if I'm wrong, but you don't seem to be actively looking for one." Not that Lauren had much time, even if she'd been inclined to go husband hunting. Completing the quilts for Rainbow's End was a more than full-time job.

"You should talk. The Matchers are going to be so disappointed when they realize that you and Blake are no longer an item."

Marisa didn't want to talk about Blake any more than she wanted to think about her father's return.

"Don't change the subject, Lauren. We were talking about you."

Her friend took another sip of juice before she responded. "I'm not going to put an ad in the paper or join one of those online dating services, if that's what you mean. I've heard too many horror stories."

"So you're just going to wait until Mr. Right appears on your doorstep." Lauren had been fortunate, because Patrick had done almost that. He'd been assigned a locker across from Lauren's, and they'd struck up a conversation his first day of school. If it hadn't been love at first sight, it was pretty close.

"That's one way to describe it."

Marisa blinked, then realized that Lauren hadn't read her thoughts. She was referring to her comment about waiting for Mr. Right. "What I'm doing is waiting until God sends the right man." To Marisa's surprise, Lauren's lips curved in an almost secretive smile. "There are days when I think he already has."

Surprise turned to shock. "You've been holding out on me. Who is this man?"

Rather than reply, Lauren rose and headed to her room. When she returned, she held out a sheet of paper with a pencil sketch. Marisa stared at it, not wanting to believe what she saw.

"Drew Carroll? You must be kidding. He's absolutely the last man you should consider marrying."

Lauren nodded. "I know. I'm not in his class. I barely finished high school, and he's a Stanford grad, but . . ."

Marisa held up a hand in the universal gesture for halt. "Stop right there. You're not the problem. He is. I heard all about him from my mom. He's arrogant, he uses people, and he thinks rules are for others." The accusations were harsh, but Marisa couldn't let her friend continue to harbor delusional thoughts about Drew Carroll.

Lauren snatched the paper back from Marisa and laid it on the table next to her plate. "I've heard that before, but I can't stop thinking about him."

"Try harder."

## 17

Blake wasn't sure how long he'd been pacing. All he knew was that it wasn't helping. He'd counted the number of steps it took to get from one end of the living area of his cabin to the door—six—and the number of steps to cross the same room from side to side—seven. What he hadn't tallied was the number of times he'd counted and how long he'd simply paced. He probably should have gone jogging, but it was raining, and even though Greg claimed that only wimps let a little liquid sunshine keep them from exercising, Blake had always been a gym person. It was one thing to run five miles on a treadmill inside a nicely climate-controlled environment, quite another to battle with raindrops and puddles all in the name of exercise.

Even if he'd gone outside, there was no guarantee that he'd have been able to banish the images that had driven him to pace. The two events were separate, and yet in his mind, they blended together, each disturbing him in its own way.

First came Marisa. "I don't want your apology or your candy," she had said when he'd tried to hand her the box of fudge he'd brought as a peace offering. There had been no warmth in her expression, nothing but the stark anguish he'd seen earlier that day, as she added, "The only thing I want is to be left alone."

Blake might have argued. Perhaps he should have, but the truth was, he had little to say. Though he could list his reasons for using a pseudonym, he knew that would not alleviate her pain. He could claim he understood about her father, but that would be a lie. Blake's father had been a stable, loving force in his life. Marisa's had not.

Blake had no words of comfort to offer, and so he'd done as she had asked. He had returned to his cabin and resolved not to seek her out. Now that Rainbow's End was officially reopened and he was taking his meals in the dining room with the other guests, Blake had no reason to see Marisa. But, try though he might, he could not forget her.

He could tell himself that she was being juvenile in her refusal to talk to him, that he was better off without her, but his heart wasn't listening. It kept remembering the good times they'd shared—everything from watching movies together to riding Lauren's tandem to simply strolling along the lake.

What he hadn't counted on was how much he would miss Marisa, how empty his days would feel without her. It wasn't only his days that were empty. He was too. Blake felt as if a part of himself had been lost, as if there were a cavern deep inside him that had once been filled with warmth and happiness. That was gone, and he couldn't change it. Not yet. Marisa needed time to recover from the shocks she had sustained.

The memory of Marisa's haunted eyes blended with the image of seeing Blondie and his companion in the supermarket and hearing what they planned. Though Blake's shock was certainly not of the magnitude Marisa had experienced, it had been an unpleasant surprise to discover that she'd been right.

He hadn't wanted to believe it possible, but the evidence was clear. Cliff Pearson had had a negative influence on at least two teenagers. The fact that the influence was unintentional didn't matter. The result was the same. Blondie and his friend wanted to be like Cliff. They saw him as a role model.

Blake stared at the window, watching drops of rain cascade down the glass, obscuring the normally peaceful view of the lake. He couldn't change what he had written. He couldn't stop Blondie and all the other impressionable people from emulating Cliff's lifestyle. But that didn't mean he had to continue making the same mistake. For it was a mistake; Blake admitted that.

What if Cliff were a different role model, one that even Marisa could admire? What would that kind of man do? Blake shook his head and resumed his pacing. Changing Cliff's behavior might have some benefits, but if he did that, Cliff wouldn't be Cliff. The whole premise of the series would have to change, and that might— in fact, it probably would—alienate his readers. There had to be another way.

Back and forth. Back and forth. Blake continued to measure the distance from one end of the cabin to the other, but the pacing had no more effect than it had when he'd been trying to overcome writer's block back in San Francisco. The view was different, but the result was the same. Nothing, nada, zilch.

Disgusted when he recognized the beginnings of a headache and knew it was caused by sheer frustration, Blake leaned against the window, pressing his head against the cool pane. There had to be an answer. He felt as if he were close, as if there were ideas just waiting to tumble over the dam, and yet those ideas remained firmly behind the barrier. It was no use. He was accomplishing nothing.

With a sigh, he opened his eyes and started to turn away from the window. As he did, he caught sight of a staff member dashing between cabins. Blake stared as his brain began to whirl. What if . . . ? Grabbing a pad of paper and a pencil, he began to scribble.

---

It was like old times, Marisa reflected as she reached for another handful of popcorn. She and Lauren were together again, laughing more than they had in years as they listened to the squeals coming from Fiona's room on the second floor.

"It sounds like the pajama parties you and I used to have," Marisa told her friend.

"Only now we're the older generation. I wonder if my mother used to stay awake during ours."

"Probably."

Fiona had invited three of her friends for a sleepover. At least that was how she'd described it. Neither Marisa nor Lauren expected there'd be much sleeping involved, certainly not for either of them. Since they both had vivid memories of forbidden candles and close encounters with curtains, they'd decided not to even pretend to sleep. Instead, they were seated in Lauren's kitchen, eating popcorn and drinking enough caffeine to keep all of Dupree awake for a week.

"I almost didn't agree to let Fiona have this party," Lauren admitted.

Marisa took another sip of coffee. "I can understand that. It's tough not sleeping when you have to open the store in another"—she glanced at the clock—"five and a half hours."

"That's not the reason. It's just that for the next week I'm going to have to answer questions about why Fiona doesn't have any sisters. It's bad enough when she visits Alice and sees baby Liam, but this will be worse. The other two girls have sisters old enough to be playmates. Fiona wants a sibling almost as much as a father."

"Not to pry, but why doesn't she have one?" It had been a question Marisa had wanted to ask for several years, but something, perhaps the hint of sorrow she saw in Lauren's eyes whenever someone spoke of babies, had kept her silent. Tonight, though, Lauren seemed almost eager to discuss children.

"I don't know," her friend said. "Patrick and I certainly wanted another child, but it just didn't happen, and by the time we started talking seriously about adoption, he was diagnosed with cancer."

Lauren ran her finger around the rim of her mug as she said,

"That's one of the reasons I think about remarrying. I'd like to have another child. He or she wouldn't be much of a playmate for Fiona now, but I think siblings are important. I always wanted one." She looked up, her lips curving into a smile as she said, "I don't know whether I ever told you, but I used to pretend you were my sister. The problem was, you had to go home. I hated that."

"Me too." Just as it had years ago when they'd been children, the late hour had freed Marisa from many of her inhibitions. "Sometimes I wonder what my life might have been like if I'd had sisters or brothers. I can't help asking whether my father would have been different." Would the responsibility of a larger family have kept him from drinking, or would it only have increased his need to escape reality? It was a question no one could answer.

Lauren rose and stretched, then poured herself another cup of coffee. "Another thing I don't think I told you is that I used to wish your dad was my father."

For a second, Marisa was too shocked to respond. When she did, the words came out in a sputter. "Why on earth would you want that?"

"Because he was so much fun." A smile lit Lauren's face as she leaned forward to lay her hand on Marisa's. "My dad was always pretty serious. Don't get me wrong. He was a good provider, and I never doubted his love, but he didn't laugh much. You never would have caught him pushing us on the swings or teaching us how to catch fireflies." Lauren threaded her fingers through Marisa's and gave them a little squeeze. "Your dad seemed like a grown-up kid to me, while mine was just grown up."

With her mind still reeling from the thought that Lauren, who knew Eric's flaws better than almost anyone in Dupree, envied Marisa her father, Marisa closed her eyes. When she did, she pictured the three of them at the school's swing sets, her father pushing first one girl, then the other. And then there were the nights when they'd carried jars into the backyard, hoping to snag at least a couple fireflies, and one special night when he'd declared them old enough for what he called a trip. That night he'd driven them into Firefly Valley to hunt for fireflies.

Marisa's smile lasted only seconds. Superimposed on those memories were ones of Eric St. George staggering into the house, occasionally collapsing on the floor before he made it to the couch or the bed. The slurred words and bloodshot eyes were bad enough, but what had hurt the most were the absences. Even when his body was seated at the kitchen table, Marisa had known he wasn't really there. And all too often, he hadn't made the effort to be present, even bodily. The most painful memories were of empty chairs.

Marisa forced her eyes open. Though Lauren was smiling, Marisa could no longer muster a smile. "At least your dad was sober."

Lauren nodded. "That's true, but from what I've heard, so is yours now."

"For how long?" That was the question. Eric had tried to stop drinking more times than Marisa could count, but each time had ended with defeat.

"One day at a time. That's all it takes." Lauren tightened her grip on Marisa's hand. "You're probably going to tell me to mind my own business, but I believe you ought to think about mending your relationship with your dad. I know it won't be easy. Believe me, Marisa, I know how much he hurt you. But I also know you've got a second chance. Not everyone gets that."

"You sound like Mom."

Lauren shook her head. "No, I sound like the voice of reason. I never thought my dad would die so young." Lauren's father had died of a brain aneurysm before she turned twenty. Though he'd lived long enough to see his granddaughter, Fiona had no memories of her maternal grandfather, only pictures of him holding her as an infant.

"I wish he were still here to watch Fiona grow up," Lauren said, her voice cracking with emotion. "One day you're going to get married. Don't you want your dad to walk you down the aisle? Don't you want your children to know their grandfather?"

Marisa blinked at the sudden change of direction. "Marriage? Children? Aren't you getting a little ahead of yourself?"

Lauren disengaged her hand from Marisa's and took another sip of coffee. "That's another thing I wanted to talk to you about. I think you're wrong about Blake. Whenever I saw you together, you two looked so happy, like you were meant for each other."

For a few days Marisa had entertained that dream. For a few days she'd thought that Mom might have been right and that Marisa had found love at first sight. Then reality had shattered those illusions.

"It's a nice thought, but Blake's not the right man for me." Marisa wasn't certain she'd ever find that man, but she knew one thing: the man she married wouldn't keep his real life secret from her.

Lauren shook her head again. "Your problem is, you're searching for perfection. You'll never find it, Marisa. Believe me. I know that. I loved Patrick dearly, but I wasn't blind to his faults. If you weren't so stubborn, you'd admit that you love Blake."

Lauren was a hopeless romantic, a woman who saw love and happily-ever-after everywhere. Marisa was a realist. "I'm not even sure I know what love is."

"It's when you think about the other person all the time."

Marisa let out a bitter laugh. "That's how I felt about Hal, and we both know that wasn't love." It had been nothing more than a foolish infatuation, the dream every teenage girl has of going to the prom with the most popular boy in the class.

"That's true, but you didn't let me finish. Love is when you care about the other person's happiness more than your own."

Marisa nodded slowly. If she had had to describe her mother's relationship with Eric, that would have been a good way, and she had no doubt that Lauren had been more concerned about Patrick than herself.

"That's not the way I feel about Blake."

"Isn't it?" Lauren's raised eyebrows underscored her skepticism. "Beneath your anger that he didn't tell you he's Ken Blake, I suspect you're worried about him. You probably believe he's selling himself short."

"He is."

"And you care."

Marisa hesitated, trying to analyze her feelings. "I do care, but that isn't love."

"Isn't it?"

———✳———

Marisa was still thinking about Lauren's question as she drove to work the next morning. She was later than usual because of the slumber party and the fact that she'd had only two hours' sleep. Once there had been no sound from the second floor for over half an hour, both she and Lauren had decided to take advantage of the girls' collapse to catch a few winks.

Being late didn't matter. Not only did she have no clock to punch, but it was Saturday. If she hadn't wanted a few uninterrupted hours to load historical records into the new accounting software, Marisa wouldn't have gone to Rainbow's End at all. As it was, it would be an ideal day to work. Kate and Greg weren't expecting her, and if she told Mom she was working, she'd respect Marisa's need for quiet.

Mom. Marisa gripped the steering wheel more tightly. Ever since Eric's return, their relationship had been strained. It was the proverbial case of walking on eggshells, with each of them being overly polite, as if afraid to provoke another argument.

After the day when Mom had said she was afraid of losing her, Marisa had tried her best to be conciliatory. That was why she had agreed to have dinner with Mom and Eric each Sunday. Tomorrow would be the first time, and though she was apprehensive, Marisa kept telling herself everything would be fine so long as she treated him like a casual acquaintance, not the man who was her father. She knew how to deal with casual acquaintances. Fathers were a different story.

Eric was sitting on the cabin steps when she parked her car. For an instant, Marisa considered choosing a different parking spot, but that would have been the act of a coward. She wasn't a coward.

"This is a pleasant surprise," Eric said as she climbed out of the car. "I didn't know you were coming today."

He rose and stood by her side, not touching but close enough that she could smell his aftershave. Old Spice, of course. Marisa remembered chiding him about using such an old-fashioned product and him telling her that if it was good enough for his father, it was good enough for him. That day he'd even tried to splash some of it on her face, causing Marisa to run to her mother, shrieking as if she were being murdered.

*There's no need to keep walking down Memory Lane*, Marisa told herself. *He's a casual acquaintance.* "I have some extra work to do," she said, her voice as cool as if she were talking to someone she'd just met.

"You always were conscientious."

She pointed the remote at the car and locked it, a habit she'd developed in Atlanta. "You can give Mom the credit for that. She kept telling me to give my employers more than they expected." Marisa had done that for Haslett Associates, and look what it had gotten her. That was another memory best left untouched.

Eric took a step toward her, then matched her pace as she started toward the office. "I'm proud of you, Marisa. You made the most you could out of a tough situation." He paused, and when Marisa darted a glance at him, she saw what appeared to be sorrow etched on his face. "I wish things had been different."

They were approaching dangerous territory. "Well, they weren't." Her voice was harsher than she'd intended. "I need to get to work."

"Sure." If he was disappointed that she didn't want to continue the discussion, Eric gave no sign. Instead, he tipped his head toward her car. "That rattle is in the drive train."

Once a mechanic, always a mechanic. Mom had been right. Eric St. George was a genius where the internal combustion engine was concerned. That was why he'd held on to his job for as long as he had. He could fix any vehicle ever made, and even when he was hungover, the quality didn't seem to suffer. If Eric had cared about her and Mom as much as he did his customers' cars, their lives would have been different. But that was another subject Marisa didn't want to address.

"It can't be serious," she said, not wanting to admit that he might be right. That would give Eric power over her, and that was one thing she would not let happen. "It got me all the way from Atlanta to Texas without any problem."

"You'd better have it looked at."

"Sure." But she wouldn't.

---

Blake stared at the stack of paper on the edge of the table and grinned. He couldn't believe it. After months without a single idea, he now had a flood of them, what some would call an embarrassment of riches. He'd been writing for more than a decade, and this was the first time that had happened. In the past, he would get an idea for one story, but in the last twenty-four hours, he had outlined half a dozen, each competing to be the first to be told.

Standing to stretch muscles that had cramped while he'd sat hunched over the table, his hand trying to capture the ideas that were racing through his brain, Blake grinned again. He couldn't remember ever being so excited about a story. His fingers practically itched to start turning his notes into a manuscript. That left only one problem.

After grabbing his cell phone, Blake sprinted toward his car and drove to the top of Ranger Hill. Though he could have used the resort's pay phone, he preferred the privacy of his car. Depending on Jack's reaction, this could be a long call.

Still grinning when he saw that Greg had been correct and that there was indeed cell coverage here, Blake opened his contact list.

"I'm sorry to bother you on a Saturday," he said when his agent answered, "but I want to run something by you."

"The concept for your next book?"

Blake heard the enthusiasm in Jack Darlington's voice. "Yeah." He tried to restrain his own excitement. So much was riding on the next few minutes. "I think it could be a winner. There's only one problem. It's different from anything I've done in the past."

"Don't tell me you've decided that Cliff Pearson should start wearing a Superman cape and tights."

Blake shook his head, despite the fact that Jack couldn't see his gesture. "It's worse than that. There is no Cliff Pearson."

"What?" He heard the intake of breath and the shock in his agent's voice. "He's your brand. You can't stop writing about him. Cliff's story is what readers want to read."

Blake waited until Jack stopped shouting, then said as calmly as he could, "I know all that, but do me a favor. Just listen. You can shout again when I'm done." Without waiting for agreement, Blake launched into an explanation of the idea that had kept him up for most of the night.

"So, what do you think?" he asked when he had finished.

The reply was instantaneous. "It's brilliant."

18

"Good morning, beautiful lady. My carriage is outside, waiting to whisk you away to a romantic dinner."

Lauren had been so absorbed by the design she was sketching that she hadn't heard the bell tinkle as a customer entered the shop. Any customer would have startled her, but this one . . . She jumped to her feet, scarcely noticing that the pencil had flown from her hand, leaving a streak through the middle of her sketch.

"Drew! What are you doing here?" Though the man had haunted her dreams and been the subject of far too many sketches, Lauren had not expected to see him again. It was true that there were times when she believed God had brought Drew into her life for a reason and times when she wished that reason were to love her, but every time she let herself dream, reality intruded. Drew had no reason to return to Dupree and many to stay away. Yet here he was.

He crossed the small reception area and leaned his arms on the counter. "I told you why I'm here," he said, his blue eyes reflecting amusement that Lauren hoped wasn't caused by her all-too-evident shock. "I came to ask you for a date."

"A date?" The words emerged as little more than a squeak. So much for her hope of appearing poised and confident.

He shrugged, the action reminding Lauren of just how broad those shoulders were and just how firm his biceps seemed to be. "It's a simple concept. You and I go somewhere. We enjoy a nice dinner. Afterward, if you like, we can go dancing or maybe watch a movie. And, if I'm very lucky, when the evening ends, you'll let me kiss you good night."

She couldn't help it. She blushed. Though the morning had been cool enough to turn on the furnace, right now Lauren wished the air conditioner were blasting. Anything to chase the telltale blood from her face.

"Why?" she managed to croak. It had been years since she'd been on a date. Oh, she and Patrick had dated when they'd been in high school, but once they married and Fiona was born, dates had taken second place to their daughter's needs.

"Why am I asking you out?" Drew leaned forward, as if trying to close the space between them. "Because I want to get to know you better. Isn't that the reason most people go on dates?"

"Yes, but . . ." Lauren couldn't recall the last time she'd felt so flustered. "Why me? There are thousands of women in California." Sophisticated women who frequented nightclubs, women who thought nothing of spending thousands of dollars on a dress, women who weren't raising a little girl alone.

He stood up straight and fixed his gaze on her, his eyes blazing with apparent sincerity. "But there was only one woman I couldn't forget, and she's right here in Texas. Say yes, Lauren. Find a sitter for Fiona and spend the evening with me."

Lauren took a deep breath, trying to calm her racing pulse. He said he couldn't forget her. Every time she'd fantasized about a future with Drew, Lauren had told herself she had been nothing more than a diversion while he was in Dupree for Greg's wedding. She had told herself that he had forgotten her by the time he boarded the plane the next morning. It seemed that she was wrong.

Exhaling, Lauren considered Drew's proposition. What he offered was almost irresistibly appealing. Marisa kept saying Lauren needed a change of pace. An evening with Drew would certainly qualify as that. And the fact that he remembered her daughter's name did more to convince Lauren of Drew's sincerity than even the distance he'd traveled to invite her out to dinner.

"Tonight?" she asked. She had never, ever had a date on a Tuesday evening.

He nodded. "Tonight. Why wait?"

Lauren had a dozen answers. Because it would be impulsive, and she was not an impulsive woman. Because it would be her first date with anyone other than Patrick, and she wasn't certain she was ready. Most of all, because she was afraid of disappointing or being disappointed. But when she looked at Drew and saw the smile that had starred in so many of her dreams, all the reasons seemed like nothing more than weak excuses.

"Let me make a couple calls," Lauren said. Two minutes later, she nodded. "Everything's set." Marisa had agreed to leave work early so she could stay with Fiona. Almost as importantly, Tuesday was normally a light day at the store, which meant there would be no problem closing a couple hours early. Nothing stood between Lauren and a date with Drew Carroll.

He grinned. "Terrific. I'll pick you up at 5:00. That'll give us plenty of time to get to San Antonio by 6:30. Oh," he said as if it were an afterthought, "you might want to wear a skirt."

Though she asked, Drew would tell her nothing more, leaving Lauren to wonder where they were going and just how fancy the restaurant was.

The rest of the day passed in a blur. Since none of her customers gave her puzzled looks, she must have sounded coherent, but all Lauren could think about was the fact that Drew had traveled thousands of miles to take her to dinner.

If it wouldn't have set the gossips' tongues wagging, she might have skipped on her way home. As it was, she set herself a brisk pace and reached her house in record time. To her surprise, Marisa was already there, relaxing in the living room.

"I didn't expect you so early." Fiona wouldn't be home from school for another hour.

Marisa shrugged. "I thought you might need help deciding what to wear."

Leave it to Marisa to reach the crux of the problem. Lauren had thought of little else since Drew had suggested a skirt. "There aren't too many choices. All I have are my church clothes." And while they were fancier than the jeans and casual skirts she wore to work, they weren't evening clothes by any stretch of the imagination.

"Or this." Marisa stood and held up a garment bag. Unzipping it, she pulled out one of the prettiest dresses Lauren had ever seen. Although to call it a dress was like calling an orchid just a flower. Made of what appeared to be pure silk, the apricot-colored creation featured a softly draped bodice, long flowing sleeves, and a skirt that would swirl around her legs. Even without trying it on, Lauren knew it would be the most flattering dress she'd ever worn, with the possible exception of her wedding gown.

"You're thinner than I am," Marisa continued, "but that shouldn't matter. The dress is meant to flow rather than cling. The salesclerk described the design as forgiving."

"I'd call it fabulous, but are you sure?"

"Of course. Don't you remember how we used to share clothes in school?"

"That was different. Those were cotton shirts, not silk dresses with designer labels." Lauren didn't have to look inside to know that it carried the name of either a famous designer or an exclusive shop.

"I sold most of my fancy clothes before I left Atlanta," Marisa explained, "but something kept me from taking this one to the consignment shop. Now I know why. If you're going out with Drew Carroll, you need to be properly dressed."

That was true. Lauren wanted him to realize she wasn't a country hick, and this dress would certainly accomplish that.

"I'm surprised you didn't try to stop me from going out with him. You've made your opinion very clear." Just as Lauren had pulled no punches when it came to discussing Blake.

Marisa's eyes held a hint of amusement. "Would it have worked?"

"No." Nothing and no one would have kept her from this date with Drew.

Marisa's smile did not falter as she said, "I didn't think you'd listen to me. I might not trust Drew, but you're old enough to make your own decisions."

She slid the dress over Lauren's head and zipped the back, then turned Lauren so she was facing the full-length mirror. Lauren stared, astonished at the difference the dress made. She'd never call herself beautiful, but the apricot silk made her look pretty.

"It's gorgeous," she said, enjoying the sensation of soft fabric against her skin.

"So are you." Marisa touched her shoulder and smiled. "I can say this in all sincerity: I hope you have a wonderful evening."

Lauren did. When Drew arrived, dressed in a dark suit and white shirt that highlighted his blond hair and blue eyes, those eyes were filled with admiration.

"You look lovely," he said softly.

Lauren felt lovely. She'd spent more time than normal on her hair, and it now fell to her shoulders in gentle waves. The makeup Marisa had insisted she wear highlighted her eyes and made her look model thin rather than simply skinny. Even Fiona, who'd voiced displeasure over her mother spending the evening with Mr. Drew, grudgingly admitted that Lauren was pretty.

Though Marisa had speculated that Drew might bring Lauren flowers, he did not. Instead he brought something that pleased Lauren even more.

"I thought you deserved a special evening too," he told Fiona as he handed her a wrapped package that turned out to be a DVD of the latest children's blockbuster movie. And Fiona, who had been pouting, grinned.

Her last lingering concern resolved, Lauren stepped out of the house, her grin almost as wide as Fiona's when she saw that Drew had hardly exaggerated when he claimed he had a carriage. There might be no horses, but he had rented a luxury car. Lauren and her borrowed finery would be transported in more comfort than her third-hand minivan afforded.

She sank into the deeply cushioned leather seats and closed her eyes for a moment, enjoying the new car smell and the soft music coming from concert-hall-quality speakers.

"So this is how the other half lives," she said as they turned onto the highway and headed south.

Drew shrugged as if cars like this were his daily form of transportation. They probably were. "I would have hired a limo, but I thought that might be over the top."

"You thought right." Lauren could only imagine how tongues would have wagged. "The only limos we see are for weddings and proms." And the occasional funeral. Funerals were one thing she didn't want to think about.

They chatted on the drive to San Antonio. Lauren told Drew about Fiona's twirling practice and the town council's hope that this year's Christmas parade would attract visitors from nearby towns, while he entertained her with stories of irate customers' complaints that they could not change screen colors to match their corporate logos. To Lauren's surprise, Drew seemed genuinely impressed with her plans to expand HCP through online sales.

"What I'm doing must seem insignificant compared to your company. My sales are measured in thousands, yours in millions. Maybe even billions." Everyone in Dupree knew that Greg Vange was a billionaire, and as his former partner, it was likely that Drew was almost as wealthy.

"The money's nice," he admitted, "but it isn't everything. I suspect you get more satisfaction from your shop than I have from Sys=Simpl for the past few months."

Though his voice was neutral, Lauren was watching him closely enough to see the flicker of pain in his eyes. "Is something wrong?"

"Nothing. Everything. It depends on the day."

The fact that Drew forced a laugh told Lauren he didn't want her to pursue the subject, and so she said lightly, "That sounds like my life. Some days it feels as if nothing's going right. Thanks to you, though, today's not one of those days."

She shifted in the seat, grateful they had turned east so the setting sun was no longer streaming through her window. Sensing that Drew needed a diversion, Lauren said, "I feel like the heroine from one of those romance novels my mother used to read. If you've ever looked at the book racks at the supermarket, you may have seen them—Cinderella stories with titles like *The Billionaire Tycoon's Shopgirl*."

"You're kidding."

"About the titles, maybe, but the rest is true. Right now I feel as if I'm living a fairy tale." So far there were no evil stepmothers in sight, nor had the clock struck midnight. Lauren was living the happy part of the story.

"Does that mean I'm Prince Charming?" Drew seemed almost amused by the thought.

"If the shoe fits . . ." As she'd hoped, he laughed.

Lauren took a deep breath when they reached the restaurant Drew had chosen. When he'd first told her they were going to San Antonio, she had thought their destination might be one of the nicer hotels in the city or one of the special places along the River Walk, but instead he'd driven to a suburban location and pulled the car into a long, winding drive flanked by live oaks. Other than a discreet sign on the brick entrance pillars, there was no indication that this was a commercial establishment, but the exquisite landscaping made Lauren thankful that Marisa had lent her a fancy gown. This, she knew instinctively, was not a place for casual clothing.

As the road took a sharp bend to the left and revealed a private club that looked like something out of *Gone with the Wind*, Lauren caught her breath. The building was as magnificent as its landscaping. Two-story-high columns supported the roof, while a wide front porch with rocking chairs beckoned guests to sit and relax a bit.

As they approached the intricately carved front door with its cut glass sidelights and transom, the door swung open, and a formally dressed man ushered them inside. Seconds later a similarly attired man led Lauren and Drew to one of what Drew said were several dining rooms. The thick carpets and original oil paintings left no doubt that the room had been designed for guests with discriminating taste, an impression confirmed by the fancy linens, fine china and crystal, and the heavy silver flatware. Not even Cinderella had had a dinner like this.

When the maître d' had seated Lauren and placed her napkin on her lap, he handed her a menu. She noted the variety of food and the absence of prices.

"I feel like a country bumpkin," she told Drew. "How do I order?" Even on special occasions like their anniversary, she and Patrick had worried about cost.

Drew's expression was kind, giving her the impression he was enjoying her introduction to luxury. "Pick whatever sounds good. If you don't like it, they'll bring something else."

There was no danger of that. The chicken and wild rice with the delicate mushroom sauce, the crusty French bread, and the roasted baby carrots and green beans were exquisitely prepared. To Lauren's surprise, a simple green salad was served after the main course in what Drew told her was the European custom. "It's supposed to help digestion," he said, "and get you ready for dessert."

Though Lauren protested that she could not eat another bite, Drew insisted on ordering a chocolate soufflé and persuaded her to try a mouthful of the delicious concoction.

"Promise you won't ever tell Carmen," Lauren said as she swallowed the decadent dessert, "but this is the most delicious meal I've ever eaten."

"Your secret is safe with me." Drew ended his declaration with a cackle and pretended to twist the corners of a nonexistent moustache, as if he were the villain in an old-fashioned melodrama.

Lauren laughed, intrigued by this new side to Drew. When she'd first met him, she'd believed him to be a somewhat self-centered man who took himself seriously. Tonight he appeared lighthearted, more concerned with her pleasure than his own. It was a dramatic and delightful change.

"Can I interest you in some dancing?" he asked when they'd finished their coffee and he'd paid the bill. "They have a small band in another room."

Giving her shoes a rueful glance, Lauren shook her head. The four-inch stilettos were the perfect accessory for Marisa's dress, but they were what Lauren's mother would have called accidents waiting to happen.

"I'm afraid not. I'd probably break a leg trying to dance in these shoes." And this was not the kind of establishment that would appreciate her dancing in bare feet.

She couldn't dance tonight, but she wished—oh, how she wished—that the evening would never end. Ever since Drew had entered her store, Lauren had felt like Cinderella. Now she was at the ball, and if dreams came true, the clock would never strike midnight.

"A stroll in the gardens, then?" The fact that Drew seemed as unwilling as she to return to Dupree made her pulse race. This truly was a magical evening.

Lauren nodded. "That sounds wonderful."

The gardens were as beautiful as the club itself. Though the roses were past their peak, they had not lost their fragrance, and the combination of moonlight and the carefully placed lanterns made the white flowers gleam, while the darker blossoms faded against the foliage, leaving their lighter-colored cousins to steal the show.

"Ready for an adventure?" Drew asked when they'd finished the circuit of the rose garden. He held out his hand, and Lauren placed hers in it.

"Of course." There was something so reassuring about having her hand clasped in his that, although Lauren had never thought of herself as adventuresome, with Drew at her side, she found herself eager for new experiences. It was probably a cliché, but the way she felt right now, she would walk to the end of the earth with this man. It was scary; it was exciting; it was a feeling she had never before encountered.

Drew's adventure turned out to be a maze formed by tall hedges, and as was true of everything the club offered, it was beautifully done. Cinderella and Sleeping Beauty hadn't had mazes, but they should have, for this was the perfect place to wander with a sweetheart.

Though lanterns marked each of the intersections, the paths were dimly lit, adding to both the mystery and the romance. Occasional benches fitted into the hedges provided places to linger, but Drew and Lauren did not. Instead, they strolled slowly, debating each fork in the path, laughing when several of them turned out to be dead ends.

"I hope you've been dropping bread crumbs," Lauren said when they made another turn, "because I have no idea how to find our way out."

Drew stopped and smiled. "I can't think of anything I'd like more than to spend the rest of my life here with you."

The words were sweet, the sentiment worthy of a fairy tale, but even though her heart longed to believe he was serious, Lauren knew a real world waited for them outside the maze. When they returned to Dupree, she would once again be a single mom and small town resident, while he was a California multimillionaire more comfortable with movie stars than country widows. It would be the modern equivalent of Cinderella's coach turning back into a pumpkin.

"You don't mean that."

Though she'd expected a quick nod, acknowledging the jest, furrows appeared between Drew's eyes. "I'm serious. I've dated a fair number of women, and I've gotten close to marrying a couple, but I've never felt like this." He reached for Lauren's hands and squeezed them. "I have to admit that it took me by surprise. This happened faster than I thought possible, but I know what I feel, and I know it's real. I love you, Lauren. I want you to be my wife."

Blood drained from Lauren's face, leaving her feeling lightheaded. In her dreams, she had imagined Drew saying those words, but never had she dreamt that she would hear them tonight. This was their first date. They hardly knew each other, and by Drew's own admission, he'd almost married several other women.

Lauren had loved only one man. And though there had been an immediate attraction, she and Patrick had not spoken of love until they'd known each other well. This was too much, too soon. Even though she wished it were otherwise, men like Drew Carroll did not marry women like Lauren Ahrens.

"This has been a wonderful evening," she said slowly. Whatever she did, she didn't want to hurt Drew. "I'll never forget this, but I'm feeling like Cinderella. The clock will strike midnight, and I'll be back in my ordinary life. I may not be a scullery maid, but I know what my future holds: a house, a small business, and a daughter in Dupree."

It was enough for her, but Drew was accustomed to more. He'd be bored and unhappy in Dupree. "That's not the life you want."

"It could be."

Lauren shook her head. "Be serious, Drew. You're a big city man; I'm a country girl. We don't have a future together."

She couldn't build her life on such a shaky foundation. It wouldn't be fair to her, to Drew, and especially not to Fiona. It was flattering—very flattering—that Drew was attracted to her, but it was too soon to know whether that attraction would turn to love and whether that love would be strong enough to enfold Fiona.

It was Drew's turn to shake his head. "That's where you're wrong. We could have a future together. I'm going to prove it to you, but first . . ." He gathered her into his arms and lowered his lips to hers.

It was the sweetest of kisses, a gentle embrace that stirred Lauren's senses and made her head spin. It might be nothing more than the moonlight and roses, the maze and its mystery, but Lauren knew this was a moment she would never forget.

"I love you, Lauren Ahrens," Drew said when the kiss ended.

If only it were true.

19

"Did you hire a handyman?" Blake shot a glance at his friend as they jogged their way to the top of Ranger Hill. Now that ideas were flowing faster than a mountain stream during the spring snow melt, his morning run with Greg was the only break he took from writing.

Greg shook his head. "No, why?"

"I saw a man hanging around Rainbow's End, and he didn't look like one of the guests. Older, about our height, with graying blond hair. I thought it might have been Marisa's father, but every time I saw him, he was fixing something."

"Must be Eric. He used to be a mechanic. Now that he's living here, he's appointed himself the resident handyman." Greg chuckled. "That used to be my role."

Blake was panting as they reached the summit. There was a reason he and Greg usually ran in silence—it was easier on the lungs than trying to carry on a conversation—but this morning had been the exception. First Greg had surprised him with the announcement that Drew had spent a night at Rainbow's End, refusing to say why he was back in Dupree, skipping both dinner and breakfast, and leaving as soon as it was light. That didn't sound like the Drew that Blake remembered, but who knew what was happening in his life? Perhaps Drew was like Blake himself and was facing personal upheavals.

Rather than think about that, Blake pictured the stranger, comparing him with Marisa. He should have guessed that he was Eric St. George. After all, Blake had known that Marisa's father was at Rainbow's End. The problem was, the man wasn't what he had expected. He'd envisioned a younger man, not one with gray hair.

"What do you know about Marisa's father?" Blake asked as he and Greg jogged in place for a minute before beginning the descent.

"Not much other than that he's a recovering alcoholic who says he's been sober for three years. He also told me we should consider buying a van so we can pick up guests at the airport." Greg rolled his shoulders. "I'm thinking about that. It's not a bad idea for when we start inviting out-of-work families. Even if they have good cars or trucks, they might not be able to afford the gas."

Blake took a swig from his water bottle. He didn't need the hydration as much as he did a chance to think. It didn't matter whether Greg bought one van or a dozen; Blake was still trying to digest the bombshell his friend had dropped on him. Marisa's father was an alcoholic. Blake's head reeled at the thought. Though Greg had mentioned it almost casually, it was the single most significant fact Blake had learned about Marisa.

No wonder she had been so upset by Cliff Pearson's vices. Marisa probably feared that Blake's books would lure others down the dark path toward alcoholism. No wonder she felt the need for control. The research Blake had done on children of alcoholics for one of his books had revealed that many had a deep-seated need for order to compensate for the unpredictability of their childhoods. No wonder Marisa had been unwilling to trust Blake. He'd thought that was the result of her father's desertion, but he suspected that had been only the culmination of years of broken promises. Poor Marisa, and poor Eric.

"Is he working?" Blake asked. He left his cabin so infrequently that he didn't know whether Eric St. George had a routine that involved a job.

Greg recapped his water bottle and started down the hill, waiting until Blake caught up with him before he spoke. "Not that I've heard. Carmen told Kate he was trying to get his old job at the service station, but the owner is leery. According to Carmen, there's no reason to worry. Eric's not drinking, and even when he was, he rarely missed a day of work. It seems the real benders were on weekends. At any rate, Kate and I've been talking about finding him a permanent job at Rainbow's End. We don't need a full-time handyman, but he needs full-time work."

Blake nodded slowly, thinking about small towns and their grapevines. Even if Marisa's father went back to work at the station, his every move would be scrutinized. Being at Rainbow's End would spare him a bit of that. "You've got to give the guy credit. It couldn't have been easy to come back to Dupree."

"The way I see it, he had two pretty good reasons: his wife and daughter. He loves them both."

"Yeah." But one of them refused to accept him. As far as Blake could tell, Marisa had left Rainbow's End rather than share the resort with her father. That must have been a blow to Eric. The man had battled demons to stop drinking; he'd returned here to make amends, but he could hardly do that when Marisa refused to be near him.

Blake had firsthand experience with Marisa's rejection and knew how painful it could be. The memory of her harsh refusal to speak to him still stung, although now that he knew more about the reasons behind it, he felt a glimmer of hope that she would be able to resolve her issues. Children of alcoholics frequently had anger management problems like the ones Marisa was exhibiting, and the fact that she'd been abandoned would only have deepened them.

Even though he'd never met the man, Blake wished he could help Eric St. George and, in doing that, help his daughter. Perhaps if the two of them worked together, they could find a way to break down the barriers Marisa had erected. Perhaps then Blake and Marisa could rebuild their relationship. But that would have to wait until he had finished his manuscript.

As if he'd read Blake's thoughts, Greg asked, "How's the writing going?"

That was a happier subject than Eric St. George. "Better than ever before. Another couple days and I'll be done."

Greg increased the pace slightly as they approached the gate to Rainbow's End. It was the final sprint of the day. Once they entered the resort, they'd begin their cooldown routine. "Any chance you'll give me a sneak peek at Cliff Pearson's next adventure?"

Blake shook his head. "Sorry. Can't do that."

And he couldn't, primarily because there was no new adventure for Cliff Pearson. Logan Marsh's adventures were as different from Cliff's as Logan himself was from Blake's first hero. Fifteen years younger than Cliff, Logan was also a crime solver but on a different scale.

Instead of foiling international terrorists and saving the world, Logan was a teenage sleuth working on more personal crimes: robbery, extortion, the occasional murder. Instead of being a debonair, movie-star-handsome adult, Logan was a teenager, suffering from the usual teenage problems of pimples, peer pressure, and puppy love. Logan's appeal was the fact that he was an ordinary teen who, thanks to his own resourcefulness, was able to do extraordinary things.

If Blake's agent was right, the Logan Marsh books would appeal to adults as well as the growing young adult market. If Blake was right, they'd show Marisa that he'd heard her concerns and that he cared enough to address them. And then . . . Blake nodded. The rest was in God's hands.

---

"Donuts?" Lauren snagged one of the chocolate chip donuts from the plate and held it under her nose, sniffing appreciatively. "Fiona will be ecstatic. She loves everything deep-fried."

Though she'd had a shorter than normal night's sleep, Lauren radiated happiness as she made her way into the kitchen, and yet instead of launching into an account of her date as she would have ten years ago, she'd focused on food. How odd. But far be it from Marisa to push her friend.

"In that case, don't tell Fiona these are baked." Marisa made a flamboyant gesture toward the small appliance on Lauren's kitchen counter as if she were the host of a TV game show pointing toward the prize contestants might win. "I was sorting through all the stuff that used to be stored in my office, hoping I could find some old records, when I found this." She opened the donut maker and used a fork to remove each of six perfectly baked donuts. "I thought you and Fiona might enjoy something different."

Lauren smiled again and poured a cup of coffee. "You've been spoiling us. I'll never get Fiona back to oatmeal. That used to be our weekday standard."

It seemed they were destined to continue talking about food. Though curiosity was consuming her, Marisa decided to wait another thirty seconds before asking about Lauren's evening with Drew.

"The trick is to put something special in it," she told Lauren, as if properly flavored oatmeal were the secret to world peace. "Applesauce and molasses are good, but dried fruit and nuts are even better."

When she'd finished chewing a bite of donut, Lauren washed it down with a sip of coffee. "Carmen must be proud of you. You're turning into a first-rate cook."

The subject had changed, but not in the direction Marisa wanted. "Mom's not real happy with me these days," she said as she added a spoonful of sugar to her second cup of coffee. "She thinks I ought to spend more time with her and Eric."

"And you won't consider it."

"Nope." Marisa sipped her coffee, then laid the mug back on the counter as she poured more batter into the donut maker. "I like being here with you and Fiona. Besides, if I were at Rainbow's End,

I wouldn't be able to quiz you about your big evening. So tell me everything." After setting the timer, Marisa took the chair across the table from Lauren and smiled.

Lauren returned the smile. "It was wonderful," she said softly, her eyes reflecting a happiness that had been too long absent. "You saw the fancy car. That was only the beginning. He took me to a private club with the most incredible food. You should have seen the place, Marisa. The rooms looked like something out of a movie, and they even had a maze." As a blush stained Lauren's cheeks, she lowered her gaze to the table.

"Let me guess," Marisa said, trying not to chuckle at her friend's reaction. Though Drew was far from the man Marisa would have chosen for Lauren, she was glad to see the flush of happiness. "Does that lovely pink in your cheeks mean that you and Drew did more than walk through the maze?"

Lauren nodded, her expression almost sheepish. "Oh, Marisa, it was like a fairy tale. He kissed me and said he wanted to marry me."

Practically choking on her coffee, Marisa lowered the mug to the table and stared at her friend. "He what?"

"I know." Lauren reached across the table and laid her hand on Marisa's, giving it a little squeeze. "I can't believe it either. Imagine a man like Drew Carroll wanting to marry me." She picked up her mug and took another sip. "I told him he was crazy. Well," she amended, "I didn't say it exactly that way, but I pointed out that this was our first date and that we're two very different people. I know we have no future, but I've got to tell you, Marisa, for a minute I wished it was different. No one's ever made me feel the way Drew did, and that includes Patrick."

Marisa hadn't realized that her gasp was audible, but Lauren nodded slowly, as if in response to it. "I loved Patrick with all my heart. You know that. But this is different. Loving Patrick was sweet and peaceful. This is exciting."

When the timer buzzed, Marisa jumped up from her chair, grateful for the interruption. Of all the things she'd expected to happen last night, Lauren's becoming infatuated was not one of them. "You hardly know the man," she protested when she'd put the last of the donuts on the cooling rack. "How can you be thinking about marriage?" Nothing was the way it should be if sensible Lauren was considering marrying a virtual stranger.

"You're not telling me anything I don't already know," Lauren said as she clasped her mug with both hands. "I even said practically those same words to Drew. You know what he said?" Without waiting for a response, Lauren continued. "He told me we were both quick learners, and by the time we got back to Dupree, I'd feel as if I'd known him my whole life."

That sounded like a salesman's pitch. "And did you?"

"Maybe not exactly, but I do feel as if I know him. We talked about everything on the drive, and we even stopped for a cup of coffee so we could talk some more. I know what kind of music he likes. I know his favorite sports and how much he hates jury duty, and he knows how important Fiona is to me. Believe it or not, Drew asked more questions about her than he did about me."

It was a clever move, the sure way to a mother's heart, but Marisa knew better than to say that. She had to say something, though, for her friend was waiting, and so she cautioned, "Be careful, Lauren. I don't want you to be hurt."

Marisa wasn't sure what game Drew Carroll was playing, but she couldn't picture him staying in Dupree and making Lauren happy. The man had "playboy" practically tattooed on his forehead. He was intrigued by Lauren, probably because she was so different from the women he'd dated in California, but that didn't mean he was looking for a permanent relationship.

Lauren shook her head. "You don't need to worry, Marisa. My head knows Drew and I have no future. Now all I have to do is convince my heart."

It was too late for that. Lauren might think otherwise, but Marisa had seen her this way once before. She looked the way she had the day she met Patrick—head over heels in love. The only thing Marisa could do was hope that Drew was sincere and that he would not hurt Lauren.

Taking another sip of coffee, Marisa tried to settle her thoughts. There must be something in the air, or perhaps it was in the water, but it seemed as if Dupree had more than its share of happy couples. Kate and Greg, Kate's grandmother and Roy Gordon. Mom and Eric had a good chance at a reconciliation, and now Lauren and Drew were talking about love. That only left Marisa. She had no happy endings in sight.

--------- ✳ ---------

Blake scowled as he looked at the fragrant flowers. It had been three weeks since Marisa refused the candy he brought her. He had thought her anger would have subsided by now, and so he'd decided to try again. This time he'd ordered a dozen yellow roses. Not only were they the quintessential Texas flower, but he thought they'd be a pleasant reminder of the skits she'd directed for Rainbow's End's grand reopening celebration. No Texan could resist yellow roses, or so he'd thought. But he'd been wrong. This time there'd been no anger, just quiet determination as she said, "No, thank you," and ushered him out of her office.

"She didn't like the flowers?"

Blake turned, startled by the man's voice. When Marisa had closed the door in his face, Blake had left the building, not sure what to do next. He'd thought about leaving the flowers in the lobby but figured Marisa might not appreciate that. Perhaps he should offer them to her friend Lauren.

He was standing in the parking lot, ambivalent, when he heard the man. Though he hadn't expected anyone to see him, once again he'd been wrong. Marisa's father stood only a yard away, his expression telling Blake he knew what had happened.

"I'm not sure the flowers were at fault," he admitted. "She doesn't like me very much."

"I know the feeling." The older man extended his hand for a shake. "I'm Eric St. George."

"And I'm Blake Kendall." Though his graying hair and the lines that creased his face made him look far older than the fifty-five Blake knew Eric to be, his handshake was as firm as a young man's.

"I haven't seen you around much, but it's good to meet you," Marisa's father said, leading the way to the small gazebo. When they were seated, Eric continued. "For what it's worth, Carmen believes Marisa will come around eventually. Personally, I'm not so sure, but I figure she's got a better chance of forgiving you for whatever it is she thinks you've done than of patching up matters with her old man."

Blake wasn't certain what surprised him more, Eric's candor or the quiet despair in his voice. All he knew was that his heart ached at the man's pain. Though he'd been consumed by his book, the rare breaks Blake had allowed himself had focused on Marisa and her relationship with the men who cared for her. Her refusal of the roses left him no doubt about her feelings for him, but he'd been praying that she would open her heart to her father.

Blake focused on Eric's words. Since the man didn't strike him as a Pollyanna, perhaps his guarded optimism had a solid basis.

"I'd like to believe that, so even though I doubt it, I'm going to defer to your judgment. After all, you know her better than I do."

Though Eric had been leaning against the back of the bench, he bent forward and shook his head. "That's where you're wrong. I remember the girl Marisa used to be. She loved to ride a bike, swing as high as she could, and she'd read *Anne of Green Gables* so often she almost had it memorized. The young woman she's become is a stranger. She doesn't even look all that much like my daughter."

Eric fixed his gaze on Blake and nodded slowly, as if he approved of something he'd seen. "If you're wondering why I'm telling you this, it's not just because misery loves company. If there's one thing I learned at AA, it's that people with the same problem need to help each other."

Blake had had the same thought the day he'd learned of Eric's past. "I don't know how to get her to listen to me," he admitted.

"Me, neither."

"So, what do we do?"

"We keep praying and we get through it, one day at a time."

# 20

Lauren frowned at the low-bobbin warning light, hoping there would be enough thread to finish this seam. The quilt she was piecing was turning out well. Unfortunately, she couldn't say the same about the rest of her life. It had been two and a half days since her dinner with Drew—two days, thirteen hours, and forty-three minutes to be precise—and she hadn't heard a word from him. At first, Lauren had been puzzled. Though they hadn't made any specific plans that night, she had thought he would come into the shop the next day or at least call her. But he hadn't. Now, though she hated to admit it, she was afraid that Marisa was right: Lauren was nothing but a brief diversion. All that talk of love, marriage, and a future together had been a lie. Lauren frowned again. She should have trusted her instincts and not let herself believe in second chances.

When the doorbell tinkled, she switched off the sewing machine and pushed back her chair. "I'll be with you in a second."

"Don't rush. I'm not going anywhere."

Lauren swiveled, hoping her shock wasn't apparent. The voice sent tremors up her spine, and her pulse began to race. "Drew!" The man she thought had disappeared from her life was back, grinning as if he'd never left. "What are you doing here? I thought you went home to California."

He stood in front of the counter, looking for all the world as if he belonged there. Perhaps because of the cold front that had come through, leaving the air cooler than in California, he wore a khaki jacket over his casual shirt. Otherwise, Drew looked exactly like the man who'd come into HCP on Tuesday.

"I did go to California," he admitted, amusement coloring his blue eyes. "But, as you can see, I'm like the proverbial bad penny. You can't get rid of me."

Lauren lowered her gaze as she tried to make sense of his statement. He'd left without a word, and now he was back, acting as if nothing had changed.

"I don't understand."

His smile made that handsome face all the more appealing. "Sure you do," he countered. "I told you what I wanted, and I'm not a guy to give up."

He'd said he wanted to marry her, but that couldn't be what he meant. Or could it? The look Drew gave her made Lauren's pulse accelerate again. He was gazing at her as if she was the most beautiful woman on earth, when she was nothing more than a single mom trying to make a living and raise her daughter.

"I realized I was moving too fast," Drew continued, "so I want to start over. Forget the whirlwind romance. We'll go slowly this time. When you say yes, I don't want there to be any doubts."

Say yes. The man was talking about marriage. Lauren hadn't imagined Tuesday night or the fact that Drew had seemed as attracted to her as she was to him.

He glanced at his watch, a gold Rolex that had probably cost more than Lauren earned in a year. "I'm sorry for the short notice, but I wondered if you and Fiona would have supper with me tonight."

She blinked. "You're inviting both of us?"

"That's what I said. It won't be fancy, because I'm cooking, but if you're feeling generous, maybe you'll give me some hints about decorating my new place."

The world was definitely spinning faster than it had five minutes ago. That was the only way Lauren could explain the dizziness that made her clutch the edge of the counter.

"Wait a minute," she said, hoping her voice didn't sound as confused as she felt. "Back up. What do you mean, your new place?"

This time there was no doubt about Drew's smile. It radiated satisfaction. "It seems the grapevine doesn't move as fast as I feared. You're looking at Dupree's newest resident."

"You're joking."

"Nope. I couldn't picture myself spending more than a couple nights at Rainbow's End, so I looked for something more permanent. I'm renting a place on Live Oak. It's only a block or so from your house."

Lauren felt as if she'd fallen down Alice in Wonderland's rabbit hole. This was becoming curiouser and curiouser. As far as she knew, only one house on Live Oak was for rent. "That's the old St. George house," she told Drew. "That's where Carmen and Marisa used to live." And Eric, of course.

Drew shrugged. "If you say so. I won't dispute the old part. The realtor told me it had mid-century charm, which roughly translated means no one had the money to update it. That's why I'd appreciate your decorating help."

He sounded as if he were planning to stay. Lauren swallowed deeply, trying to imagine what it would be like having Drew practically around the corner from her.

"What about your job?"

He shrugged as if the need to earn a paycheck was of no account. "That's not an issue. Now, can I pick you up at six?"

Though her head was whirling at the possibility of Drew living so close, Lauren shook it. "It's less than a five-minute walk." The year they'd both gotten watches for Christmas, she and Marisa had timed the walk and had discovered that it took two minutes and thirty-seven seconds at their normal pace.

"All right. We'll skip the chauffeur service, but you'll still come, won't you?"

Lauren nodded.

———— ✳ ————

Blake never took breaks like this when he was in the middle of a manuscript, but ever since Eric St. George had mentioned Marisa's childhood fascination with *Anne of Green Gables*, Blake had found himself wondering whether he'd find a clue to her in the book. He'd downloaded a copy and had spent more hours than he should have reading the adventures of a red-haired girl with a vivid imagination and a quick temper.

What he'd read hadn't encouraged him. If Anne had held a grudge against Gilbert for years—years!—just because he teased her about her hair, how long would it take Marisa to forgive him for creating a hero who drank? There were some questions a man shouldn't ask.

———— ✳ ————

"It'll be boring," Fiona whined as Lauren ushered her daughter toward the front door. She had been complaining ever since Lauren had told her they were having supper with Drew. It seemed that the allure of the DVD he'd given her had worn off and Fiona was back to disliking Drew. That did not bode well for the evening or for any future Lauren might have with him.

"There won't be anyone for me to play with," Fiona continued.

"There's no one for you to play with here, either."

"Yeah, but I have my books and toys here. I don't have to listen to you and Aunt Marisa talk grown-up talk."

Her point was valid. "All right," Lauren conceded. "You can take a book with you."

When Fiona scampered into her room to select a book, Lauren

sighed. The truth was, she was more nervous about this evening than she had been about her official date with Drew, because tonight involved Fiona. Fiona, Lauren's wonderful but whiny daughter, the girl who wanted a new daddy but didn't consider Drew a contender for that role.

Lauren, too, had reservations about Drew as a possible step-father. He had admitted that he had little experience with children and that it had been a colleague's advice that had led to the DVD purchase. Tonight would be more challenging. There'd be no colleague to coach him on the art of conversation with a child.

Apparently pacified by the fact that she had her favorite book clutched in her hand, Fiona grumbled only a few times as they walked to Drew's new home. Lauren felt apprehensive as they climbed the front steps. She'd done that hundreds of times when Marisa had lived here, but tonight was different. Very different.

Within seconds of their knocking, Drew opened the door. "Welcome to my humble abode."

The front door opened directly into the living room, the place where Lauren and Marisa had watched TV and played games. Lauren looked around, cataloging the differences. The St. Georges' furniture was gone, replaced by what Lauren would call motel-modern. The walls that had once sported fading wallpaper were now painted the off-white decorators advised for rental property, and the floor was covered with industrial carpeting chosen for its durability rather than its style. A quick glance into the kitchen revealed that nothing had been upgraded, although the avocado appliances had been spray painted white, as had the oak cabinets. Everything about the once charming house now shrieked low budget.

"I don't imagine your home in California looks like this." Lauren envisioned sleek furniture, lots of stainless steel and granite, expansive views of either the ocean or the mountains. This shabby little bungalow was the antithesis of Drew Carroll.

He shrugged as if the humble surroundings didn't bother him. "Not quite, but it'll do for the present."

"Speaking of which, we brought you a housewarming present."
She handed him the gift bag.

"She let me pick it out," Fiona declared, her pride evident in the
way she straightened her shoulders.

Drew gave her a conspiratorial smile. "Then I know I'll like it."
He reached into the bag and pulled out a set of quilted coasters,
each featuring one of the six flags that had flown over Texas.

When Kate had approached Lauren with the idea of selling
merchandise at Rainbow's End, Lauren had designed a series of
coaster sets. Since they were smaller than a pillow and more affordable than a full-sized quilt, she'd hoped they would appeal to the
resort's guests, and they had. Marisa had reported that they were
currently the bestselling item at the gift shop.

"Mom thought you might like cowboy boots, but I figured these
were better," Fiona told Drew.

"You figured right, Fiona. I'm not a boot man." As if to prove
his point, he extended one loafer-clad foot. "Thank you both. Of
course, you do know that I won't ever use these."

"Why not?" Fiona seemed to think that the comment had been
directed at her.

"I might get them dirty."

She shook her head and wagged a finger at him. "You're silly,
Mr. Drew. That's what washing machines are for."

He thumped his forehead in mock dismay. "Duh! I should have
known that."

Fiona's giggle told Lauren her fears had been ungrounded. Somehow Drew had known exactly the right way to approach Fiona,
and her daughter was now as charmed by Drew as she was.

The question was how long it would be before the charm wore
off for Drew. Fiona could be demanding, and when she was in a
snit, there were times when even Lauren did not want to be with
her. She wouldn't be surprised if Drew discovered that a seven-year-
old child was more than he'd bargained for and he left Dupree as
suddenly as he'd arrived. What Lauren feared most was the effect

that might have on her daughter. It was one thing for Lauren to have a broken heart, but she couldn't let Drew hurt Fiona.

---- ✳ ----

"Your car needs work. I wish you'd let me look at it."

Marisa felt a tingle of annoyance slide down her spine as she approached the car. It wasn't the first time Eric had said that, just as it wasn't the first time he'd appeared to be waiting for her when she left her office. Most days he simply greeted her, then went back to whatever he'd been working on, but some days he patted the car and repeated his statement that it needed to be repaired. He might be right about that, because the rattle seemed to be worsening. The problem was, Marisa didn't want to be beholden to Eric for anything.

It was bad enough that he was now on the Rainbow's End payroll. Marisa had been shocked the day Greg had appeared in her office, leaning casually against the door frame as he said, "Ledger Lady, I've bought a van and hired a new employee. I need you to do the paperwork."

Predictably, Mom had been thrilled that Eric had a full-time job and that the whole family now worked at Rainbow's End. Marisa was less excited. Having Eric on the payroll meant that he had valid reasons for wandering around the resort, and that meant she saw him frequently. Marisa had started closing her door simply to avoid unplanned encounters, but she couldn't stop him from meeting her in the parking lot.

She gripped her shoulder bag as if it were a lifeline while she looked at the man she'd once adored. Perhaps it was time for answers.

"I don't need you to fix my car," she said when she was only a foot away from him, "but there is something you can do for me."

The eagerness in his eyes made Marisa cringe. On a grown man that vulnerability was pathetic. "Anything, Marisa. Just tell me what it is."

"You can give me some answers," she said, pleased that her voice was cool and calm. She glanced at the cabin, then shook her head. She didn't want to go there, but they needed to sit down. What she wanted to know would take more than a few seconds. Though the lodge was a logical choice, they faced the possibility of interruptions there. As her eyes lit on the gazebo, Marisa nodded. It might be cold, but at least they'd have privacy.

"Let's sit in the gazebo."

When they reached the small structure, Eric waited until she'd chosen a seat, then perched on the opposite side of the bench, almost as if he realized she didn't want to be touched. Or perhaps he preferred to be far enough away to see her expression. The reason didn't matter. The effect was what she needed: distance from the man who still had the power to break her heart.

"If you're going to ask why I started drinking, I can't answer that. I wish I knew what happened, but I don't." The pain in his eyes mingled with resignation, as if he'd struggled but had accepted the outcome.

"That wasn't my question," Marisa said softly. "I learned enough from Al-Anon to know there is no one reason."

Eric made no effort to hide his surprise. "You joined Al-Anon?"

"Yes. I was looking for answers when I was in college, and that seemed like a place to start. Later I tried different support groups." She wouldn't tell him about Trent and how he'd duped her. That was none of Eric's business.

"I wish you hadn't had to go through that."

Marisa felt the blood drain from her face. How did he know about Trent? Then she realized that Eric was referring to Al-Anon. After taking in a deep breath, she let it out slowly, willing herself to relax.

"Me too. I would have given almost anything to have had a normal childhood, but that wasn't in my power." She swallowed to dislodge the lump that had taken up residence in her throat. "That's not what I wanted to talk about. The question I've never been able to answer is why you left on graduation day. Didn't you know how much I needed you that day?" When she'd accepted her diploma, only Mom had been there to cheer, and afterwards when the other graduates had been surrounded by their families, Marisa had insisted on leaving, not wanting to admit that her father hadn't cared enough to celebrate with her.

Though he flinched at the accusation he heard in her voice, Eric nodded slowly. "Leaving you and your mom was the hardest thing I've ever done, but I had to. I couldn't embarrass you again. When I heard what happened at your prom, I knew I was no good for you."

Marisa gripped the edge of the bench, the rough texture less painful than her thoughts. "How did you find out about that? Mom promised she wouldn't tell you."

"She didn't. Even though I was three sheets to the wind, I heard you crying. The next day I realized you hadn't left the house. Carmen wouldn't say anything, so I went to the Lundquists to see what had happened."

Marisa closed her eyes, her all-too-active imagination picturing the scene at the mayor's home. "Hal wouldn't have been there. He and Tiffany went to an all-night party."

Eric nodded. "Yeah, but Mayor Lundquist was there. He laughed in my face and told me you were a fool if you thought he'd let his son be seen with the daughter of a no-count drunk." Those eyes so like Marisa's own reflected remembered pain. "That's when I realized the best thing I could do for you was to leave. I didn't want to, but I really believed that I had to do it for your sake."

Pain speared through Marisa as she thought of that day and all the days that had followed. Eric was wrong. So very, very wrong. "But you didn't think about what it would be like for us, not knowing whether you were dead or alive, did you?"

She had thought he would deny it, but instead Eric fixed his gaze on her, shame and regret etched on his face. "To be honest, Marisa, I didn't do a lot of thinking about anything except where I was going to get my next drink. I spent five years trying to drown the pain until eventually I hit bottom. That's when I knew there was no way to escape what I'd done. Fortunately, I found AA." His eyes shone with unshed tears. "Thanks to God and the people I met at AA, I've been sober for three years."

Marisa looked at the man whose disappearance had shaped so much of her life. He appeared genuinely contrite, and yet she wasn't convinced that would last and that he wouldn't pick up a bottle again.

He extended a hand toward her before letting it drop. "I know I don't deserve your forgiveness any more than I deserve God's mercy, but I'm asking for it. Can you forgive all the things I did and the ones I should have done but didn't? Can you let me be your father again?"

Part of her wanted to say yes. Part of her wanted to close the distance between them, to be held in her father's arms again. But the other part couldn't forget how many times he'd promised to stop drinking and how many times he'd broken that promise.

"I don't know, Eric," she said slowly. "I want to believe you. I want to trust you, but I'm just not ready."

# 21

He seems like a different person."

Marisa nodded, admiring the way Lauren sliced cucumbers for the steak salad they had agreed would make an adequate supper. Unlike the zucchini Marisa had cut, each slice of cucumber was the same thickness as the others. Mom would be proud that at least one of the girls she'd taught to cook had learned the art of vegetable preparation without the aid of a food processor. Marisa gave her zucchini an appraising look, then began to turn the slices into chunks. The imperfect cuts would be less apparent that way.

"I want to believe that," she told her friend, thinking of the changes she'd seen in Eric since he'd returned to Texas. At least on the surface, there had been no sign of the man who'd once hidden in a closet with bottles of cheap whiskey half concealed in brown bags. "The problem is, I'm not sure people can change. Not fundamentally."

Lauren reached for an onion and began peeling the skin. "I know you were worried about it, but there's been no sign of drinking."

"Mom said the same thing."

Though she'd been intent on the onion, Lauren paused and looked up at Marisa, her eyes wide with surprise. "How does your mom know anything about Drew?"

"Drew?" It was Marisa's turn to be surprised. "I thought we were talking about my father." In the three and a half weeks since he'd come to Rainbow's End, not only had he not taken a drink, but he'd accompanied Mom to a party where the beer had flowed freely, and he'd declined every offer of a longneck bottle, saying he was an alcoholic.

When Marisa had heard the story, she'd been astonished by the fact that Eric hadn't tried to hide his past but had spoken of it as matter-of-factly as if he'd been announcing that he had blue eyes and gray hair. "It's not just his past," Mom had said firmly. "It's his present and future too."

Resuming her peeling of the onion, Lauren nodded. "I'm glad to hear your dad's staying sober. That's good for him."

"It's good for Mom too."

"What about you?"

Marisa stared out the window, trying to concentrate on the antics of a woodpecker attempting to chase a second one from the tree they'd both claimed. It was easier to think about wildlife than her father. Though she knew the response Lauren expected, she couldn't give it.

"I don't think I could bear to be hurt again," Marisa said, thankful that there was no danger of being overheard. Fiona was eating with Alice, and for once Lauren did not have a date with Drew. It was girls' night at home.

"No one wants you to be hurt, but I'm worried that you're giving up a chance for happiness." Lauren made no effort to hide her disapproval. "Life has plenty of pain—believe me, I learned that when Patrick was so sick—but there's joy too if we look for it."

Marisa stared at her friend, wondering whether the moisture in Lauren's eyes was caused by the onion she was peeling or memories of her husband. Though Marisa had seen no sign of tears since she'd moved in with Lauren, that didn't mean the sorrow was gone.

"Even if I'd known Patrick was going to die so young," Lauren continued, "I wouldn't have done anything different. I may not have him with me any longer, but I have memories of all the wonderful times we shared." She pointed her knife at Marisa, her expression stern as she said, "I hate to see you cutting yourself off from happiness. You're too young to give up on life."

The words sliced deep inside Marisa. They weren't true, no matter what Lauren thought. Marisa was being cautious—any sane person would be—but that didn't mean she'd dismissed her hopes of happiness. "I'm not doing that."

"Aren't you? You ran away from Blake at the first sign of trouble, and you won't give your father another chance." Lauren sniffed as she laid the knife on the counter and reached out a hand to cover Marisa's. "You're my best friend, and I love you dearly, but I think you're wrong about both of them. Open your heart, Marisa. You won't regret it."

Marisa wished she could believe that.

---- ✦ ----

Blake stared at the computer screen, knowing he ought to take a break but unwilling to stop until he'd finished the chapter. The book would be done as soon as he completed this final read-through, and he had only ten chapters left. Then would come the hard part: waiting for his agent's reaction, followed by his editor's opinion. But first he had to convince himself that the story was as perfect as he could make it, that each word was the right one, that his characters rang true.

He could feel the furrows forming between his eyes as he reviewed the text that had flowed so easily one day only to leave him feeling stymied the next. It was always that way. He agonized during writing, but once he sent the manuscript to his agent, he would forget the struggles and remember only the productive days. And then the cycle would repeat itself with the next book.

The knock on the door broke his concentration. Groaning, Blake looked at his watch and saw that it was past seven. He'd been working considerably longer than he'd realized; he had only two chapters to go. Once he finished them, he'd email the manuscript to his agent, and then he could get some much-needed sleep. He stretched as he walked to open the door, then blinked in surprise at the sight of Eric St. George on the front porch, a tray with covered dishes in his hands.

"Carmen said you missed dinner," Marisa's father explained as he entered the cabin and laid the tray on the table Blake had been using as a desk. "She was convinced you were going to waste away, so she insisted I bring you some of her vegetarian chili, a couple pieces of cornbread, and some chocolate pound cake."

Eric gestured toward the thermos. "That's sweet tea, with the emphasis on sweet. Every time I drink some, I'm convinced the American Dental Association is going to outlaw it, but Carmen insists it's a valuable source of energy."

As Eric's gaze roamed around the cabin, lighting on the laptop and the pile of paper on the opposite side of the table, Blake knew he'd made a mistake letting Eric enter the cabin. Each time he left, Blake was careful to lock all evidence of his writing in his suitcase. So far it had worked, and no one had learned that he was a writer, but the scribbled notes and the research books would be difficult to explain away.

Blake tried to deflect Eric's attention. "I'm sorry to have worried your wife. The food smells delicious, though."

Marisa's father did not take the bait. "There's been some specu- lation about what you do here all day. One theory is that you're part of the CIA on some kind of stakeout." Eric snorted. "I've got to tell you that's the most ridiculous thing I've heard. Imagine a spy ring in Firefly Valley! I kinda liked the idea that you were in the witness protection program, but I figured that was pretty far- fetched too. Now it looks like everyone was wrong." He nodded at the dog-eared thesaurus Blake preferred to the online version. "You're a writer, aren't you?"

It was futile to deny it. Though he felt a pang of regret that Marisa's father was learning about his writing career before his own father did, Blake nodded. "That's a well-guarded secret, but yes, I am."

"If you ask me, that's better than the CIA." Obviously intrigued, Eric stared at the laptop with its kaleidoscope screen saver. "What kind of books?"

"Ones your daughter disapproves of." Except for this one. Blake doubted even Marisa could find anything objectionable in it. Unfortunately, she hadn't let him tell her about the new direction his writing had taken, so she had no way of knowing that he wasn't creating another Cliff Pearson adventure.

Eric was silent for a moment. Then he leaned back against the table, crossing his arms. "What did you do—have a character who drank?"

Blake nodded. "Yeah, along with various other vices. He saves the world or at least significant parts of it, but all too often, he has a cigarette or a drink in his hand. He's what reviewers call a flawed hero."

"I can see why that would bother her." Eric's expression held more than a hint of sadness. "You can blame me for that."

"I don't blame you, Eric, although I'm sorry for what you and your family have gone through and the effect it's had on Marisa. The truth is, I admire you for admitting you had a problem and overcoming it." The change in Eric's demeanor was subtle but unmistakable. Apparently it had been a long time since anyone had told Eric St. George that they admired him.

"The struggle's not over yet. It won't be until the day I die, but God's given me the strength to say no. Now I'm praying that he'll soften Marisa's heart enough that she'll forgive me."

Eric swallowed, the depth of his emotion evident in the pain that radiated from his eyes. "From the day she was born, I pictured myself walking her down the aisle. I don't imagine that'll happen now."

Blake nodded, once again feeling a connection with Marisa's father. They both loved her, and they'd both been rejected. Eric knew about Blake's alter ego. He might as well learn more about Blake. "For a time, I pictured myself standing at the altar, waiting for her to come to me." But that was before he discovered the other side of Marisa, the harsh, angry side that revived painful memories of Grandfather and Ashley.

Marisa's father gave Blake an appraising look, as if assessing his qualifications for the role of son-in-law. "It was that serious, huh?"

Blake nodded again. "For me, at any rate. I've never met a woman like Marisa, and my gut tells me I never will again. I know she's got her issues, but I don't want to give up. The problem is, I don't know what to do when she won't even talk to me."

Laying his hand on Blake's shoulder, Eric shook his head slowly. "I've told you this before. There's only one answer for either of us."

"Prayer."

———— ✦ ————

Marisa switched off the car radio seconds after pulling out of her parking spot. Though she usually listened to music on the way from Rainbow's End back to Lauren's home, today it seemed more annoying than soothing. If only she could turn off her thoughts as easily.

*Open your heart.* That was what Lauren had advised. The problem was, that was exactly what had landed her in this situation. She'd loved her father with every ounce of her being. If she hadn't, perhaps it wouldn't have hurt so horribly when he'd left. As it was, he'd broken her heart and left her believing that if only she'd done something differently, if only she'd been a better daughter, he would have stayed.

And then there was Blake. Though she should have known better, Marisa had let herself fall in love with him. She'd dreamt of weddings and happily-ever-after until she'd learned that once again she'd been a poor judge of character.

Blake wasn't the man she thought he was any more than Eric had been the kind of father she'd longed for. She'd been foolish, and now she was paying the price. The Matchers were wrong if they thought Marisa was marriage material. She wasn't destined for marital bliss any more than she was meant to be a part of a perfect family.

Her hands gripping the steering wheel far more tightly than necessary, Marisa headed toward Dupree and her hair appointment. At least that was one place she would not be disappointed. The town might have only one hairdresser, but she was good. Though Ruby of the eponymously named Ruby's Tresses could have landed a spot in one of the most exclusive San Antonio salons, she'd preferred to remain at home, coaxing blue-haired ladies into more modern styles and assuring teenagers that she could cover up the disastrous effects of their attempts at home coloring.

Ruby had had moderate success with both campaigns, but she'd failed utterly in her attempts to convince Marisa to return to her natural hair color. As if it mattered what color her hair was. What mattered was the state of Marisa's heart.

She'd forgotten how long the emptiness lasted. She'd forgotten how easily even the slightest thing could trigger unwelcome memories. No matter what she did, thoughts of Blake popped up when she least expected them, ambushing her already vulnerable heart. Last night when she'd taken a bag of garbage to Lauren's garage, Marisa had spotted the tandem leaning against the far wall, and that had set off memories of the days she and Blake had ridden, the fun they'd had coasting down hills, the confidences they'd shared on their breaks.

Two days ago, she'd caught the scent of the roses Drew had brought Lauren, and that had unleashed another set of memories, less pleasant ones this time. Try though she might, Marisa couldn't forget the pain in Blake's eyes when she'd refused his flowers, and though she knew she was right to return them, she'd hated the fact that she'd hurt him.

Even the sight of Eric reading a book—any book, not simply a Ken Blake book—triggered thoughts of Blake, making Marisa wonder about the story that occupied Blake day and night. Mom said he rarely left his cabin, even to eat, and that everyone wondered what he was doing.

Marisa didn't wonder. She knew, but she wouldn't tell anyone.

It wasn't her secret to reveal. Though she told Mom not to worry, her mother did not listen. Instead, she did what she did best: she cooked. Each night she left a plate of dinner in the refrigerator so Blake could reheat it whenever he felt hungry, but some nights he forgot. So Mom had started sending Eric with a tray of food.

Marisa couldn't imagine being so caught up in work that she forgot to eat for more than a couple hours, but Blake was very different from her. She'd known that from the beginning. It was part of his appeal, part of the reason she wanted to be with him.

Her heart ached to close the distance between them, to knock on his cabin door and ask him what it was he'd wanted to say to her the days she'd refused to let him talk. Her head knew just how foolish that would be.

No matter what Blake might say, Marisa wasn't sure she could trust him. Instead, after what had happened between them, she feared that she would always wonder if he was hiding something important from her. Colleen would tell her to take a leap of faith, but Marisa wasn't a leaper. It was time to accept the fact that she and Blake had no future.

Biting her lip to keep from crying, Marisa forced her attention to the road ahead of her. She was approaching the summit of Ranger Hill. This was where the car's rattle would turn into a shake and she'd turn up the radio volume to avoid listening to it. But today there was no radio and, she realized, no rattle. She blinked, wondering if she'd missed it. But as she crested the hill and began the descent into Dupree, Marisa realized that the rattle was gone.

Her frown deepened. Even though she'd told him not to, Eric must have worked on her car while she was in her office. What she had tried to avoid had happened: she was beholden to him.

As her fingers tightened their grip on the steering wheel, memories began to whirl through Marisa's brain. She had been descending this hill, her legs pumping as fast as they could to give her the fastest, longest coast, when the accident had occurred. She'd hit something—perhaps a rock—and she and the bike had flown in opposite directions. Though Marisa had suffered no more than scrapes and cuts, the yellow bike that had been her pride and joy hadn't fared as well. The crash had bent the front fender so badly that it rubbed on the tire. Marisa had walked home, dragging the bike with her, devastated as only an eight-year-old could be. Thanks to her, she and Lauren would not be able to take the special ride they'd planned for the next day.

As Marisa had expected, Mom had been unhappy about the accident, but by some miracle, she hadn't grounded Marisa, instead saying that not being able to ride was punishment enough. It would be at least a week before the bike could be fixed, because Marisa's dad was working extra shifts each day and would have no time to look at the result of his daughter's foolishness.

Marisa had been asleep before Eric returned that night, and he was gone when she wandered into the kitchen for breakfast, but when she looked outside, her eyes had widened with surprise and delight. Her bike was leaning against the garage, both fenders looking as good as new.

Afterwards, Mom had told her that Eric had stayed up all night, fixing the bike and insisting that "good enough" wasn't good enough for his daughter. Instead of simply straightening the fender, he'd spent an extra couple of hours to give it several coats of chrome paint, his meticulous work hiding all evidence of Marisa's crash.

As a lump lodged in her throat, Marisa pulled into one of the parking spots in front of Ruby's Tresses, forcing her lips into a smile as she entered the small salon.

"Same as always?" Ruby asked when she'd draped a cape around Marisa's shoulders.

Marisa started to nod, then shook her head. "No," she said firmly as she removed the colored contacts from her eyes. "I want to be a blonde again."

Ruby stared at her as if she'd started speaking Swahili. "You do?"

Marisa nodded. "Yes. It's time for a change."

unt Marisa!" Fiona's voice held both curiosity and concern. "What did you do to your hair?"

That was the question Marisa had asked herself when Ruby swiveled the chair to face the long wall of mirrors. The woman she saw reflected in the glass had familiar features, and yet for the briefest of moments, Marisa had felt as if she were gazing at a stranger. The often painful experiences of the last eight years had left their mark. Fiona didn't see that. All she saw was that the woman she'd known as a brunette now had blonde hair.

"Ruby colored it," Marisa told her. "Actually, she removed color. Believe it or not, Fiona, this is the hair I was born with."

"Really?" Fiona touched Marisa's hair, as if she expected it to have changed texture as well as color.

"Really what?" Lauren demanded as she descended the stairs, now clad in her work-at-home attire of sweats and sneakers. Her eyes widened when she saw Marisa's hair, and a smile lit her face. "It's about time."

As she'd feared, Marisa's hair caused a stir when she arrived at Rainbow's End the next morning. Mom had hugged her, repeating "I'm so glad" so many times that Marisa began to lose count.

Perhaps because his wife was so vocal, Eric had said nothing, but the gleam in his eyes left no doubt that he was pleased. Kate had hugged Marisa, saying she was glad to have another blonde on the staff. Even Greg had commented on how nice Marisa's hair looked.

The only one who hadn't weighed in was Blake. Marisa hadn't caught a glimpse of him in days. Not that she cared. Of course she didn't. And yet she couldn't help wondering what he'd think.

———————— ✳ ————————

"I'm glad you could join us." Kate gave Lauren a warm smile that said she appreciated her closing HCP for an hour so she could be part of the Thanksgiving planning committee. That was the name Kate had given to herself, Marisa, Lauren, and Carmen. The four women had gathered in Marisa's office. Though a bit crowded, it was one of the few places at Rainbow's End where they could be assured of no interruptions. "I want to be certain everything's ready," Kate added.

Marisa knew Kate was nervous about the upcoming holiday. It would be the first time Rainbow's End had nonpaying guests. Although Kate and Greg's original plan had been to offer half of the cabins at reduced rates or even for free, Kate had insisted that they wait until all the glitches had been worked out before they invited unemployed and underemployed families. Her rationale was that if something went wrong during a stay, they could offer refunds to paying guests, but they had only one chance to make a good impression on those less fortunate.

"Have y'all seen the new van?" Kate asked, feigning a Texas drawl. "Greg and I think it turned out well, but we might be a tad prejudiced."

Marisa couldn't help it. She smiled at the thought of the now brightly colored van. "It's fabulous." A week ago it had been a plain white van. Now it was both unique and eye-catching.

"You can thank your father for that."

Marisa blinked as Kate's words registered. "What did he do?"

She knew it had been Eric's idea to buy a van, but this was the first Marisa had heard that he'd played any role in its decoration.

"I was going to put a small logo on the driver's side, but he convinced me to turn the whole van into a rolling advertisement for Rainbow's End." Kate laughed. "You'd never know I used to be an advertising executive, would you? I should have been the one to think of that."

Marisa looked at her mother, who'd brought in her favorite chair from the kitchen to complement the two guest chairs Marisa's office offered. Mom shrugged her shoulders, as if she hadn't known about Eric's involvement. The van had been transformed into what appeared to be a motorized ark, with the Rainbow's End logo covering not only the sides but also the front and back. There was no question that it would turn heads wherever it went.

"We're talking about having a float for the Christmas parade," Kate continued, "but first things first. Let's review where we are for Thanksgiving. Why don't you start, Carmen?"

Mom nodded. "The menus are complete, and the food's been ordered. I'm still waiting for final confirmation on the tablecloths and napkins, but the supplier assured me there'd be no problem having them delivered by Monday of Thanksgiving week."

Marisa watched a slow smile spread across Kate's face. Though the round tables with lazy Susans in the center were normally left bare, Kate was determined to have linen tablecloths for Sunday dinners and had decided that Thanksgiving weekend would be the ideal time to inaugurate them.

Marisa had volunteered to look for tablecloths, but Mom had insisted that she wanted to do it, citing Marisa's other responsibilities. She had wound up spending hours calling commercial linen supply houses to no avail but had finally found a small manufacturer in Dallas who'd agreed to produce the desired table coverings. Though the price had been higher than Marisa had expected, Kate had approved it, claiming she wanted guests to feel pampered.

"Excellent," Kate said before turning to Lauren.

"The Christmas ornaments are half done," Lauren said, referring to the quilted stars and angels that would be gifts for each of the guests. "There'll be no problem finishing them before anyone arrives. My only question is whether you want them wrapped."

Kate looked at Marisa. "What do you think?"

"It'll be more fun for them if they're wrapped."

"You've got your answer," Kate told Lauren. Turning back to Marisa, she raised an eyebrow. "How are the skits coming?"

"It's a piece of cake. Chocolate pound cake," Marisa amended, giving her mother a fond glance. "None of the guests are repeats, so we're going to do the same ones as the grand opening. All that's new is the finale."

Since Thanksgiving marked the official start of the Christmas season for retailers, Marisa and Kate had decided that it should be the beginning of Christmas at Rainbow's End too. "We'll have the unveiling of the tree, and the youngest child will get to place the star on top. After that, we'll sing a few carols, then distribute the gifts. The good news is that we can use the same finale for Christmas, even though the tree will already be there."

"I'm planning to serve hot chocolate and spiced cider along with those frosted cookies you used to like," Mom told Lauren, who was the only one who hadn't heard about the refreshments.

Though Mom had wanted to make a variety of cookies, Kate had suggested that this was one time when less was more. "I don't want there to be any fighting if one kid doesn't get the flavor he wants," she explained. Mom had acquiesced, even agreeing to make only stars rather than the assortment of stars, angels, and nativity scene figures that had been a highlight of Marisa's childhood.

"It all sounds perfect," Kate said. "I know everyone will enjoy it and that it'll give our guests what they need: a break from the stress and worry of their ordinary lives." Kate's expression turned wistful. "I only wish Gillian could be here to see how you've incorporated her music. That was pure genius on your part."

Marisa shook her head, unwilling to take credit for what had been a group effort. "Everyone pitched in with ideas for the skits, and Gillian's music tied everything together."

Kate appeared unconvinced. "The concept was yours. Gillian would have loved it."

Lauren tipped her head to one side, a sure sign that she was pondering something. "Why don't we record the program?" she asked. "Some of the guests might want copies, and you could send one to Gillian."

Kate squealed in delight. "What a great idea! We're selling CDs of the music. A DVD would be the perfect companion." She thumped her forehead. "Why didn't I think of that?"

"You've been a bit preoccupied." Marisa had caught Kate staring into the distance several times, a small, almost secretive smile on her face. Though Kate had dismissed it as nothing more than daydreaming, Marisa wasn't convinced. Still, she knew better than to pry.

"How is Gillian?" she asked.

"It's too soon to know the long-term prognosis," Kate said. "The cast is off, but now she's facing months of physical therapy."

Lauren nodded. "Healing's a slow process."

"Especially for people who are as impatient as my daughter." Mom's smile took the sting out of her words. "I'm glad Marisa didn't suffer anything more than sprains when she was growing up. I can't imagine what it would have been like to deal with a fracture. I'd have been gray before I was thirty."

Everyone was laughing when the door opened and the teenager who'd been manning the front desk popped her head in. "I know you didn't want any interruptions, but it's an emergency." Her gaze moved to Lauren. "Your daughter fell off a swing. They think her leg is broken."

<hr />

Blake put the car in park at the top of Ranger Hill and checked for cell service. Perfect. There were plenty of bars. Jack would have no trouble getting through to him.

Blake took a deep breath, trying to calm his nerves. This wasn't the first time he'd emailed a manuscript to his agent. It wasn't the first time they'd discussed a story. But it was the first time he'd sent Jack a manuscript like the current one. Feeling more nervous than he could recall, he'd pushed the "send" button yesterday morning, suggesting they talk about it after Jack had had a chance to read the first few chapters and proposing this time for a call.

Glancing at the time display on his phone, Blake swallowed again. If Jack was prompt—and he normally was—the phone would ring in thirty seconds. It did.

"Kendall here."

"Darlington here." It was their normal greeting, but today Jack's voice had a different tone. The fact that Blake could not pinpoint the reason for the difference set his nerves on edge.

"I'm going to conference Heidi in if that's okay with you," Jack continued. Heidi Goldberg had been Blake's editor for all of the Cliff Pearson books and was the one who would ultimately decide whether or not to accept the new one. While they had occasional conference calls, they were normally later in the production process. Blake's sense of unease grew.

"Sure, but wouldn't it make more sense to wait until she's read it?"

"She has." There it was, the same odd tone to Jack's voice, almost as if he were trying not to laugh. Blake saw nothing humorous about either the manuscript or the situation.

"I read the first three pages and knew she had to see it," Jack said. "Heidi did the same thing I did and stayed up most of the night reading."

"You've finished it?" That was more than Blake had expected. It typically took Jack a couple days to read a manuscript, then a couple more to formulate his thoughts.

"You bet."

"And you liked it?" That he'd sent it to Heidi without discussing it with Blake seemed to indicate that, but Blake didn't want to jump to conclusions. Although he wasn't normally insecure about his writing, this book was so different from everything else he'd written that he wanted confirmation.

"Sure, I liked it, but let's let Heidi tell you what she thinks. Hang on." Blake heard a click, a second or two of silence, then Jack's voice. "You there, Heidi? Great. I've got Blake on the line."

"Is it true that you're holed up somewhere in Texas?" Blake's editor asked. While Heidi never put much emphasis on social niceties, this was abrupt, even for her.

"Yes, it's true, but why are you asking?" Blake had thought she would say something about the book, not about the location where he'd written it.

"Stay there." Heidi sounded like a drill sergeant issuing a command. "Whatever it is about the place, it's working. Blake, your book is incredible, and you know I don't say that lightly."

Blake inhaled slowly, trying to control the emotions that had begun to run wild. Pleasure and excitement combined with the fear that he would be unable to re-create the same enthusiasm for a second book had set his heart pounding at what felt like twice its normal pace.

"I didn't think you could surpass Cliff Pearson, but you did." Heidi was still speaking, her voice now warm with approval. "This has the action and intrigue of the Pearson books, plus what I'm calling heart."

Blake's own heart skipped a beat, then began a slow thudding. This was what he'd hoped for, that both his agent and his editor would approve his change of direction. He stared into the distance for a second, his eyes drinking in the beauty of Firefly Valley. Heidi was right. Being here was why his writing had changed so dramatically. Jack's and Heidi's enthusiasm confirmed what Blake had thought, that this was the kind of book he was meant to write.

"I'm glad you like it." That was a major understatement, but though Blake made his living with words, he could think of nothing else to say.

Heidi took a deep breath and let it out slowly. "It only needs one thing to make it a perfect package."

Blake hoped he was wrong about what she was going to say. "And that would be . . ."

"Promotion. I'm not asking you to go on a tour, but if you'd reveal your identity and do a couple talk shows, your sales could rival J. K. Rowling's."

That was a gross exaggeration. The Logan Marsh books might be good, but they wouldn't have the audience Harry Potter did, even if Blake went on a worldwide tour.

"I'm sorry, but the answer's the same as it's always been: no." Although his grandfather's disapproval was no longer an issue, Blake had Marisa to consider. If they were going to have any kind of relationship—and he hadn't given up hope that they would—he knew it would be more difficult if every time they went somewhere, he was recognized and asked for his autograph.

He heard Heidi's sigh.

"Blake and I'll discuss this off-line," Jack told her.

Blake shook his head. "There's nothing to discuss."

# 23

Dr. Santos slid his hands into his pockets and leaned against the wall rather than taking the chair behind his desk. Though his posture was casual, the expression on his face told Lauren she wasn't going to like his words. She'd been concerned when the nurse had ushered her into the doctor's office rather than leading her to the treatment room where Fiona was waiting. Lauren's worries increased when she saw the furrows between the doctor's eyes. This was the man who'd delivered Fiona and who'd treated her few ailments. Never before had he looked so concerned.

Lauren had refused Marisa's offer of a ride to the small clinic that was Dupree's only source of medical care, telling her friend that kids broke legs all the time and that she was perfectly capable of driving herself. This wasn't a big deal, or so she'd thought. Now she was reconsidering.

"I'm not going to sugarcoat this," the doctor said. "Fiona has a serious fracture. I could set it for you, but if I do that, I can't guarantee it'll heal properly."

He walked to the desk and swiveled the computer monitor so Lauren could see it. "Here's the break," he said, pointing to a line on the X-ray. "This isn't a hairline fracture. It's a complete break."

Dr. Santos rattled off a few medical terms that meant nothing to Lauren. She was still trying to register the fact that Fiona's injury was serious. *It's not life-threatening*, she told herself, remembering the day she and Patrick had sat in this office, hearing the diagnosis that had changed their lives.

"I've given Fiona a shot for the pain," the doctor continued, "but I didn't want to do anything more without talking to you."

Gripping the sides of the chair as if they were lifelines, Lauren looked up at the kindly man who'd reassured her so many times in the past. "So what do I do?"

"First of all, take a deep breath. I don't need you fainting. One patient per family is my limit." Doc punctuated his words with a smile. "I think you should take Fiona to an orthopedic specialist." He handed Lauren a business card. "I've already called, and they can fit you in this afternoon. They're among the best in Texas."

A specialist. That was the way it had started with Patrick. Lauren took another deep breath, reminding herself that, while serious, a broken leg was not in the same category as cancer.

She glanced at the card. As she'd feared, the address was in San Antonio. Fortunately, the map on the back showed that it was on this side of the city, which meant she wouldn't face too much traffic.

"All right," she said. "I think we should tell Fiona together, and then I need to make a couple calls." Lauren wouldn't trust herself to use the phone while she was driving her daughter to the city. She'd need all her attention focused on the road and minimizing Fiona's pain.

"I'm sorry, Drew," she said after she'd told Marisa of the diagnosis and that she would be late getting home, "but I have to cancel our dinner tonight." In return for all the meals Drew had provided, Lauren had invited him to join her and Fiona for supper tonight. "Fiona broke her leg, and I'm taking her to a specialist in San Antonio." Lauren hated the way her voice wavered, but she couldn't stop thinking about how painful the injury must have been. According to Alice, they'd both heard the bone crack.

Lauren heard Drew's intake of breath. "The poor kid doesn't need this, and you don't either." Without so much as a pause, he added, "I'll drive."

She shook her head before realizing he had no way of seeing the gesture. "You don't need to do that."

"Yes, I do," he countered. "The alternative is staying here and worrying about you being on the road. You can't tell me you wouldn't be a distracted driver."

"That's true," Lauren admitted. With her maternal instincts in overdrive as they were now, she had trouble thinking about anything other than her daughter.

"Besides, my rental's more comfortable. That'll be better for Fiona, so just tell me where you are and I'll be there in five minutes."

When he arrived, Lauren wheeled Fiona out of the clinic. Doc had stabilized her leg with a splint, leaving Fiona unable to bend her knee, but he'd assured both her and Lauren that the worst of the pain was over.

Though Fiona was more subdued than normal, perhaps because of the meds, she grinned when Drew asked if she'd been swinging. "Yeah, how'd you guess?"

"Just lucky. The question is, did you get to touch the sky?"

Lauren's eyes widened at the realization that Fiona had confided her dreams to Drew. It had been Patrick who'd told her that if she swung high enough, she could touch the sky, and for years Fiona had pumped her legs harder and harder, hoping to reach the top of the swing set frame. That, Patrick had said, was where the sky began. Since his death, Lauren hadn't heard her daughter mention reaching for the sky, but it appeared that she had told Drew about it.

Fiona's grin was weak but triumphant. "Yeah. It was cool."

"Then give me five." Drew held up his hand for a slap.

After settling Fiona onto the backseat, Drew climbed into the driver's seat. To Lauren's amazement, he practically ignored her, spending the entire drive to San Antonio regaling Fiona with tales of his skiing, surfing, and dirt bike accidents. Though Lauren suspected they were exaggerated if not downright imaginary, she wasn't complaining, because the wild tales of injuries and the almost miraculous recoveries that followed them were helping Fiona relax.

When they reached the clinic, Drew refused to wait for a wheelchair but carried Fiona in, then insisted on getting a cup of coffee for Lauren once Fiona had been admitted.

She took a sip and wrinkled her nose. "This is awful." Strong, bitter, and overly sweet, it was the poorest excuse for caffeine she'd had in a long time. "I didn't think it was possible, but this is worse than the Sit 'n' Sip's." Though the food at Dupree's only diner was excellent, everyone in town knew to avoid the coffee.

"That's by design." Drew settled into the chair next to Lauren, stretching his legs out in front of him. "You're supposed to concentrate on the coffee and not think about what's going on behind those doors."

If that was the goal, it didn't work. "How long do you think it'll take?"

"There's no telling. You heard Dr. Talbot. It can vary by hours, depending on what they find. But you don't want them to rush, do you?"

Lauren shook her head. "Of course not. I just want Fiona to be well again."

"In the meantime, you need to relax." As if he knew that wasn't going to be easy, Drew leaned forward, wrapping his hand around the cardboard coffee cup. "This is my first time in a hospital waiting room, so I don't know the protocol, but I'd suggest we talk about anything other than broken bones."

He stared into the distance for a second, then returned his gaze to Lauren. His expression was gentle, and she saw what appeared to be genuine interest in his eyes. "We've talked about a million things," he said slowly, "but you've never told me how you got started quilting."

And so Lauren found herself recounting stories of her grandmother and how she passed on her love of needle arts to her granddaughter. "Next to Marisa, my sewing machine was my best friend," she admitted. "I love creating things from pieces of fabric."

The time passed more quickly than Lauren had thought possible as she and Drew discussed everything from sewing to scuba diving, from picnics in the park to parasailing over the Pacific. Some of the topics were silly, others serious, but throughout it all, Lauren found herself entranced by the man who against all odds was keeping her from dwelling on what was happening to her daughter.

"Ms. Ahrens."

Lauren rose as the surgeon entered the waiting room, her blonde hair still covered by her surgical cap, her expression inscrutable.

"How is she?"

"She's sedated," Dr. Talbot said, "but you'll be able to see her in a few minutes. In the meantime, I want to discuss what we did. Dr. Santos was right to send her here. The fracture was comminuted, which means the bone had broken into more than two pieces, and since it was her femur, I was particularly concerned about proper healing. That's why we have her in traction."

As images of ropes and pulleys flashed through Lauren's mind, she started to tremble. Drew wrapped his arm around her and guided her back to the chair.

"How long?" Lauren asked when the blood returned to her head.

Dr. Talbot's eyes radiated compassion. "The good news is that it's not as long as it would have been twenty years ago. The bad news is that I want her in traction for at least two weeks. I can recommend a couple of rehab centers that have experience with children."

Lauren closed her eyes for a few seconds, praying for strength. The thought of nursing homes brought back memories of Patrick's final month, when he'd been too ill to remain at home. Though closer than San Antonio, the nursing home had still been a half hour away. Lauren and Fiona had made the drive every day, wanting to spend as much time with Patrick as they could, but hating the fact that he was in an institution.

"I don't like the idea of leaving her there," she admitted.

Dr. Talbot nodded. "There are hotels practically next door to each of the facilities I've suggested. If you stayed at one of them, you could be with Fiona all day long." But it would still be an institution.

"Is there no other choice?" Lauren couldn't imagine how Fiona would cope with being in a hospital-like environment. Ever since Patrick's death, she'd refused to even watch TV shows set in hospitals, and she'd been trembling with fear when Drew had carried her into the clinic.

Though her expression said she wished there were another answer, Dr. Talbot shook her head. "I'm afraid not. Without the traction, we're risking her leg not healing straight."

And that was a risk Lauren wouldn't take. No matter how difficult the next two weeks would be for both her and Fiona, she had no choice.

Drew slid his arm around Lauren's shoulders and gave them a little squeeze. "What about renting a hospital bed and the traction equipment and hiring a nurse so Fiona can heal at home?"

Dr. Talbot was silent for a moment, obviously considering his question. "That could work. You'd need to transport her by ambulance and hire an expert to set up everything, but after that you wouldn't need a full-time nurse. The important thing is to have someone stay with Fiona. Kids her age are restless and inquisitive. Even the best behaved will try to get out of traction. That's why she needs adult supervision."

"I can provide that."

Lauren stared at Drew, astonished by the offer. "But . . ."

He looked up at the doctor. "Would you give us a few minutes alone?" When Dr. Talbot left, he turned so he was facing Lauren. "We both know you and Fiona would be miserable staying here. At least if she's in Dupree, her friends can visit. We also know you have commitments to meet if you're going to keep your business alive. You can't afford two weeks without work."

Lauren couldn't dispute anything he'd said. It was true she had to work, and she couldn't help worrying about how much of the nursing home costs would be covered by insurance. Though it was awful to have to worry about costs when her daughter's health was concerned, Patrick's illness had taught Lauren the high price of being sick.

"You're right, but I can't ask you to play nurse."

Drew reached for her hand and threaded his fingers through hers. "As I recall, you didn't ask. I volunteered. If I stay with Fiona during the day, you'll be able to keep your store open. Didn't you tell me this is one of your busiest times of the year?"

She nodded. "What you're proposing solves my problem, but what about you? You must be busy with your business."

A spark of something that looked like annoyance flitted across Drew's face. "I never said I was working."

It was possible he was taking an extended vacation, but Lauren didn't think so. The town scuttlebutt said that though he had a month-to-month lease on Marisa's former home, he'd indicated that he planned to stay in Dupree indefinitely. "I assumed . . ."

"Incorrectly. The truth is, I'm unemployed." When Lauren gasped at the unexpected revelation, Drew tightened his grip on her hand as he said, "The official story is that I'm devoting myself to other ventures, but the reality is that the new owners and I had very different expectations. Greg tried to warn me, but I was too stubborn to listen. It turns out he was right. When the differences became irreconcilable, I was fired." Drew clenched his free hand. "Oh, I got a nice severance package, but the result is the same. I'm not working and haven't been since a couple weeks before I moved to Dupree."

Lauren couldn't imagine that. The few times they'd discussed work, it had been clear that Drew thrived on being busy. That was why she'd thought he was telecommuting, although now that she thought about it, he'd always used the past tense when speaking of his job.

"Oh, Drew, I'm so sorry."

His response surprised her. "I'm not. Being fired was the best thing that could have happened to me. Losing my job forced me to take a long look at myself. When I realized that I didn't like what I saw, I knew I had to change." He lowered his gaze for a moment, then met Lauren's, the corners of his lips turning up into a faint smile. "I'm still working on it, but with God's help, I'm becoming a person I can like."

She nodded slowly. Her instincts had told her something was different, and now she knew what had changed. The Drew who'd rented Marisa's old home was not the same man Lauren had met last spring.

"For what it's worth, I like the new you," she said softly. "I like him a lot."

Drew's smile lit his face. "Then you'll let me stay with your daughter while you're at work?"

"I will."

## 24

Ambushed. That's the way Marisa felt. She had just entered her office when Blake arrived. This was not what she needed, especially not first thing in the morning. She needed another cup of coffee, at least one cinnamon bun, and another month or so before she dealt with him.

Ever since the day she'd told Ruby it was time to become a blonde again, Marisa had found herself remembering her reaction when she'd learned of Blake's dual identity. The white hot anger she'd felt that day had cooled, leaving her to wonder if she'd overreacted. It was true that she'd been shocked by the revelation, but it was also true, as Lauren had reminded her several times, that she'd fallen in love with Blake, the man. That he was a writer was secondary.

As the days had passed, Marisa had admitted to herself that while she might believe that writing was who Blake was rather than what he did, it was possible that she was wrong. Writing might be nothing more than a career, like his work as a financial planner. And if that was the case, she owed him an apology.

Colleen would say that Marisa owed him an apology in any case, simply because she'd let her temper get the better of her. But Marisa wasn't ready to apologize. She had more than enough turmoil in her life right now between Eric's return and Fiona's accident.

Though Drew tried his best not to disrupt their schedule, everything had changed. Not only was Fiona hooked up to pulleys and cables, but the family dynamics had altered. Fiona now looked to Drew for comfort, whereas in the past she'd sought only her mother. And then there was Lauren's relationship with Drew. Marisa would have had to be blind to miss the tender looks they exchanged or the way Drew's hand lingered whenever he touched Lauren. Everything was changing, leaving Marisa feeling more than a little overwhelmed.

She needed time to adjust, and she definitely needed time to prepare herself for an encounter with Blake. But the determination she saw on his face and the way he leaned against the door frame told Marisa he had no intention of letting her escape. Whatever he wanted to say, she would have to listen, unless she did something childish like plugging her ears.

The corners of Blake's lips twitched, almost as if he'd read her mind. Perhaps he was reacting to her hair color. Though his eyes had widened when he opened the door, he'd said nothing about the change.

"I know you said you didn't want to see me again, but I brought something I hope will change your mind." To Marisa's surprise, Blake held out an object she had no difficulty identifying.

"An e-reader?" She already owned one.

As he shook his head, a shock of light brown hair tumbled across his forehead. "The reader's not the gift. It's the book that's on it that's important."

Flowers, candy, and books. Mom claimed those were traditional courting gifts. Blake had already offered Marisa flowers and candy. This must be the twenty-first-century substitute for a book of poetry.

Though she wanted to refuse, Marisa found herself intrigued. Without turning on the machine, she wouldn't know which book Blake had chosen for her.

"I'm not a big fan of poetry," she told him.

"This isn't poetry."

"Romance?"

"No."

"Science fiction?"

"No."

When she'd exhausted every category she could recall, each time eliciting a shake of the head and the hint of a smile from Blake, Marisa nodded. "Then it must be some sort of self-help book." She'd read more than her share of them when she'd been trying to understand her father's behavior.

"Not exactly," he said. "Although writing it did help me."

For a second, Marisa was silent, absorbing the unexpected response. Perhaps if she'd had a second cup of coffee, she might not have been so dense. "It's your new book."

"Yeah." Blake's expression turned solemn. "I won't say anything about it other than that I hope you'll read it. And if you want to talk when you're done, you know where to find me." His eyes narrowed, and this time there was no doubt about it: Blake wanted to smile. "For the record, you look great as a blonde."

Without waiting for a response, he left, closing the door behind him and leaving Marisa alone with his gift and a Texas-sized supply of curiosity. Blake knew how she felt about his books, so why did he want her to read this one? And why now? Marisa didn't know a lot about writers, but she had heard that few shared their stories with anyone other than their agents and editors, not wanting the plot to be leaked to the public.

What had he written? It had to be another Cliff Pearson story. That was his brand. But if it was, it made no sense that Blake wanted her to read it. Marisa started to put the e-reader aside, then switched it on. She would read the first page. That was all. An hour later, when the phone rang, she realized she was supposed to be working, not reading Blake's book.

Reluctantly, she answered the call. Though she forced herself to follow her to-do list, for the rest of the day Marisa found herself thinking about Blake's characters. She had read engaging books before, but this was different. Blake had hooked her on the first page, and no matter what she did, she couldn't stop wondering what was going to happen next.

The next morning, bleary-eyed from too little sleep, she knocked on Blake's cabin door.

"Let's talk," she said when he opened the door.

The smile that lit Blake's face left no doubt of his pleasure. "I was hoping you'd say that. Do you want to walk while we talk?"

Marisa shook her head. Fatigue had made her legs weak. "Why don't we just sit on your porch?" She'd worn a hooded sweatshirt to ward off the early morning chill.

"Great." Seconds later, Blake zipped his jacket closed as he took the second Adirondack chair.

"I read it," she said as she handed him the e-reader. "I'm not sure what I was expecting, but it wasn't that."

Blake simply raised an eyebrow, encouraging her to continue.

"It's good," she said, then shook her head. "No, that's not true. It's wonderful. Once I started reading, I didn't want to stop, and when I finished, I was tempted to start all over again."

Marisa smiled, wanting him to understand how much she'd enjoyed his story. Unlike Blake, she wasn't a master with words. "I can't remember when a book affected me like this. I loved the characters." Marisa wrinkled her nose and amended her statement. "Well, not the villain. I was afraid of him, and that was good too, because I know that's what you intended."

Though Blake said nothing, as if he knew she wasn't finished, Marisa watched the tension drain from him. His hands were no longer gripping the chair arms, and his shoulders had relaxed.

As the morning chill settled over her, Marisa slid her hands into the kangaroo pockets of her sweatshirt. She'd go back to Lauren's once she told Blake everything she felt about his book. "The story kept me totally engrossed, but what I liked best was the way you delivered a message without being heavy-handed." Marisa paused for a moment to emphasize her next words. "This is a fabulous book, Blake."

His eyes shone with pleasure. "Better than *Anne of Green Gables*?"

She stared at him, startled by the question. "Who told you about that?" Marisa knew she'd never mentioned her love of the classic, and it was hardly a subject that would come up in casual conversation with anyone else.

"Your dad. He said it was your favorite book." Blake's lips turned up in a mischievous smile. "I learned a few things from it, like not to comment on a woman's hair color unless you're very sure she's happy with it."

So that was why he hadn't said much about her new look. "I'm happy being a blonde again," she told him. "What surprised me is that you actually read *Anne*."

"I did. It's not my normal fare, but I can see why you enjoyed it." Blake clasped his hands around his knees as he said, "So, tell me. How does mine compare?"

"Nothing can top *Anne*," Marisa said, staunchly defending her childhood reading, "but your story is a close second. I really enjoyed it."

For the second time in only a few minutes, Blake said, "I was hoping you'd say that. My agent and editor like it, but it's your opinion that matters most."

The rush of warmth that flooded Marisa's face had nothing to do with the rising sun. "That's very flattering, but why?"

"Because you're the reason I wrote this story and not another Cliff Pearson."

"I don't understand." The day she'd learned that he was Ken Blake, Marisa had believed Blake saw nothing wrong with his fictional hero. Now it appeared that he had listened—really listened—to what she'd said.

"Your reaction to Cliff made me look at my books differently."

Blake stared at the lake for a moment before turning back to Marisa. "I didn't agree with everything you said, and I still don't, but when I heard two teenage boys trying to buy Cliff's whiskey and cigarettes, I thought about what you'd said. That was when I knew he wasn't the best role model." Blake leaned forward to close the distance between them. "Thank you, Marisa. You opened my eyes."

Marisa's heart soared, then plummeted. While it was flattering to know that she had been able to influence Blake, the new book only reinforced how wrong she'd been.

"I'm glad you're writing about Logan Marsh instead of Cliff Pearson." That was half of the story. Taking a deep breath, Marisa tried to slow the racing of her pulse. What she was about to say was sorely overdue. "I owe you an apology, Blake, a huge apology. I had no right to say the things I did about your writing. All I can say in my defense is that I'm not totally rational when drinking is involved."

He nodded slowly, his eyes solemn. "That's understandable."

"But not excusable. I should have realized that you're not Cliff Pearson and that I had no right to judge the way you make your living." When he said nothing, she continued. "Can you forgive me?"

"Of course." His lips curving into a smile, Blake tipped his head to one side. "I hope this means that we can be friends again. Even though I've been writing night and day, I've missed you."

And she had missed him. Though she had tried to deny it, Marisa had felt as if a part of her heart had been torn away.

"I thought the time we had together before Ken Blake got in the way was special," Blake continued, "and I want to recapture that."

If Marisa had learned one thing, it was that you could not recapture the past. Fortunately, there was always the future, and right now that future looked bright.

"I'm not sure we can recapture anything," she said, not wanting to mislead Blake. "We're not the same people we were a month ago. Instead of looking backward, I'd suggest we move forward."

"That sounds like a plan to me." Blake's smile turned into a mischievous grin. "Can we start by going to dinner tonight? I've heard there's a good French restaurant in Blytheville."

As she thought about Strawberry Chantilly with its reputation for superb food and a romantic atmosphere, Marisa smiled. "You sure know how to impress a girl."

Blake smiled. "So you'll go with me?"

"Of course."

———————— ✳ ————————

"Hey, Fiona, did you see any pigs fly by?" Though Lauren pretended to be serious as she entered her daughter's room, Marisa knew she was trying to make her laugh. Even though Fiona was reacting better than anyone had thought possible to her enforced inactivity and the discomfort of having a leg in traction, she needed frequent distractions.

"Don't be silly, Mom," Fiona said with a giggle. "Pigs don't fly."

"I'm not so sure about that. Your Aunt Marisa is doing something I didn't think would happen until pigs flew."

Fiona's eyes grew wide and she stared at Marisa. "What are you doing?"

"It's only dinner."

"Dinner at the fanciest restaurant this side of San Antonio with a man you haven't spoken to for the better part of a month," Lauren countered. "Now, what are you going to wear?"

Marisa's choices were fewer than they'd been a year ago, thanks to all the outfits that had gone to the consignment shop. "I have a dark blue velvet skirt and a white silk blouse that I thought might work."

"I like velvet," Fiona told her, "but Mom says it isn't practical."

"Aunt Marisa isn't trying to be practical tonight. She's trying to impress a gentleman."

"I am not." Well, not too much. Even though the fabrics were luxurious, the outfit was not as fancy as the apricot dress she had lent to Lauren for her date with Drew.

Lauren pretended not to hear Marisa. "I've got one of those pretty crocheted necklaces that might go with it. I'll meet you in your room."

As Lauren headed for her bedroom, Fiona reached for the book she'd been reading when Marisa had first come in. "Will you come see me before you leave?"

"Of course I will. You're my fashion consultant." Marisa pointed to Fiona's feet with their mismatched socks. When he'd realized that Fiona's normal socks wouldn't fit over the cast, Drew had somehow found a number of oversized socks in the wildest colors Marisa had ever seen. Paired with the socks Fiona already owned, they were a guaranteed topic of conversation.

"Here you go," Lauren said a minute later as she entered Marisa's bedroom, the necklace in her hand. Placing it next to the skirt Marisa had laid out on the bed, she nodded. "A perfect match."

"Like you and Drew?" Marisa asked, raising one of her eyebrows. "It hasn't escaped my notice that you two are acting like lovebirds."

Lauren looked as if she didn't know whether to be embarrassed or pleased. "I didn't know it was so obvious," she admitted, smiling as she ran her hand over the soft velvet of Marisa's skirt. "I can't quite believe it, but I'm in love, and it's just as wonderful as the first time."

She took a deep breath. "It may even be better, because I'm old enough to know how special love is." Fixing her gaze on Marisa, Lauren said, "I know you didn't like Drew at first, but I hope you'll be happy for us if this works out."

Marisa reached for the blouse and slid her arms into it. "It wasn't a matter of not liking Drew," she explained. "I was worried that he might hurt you, but even a cynic like me has to admit that he's been a real Prince Charming taking care of Fiona." Marisa couldn't imagine any of the men she'd met—and that included Blake—being so patient, but Drew never complained, not even when Fiona was cranky.

"He is wonderful," Lauren agreed. "I don't know how I got

so lucky as to find two wonderful men." She handed Marisa the necklace and watched while she adjusted the length. "I don't know what makes me happier: the fact that Drew is part of my life or that you're back with Blake."

"Aren't you getting ahead of yourself? It's only dinner."

"Right. You can say what you want, but I know what I see. The pigs are definitely flying."

## 25

It would probably be rude to whistle, so all I'm going to say is 'wow.'"

Marisa smiled as she ushered Blake into Lauren's house. She could say the same thing to him. Dressed in a suit and tie, he looked more handsome than usual, the dark blue of his suit and the white of the shirt highlighting the tan he'd acquired while in Texas.

"I hope you're not allergic," he said as he handed her what was obviously a florist's box.

Marisa opened it, sighing with pleasure when she saw an assortment of roses. Other than the single red carnation that Dupree High School's graduates were expected to pin on their gowns and the yellow roses she'd rejected, these were the only flowers she'd received.

She had bought Hal a boutonniere carefully dyed to match her prom dress and had expected him to bring her a corsage when he picked her up for the dance. He'd asked her about her dress color enough times that she'd believed he had something special in mind, and he had. It simply wasn't the surprise Marisa had expected.

As she looked at the gorgeous roses with their velvety soft petals, Marisa was thankful Hal had not given her flowers. It seemed right that Blake was the first.

"They're beautiful, Blake," she said with another smile. Lauren might be right. Pigs must be flying, because once again Marisa felt as if she were falling head over heels in love with this man. "Thank you, and no, I'm not allergic to flowers."

Marisa led the way into the kitchen, pulled a vase from the cupboard, and carefully arranged the flowers in it. "I can't imagine where you found roses like this in Dupree."

"Who said anything about Dupree? There's a full-service florist in Blytheville. They made it up while I waited."

The frisson of pleasure that had slid down her spine when she'd opened the florist's box intensified at the realization that Blake had invested not only his money but his time to make this a special evening. It seemed he'd been genuine in both his acceptance of her apology and his belief that they could begin again.

"That's the nicest thing anyone's done for me in a long time," Marisa said softly. "Thank you, Blake."

She smiled at him, noticing the tiny nick on the edge of his chin, evidence that he'd tried for a particularly close shave. Somehow that touched her even more than the flowers, and she was tempted to press a kiss on the sore spot. She wouldn't, of course. That would be too much too soon. Instead, she deliberately changed the subject.

"Do we have time for a brief detour?" she asked. "I don't know how much you've heard, but Lauren's daughter broke her leg and is in traction. I know she'd enjoy seeing the flowers and meeting you."

"Sure. Lead on, Macduff. Or is it lay on?"

Marisa raised her hands in mock surrender, thankful that the diversion had worked and her pulse had resumed its normal beat. "I'm not going to have the Macduff discussion again." She led the way to Fiona's bedroom, where Lauren was playing a game of Parcheesi with her daughter. Drew had left as soon as Marisa arrived, but she wouldn't be surprised if he returned for supper. The man was definitely persistent in his courtship.

"Look at the pretty flowers Mr. Kendall brought me," Marisa said, holding out the vase as she and Blake entered the room. When

Fiona had sniffed the flowers, she looked up at Blake, her brown eyes serious. "Are you gonna marry Aunt Marisa?"

For a second, there was total silence. Marisa felt the blood drain from her face, then rush back, flooding her cheeks with color. What could she say? What could Blake say?

Lauren shook her head at Fiona. "That's not a question you should be asking."

Although Marisa had expected him to share her embarrassment, Blake appeared unconcerned by Fiona's bluntness. "It's all right, Fiona. I'd answer if I could, but it depends on Marisa." That wasn't the response Marisa had expected, but perhaps Blake was trying to deflect attention from himself. One thing was certain: she wouldn't take the bait, if that's what it was. Not here, not now.

Nodding solemnly as if the answer pleased her, Fiona fixed her gaze on Marisa. "You should marry him, Aunt Marisa. You need a husband."

As Lauren shrugged and mouthed "Junior Matcher," Marisa knew it was time to make a quick exit.

"Good night, Fiona." She kissed the girl's forehead, then hurried out of the room, grabbing Blake's hand and propelling him to the front door.

He was chuckling as he helped Marisa into his car. "Greg warned me about the matchmakers in Dupree, but I didn't know they started so young."

"Fiona has daddies on her mind."

"So I've heard. Greg says things are pretty serious between Drew and Lauren. There must be something in the air in Dupree," Blake said as he started the ignition. "Two confirmed bachelors, one married, the other well on the way."

*Where are you on that continuum?* Marisa wondered, though she had no intention of asking. She and Blake were starting over, and they needed to proceed slowly.

Once they were headed north on the highway, Blake turned to glance at Marisa. "Greg warned me about deer accidents on this road, especially at this time of the day." The sun had just set, and though the road wasn't yet dark, visibility was reduced. "Let me know if you see any animals."

Marisa nodded. "Sure." The thought of deer reminded her of Blake's new book. That was a safer subject than marriage. "Is Greg's warning why you wrote the scene with the deer?"

A small smile was Blake's first response. Then he spoke. "Short answer: yes. The long answer is that even though I've been fortunate enough never to have had a close encounter with one of Bambi's relatives, knowing how common deer-car collisions are piqued my imagination."

Blake's explanation piqued Marisa's imagination. "I've always wondered how much of their real lives writers included in their books." That was part of the reason why Cliff Pearson's vices bothered her so much. Though she'd seen no sign that Blake drank here, she wondered if that had been part of his life in California.

He sped up to pass a slow-moving farm vehicle. When they were back in the right lane, Blake spoke again. "I can't speak for anyone other than myself, but for me it's only bits and pieces. My characters aren't based on real people, and the things that happen to them never happened to me."

"So it's all your imagination?"

Blake nodded. "Does that surprise you?"

"A bit." Marisa had read somewhere that writers were advised to write what they knew and thought that meant most stories were based on real-life experiences. That was the reason that knowing Blake had created Cliff Pearson had bothered her so much.

"I play games of what-if." Though his attention remained focused on the road, Blake's grip on the steering wheel was relaxed. "When Greg told me about the number of deer accidents in this part of the Hill Country, I started asking myself what would happen if my hero were the first to arrive at the scene of an accident. What would he do? And would his decision be different if there were a reason why he shouldn't have been there?"

"He did the right thing." Though he knew there would be serious repercussions when his family learned he'd violated his curfew, Logan hadn't left the injured motorist. Instead, he'd called 911 and given CPR, keeping the man alive until the emergency responders arrived.

"But it wasn't an easy decision."

"That's what made the scene so powerful. Logan had to weigh right and wrong." Marisa settled back in the comfortable seat, her attention once more on the man at her left. As had been the case for a day and a half, ever since he'd given her the e-reader with his manuscript, her thoughts revolved around the story and the man who'd written it.

The Logan Marsh story had the action and excitement of Blake's Cliff Pearson books. It also had a hero who overcame seemingly insurmountable odds, the way Cliff did. The difference was that Logan made mistakes, and he learned from them. In Marisa's eyes, that made him far more heroic than Cliff.

She turned to Blake and asked him one of the questions that had been floating through her mind ever since she finished reading the manuscript.

"Are you going to use your real name for this book?"

Blake shook his head. "No. It will be another Ken Blake story."

"Why? There's nothing to be ashamed of in this one."

Blake's lips tightened momentarily. "You may not believe this, but shame wasn't the reason I chose a pseudonym." He stared out the windshield, then shifted his glance toward Marisa. "Do you remember my telling you that my grandfather lived with us?"

"Yes. I also remember that he sounded like a difficult man."

"That he was, in many ways." Blake swallowed before continuing. "Grandfather was very opinionated, and one of his opinions was that fiction is the work of the devil. I don't agree, and my dad doesn't, either, but if Grandfather had known that I wrote novels, he would have been furious. He would have called me and ranted until he was hoarse. Then, because I wasn't there, he would have made my father's life miserable. There would have been tirades, little digs, even full-fledged sermons about how wrong I was."

Blake took a shallow breath. "Trust me, Marisa. It wouldn't have been a one-time occurrence. Grandfather would have found a way to tell my dad every single day that he'd obviously failed as a parent. I couldn't subject my father to that, so I chose a pseudonym and insisted on anonymity. I haven't even told Dad, because I didn't want him to have to keep a secret from his father."

Though Blake had alluded to his grandfather's abrasive personality, Marisa hadn't realized it had been so extreme.

"Why did your father put up with that kind of behavior?"

As he clenched the steering wheel, Blake frowned. "I think it was a sense of duty. My grandmother died only a couple months after my mother, and Grandfather was lost. Dad's never really said so, but I believe he was worried about his father, so he invited him to live with us. Once he was there, it seemed there was no going back."

"I'm sorry. Life with Eric wasn't always easy, but at least he wasn't abusive."

Blake's smile was warm and reassuring. "It's over. And now can we talk about something more pleasant than me? Tell me what's going on at Rainbow's End. Even though Greg and I jog almost every morning, we don't talk much."

And so Marisa told Blake about the plans for Thanksgiving weekend. "It's amazing to me, but even with the expense of renovations, if we continue at our current pace, Rainbow's End will break even by the end of next year."

"I'm not surprised. Both Greg and Kate are shrewd at business, and they're doing God's work at Rainbow's End. I would expect it to thrive." Blake turned to glance at Marisa again. "What about you? Are you enjoying what you're doing?"

"Surprisingly, yes. The accounting isn't especially challenging, but I have the chance to do so much more."

Though he kept his eyes on the road, Blake's lips curved in a smile. "Like arranging entertainment for the guests."

"And helping with the hiring. I even do procurement." Marisa smiled, thinking of the calls she'd made and the impromptu visits to some of Dupree's merchants. "It's been fun, trying to find local suppliers." While she'd known there would be challenges, she had fully supported Kate and Greg's desire to locally source as many things as possible. Their goal, they'd explained, was to benefit Dupree as well as their guests.

"So you're glad to be back home?"

Marisa was silent for a moment, considering the question. "Most of the time, yes." But as the image of her father skittered across her mind, she started to shake her head. The truth was, she wasn't sure how she felt about being back in Dupree with him here. Though it was wonderful to see Mom happier and more relaxed than she'd been in eight years, Marisa wasn't yet ready to admit that the changes she'd seen in Eric were permanent. She still feared that he'd take a drink, then another, and that the nightmarish pattern of her teenage years would repeat itself.

Unwilling to spoil the evening, Marisa changed the subject, telling Blake how glad she was that she was living with Lauren and could help her care for Fiona. By the time she'd exhausted the topic, they were pulling into the parking lot of what was considered to be one of the most elegant restaurants in the Hill Country.

Strawberry Chantilly lived up to the hype. With formally clad waiters, fine linens and china, and tables set far enough apart to ensure privacy, it was the perfect spot for a romantic evening. Plush carpet and heavy draperies muffled the other guests' conversations, while the soft music added to the atmosphere.

Marisa might have been ambivalent about living in Dupree, but there was no question that dinner with Blake was the most enjoyable evening she'd spent in a long time. The food was delicious, the service attentive, the company wonderful.

She and Blake talked about everything from politics to pasta, and though they didn't always agree, that didn't matter. What mattered was that they were sharing parts of themselves. They picked up where they had left off before she had let Ken Blake get in the way, but tonight's discussion was at a deeper level.

The fact that there had been a rift between them gave everything they said a heightened importance, as if they were seeking to ensure that there would be no further misunderstandings. And though there were a few moments of awkwardness when Marisa recalled how she'd misjudged Blake, they were soon outweighed by the sheer pleasure of candlelight, crystal, and fine cuisine.

When they'd savored the last bite of dessert and drained their coffee cups, Blake rose and pulled out Marisa's chair, leading her outside. Perhaps it was because the evening was cool; perhaps there was another reason Blake wrapped his arm around her shoulders and drew her close to him. The reason didn't matter. What mattered was that Marisa felt cherished as they walked slowly toward his car. Blake's gentle embrace deepened that feeling, warming her more than she had believed possible.

Stars sparkled in the moonless sky, a light breeze rustled the trees, nocturnal animals scurried across the ground. It was an ordinary autumn evening, and yet it was anything but ordinary for Marisa. For the first time ever, she felt as if she were where she was meant to be. For the first time ever, she felt as if she were with a man who would not betray her, a man who just might be the one man in the world meant for her. For the first time ever, she felt beautiful, and it was all due to the man at her side.

When they reached the car, Blake paused. Turning to face Marisa, he placed his hand beneath her chin, cupping it, sending shivers of delight through her veins as he caressed her skin.

"I want to kiss you," he said softly, "but I won't if you don't want me to."

Her heart beating so wildly it threatened to burst through her ribs, she smiled at him. "Kiss me, Blake," Marisa said, amazed that she could form a coherent sentence when all she could think about was being kissed by Blake Kendall. "Kiss me," she said softly, and he did.

His lips were tender, tasting of the praline pastry he'd had for dessert. His hands were firm, their warmth comforting her as he drew her closer to him. His embrace was everything she'd dreamed of and more.

As their lips met, Marisa wrapped her arms around Blake's neck, savoring the faint prickle of his hair beneath her fingertips. And for a moment, nothing mattered but the fact that she was with Blake, feeling his heart beat, smelling the spicy scent of his aftershave, hearing the soft rustle of his suit coat as he raised his hand to caress her hair. This was the perfect way to end the day.

# 26

Marisa was still smiling the next morning. When she thought about the kiss, all she could do was smile. It had felt so good, so right, to be in Blake's arms with his lips pressed to hers. The drive back to Dupree had been almost as wonderful. They'd talked and talked. They'd talked about little things, about big things, about how sometimes silence was as powerful as words. And while they'd both agreed they couldn't start over, they were equally determined to give their relationship a second chance.

Marisa liked the sound of that, she reflected as she slid behind the wheel of her car. Though she wasn't sure what the future would bring, whether it would lead to marriage as Lauren predicted, right now, it felt good to live one day at a time. Marisa's smile turned to a frown. She was starting to sound like Eric. That was what he claimed he and all recovering alcoholics did: live one day at a time.

Marisa didn't want to spoil her day by thinking about Eric, but she couldn't stop. Every time she drove, the absence of the familiar rattle reminded her that, even though she hadn't asked him to, he had repaired her car. She appreciated that. That was why she'd given Eric a bottle of Old Spice.

It had been common courtesy, nothing more, no reason for his eyes to mist. Marisa had said thank you—she'd even smiled a bit more than normal—but that didn't mean she was ready to let Eric into her heart again. That was the road to heartache, and that was a road Marisa had no intention of taking.

A few minutes later, her smile once more restored as she thought of Blake and the fact that he'd suggested they schedule another movie and sundae evening, Marisa parked the car in its usual spot and headed into the lodge. To her surprise, her mother appeared to be waiting for her, her normally placid face twisted into a frown.

"I can't believe it!" Mom cried, her distress evident by the heavier than normal accent. "They promised me!" She followed that statement with a volley of such rapid Spanish that Marisa struggled to understand it.

"Slow down, Mom. Start from the beginning and tell me what happened." She drew her mother into her office and urged her to sit down. Though Mom sat, she continued to twist her apron in an uncharacteristically nervous gesture.

"The company in Dallas called. They said their shipment of linen was delayed and they won't have the tablecloths to us in time."

No wonder Mom was so upset. She'd been the one to select this supplier. Though Marisa had offered to help, Mom had insisted that she could handle it, pointing out that Marisa had enough to do without trying to find tablecloths.

Unlocking her desk, Marisa pulled out the file. "Let me call them and see what I can do. Maybe I can threaten them with breach of contract." Not that doing so would make the tablecloths suddenly appear, but it might encourage the supplier to propose alternatives.

Half an hour later, Marisa was as frustrated as her mother. The ship carrying the linen destined to be turned into tablecloths for Rainbow's End had been delayed by a hurricane. That made it an act of God, one of the specific exclusions in the contract. Even worse, the supplier had no suggestions for other sources of table linens.

"I hate having to tell Kate," Mom wailed when Marisa explained what she'd learned. "She'll be so disappointed."

Though it might seem like a small thing to others, Marisa knew how much Kate had been counting on the tablecloths. She wanted everything to be extra special for Thanksgiving, to make it a celebration for the guests who might otherwise not have had much of a holiday.

"There's got to be a way to fix this," Marisa said, although her brain refused to provide a solution. The fact that her mother was so upset bothered her more than Kate's possible disappointment. "Don't say anything to Kate yet. I want to think about it, and you've got some meals to prepare." Perhaps if Mom returned to the kitchen and started cooking, she'd be able to relax and Marisa would be able to find an answer.

Armed with a pad of paper, a pencil, and a pair of scissors, Marisa walked down the short hallway to the dining room. The tables had started their lives as ordinary round pine tables. What made them unique was the addition of a lazy Susan in the center. It was a wonderful way of serving food family style, eliminating the constant stream of "please pass the butter" requests and the question of where to store the various bowls and platters. But, while the Susans worked admirably for serving, they also made fitting tablecloths a challenge. Somehow, the cloth had to fit underneath the Susan and around the pole that attached it to the table. And that, Marisa suspected, was not easy. That was probably the reason none of Rainbow's End's previous owners had used tablecloths.

Marisa sat at one of the tables and stared at the Susan. She wasn't certain what the supplier in Dallas had planned to do, but she could think of only one way to make this work. She would have to cut a hole in the center of a round tablecloth to provide space for the rod, then slit the fabric to maneuver it underneath the Susan. She ripped a piece of paper from the pad and started to cut it into a circle.

"I didn't know I was missing arts and crafts time."

Marisa looked up and smiled. Blake might not be able to solve her problems, but just having him in the same room boosted her spirits. "I wish it were that simple. I'm trying to figure out how to make cloths for these tables."

"I can see where that would be a challenge. They're like outdoor umbrella tables."

"You're right." Marisa shook her head, wondering why she hadn't recognized the similarity. It wasn't as if she'd never seen an umbrella table. For the first time since Mom had told her about the problem, Marisa felt a glimmer of hope. The tables themselves were a standard size. Perhaps there were ready-made tablecloths she could have shipped to Rainbow's End in time for Thanksgiving. They might not be as nice as the ones Mom had ordered, but at least they'd cover the tables and make the day a bit more special.

"I need to do some online shopping." Marisa headed back to her office and its computer, smiling when Blake followed her and pulled a chair next to hers. Though he admitted that he'd never shopped for table linens, he claimed everyone needed moral support. He provided that, making Marisa laugh even when she realized that none of the commercially available umbrella cloths would meet Kate's expectations. The fabrics were too casual, and the exposed zipper was definitely not a look Kate would approve.

"What about place mats?" Blake asked. "That's what my dad uses for special occasions. I don't think he ever owned a tablecloth."

Marisa wrinkled her nose. "Spoken like a man. You didn't see place mats at Strawberry Chantilly, did you?"

"Do I get points for saying that I didn't notice anything other than the beautiful woman who was my companion?"

"You get points," Marisa agreed, flattered by his sweet words, "but Kate still wants tablecloths, and the last time I checked, she was still my boss. I need to find a way to make her happy."

Marisa clicked on the site that offered the least offensive tablecloths and studied it, trying to convince herself that oilcloth would be acceptable for one weekend. She failed. As much as she hated to, she was going to disappoint both Mom and Kate.

She was about to close the browser window when a small ad on the right caught her eye. Marisa grinned.

"If you were a writer, I'd say inspiration just struck," Blake said when she clicked on the ad.

"It did." Marisa pointed to the monitor. "I realized that I can buy regular round tablecloths and modify them. I'm not a master seamstress like Lauren, but I know how to use a sewing machine. All I need are the right materials."

"What do you think?" Marisa asked a few minutes later when she found a supplier in San Antonio who promised overnight delivery anywhere in the US. They had a variety of round tablecloths in the correct size, including one in the ivory linen Kate preferred.

"It looks good," Blake agreed, "but you won't be able to judge the quality until they arrive. Why don't we pay them a visit? You can see if you like the fabrics, and if you don't, they may have other merchandise that's not listed on the website."

"You're right." Marisa switched off her computer and reached for her purse. "I'm on my way."

Blake feigned a pout. "Did you miss the part where I said 'we'? I'll drive."

The restaurant supply house in San Antonio proved to be even better than Marisa had expected. Blake had been correct. They did have items not shown online, and since Marisa needed only eight of each design, she had more choices than she'd anticipated.

"What exactly are you going to do with them?" the clerk asked. "You said the tables were special."

"They have lazy Susans in the center, so I need to cut a hole and make a slit to get them onto the table. I thought I'd use invisible zippers to close them."

The clerk shook her head. "That won't work. The fabric won't lay flat once you've inserted the zipper. That's why umbrella cloths have exposed zippers. They make up for the fabric that's turned under in the seam allowance."

Marisa frowned. If she'd been as experienced at sewing as

Lauren, she would have realized that and not have wasted her and Blake's time.

"The owner has her heart set on having formal tablecloths. A wide exposed zipper isn't what she's expecting."

Though the clerk looked sympathetic, she offered no suggestions, perhaps because there were none.

"Here's what the tables look like," Blake said as he showed her one of the pictures he'd taken with his cell phone.

The clerk studied it for a moment. "It's pretty. Do you always have eight settings at the table?"

Marisa shook her head. "Not always, but we will when we use the tablecloths. Why do you ask?"

"I have an idea. It'll be more work, but you could use a piece of trim to cover the zipper. If you do that, I suggest adding seven more like spokes on a wheel. That way the zipper wouldn't be obvious."

"And we'd have clearly defined place settings." It was a wonderful idea and one that might not have occurred to the clerk if Blake hadn't shown her the picture. Marisa smiled as she envisioned the finished product. "I like it. Do you by any chance sell trim?"

"No, but there are a couple of great places in the city." The clerk scribbled names and addresses on a piece of paper.

When they were back in Blake's car with their purchases safely stowed in the trunk, he shot Marisa an amused glance. "When you told me you enjoyed procurement, I didn't realize what it involved."

"Neither did I. I feel as if I'm on a treasure hunt, and thanks to you, we have a good chance of finding that treasure." Marisa settled back in the seat after entering the address of the first notions store into the car's GPS. "This is more fun than preparing tax returns."

By noon, they'd acquired everything Marisa needed, and after visiting the drive-through lane of a fast-food restaurant, they took their lunches to a small park.

"This is hardly competition for Strawberry Chantilly," Blake said as they spread their food on one of the tables overlooking the pond, "but the shake isn't bad."

"And we get live entertainment." Marisa pointed at the pair of ducks that was squabbling over a piece of bread left by a previous visitor.

Though loud, Blake's peal of laughter did not appear to faze the ducks. "That's one way of describing it," he said with another laugh. "You're amazing, Marisa."

"Hardly."

"Yes, you are. You're the only person I've dated who looks just as happy sitting on a metal bench eating a greasy burger as she did dining at a fancy French restaurant."

Keeping a firm grip on her burger, lest the ducks that were waddling ever closer decide to snatch a bite, Marisa smiled at Blake. "It's the company that makes the difference."

---

"Does Kate know you're doing this?" Lauren asked as Marisa spread the first tablecloth on the cutting table in the back of HCP.

Marisa shook her head. "I thought I'd wait until I had a finished product to show her. I told Mom, so she's no longer worried, but as far as Kate knows, we're still expecting the custom cloths she approved. I want to surprise her."

Though the original plan had been to have only one set of ivory tablecloths with matching napkins that could be used on Sunday and for holidays, Marisa had ended up buying three sets. The ones she'd chosen for Thanksgiving were printed with cornucopias and other autumnal motifs in seasonal colors. Those would have a dark brown braid covering the zipper and marking each of the place settings.

Unable to resist the idea of special table coverings for Christmas as well as Thanksgiving, Marisa had been disappointed to learn that the store had only four red cloths, but when she'd found four green ones in the same fabric, she had snatched them up and had bought gold trim to give them a festive look. And, keeping in mind Kate's wish for Sunday dinners with linen tablecloths, she'd selected plain ivory cloths with a fancy woven braid in the same shade. Those would be subtle but elegant, exactly what she thought Kate had envisioned.

"I wish I could help you with this," Lauren said, her expression telegraphing her disappointment, "but . . ."

"You've got your own work, not to mention taking care of Fiona." When she'd embarked on this project, Marisa had known she would have to do it alone. Undoubtedly, Lauren would have been able to make the modifications to the tablecloths faster than Marisa, but she had other commitments, and the town's one seamstress had just had carpal tunnel surgery.

Lauren glanced at her watch and frowned. "I've got to run. Betsy Lenhardt is staying with Fiona this afternoon, and you know what a clock watcher she is. I'll never hear the end of it if I'm late."

"Where's Drew?" As far as Marisa knew, he never took a day off.

"He said he had to talk to Greg about something. I didn't want to pry."

"Of course not." Marisa wouldn't be surprised if Drew was actually talking to Mom, trying to get ideas about Christmas gifts for Lauren and Fiona. He'd mentioned something about the number of shopping days until Christmas.

As she reached for her bag, Lauren frowned. "I forgot to tell you. Maggie Roberts was in this morning. She said Hal and Tiffany are coming for Christmas. She made a point of mentioning that Hal was surprised to learn you and your dad are back in town. Apparently, he wants to see your father."

Marisa felt her heart sink. "That can't be good news."

"Exactly what I thought."

# 27

"Dinner call." Blake knocked on the door to Lauren's shop. Even though the shades were drawn and the sign read "closed," he knew that Marisa was inside, taking advantage of Lauren's sewing equipment, and that she was expecting the delivery.

"Thanks," she said as she opened the door. "I'm glad you came." Though a sweet smile lit Marisa's face, highlighting those blue eyes that haunted his dreams and his waking thoughts, Blake thought she looked preoccupied, maybe even a bit worried. That was only natural, considering all that she had to accomplish in a few days.

"Mom won't admit it," she continued, "but she doesn't like driving at night, even just the short drive to Dupree."

"Her loss is my gain."

When Carmen had told Blake that she was sending dinner because she doubted her daughter would take time to eat otherwise, he had jumped at the chance to spend more time with Marisa. "I thought you might appreciate some company," he said, "especially since it looks as if we're not going to get our movie and sundae evening this week." Blake lifted the insulated container onto the counter. "Your mom said she'd sent enough food for both of us."

Marisa chuckled as she pulled the plates and utensils from the side pockets. "This is my mother we're talking about. There's probably enough for at least four hungry lumberjacks."

"You could be right. It's pretty heavy." He unzipped the top and sniffed appreciatively. "It smells good."

"Chicken fricassee. That means there's chocolate pound cake too." Marisa chuckled as she arranged place settings on the counter. "I may actually survive the night."

After Marisa gave thanks for the food, she opened the containers her mother had sent, urging Blake to take large servings. "Mom may not be able to sew a straight seam, but no one has ever challenged her title as the culinary queen of Dupree."

It took only one bite for Blake to agree. Though it would be difficult to say which of Carmen St. George's meals was the best, this was in the top five. But Blake hadn't come here for food. He wanted to help Marisa. He glanced through the doorway into the large workroom that formed the back of Lauren's shop, seeing one of the Thanksgiving tablecloths spread out on a large work surface.

"I don't know anything about sewing. Is it hard work?"

Marisa appeared surprised by the question. "It's not physically demanding, but it requires a lot of precision."

"Like accounting, I would imagine."

"I suppose." Marisa sliced another of the flaky biscuits her mother had sent and covered it with the delicately flavored fricassee. "Somehow it seems more difficult to keep a piece of braid straight than to generate income and expense sheets."

"It'll probably get easier with practice."

Wrinkling her nose, Marisa pretended to frown. "I'll have plenty of that. I can't believe I committed to making eight tablecloths before Thanksgiving."

"Is there any way I can help?" Blake doubted she'd accept his offer. If Marisa was anything, it was fiercely independent.

To his surprise, she appeared to consider the question. "Would you mind holding the trim while I pin it?"

Elated by her willingness to include him in the project, Blake grinned. "Just show me how."

And so, after they'd finished their supper and packed away the dishes, Blake found himself leaning over a large worktable, holding the end of a piece of dark brown braid. His grandfather would have had something derogatory to say if he'd seen Blake doing what he'd have called women's work, but Blake didn't care. He was having too much fun watching Marisa.

He memorized the way she pursed her lips as she placed each pin, taking care to position it at a precise right angle to the braid. Though Blake doubted that the precision was necessary, he wouldn't say anything to disturb her concentration. Marisa was treating this tablecloth as if it were the space shuttle, acting as if human lives depended on everything being absolutely perfect. That was, he suspected, her way of trying to control a world where so much was out of her hands.

When the eight pieces of braid were aligned to Marisa's satisfaction, Blake helped her carry the tablecloth to the sewing machine, being careful not to dislodge any pins. She perched on the edge of the chair and leaned forward, guiding the fabric under what she told him was the presser foot.

Sewing seemed to relax her a bit, but when Marisa glanced up at him, Blake noticed that the same faintly worried expression he'd seen when he'd entered the shop was back.

"Is something wrong?"

She looked up, obviously startled by the question. "Why do you ask?"

"Because you seemed preoccupied when I came in, and now you're looking that way again."

Still feeding the fabric through the sewing machine, Marisa gave a short nod. "Oh, that. I heard that someone I don't particularly like is coming back to town."

The faint tremor in her voice told Blake this was more serious than she wanted to admit. "Who's that?"

She looked up, her lips twisted into an ironic smile. "The boy who stood me up for our senior prom."

"Tell me you're joking." Blake couldn't imagine anyone standing up a girl on such an important night. Melody, his date for their prom, had told him that she and her mother had spent two months preparing and that they'd wished for more time. For his part, Blake hadn't understood why it was such a big production, but he'd accepted the fact that fancy clothes, the right makeup and hairstyle, even the correct height of heels, were important to the female of the species. He'd been more worried about remembering the steps to the various dances Melody had said were her favorites.

"I'm not kidding."

As she continued to speak, telling him what had happened that May night eight years ago, Blake felt his anger rising. He knew people could be cruel—he'd made a small fortune writing about the various kinds of cruelty one person could inflict on another—but what Hal Lundquist had done to Marisa seemed especially mean.

If the man had been in Dupree today, Blake would have paid him a visit, demanding he do something to make up for the pain he'd caused Marisa. But Hal wasn't here, and Blake could do nothing other than sympathize with Marisa.

"I hope someone took him to task." Even as he pronounced them, the words felt inadequate. Hal had been the mayor's son, and from what Marisa had said, the mayor had ruled Dupree the way a medieval king ruled his country. No one would have dared to cross him or his son.

Marisa's smile was bittersweet. "My dad tried to talk to his father, but it didn't accomplish anything."

Eric St. George rose another notch in Blake's estimation. It must have taken a lot of courage to confront Hal's father.

"At least he tried." And that showed not simply courage but love. Blake wondered if Marisa realized how much her father loved her or whether she believed, as some children of alcoholics did, that that love had been replaced by love of the bottle.

Though Marisa nodded, the furrows between her eyes remained, leading Blake to believe that it was the present, not the past, that bothered her. "There's no reason you have to see Hal," he told her.

"I know, and I have no intention of looking for him. As far as I'm concerned, the past is the past." They were brave words, spoken with conviction, but Blake did not believe them. Marisa's expression said otherwise.

She shook her head slowly, almost as if she'd read his thoughts. "Meeting Hal is not what's worrying me. His mother-in-law said he wants to see my father."

"Why?"

"I don't know, but I don't like the possibilities."

She might not like the possibilities, but the concern he saw in Marisa's eyes encouraged Blake more than anything she had said. Whether she would admit it or not, Marisa still loved her father. The trick would be getting her to recognize that love.

———————✳———————

"You can open your eyes now."

It was Thanksgiving morning, and though it was hours before the dining room would be prepared for dinner, Marisa and her mother had set up one table to show Kate the new tablecloths and napkins. Though Marisa had worried about whether or not she would be able to keep the tablecloths a surprise, Kate hadn't asked to see them. She'd been so busy with other plans that all she'd cared about was whether or not there would be linens on the tables for Thanksgiving dinner.

Even with Blake's help, the sewing had taken longer than Marisa had expected, and she'd finished the final tablecloth only last night. But now the linens were ready, and if Marisa said so herself, they formed a striking background for the resort's white dishes.

Once everything was arranged, Marisa had knocked on the door to the owner's suite and told Kate she wanted to show her something. Her face paler than normal, Kate took a sip of what smelled like peppermint tea and followed Marisa down the stairs. When they reached the dining room door, Marisa insisted that Kate keep her eyes closed as she led her to the table, then urged her to open her eyes.

Kate did. The shock and disappointment were momentary, but Marisa saw them. Before she could explain, Kate nodded.

"It's beautiful and perfect for Thanksgiving," she said slowly, obviously choosing her words carefully, "but I'd be lying if I didn't tell you it's not what I expected. I thought we all agreed on plain white or ivory that we could use on Sundays."

Why had she thought that surprising Kate was a good idea?

"I'm sorry," Marisa said. "I should have told you what I was doing. The original supplier couldn't deliver, so I had to go with Plan B. This is part of it. We've got red and green for Christmas, plus a nice ivory for Sundays and other occasions. All three sets cost a bit less than the original supplier was going to charge for one."

Kate's hesitance disappeared, and she flung her arms around Marisa, giving her a big hug. "You're a wonder!" she declared. "Hiring you was the best thing Greg and I did."

Marisa felt herself flushing with pleasure. She'd worked long hours for Haslett, but she had never felt as fulfilled and appreciated as she did right now. It hadn't been a mistake, coming back to Dupree.

When Kate had oohed and aahed over the tablecloth and napkins, Marisa returned to the kitchen, intending to tell her mother that Kate was pleased. "Mom . . ." Her voice faded and the rest of her words deserted her as she walked through the doorway. Mom was standing next to the sink, her arms wrapped around Eric, her lips pressed to his.

"Sorry," she said and started to turn.

Though Marisa had obviously interrupted a tender moment, Mom didn't seem to care. Keeping her arms around her husband, she turned toward Marisa. "There's no need to leave."

Her voice was different, softer and sweeter than Marisa had

ever heard it. Her face was different too, glowing with happiness. The man at her side was equally at ease, his smile as radiant as a bridegroom's. Years may have etched lines in their faces, but their eyes had lost the faintly haunted look that Marisa had thought was normal for them, leaving them looking almost carefree.

"I just wanted to tell you that Kate's happy with the tablecloths," she said as she spun on her heel and left.

She was only a few steps down the hallway when Eric caught up with her. "I'm sorry if we embarrassed you." Though he started to put his hand on her arm to stop her, he pulled back at the last second. "I know it's hard for some kids to realize that their parents aren't strangers to romance."

That wasn't the issue. Marisa had come to terms with the fact that her parents had once been in love. It was the way that love had ended that concerned her. "I'm worried about Mom. I've never seen her so happy."

Eric looked surprised. "Why would that worry you?"

"Because it might not last. What will she do if you leave again?"

His eyes clouded for a second, and he lowered them to keep Marisa from reading his thoughts. When he met her gaze again, Eric's expression was solemn. "I'm not leaving, Marisa. You've got to trust me when I say that I won't do anything to hurt either your mother or you."

Trust him. If only she could.

In case you haven't figured it out, I'm wooing you."

Marisa caught herself just as her foot started to tangle in a tree root. If there were a more unusual setting for a declaration of courtship, she didn't know what it would be. No moonlight and roses, not even a romantic table for two. Instead, she and Blake were hiking in a small forest. The scent of cedar mingled with the dusty smell of dried leaves underfoot, while the less pleasant aroma of a skunk lingered in the air. They were walking side by side, and they'd been chatting until he startled her with his unexpected words. There was nothing passionate about Blake's declaration. It was a simple statement of fact.

Marisa decided to respond in kind. "That's what Lauren said." Fortunately, her voice remained even, not betraying the sudden acceleration of her pulse. "Of course, Lauren has love and marriage on her mind."

She might claim otherwise, but Marisa was certain Lauren hoped Drew would repeat his offer of marriage. If he did, Lauren's answer would be very different from the first time.

Grabbing the branch blocking the path, Blake held it aside so Marisa could pass by. "I can't believe the change in Drew," he said when they resumed their previous pace. "He looks the same, but his behavior is so different that if it weren't for the physical proof, I wouldn't recognize him as the man I knew at Stanford."

The day Fiona had been released from traction, Lauren and Drew had taken her to a movie and had invited Marisa and Blake to join them. It had been the first time Marisa had seen the two men together since Kate and Greg's wedding, and she'd found the contrast between them intriguing. On the surface, Drew appeared more gregarious, and it was obvious that he doted on Fiona, but Marisa still worried that he would become bored with Dupree and leave Lauren with a broken heart.

"Do you really believe Drew has changed?" Lauren said he wasn't the same man he'd been last spring, but Lauren was looking at Drew through the eyes of love, and they were as unreliable as rose-tinted glasses.

"Yes." There was no hesitation in Blake's response. "He's kinder. I'd even go so far as to say that he's a better person than he used to be."

"I hope so for Lauren's sake, but I'm not convinced that people can change. Not fundamentally." Marisa had heard Eric's protestations that he would change, that this time would be different, too many times to believe they were more than empty words. Though he seemed different since he'd returned, more like the daddy she remembered from her earliest childhood, she was afraid it would not last.

"Why not?" Blake stopped to flip open his water bottle and take a long swig. They'd been walking for close to an hour on what he'd told Marisa would be a three hour round-trip hike.

"I've changed," he said, "and it's not simply the direction of my writing. Your questions made me look at my whole life differently."

"Are you saying that I was responsible for the change?" Marisa couldn't believe that. She'd begged and begged Eric to stop drinking, but no matter how she pleaded, it had never been enough.

"No." Blake shook his head. "No one can change another person. That's up to the individual and God. But you pointed me in the right direction." And unlike Eric, Blake had listened to Marisa.

"Is that why you're wooing me?" She tried not to giggle at the word.

Wooing and courtship sounded like terms from a historical romance novel, not a conversation taking place in the twenty-first century.

"No. I'm grateful for that, and I'd even call you my muse, but that's not a reason for wooing or courtship or any of those old-fashioned words."

Marisa smiled at the realization that Blake shared her opinion, at least on that particular terminology. He stopped and faced her, his expression solemn.

"The fact is, I'm attracted to you. Not just your beautiful face, but what's inside you. I'm attracted to the woman who goes out of her way to make a little girl feel like a princess. I'm attracted to the woman who'd endure sleepless nights and countless pinpricks so that her friend could have special tablecloths. I'm even attracted to the woman who was willing to wear a silly costume to entertain less fortunate families and help make their Thanksgiving a memorable one."

They were beautiful words, wonderful words, words that made Marisa want to shout with joy.

Blake stretched his hand out and clasped hers. "You're a very special woman, Marisa. I felt that the first time I saw you. That's why I want to spend more time with you, so we can learn whether we have a future together. That's why I'm trying to woo you."

As he'd spoken, a lump had risen to fill Marisa's throat. No one had ever said such things to her. They made her feel as if she, not Fiona, was the princess. Marisa had given Fiona a sparkly tiara to wear while she was lying in bed, but Blake had given Marisa a priceless crown of heartfelt words.

"I wish I were as eloquent as you," she said, swallowing to dislodge the lump. They had resumed walking side by side, their pace a bit slower than before, as if neither one was in a hurry to reach the summit of the small hill that Blake had said was their destination. "I'm not a wordsmith like you. I make my living with numbers, and numbers aren't a lot of good where feelings are concerned."

"What do your feelings tell you?"

*That there's something incredibly wonderful about being here, my hand in yours. That I'm beginning to understand the adage that it's the journey that's important, not the final destination. That I wish this day would never end.* But Marisa said none of those things. Instead she gave Blake's hand a little squeeze and said, "That I like you very much and that I want to spend more time with you."

Perhaps she should have stopped there, but she'd been raised to be honest, and so she continued. "I have to warn you, though. I'm not the wonderful person you described. Deep inside, I'm scared." Marisa paused, not wanting to say anything more but knowing that she owed him a full explanation. "I'm afraid of being hurt the way my mother was."

Blake nodded as if he understood. "I'm not an alcoholic, Marisa."

"Eric wasn't either at the beginning."

"If we get to the point of marriage—and I hope we will—I promise you that I will never abandon you."

And that was the crux of her fear. The first therapist she'd seen had told Marisa that her fundamental fear was of abandonment and that until she overcame that, she'd be unable to form a lasting relationship. Colleen had agreed and had insisted that Marisa's problems with anger were the result of those fears. "You can't solve one without solving the other," Colleen had said.

"I want to believe you. I do." Perhaps that was why Marisa was clinging to Blake's hand right now.

"That's what courtship is all about." He stopped, disengaging his hand from hers, and turned so he was facing her. "It's a chance for us to learn about each other, to learn to trust." As the corners of his lips curved into a smile, he added, "A chance for a few other things too."

Slowly, as if he were approaching a skittish animal, Blake raised his hand to touch Marisa's cheek. For a long moment, he said nothing, simply smiled as he caressed her skin. Then his fingers wandered to trace the outline of her lips. It was less intimate than a kiss, and yet the touch of his fingertips sent the same shivers of pleasure through Marisa that his kisses had. She gazed at him, wondering if he would kiss her. Instead, he began to speak.

"I probably shouldn't admit this." He gave her an almost sheepish look. "It's not exactly a macho thing to say, but this is scary for me too. I'm thirty-two years old, and this is my first experience with love. Growing up in an all-male household, I didn't have a good role model for love."

Marisa nodded, remembering Blake's stories of his grandfather's unreasonable demands.

"I dated a bit in high school and college," Blake continued, "but it was never serious. Then, once I was on my own, I met a woman I thought might be the one." He shook his head. "She wasn't. Neither was the second one. Afterwards I realized that what I'd felt for them had been attraction, not love."

Blake's expression softened as he cupped Marisa's chin. "It's different this time. I don't know where we're headed, but I do believe that God brought our paths together for a reason."

She wanted to believe it. Oh, how she wanted to believe it. Marisa managed a small smile. "I thought you were special the day we met, and that scared me. I'm still scared now."

His hand moved, gliding gently along her neck. "Don't be scared. I love you, Marisa. Let me show you how much."

And then he lowered his lips to hers, giving her the kiss she longed for, sending sparks of excitement to every nerve ending, warming her more than the Texas sun. Birds chirped, squirrels scampered, and Marisa sighed with pleasure as the man she loved held her in his embrace.

———— ✦ ————

"You look like a woman who's dreaming about the man she loves." Kate cut a tiny piece from a slice of pineapple and speared it with her fork.

"And you look like a woman who's not feeling well." Though

this was supposed to be a breakfast meeting to finalize the Christmas celebration, Marisa appeared to be the only person eating.

Kate shook her head. "I'm fine. It's just that I'm not much of a breakfast person. But don't let that stop you." She gestured toward the buffet with its selection of pastries, cereals, and yogurt. "You'll need energy for all that we have planned, starting with the parade and the costumes for the float, but before we talk about Christmas, tell me about you and Blake. From an outsider's view, it looks like something has changed."

Lauren had said the same thing when Marisa returned from the hike. "There's not much to tell," Marisa said, repeating the story she'd given Lauren. "We're trying to figure out whether we have a future together." They'd been doing that ever since the day they'd gone to Strawberry Chantilly, but the hike and the conversation they'd shared had drawn them closer and had deepened their relationship.

"You're giving an awfully good imitation of two people in love." Kate took another bite of pineapple, washing it down with a sip of herb tea.

"Does love mean being confused? That's the way I feel." When Kate merely crooked an eyebrow, encouraging Marisa to continue, she did. "I've never felt like this before. I love the time we spend together, and now I'm worried about what it'll be like when Blake goes to Pennsylvania. I hate the idea of being apart for two weeks."

That was part of what confused Marisa, that and the fear that this was nothing more than a dream and that she'd wake to discover Blake had never existed. Marisa didn't know how she'd bear that. In the past, she'd prided herself on her independence. She hadn't needed anyone to make her life complete, but now Blake had become such an integral part of her life that she dreaded being separated.

Kate nodded. "Greg mentioned that he was going away. Blake said we could rent out his cabin while he's visiting his dad, but neither of us wants to do that." She chuckled. "We've started calling it 'Blake's cabin' rather than its official name. But I'm digressing. Is there anything I can do to help unconfuse you?"

"I don't think so. It's something I need to work out on my own."

"I know you probably don't want any advice, but I'm going to give it anyway. Don't let Blake slip away. Greg says he's one of the good guys."

"That's what I think too."

✳

"You look especially happy, Fiona." Lauren smiled at her daughter, who was sitting in the living room watching one of her favorite movies for what had to be the hundredth time. "Did you have a good time with Mr. Drew?"

"The best. He bought me lunch." Now that she was out of traction and back to school, Drew no longer spent his days with Fiona, but today was an exception. With the teachers having an in-service day, Drew had resumed his babysitting duties.

"Where did you go? The Sit 'n' Sip?" There wasn't much question about that, since the small restaurant was Dupree's only eating establishment.

Fiona shook her head so vigorously that her braids slapped against her cheeks. "Oh no. Mr. Drew took me to Blytheville. Did you know they have a real diner there? It's all silvery on the outside, and we had the best burgers and shakes, and he even showed me how to play the jukebox."

This was vintage Fiona, talking a mile a minute. It was no wonder she looked so happy. There hadn't been time or money for excursions like that for quite a while. Though the diner wasn't especially expensive, the cost of two meals combined with the gas to get to Blytheville had been beyond Lauren's budget.

"That must have been fun. I hope you thanked him."

Fiona rolled her eyes, as if the answer should be apparent. "Yes, Mom. I know my manners." She was silent for a few seconds, fiddling with the remote. When she looked up, Lauren saw an almost calculating expression in her eyes. "What are you gonna wear tonight?"

"I haven't decided." Drew had invited her to dinner at Strawberry

Chantilly, saying he wanted to see if it lived up to the hype and declaring that since he couldn't possibly eat there alone, Lauren would be doing him a big favor if she agreed to be his date. Trying to avoid the impression she was a love-struck teenager eager to spend time with her boyfriend, Lauren had simply agreed that she'd enjoy the evening out.

"I think you should wear Grandma's old dress," Lauren's fashion consultant/daughter announced.

Lauren hadn't thought about the dress in years. It probably fit, because she'd regained some of the weight she'd lost during Patrick's illness, and it was a beautiful gown. Made of ivory satin, it had a tea-length skirt, the full sleeves that were so popular in the eighties when Mom had bought it, and heavy ecru lace trim on its bodice and deep cuffs. Though hardly the height of current fashion, it was old enough to have a vintage appeal. Even better, it was a dress Drew hadn't seen.

"That's a great idea." Lauren brushed a kiss on Fiona's head. "I think I will."

Two hours later, Drew gave her an appreciative look as he entered the house and whistled. To Lauren's surprise, he also winked at Fiona.

"Told you so," Fiona said with a grin that would have put the Cheshire cat to shame.

Lauren gave her daughter a stern look. "What did you tell Mr. Drew?"

Feigning innocence, Fiona said, "That you had a real pretty dress." She looked up at Drew, as if asking him to corroborate her story. Something was definitely going on here, but Lauren suspected she would have to wait until she got her daughter alone to get to the bottom of it.

"The dress is pretty," Drew agreed, "but the woman inside is beautiful." Though the words were sweet, it was the look that accompanied them that made Lauren blush.

"You're a smooth-talking man," she said, wishing she could blame the color in her cheeks on the heat. When she heard a car engine stop, she gave Fiona a kiss and turned to Drew. "Marisa's here, so we can leave."

It must be her imagination that Drew, never at a loss for words, seemed quieter than usual, Lauren told herself as she settled back in the comfortable seat and prepared to enjoy the drive to Blytheville. But when she tried to introduce subjects, even ones as innocuous as his lunch with Fiona, Drew's replies were terse.

How strange. It was only when they reached Strawberry Chantilly and were seated at a secluded corner table that Drew leaned forward.

"We need to talk," he said abruptly. "I know I didn't say much on the drive, but that wasn't the right time or place. This is better."

Lauren tried to keep her expression neutral while she felt panic make its way through her veins. Drew was about to deliver bad news, and she had a good idea what it was. He was leaving Dupree. This would be their final evening together.

She should have listened to Marisa. But Lauren had let herself dream, especially when Drew had been so kind to Fiona. Now those dreams were ending.

Though she wanted to say something, Lauren could not force the words out. Instead, she simply nodded at Drew, encouraging him to continue. There was no point in delaying the inevitable.

Drew's eyes were solemn as he said, "Ever since I arrived in Dupree, I've been thinking about my future. You know I was at a crossroads when I arrived. I'd lost my job and wasn't sure what I was going to do with the rest of my life."

"Now you've made a decision." The way he looked, the way he spoke, told Lauren he had chosen his direction.

To her surprise, Drew shook his head slightly. "No, but I have a few ideas. I've been thinking about opening a web design and hosting service. It wouldn't be huge, but even fifty employees would be good for Dupree."

It took a second for his words to register, and as they did, the dread that had threatened to choke her began to subside. She'd been wrong, at least about one thing.

"You want to start a business in Dupree?" This was more than Lauren had hoped for. When she'd dreamt of a future together, she had thought it would involve moving to California. She'd told herself that Fiona would adjust to a new home and that she'd make friends quickly. She'd tried to convince herself that she would enjoy opening a shop in a new area. Lauren had never allowed herself to hope that the three of them could forge a future in Dupree.

Drew nodded slowly. "That depends."

"I'm sure there won't be any issues with zoning or permits." The mayor and town council would be so thrilled with the idea of a successful entrepreneur like Drew Carroll settling in their town that they'd offer him anything he wanted.

"I wasn't worried about them."

Though her throat was dry, Lauren was afraid to take a sip lest her nerves choke her. "Then what are you worried about?" she asked as calmly as she could.

"You." Drew edged closer, his blue eyes serious as he said, "When I think about the future, much of it is fuzzy, but one thing is clear: I want you to be part of it." He paused, giving her a little smile before he continued. "I love you, Lauren, and I want you to be my wife."

This was the second time he'd said that. The first time she hadn't dared to believe he was serious, and she'd known she wasn't ready. This time, Lauren had no doubts. Marriage to Drew was everything she wanted, her fondest dreams coming true. She had seen him with Fiona, and she knew he'd be kind to her. He might not love Fiona as Patrick had, but Drew would be a positive role model, as good a stepfather as Lauren was likely to find for her daughter. "I—"

He held up a cautioning hand. "Please let me finish. It's not just you I love. I also love your daughter." Lauren started to gasp, then forced herself not to react. Let him finish, he'd asked, and she would.

"I would never have wished that broken leg on her," Drew continued, "but it turned out to be a blessing. It gave us time to get to know each other. I learned that I love Fiona, mismatched socks and all. I love her almost as much as I love you." He paused, his gaze fixed on her. "Will you do it, Lauren? Will you marry me?"

Yes, yes, yes! Though she wanted to jump out of her chair, throw her arms around Drew, and accept his proposal, Lauren knew there was one step she had to take before she did any of that. "I love you, Drew," she told him, hoping he'd read the sincerity in her eyes. "I want to marry you, but first I need to talk to Fiona."

The little smile she'd seen teasing his lips turned into a grin. "No, you don't. I've heard that in the past a man would ask his prospective bride's father for permission to marry her. I couldn't do that, so I did the next best thing: I asked your daughter. That's why I took her to lunch today, to see if she was willing for me to be her new daddy."

"And she agreed." The giggles and the wink were starting to make sense. This was why Fiona had been so excited this afternoon.

"See for yourself." Drew reached into his coat pocket and handed Lauren a piece of paper.

She recognized the lined sheet as one from Fiona's school pad. Unfolding it, she saw her daughter's sloppy handwriting and words that made her catch her breath.

*Dear Mom,*
*I want Mr. Drew to be my new daddy.*

*Love, Fiona*

Tears of joy pricked Lauren's eyes. "Oh, Drew. I don't know what to say. You thought of everything."

Reaching into his other pocket, he pulled out a square jeweler's box and opened it to reveal the most magnificent emerald ring she'd ever seen.

"Say yes," Drew urged as he slid the ring onto her left hand.

Lauren did.

29

O h, Lauren, I'm so happy for you!" Marisa gave her friend another hug, smiling at Lauren's exuberance. She'd been doing
an imitation of the Snoopy dance ever since she'd returned from
dinner with Drew, sporting what had to be a three-carat emerald
ring. Any doubts Marisa might have had about the match vanished
at the sight of Lauren's happiness and the love she'd seen glowing
from Drew's eyes when he'd left his fiancée a few minutes after
accepting Marisa's congratulations.

"I don't think we surprised you."

"You didn't. You might say I had some insider information."
When Lauren raised a questioning eyebrow, Marisa continued.
"Fiona told me she and Drew discussed more than burgers and
jukeboxes at lunch. I've never seen her so excited." And that was
saying a lot, because Fiona was a naturally excitable child, or she
had been before Patrick's death.

"The front door had barely closed behind you when she told me
Drew was going to be her new daddy. I heard all about how Fiona
wants to be your flower girl and how she'll even wear matching
white socks if you let her have the frilly pink dress she saw in a
magazine."

"Matching socks, huh? This is serious." Lauren sank onto the couch and extended her left hand, staring at the ring as if she couldn't believe she was now an engaged woman. "Drew and I were thinking about a very small wedding."

"You might want to rethink that. I got the distinct impression that Fiona has her heart set on this. She has visions of the church filled with people as she walks down the aisle. She told me she'd agree to a blue dress if you insisted, and you know she doesn't like blue this week."

Fiona's tastes seemed to change more often than the weather, making it a challenge to get her ready for school. Church was easier, because she had only two dresses to choose from, and neither was blue.

Lauren nodded slowly. "It would be nice to have all of Dupree there. The townspeople supported me when Patrick was so ill and afterward. I'd like to have them share the beginning of my new life." Lauren fingered her ring again. "I have to talk to Drew, but if we go ahead with a big wedding, will you be my maid of honor?"

Pretending to consider the question, Marisa tipped her head to one side and feigned a serious expression. "Do I have to wear matching socks?"

Lauren's reply was instantaneous. "You can wear striped socks like the wicked witches from *The Wizard of Oz* if that makes you happy. I just want you at my side."

"Of course I'll be your maid of honor. Again." Though she'd been devastated by the prom debacle and her father's disappearance, Marisa had put on a smiling face for Lauren and Patrick's wedding, wearing the cranberry taffeta gown Lauren had designated for her maid of honor, while the bridesmaids wore pink.

"Thank you." Lauren gave Marisa another hug, then settled back on the couch. "I know you didn't like Drew at first, but he's changed. The new Drew is everything I want in a husband and a father for Fiona."

"It wasn't so much that I didn't like Drew," Marisa said, wanting her best friend to understand. "It was that I was afraid he'd hurt you. All I ever wanted was for you to be happy."

"I am. I'm so happy I feel as if I could explode."

"I'd rather you didn't. That would be messy." They both laughed.

Marisa wasn't laughing an hour later as she began to wash her face. Was Lauren right? Did people change? Blake claimed he had, and Eric said he was a different person. Was it true, or were they simply empty words?

Blake was a simpler case. Marisa didn't believe he'd made a fundamental change. It was more a change of direction, getting back on the right track. Eric was different. If he really wasn't drinking and was determined that he'd never again take a drink, that was almost like a river suddenly flowing upstream. It couldn't happen without an enormous amount of inner strength. The question was whether Eric had that strength. Patting her face with a towel, Marisa admitted that she didn't know. Her heart and her head were telling her two different things. Which one was correct?

Returning to her bedroom, she knelt and bowed her head. *Dear Lord, I'm confused. I want to believe him. I know that you can wash away sins and create a new person. What I don't know is whether that happened. Help me understand. Please.*

———— ✳ ————

It had been a wonderful week, Blake reflected as he walked toward Marisa's office. Though both he and Marisa had been working—she on plans for Christmas, he on the second Logan Marsh book—they'd managed to spend time together each day. One night they'd had supper at the Sit 'n' Sip. Another they'd gone to the Bijou for a movie. Other evenings they'd simply walked around Rainbow's End, watching the stars reflecting on the lake. They'd talked about almost everything imaginable. Blake now knew that red was not Marisa's favorite color, and she knew that one puff of a cigarette when he was nine was enough to convince Blake not to smoke.

He knew Marisa was surprised that she didn't miss Atlanta. "Looking back, I realize I was lonely there," she told him. "I'm not lonely now." Nor was Blake. How could he be lonely when he was falling in love with this beautiful and complicated woman?

Blake took a deep breath, exhaling slowly. Greg had told him that if what he felt was true love and not mere infatuation, he would know. Blake did. He loved Marisa. He loved the caring she lavished on her friends and her dedication to her job. He loved her strong sense of right and wrong. He even loved her occasionally twisted sense of humor.

Blake loved everything about Marisa except her attitude toward her father. But that would change. It had to change.

The fact that she was no longer dyeing her hair and wearing colored contacts was a major step forward, at least in Blake's opinion. Surely the rest would follow. Surely she would overcome her anger and her fears and let love fill her heart. Surely this wonderfully warm and caring woman couldn't go through the rest of her life estranged from her father. And if she thought she could, everything Blake believed about her was called into question.

The door to her office was open. "Ready?" Blake asked as he stood in the doorway. An hour ago there had been papers strewn over the desk and sticky notes decorating her monitor, but now the office was in perfect order. Typical Marisa. She thrived on organization.

Grabbing her purse and a notepad, she nodded. "Let's escape before Kate remembers another person who needs a gift."

They were headed for an Angora goat farm with what was reputed to be the best gift shop in the area, planning to buy Christmas presents for Rainbow's End's staff and guests.

"I'm glad Kate agreed that Lauren couldn't make everything," Marisa said as she buckled her seatbelt. She was wearing a calf-length denim skirt and a chunky Irish knit sweater in deference to the Norther that had swept through the Hill Country yesterday. "Lauren was already overloaded, and now she has a wedding to plan."

Blake nodded. When he and Greg had jogged this morning, Greg had mentioned how pleased he was that Drew was settling down in Dupree.

"I heard your mom say she was going to make the cake."

"And cater the reception. Mom considers Lauren her second daughter. Even though she's like Lauren and has too much to do, she'd be hurt if Lauren didn't let her provide all the food."

Blake had heard Carmen mutter something about fearing she'd never have the opportunity to bake her own daughter's wedding cake. Though Blake didn't consider twenty-six old, in Carmen's mind, Marisa should have been married at least four years ago. But Blake wouldn't tell Marisa that her mother had confided such thoughts to him, and he certainly wouldn't admit that thoughts of weddings had been ricocheting through his brain and disturbing his sleep. He'd even given serious thought to engagement rings and honeymoon destinations.

"Mom's trying to figure out how we can throw a surprise shower." Blake was grateful that Marisa continued to talk about Lauren's engagement and appeared oblivious to the direction his thoughts had taken. "As you've probably figured out, it's tough to keep anything secret in Dupree."

Which was precisely the reason Blake hadn't told anyone other than Marisa and her father that he was also Ken Blake. Every time he and his agent spoke, Jack urged Blake to reveal his identity, saying it would be good for sales and for Blake himself. But he wasn't convinced, and he definitely was not ready for the media hoopla from such a revelation.

"Does that mean that everyone on your Christmas list will expect an angora sweater once they learn where we're going?" Blake asked.

Marisa shook her head. "Of course not. They'll expect mohair." When Blake looked confused, she chuckled. "They're Angora goats, but they produce mohair. Angora only comes from rabbits."

"My factoid for the day."

"I can give you a couple others, just in case you need some conversation starters. Angora goats are named for Ankara, the part of Turkey where they were developed. And, did you know that a mature doe can produce six to ten pounds of mohair a year?"

"All that from a diet of tin cans?" Blake wasn't remotely interested in Angora goats, but he wasn't going to discourage Marisa. The truth was, one aspect of her personality that he admired was her ability to absorb new information. He suspected she'd been researching goats online when he'd arrived, just so she could entertain him with trivia.

She laughed. "No tin cans. They like high protein diets, which include woody plants."

And the Hill Country had its share of that. No wonder there were so many goats here. Marisa had already told Blake that the Hill Country was a major source of mohair in the US.

"Here we are." Marisa pointed to the sign with its picture of the most unusual goat Blake had ever seen. Though he recognized the muzzle, beard, and floppy ears, the coat with its long curly fleece was far different from the goats he'd seen in Pennsylvania. So this was the source of the lightweight but warm sweater he'd received for his birthday one year.

"I've got my list," Marisa said as they entered the store. From the outside, it looked like an ordinary barn, but once they were indoors, Blake found his senses assaulted by a rainbow of colors. Tables piled with a seemingly endless variety of merchandise, racks bearing sweaters in every size and style imaginable, and bins filled with skeins of yarn all competed for his attention. As if she recognized his sensory overload, Marisa laid a hand on Blake's arm. "Do you want to wait outside?"

He shook his head. Perhaps he'd buy his-and-hers sweaters for Dad and Hilary. That would be his way of saying he didn't mind that they were a couple. Though he was naturally curious about the woman who now figured so heavily in Dad's conversation, Blake would be a hypocrite if he withheld his approval when he was hoping his father would approve of his relationship with Marisa.

Despite the plethora of choices, Blake made his selection within five minutes, thanks to a helpful clerk who, when learning his father's age and coloring, steered him to a conservative hunter green. It would take Marisa considerably longer, since there were thirty people on her list, so Blake settled on one of the benches near the window and watched.

By the end of half an hour, she had piles of garments on the counter and had returned her list to her bag. Though Blake thought she was ready to check out, she wandered to a table of men's scarves and fingered one in what Blake considered a particularly attractive shade of blue.

"Who's that for?" he asked, joining her by the scarves.

Marisa hesitated, her face clouding as she laid the scarf back on the pile. "No one."

Blake wasn't buying that story. "You looked like you were ready to take it."

She touched the scarf again before shaking her head. "I was, but he . . ." She broke off, clearly not wanting to say more.

Though he was afraid he knew the answer, Blake had to ask. "Who?"

"Eric."

The word came out as little more than a sigh. It was Blake who wanted to sigh at the realization that Marisa still refused to refer to Eric as her father. It was clear that the change he'd prayed for would be slow in coming.

"We need to talk. I'm worried about you."

Though she'd been staring at the scarf, Marisa raised her gaze to meet Blake's. "What do you mean?"

A busy store was not the place for what he needed to say. "Let's pay for these things and go outside."

When they'd loaded their purchases into the car, Blake led Marisa to a bench by the pasture where a dozen goats were grazing. Though their fleece wasn't as long as the pictures that decorated the shop's walls, it was clear that they hadn't been shorn for a few months.

One of the placards in the store had said that shearing typically took place in February and August. At the time he'd read it, Blake had wondered if Marisa would like to return in February to watch some of the goats being shorn. Now he wondered if, once she heard what he had to say, they'd still be a couple in February.

"I'm worried about you," Blake repeated when she was settled on one end of the bench. He took a seat a foot or so away from her, angling his body so he could watch her expression.

"Why? Just because I decided not to buy that scarf?"

He shook his head as he prayed for the right words to make her understand. "It wasn't the scarf. It was the anger I saw in your eyes. At that moment you reminded me of my grandfather."

The blood drained from Marisa's face, then rushed back as she glared at Blake. "How dare you say that? I'm not like your grandfather. He was a horrid man."

"He was an angry man," Blake corrected, "and he let his anger destroy all the good parts of his life. I don't want to see that happen to you. To be very blunt, Marisa, I don't want that to happen to us."

As her expression softened ever so slightly at his use of the word *us*, Blake continued. "I told you that I dated two women seriously. What I didn't tell you was that after we'd been dating for a couple months, the second one—Ashley—changed. She started blowing up over what seemed like the slightest thing. One day she yelled at a waiter because her coffee wasn't hot enough. Another time she started screaming when a school bus stopped in front of our car and we had to wait for the kids to get off it."

"What's your point, Blake?" Though her voice was even, the way Marisa gripped the edge of the bench told him her anger had not dissipated. "You surely don't think I'm acting like that."

"No, you're not," he admitted, wishing this were a scene in one of his books. If it were, he would be able to control the way it ended. As it was, he felt as if he was stumbling in the dark. "I don't think you're like Ashley, and I don't think you're like my grandfather, but I wouldn't be honest if I didn't tell you that I worry about what it would be like living with your anger. I spent the first eighteen years of my life walking on eggshells. I don't want to ever do that again."

She stared at him for a moment, her eyes filled with anger and something else, something he couldn't identify. "What are you asking me to do, Blake? Is this where you tell me I need to forgive and forget? It's not that simple."

A young mother wheeled her stroller past the bench, increasing her pace when she saw Marisa's forbidding expression. Blake didn't blame her. Marisa was looking at him as if he were the most unreasonable person on the planet. He took a deep breath as he searched for the right words.

"I know it isn't easy," he said, hoping his conciliatory tone would convince her that he wasn't attacking her. "It took me years to forgive my grandfather for the way he made my father's life so miserable."

Marisa's lips flattened. "You say that, yet you expect me to turn on a dime, to welcome Eric back with open arms just because he decided it was time to make amends. I'm sorry, Blake, but it doesn't work that way."

He was an idiot. Though he'd hoped that telling Marisa of his worries would help defuse her anger, he'd only stoked it. He should have kept his mouth shut.

"That isn't what I meant."

She glared at him, her expression so fierce that he almost recoiled. "I think it *is* what you meant. Maybe it's a good thing you're going away. Maybe we both need time to think."

Maybe they did.

# 30

Marisa stared at the open doorway to her office, knowing how unlikely it was that she'd ever see Blake standing there, waiting for her to finish work. He was gone, and if he did return, it would be to visit Greg, not Marisa. She knew that from the way they'd parted. They'd barely spoken on the drive back from the goat farm, and the way he'd said good-bye after he'd helped her carry the gifts into her office had been so final that Marisa had known he had no intention of returning from Pennsylvania. After Christmas, Blake would head back to his home in California.

She couldn't blame him. After all, she was the one who'd said it was good that they were having a time-out. She was the one who'd lashed out in anger, not stopping to think of how anger had shaped Blake's life and how he might react to it the way she reacted to the thought of someone drinking.

Marisa was wrong. She knew that. But she also knew that an apology wouldn't be enough this time. Blake needed more than words. He needed proof that she wasn't like his grandfather and Ashley if they were going to have a future, and that proof was something she couldn't provide.

Marisa knew it was important to forgive Eric. She had tried—oh, how she had tried—but every time she did, anger bubbled up inside her, erupting with more power than the geysers in Yellowstone. Nothing Colleen had taught her helped. Colleen had had fancy words for the techniques she taught, terms like cognitive restructuring, but none of them worked.

How could Eric have missed all those school plays and the spelling bees? How could he have wasted his pay on whiskey, leaving Mom with barely enough money to buy groceries and not enough to give Marisa a new back-to-school outfit? How could he have deserted them? And how could he have hidden so completely that Marisa had been unable to find him? The unanswered questions swirled through her mind, replacing every kind and gentle thought with sharp edges of anger. The pain that anger inflicted was so intense that Marisa knew only one way to avoid it. She would resort to the one technique that worked: she would not even think about forgiving Eric, for to do so was to wound herself again.

Marisa closed her eyes and took a deep breath, exhaling slowly as she tried to corral her emotions. She had a job to do, and she couldn't let either Eric or Blake interfere with that.

"Are you ready?" Mom appeared in the doorway, and for once she was not wearing her apron. Not only that, but she'd applied fresh lipstick, and if Marisa wasn't mistaken, she had spritzed herself with perfume. Mom was ready for Kate and Greg's wrap party.

When she'd first proposed it, Kate had been quick to explain that this was not like a Hollywood wrap party, where the cast celebrated the successful end of filming. Instead, the Rainbow's End staff would be wrapping Christmas gifts for the expected guests. Everyone was invited to gather in the dining room for what Kate had promised would be no more than half an hour with paper, scissors, and bows followed by a lunch buffet.

Mom had gotten to work extra early that morning to prepare the food, because even though Kate had insisted they could serve ready-made dishes or simply offer cold cuts and sandwich makings, Mom had wanted this to feel like a real party with special food and beverages. Classic Mom.

"I'm ready," Marisa said with a quick nod. "Lauren hasn't finished everything, but I have what's done." She reached behind her desk and grabbed two large shopping bags filled with items from HCP that she'd brought with her today. The gifts from the goat farm had already been placed in the dining room.

"I heard Blake left this morning," Mom said as she closed the door behind Marisa.

The change of subject startled Marisa, leaving her feeling as if she'd been washed up on a strange shore. "What does Blake have to do with wrapping Christmas presents?" she demanded, trying to regain her equilibrium. She did not—she absolutely did not—want to discuss Blake or the fact that he'd left Rainbow's End.

"Nothing," Mom admitted, "but he has everything to do with the pain I see in my daughter's eyes. What happened?"

"He's spending two weeks with his father. Everyone knows that."

Mom shook her head and refused to budge, though the excited chatter from the dining room left no doubt that the party had begun. "That doesn't explain why he emptied his cabin. A man who plans to come back doesn't do that."

Taking a deep breath, Marisa nodded. She'd been right. Whatever there had been between her and Blake was over. And it was her fault.

"What happened, *mi hija*? What went wrong?" Mom laid her hand on top of Marisa's, giving it a little squeeze.

Though Marisa wished she could ignore the question, she knew Mom would not permit that.

"We disagreed," she said, hoping her mother would recognize the finality in her voice. This was a conversation Marisa did not want to have.

Mom did not take the hint. "Everyone disagrees from time to time, but that doesn't mean they give up." She raised her gaze to meet Marisa's. "If you love Blake—and I think you do—you need to fight for him. Don't let your chance at happiness slip away."

"It's not that simple, Mom."

"Isn't it? Think about it. Love is a gift, a wonderful, precious gift. Don't throw it away."

Before Marisa could respond, Kate poked her head out of the dining room. "There you are. We're waiting for you."

Feeling as if she'd been reprieved, Marisa nodded. She doubted this was the last time Mom would ask about Blake and give her advice, but at least the discussion was over for now.

The next half hour was filled with laughter and chatter as everyone wrapped gifts. The only employee who hadn't come was Eric. According to Mom, he'd had to make an emergency trip to San Antonio to get parts for the parade float. When they were finished wrapping, some of the bows were crooked and some of the ribbons clashed with the paper, but Marisa was certain no one would care. Come Christmas morning, the guests would be too caught up in the excitement of unexpected gifts to notice much more than the fact that they were wrapped.

Once the last item was wrapped, tagged, and placed on the long folding table Kate had designated for finished gifts, Greg rose, drawing his wife to his side.

"Thank you all," he said, his smile warm and welcoming. "I want to thank you not just for this morning's work but for everything you've done to make Rainbow's End a success. Kate and I couldn't have done it without you." He smiled again as his gaze moved from one person to the next, making the message personal.

"And now, before we enjoy the delicious food Carmen has prepared for us, I have an announcement." Wrapping his arm around Kate's waist, Greg took in a shallow breath. "I want you to be among the first to know that next June Rainbow's End will become a true family resort—the Vange family resort. Yes, Kate and I are expecting our first child."

Marisa smiled as the last piece of the puzzle fell into place. No wonder Kate had looked pale so many mornings; no wonder she had been careful about what she ate for breakfast; no wonder she drank herbal tea. The signs had been there all along.

Clapping turned to cheers, and before Marisa knew what was happening, everyone was crowded around Kate and Greg, offering their congratulations. While the happy couple deflected questions about gender preference and possible names, Marisa tried not to sigh. She smiled as she shook Greg's hand and hugged Kate, but though her wishes were sincere, she could not deny the emptiness deep inside her and the fear that, no matter how she longed for it, she would never know this kind of happiness.

———————— ✳ ————————

"Marisa!"

It had been eight years since she'd heard his voice, and yet she knew without a doubt who was calling her name from the other end of the parking lot. She'd just skirted the gazebo and was almost at the main entrance to Rainbow's End. For a fleeting moment, Marisa considered ignoring him, heading straight into the lodge, and barricading herself behind her office door, but only a coward would do that. And, whatever else she was, Marisa St. George was not a coward. She turned to face the man who'd made the end of her senior year so embarrassing: Hal Lundquist.

She would have recognized him even in a crowded mall. At six feet six inches, he was tall, even in a state known for its tall men. His features were just short of movie-star handsome, his hair still the golden blond that had made almost every girl in school sigh with envy. He looked like the Hal Lundquist who'd been the object of Marisa's teenage crush, and yet he didn't.

Hal wasn't simply eight years older; he was somehow different. It wasn't only the unfashionably short hair or the scar that marred his left cheek. His demeanor had changed. What had been a swagger now looked like a self-confident stride, and his expression held none of the defiance or scorn she'd seen at school. Instead, it seemed oddly hesitant, as if he were unsure of his welcome. As well he should be.

"You're just the person I want to see," Hal said, his voice as compelling as it had been when he'd led the football team to the county championships. "Well," he amended, "you and your father."

Marisa could feel her hackles rise as she remembered the number of times Hal had settled arguments with his fists. There was no way of knowing if he still did. "What do you want with Eric?"

"We need to talk." That was what Blake had told Marisa, and that particular conversation hadn't turned out well. She did not hold out much hope for this one either.

"About what?"

Hal took another step toward her, his boots crunching on the stone driveway. "I don't remember you being so suspicious," he said with what might have been intended as a placating smile. If he'd hoped to disarm her, he'd failed.

"You probably remember that I was gullible and trusting. I'm not anymore." *Thanks to you.*

Nodding as if he'd expected her response, Hal said, "I didn't think you'd be the same. I'm certainly not. Now, where is your father? I really need to see him." The gloves were off. Though Hal might still be smiling, his tone of voice was pure steel.

Marisa took a deep breath, trying to calm her nerves. Nothing would be gained by shrieking at Hal, and though she wanted to prevent him from seeing Eric, that didn't seem feasible.

"Don't you dare hurt him," she said, her voice low but seething with passion. The anger that accompanied so many thoughts of Eric had disappeared for the moment, replaced by fear of what Hal's fists might do. He was young and in obviously good shape, while Eric was a middle-aged recovering alcoholic who'd never been an athlete. "The man has had enough trouble in his life without you stirring up the past."

Hal raised both hands in a gesture of surrender. "I'm not here to hurt anyone."

And oddly, Marisa believed him. Almost. When she'd heard that he was coming to Dupree and wanted to see Eric, she'd feared Hal was still resentful of Eric's confronting his father and that he might seek vengeance. But the man standing only a few feet from her did not seem like the spoiled, self-centered boy she'd known.

"All right," she said. "Come with me."

Marisa retraced her steps to the parking area where she'd left her car and led the way to the cabin her mother now shared with Eric. After knocking on the door, she waited for Eric to open it.

"Marisa!" His eyes lit with pleasure. "I didn't expect you." He looked beyond her, his expression becoming guarded at the sight of Hal. "Who's this?"

Not waiting for Marisa's introduction, Hal stepped forward and extended his hand. "Hal Lundquist, sir. I wasn't sure whether you'd recognize me."

Marisa blinked, startled by Hal's use of "sir." The Hal she'd known had shown little or no respect for his elders, and he'd had nothing but disdain for her father, calling him the town drunk and a disgrace to Dupree. This Hal seemed conciliatory, almost as if he were meeting someone he thought might become a friend.

Eric shook his hand as he scanned Hal's face. "Can't say that I do. You don't look much like your father."

"I've been told I favor my mother."

Marisa looked at her father. "Shall we go inside and sit down?" This was not a conversation she wanted to have overheard.

"Of course." Eric opened the door wider, waiting until both Marisa and Hal were seated before he turned to his guest. "Can I offer you some tea or coffee?"

"No thank you, sir." There it was again, that polite formality. "I won't take much of your time, but there's something I need to tell you—both of you." He'd chosen one of the chairs and positioned himself so he was facing both Marisa and Eric, who sat on opposite ends of the couch.

"Marisa, I'm sorry about what happened at the prom." The words rang with sincerity, and that surprised her. Though the humiliation had colored her life for years, she had always suspected that Hal had dismissed it the way he would have any other insignificant event. She wasn't even certain he'd remembered it a month later, but today he seemed genuinely repentant.

"It was a stupid teenage prank," Hal continued. "At the time, I was too dumb to care how much it must have hurt you." He paused for a second, never letting his gaze drop. "I know there's nothing I can do to make it up to you, but I hope you'll accept my apology."

It was more than she'd ever expected. The Hal she'd known was not one for apologies, and yet the new Hal seemed comfortable with them. Marisa nodded. The pain she'd once felt was gone; there was no reason to cling to the memory.

"Apology accepted," she said softly. It was time to put prom night behind her, and thanks to Hal, she could do that.

Marisa gave Hal a small smile, thankful he could not read her thoughts. He might not appreciate realizing that seeing him again made Marisa wonder why she'd been so infatuated. Although he seemed to have grown into a decent man, when he'd been in high school, all Hal had had to offer were his good looks and his prowess on the football field. That might have been enough then, but it wasn't now. Now Marisa knew that what mattered was a man's character, not his external trappings. Hal seemed to have developed the strength of character he'd lacked in high school, but he no longer touched her heart.

At the other end of the couch, Eric unclenched his fists. "I'm glad to see you finally came to your senses, Hal." His voice was brusque and filled with an emotion Marisa couldn't identify. "I wanted to beat you to a pulp for the way you treated my little girl."

Hal inclined his head slightly. "I know that, sir. I also know you went to see my father. That's why I'm here." To Marisa's relief, she heard no hostility in Hal's voice. If anything, he sounded humble.

"I want to thank you." Hal's lips curved into a wry smile. "Oh, I didn't feel that way at the time, but the fact that you confronted my father was the best thing anyone's ever done for me."

Marisa stared, amazed by the words coming from Hal's mouth. "I don't understand."

"Me either," Eric said. "You lost me there."

"I doubt he'd admit it to you, but my father was furious after your visit—worried about what my stupidity would do to his hopes for reelection. By the time I got back from prom weekend, my fate was sealed. He marched me to the army recruiting office the next day and gave me a choice: enlist or try to live without any support from him. I picked the army."

Hal took a deep breath before leaning forward. "It wasn't always easy, especially at first, but I learned a lot about myself. I'd like to think I'm a better man now." He directed his gaze at Eric. "If I am, it's thanks to you. Thank you, sir."

As Marisa watched, her father's demeanor changed, and her heart warmed at the realization that her fears had been unfounded. Hal had brought healing rather than hurt. Eric's shoulders straightened; he held his head higher; his hands were relaxed. But the biggest change was his expression. His eyes reflected pride mixed with humility. For the first time in more years than Marisa wanted to count, he looked like the man she'd once loved. Though his hair was grayer and his face more wrinkled, Marisa saw the man she remembered from her early childhood.

She closed her eyes, not wanting the moment to end, and as she did, memories came rushing back. Holding her father's hand as she walked to school for the very first time. Laughing as he pushed her higher and higher on the swing. The two of them running through the backyard, mason jars clutched in their hands as they chased fireflies.

"Thank you, Hal," she said softly.

# 31

ou look good, son."

Blake tried to smile as his father grabbed him in a bear hug the instant he set foot inside the kitchen. The truth was, he didn't feel good. He felt empty. He hadn't thought it would be so painful, but nothing had seemed right since he'd left Rainbow's End. He hadn't expected Marisa's anger to resurface, and he certainly hadn't expected her to shut him out the way she had.

He returned his father's hug and clapped him on the back. "I had a pretty easy flight," he said as he stepped back. He'd flown to Newark and rented a car. Even with the traffic leaving the airport and the typically congested roads in New Jersey, it had been faster than making connections to land at ABE, the smaller airport that served Allentown, Bethlehem, and Easton. "The plane was crowded, of course, but I expected that."

Blake glanced around the small kitchen where he'd eaten countless meals. It looked just as he'd expected: the slightly worn linoleum floor and Formica countertops spotlessly clean, even though they were decades out of style; the jar of sun tea sitting in the center of the table; the plates and silverware ready for supper. What he hadn't expected was that there were only two plates.

"Looking for Hilary?" his father asked.

Blake nodded. "I didn't realize I was that obvious, but yes. I want to meet the woman who's caught your eye."

"She's done more than that. She's snared my heart too." As he pronounced the words, Gus Kendall's face lit with happiness, giving him the appearance of a man at least a decade younger than his actual sixty-four. The hair that had once been a darker brown than Blake's was now iron gray, and his brown eyes had faded a bit over the years, but he looked almost carefree as he clapped his son on the shoulder and leaned against the counter.

"She'll be here tomorrow. I figured you had some things you wanted to tell me and that was best done alone."

Trying to contain his surprise, Blake raised an eyebrow. "I do, but how'd you know?"

"You're my son." His father let out a low chuckle. "We may not live together anymore, but I still have a pretty good idea of how your brain works. The way I figure it, you've got two things to tell me. One's about a woman and the other . . . Well, I'll let you talk about that when you're ready. In the meantime, I've got some kielbasa we can cook on the grill, and Hilary left some potato salad that's almost as good as your mom used to make."

Dad gestured toward the small hallway leading to the staircase. "Why don't you take your bags upstairs, and I'll fire up the grill?"

Blake couldn't believe the difference in his father. Oh, he grumbled as he always did that the grill didn't heat properly, and he claimed the bakery had sold him day-old rolls but charged him for fresh ones. Blake dismissed that, knowing the comments were no more than his father's good-natured grousing. What impressed Blake was that the man who said all the same things also peppered his conversation with "Hilary says" and "Hilary and I." That, the twinkle in his eyes when he spoke of her, and the way he laughed more than Blake could ever recall told him his father was happy. And, though he didn't say it, Blake had no doubt that his father intended to marry Hilary. He wouldn't be surprised if he planned to give her a ring for Christmas.

"Do you want to review your portfolio?" Blake asked when they were seated at the table, the simple but familiar meal in front of them.

They'd chatted about casual things while the sausages had cooked. Dad wasn't one to push, and Blake knew Dad would wait for him to talk about Marisa and "the other thing." The problem was, now that the time had come, Blake wasn't ready, and so he'd resorted to a diversion. It wasn't a red herring. He wanted to be certain his father realized just how comfortably situated he was. He could afford to give Hilary a large diamond, if that's what she wanted, and they could move to a more modern home, one that held no memories for either of them.

Dad shook his head. "No need. I do read those monthly statements you send." He took another bite of potato salad and grinned, leaving Blake to wonder whether it was the flavor of Hilary's salad or the size of his brokerage account that pleased him. "I still can't believe how much that initial investment has grown. You're a genius at managing money, son. I haven't said it enough, but I'm proud of what you've accomplished."

Blake couldn't ignore the fact that his father had given him the opening he needed. The compliment would provide the perfect segue for what he wanted to tell his dad. Blake took a deep breath and then exhaled slowly, trying to calm the butterflies that had suddenly filled his stomach. "I hope you'll be equally proud when you hear about my other venture."

His father took another helping of potato salad, nodding as he said, "I'm sure I will. I can't imagine you doing something I wouldn't approve of."

That remained to be seen. Marisa certainly hadn't approved. "Grandfather wouldn't have liked it."

Dad shrugged. "But I'm not my father any more than you're me. We're different, and I for one am glad about that. The world would be boring if we were all the same." He leaned forward, resting his elbows on the table. "So, what are you going to tell me? I'm pretty sure you're not a serial killer."

Marisa had thought he was almost that bad. Though Blake wasn't a serial killer, he'd written about them. "I'm a writer. A novelist, actually."

Dad said nothing, and his expression remained neutral, as if he were waiting for Blake to finish before he reacted. "I do know something about serial killers, though. I write—I wrote"—Blake corrected himself—"thrillers."

This time Dad nodded. "That must mean you're Ken Blake. I thought so."

It was not the reaction Blake had expected. He'd expected surprise, perhaps a bit of disbelief, possibly mild disapproval. What he hadn't expected was this calm acceptance.

"You knew and you never said anything?"

"I didn't know for certain, but I couldn't ignore the similarity in names and the fact that Ken Blake's photo looked a lot like my son. That intrigued me enough that I bought the book." Dad smiled. "When I read the first one, I could practically hear you talking, and that reminded me of how you used to tell stories when you were a kid."

Dad had read his books. The thought was mind-boggling. Not once had Blake considered that possibility. As far as he knew, his father rarely read anything other than the Bible. But Dad, it seemed, had secrets of his own. "You didn't say anything."

"No, because for whatever reason, you were keeping it secret. I respected your desire for privacy, but I wondered why you felt the need for it."

The answer was simple. "Grandfather."

"That's what I thought, and you're right. He would have disapproved, just as he disapproved of all fiction." Dad smiled again. "The truth is, I brought your books into the house in brown paper bags and read them in my room so he wouldn't know what was going on. I understand why you didn't want to listen to him telling you how wrong you were and that fiction was the devil's work."

Dad pointed a finger at Blake. "It's not, you know. Jesus used parables—you could call them fiction—to help people understand his teachings. Of course, if I'd told your grandfather that, he would have said you weren't Jesus and then gotten onto his soapbox. I don't blame you for not wanting to deal with that."

Still amazed at how easily this whole conversation was going, Blake shook his head. "I wasn't concerned about myself. I've got a tough hide." Or he thought he did. "I didn't want Grandfather taking out his anger on you." It was Dad who had had to deal with the man every day; Blake had been thousands of miles away and saw him only a few times a year.

"I could have dealt with it. Like you, I've developed a tough hide too. I needed to with him as a father." Dad reached for the jar of tea and refilled his glass. "I've got two questions for you. You said you wrote thrillers, past tense. Does that mean you're no longer writing?"

"Not at all. It's just that the new books are different." Blake explained the concept of the Logan Marsh stories. When he finished, his dad was grinning.

"I can't wait to read the first one."

"You won't have to go to the store for it," Blake promised. "I'll send you one of my author's copies as soon as they arrive."

"Autographed?"

"If you like."

"I'd like that." Dad took a long slug of tea, then leaned back in his chair, apparently content to wait for Blake's next revelation.

"You said you had two questions," Blake said when the silence became uncomfortable.

"I did. The second is whether you're going to use your real name now."

Neither Jack nor Heidi had suggested that. They simply wanted Ken Blake to reveal his face and his personality, preferably on national TV.

"I hadn't planned to. Ken Blake has a good following." That was an understatement, and Blake suspected his father knew that. If his dad had been tracking his career as it seemed he had, he knew that each of the Ken Blake books hit the top ten on the bestseller charts.

"It's true that the new books have a different target audience, but I think a high percentage of my current readers will follow me to the Logan Marsh stories. And, the truth is, I like my anonymity."

"So I can't tell my buddies that my son is a bestselling author?"

"I'd prefer you didn't." Blake leaned forward, narrowing the distance between them. Though his father's expression was neutral, Blake thought he heard a note of disapproval in his voice. "Is that a problem?"

"Not really. I've kept my suspicions to myself for years. I won't even tell Hilary unless you say it's okay."

"Hilary." Blake smiled. "It seems we're both good at secrets. I had no idea you were seeing anyone until you mentioned her this spring. Where did you meet?"

"On a church retreat. It was one of those weekend deals with a dozen or so churches from the region. Something about her attracted me from the beginning."

Nodding, Blake said, "It was like that with Marisa."

"So that's her name."

"Marisa St. George, but we were talking about Hilary. I guess things moved pretty quickly." As they had with him and Marisa—until everything had come to a dead end.

A chuckle that turned into a guffaw was Dad's response. "If you call three years quick. The retreat was three years ago last spring."

"Three years? Why didn't I hear about Hilary before this?"

Dad gave him one of those "you ought to know the answer" looks that Blake had seen so often as a boy. "Your grandfather. I couldn't subject Hilary to him."

Blake didn't doubt that Grandfather would have found fault with her the way he had with the few girls Blake had brought home. As a teenager, Blake had thought it a minor miracle that Grandfather had ever married, but Dad had assured him that he hadn't been as bitter when his wife was alive.

"It seems we were both enablers."

For the first time that day, Dad looked puzzled. "What's that?"

"It's a term I learned from Alcoholics Anonymous. It means—"

The blood drained from his father's face, and he gripped the edge of the table. "Wait a minute," Dad said, his voice surprisingly weak. "What's this about AA? I didn't know you drank. When did this start?"

"I don't drink. Never did." Blake was quick to reassure his dad. "The reason I know about enablers is that Marisa's father is a recovering alcoholic. I knew a bit about them from research I did for *Quicksilver*." Dad nodded, confirming that he'd read the book.

"When I learned about Marisa's father, I did more research to understand what her life and his had been like. An enabler ensures that the person doesn't have to face the consequences of his actions. That's what you and I did with Grandfather. Neither of us confronted him with the fact that he was wrong. Instead, we appeased him, and so he continued to do things we both hated."

Dad nodded, his eyes thoughtful. "It seemed like the right thing at the time."

"Or the easiest."

"That too, but there's nothing we can do to change that now. I'd rather hear about your Marisa and why you look so sad every time you mention her name."

His Marisa. There'd been a time when Blake had thought of her that way, but it was over. He explained what had happened—how he'd met Marisa, fallen in love, then been confronted with the reality of her anger—concluding with, "I don't know if I can live with that."

Dad was silent for a moment, his expression leaving no doubt that he was concerned about Blake's revelations. "I wish I could help you, son, but there's only One who can change Marisa. Have you prayed about this?"

"Constantly, but there's been no answer."

"Then it's not yet the right time. Have faith, my boy. Have faith."

"I'm trying."

The house was quiet. Lauren and Drew had gone somewhere and Fiona was asleep, leaving Marisa alone with her thoughts. Tonight they were uncomfortable companions. She'd tried reading but couldn't concentrate. TV hadn't kept her attention, either, so she had finally decided to wrap gifts and had dragged the shopping bags filled with presents to the kitchen table along with rolls of paper and ribbon. Even if she couldn't corral her thoughts, at least she could accomplish something.

As she'd feared, her mind continued to whirl. She measured a length of ribbon, then began to wind it into a bow, wishing it were that easy to arrange her thoughts. Instead, memories of Blake's face when he'd said good-bye were juxtaposed with Eric's expression when Hal declared that he'd set him on the right path.

Marisa snipped the ends of the ribbons, admiring the way they curled. Fiona would enjoy ripping this bow from the package of half a dozen pairs of socks in assorted bright colors. There was enough variety that they could clash with everything Fiona owned. Smiling at the thought of the child wearing orange and purple socks with lime green shorts, Marisa reached for the next box. It had been more difficult to find something for Lauren, but when she'd seen the apricot sweater at the goat farm, Marisa had known it was the perfect gift for her friend.

Angora. Blake. Eric. Hal. One memory led to the next, creating a tangle of thoughts worse than the ball of wool her neighbor in Atlanta's cat had decided was a plaything. Determined to unravel the mess, Marisa focused on the easiest part: Hal.

Perhaps it was because she had less invested in him; perhaps it was because he had obviously changed. Marisa wasn't sure of the reason why it had been so easy to accept his apology. All she knew was that when she and Hal had said good-bye, she had felt a sense of completion. The past they'd shared, brief and painful as it had been, was over. There was nothing left to regret.

She couldn't say the same thing about Eric. Like Hal, it appeared that he had changed. Like Hal, he'd apologized. But though acceptance had been easy with Hal, Marisa was unable to take that step toward Eric. Why not? She'd trusted both men, and they'd both betrayed her. Admittedly, it had been on a different scale. With Hal, it had been one time, not a matter of many years and many, many instances. Her relationship with Hal had been casual, not the deeply intimate relationship she'd had—or wanted to have—with Eric. But even considering those differences, Marisa couldn't explain why it was so difficult to offer Eric forgiveness.

As odd as it seemed, she felt as if there were an iron gate between her and that forgiveness. Though the anger that had always erupted at the thought of Eric had dissipated, a barrier remained. She could see her goal, but she could not reach it. Why not? Marisa closed her eyes, trying to understand, and as she did, the scene changed. The gate vanished, replaced by a wall covered with shiny stainless steel, a wall that reflected her image. She was the barrier.

But that made no sense. Her eyes flew open and she shook her head. Where her relationship with Eric was concerned, she wasn't at fault. She wasn't the one who'd ignored a daughter's cries. She wasn't the one who refused to change, no matter how many pleas a child uttered.

This was crazy. Marisa looked down at the ribbon that she'd twisted into a mangled mess. If she continued at this pace, she'd need to buy more wrapping supplies. Disgusted, she rose from the table, pulled a saucepan from the cupboard, and splashed some milk into it.

When Marisa had had trouble sleeping as a child, Mom would make her a mug of warm milk. Not ordinary milk, though. Mom always added a dash of cinnamon, claiming it was the spice that brought slumber. Dad—Eric, Marisa corrected herself—insisted that nutmeg was better, so Marisa's warm milk had had both spices. She opened the cabinet door and stared at the spices, sighing softly as she added both cinnamon and nutmeg to her milk.

A few minutes later, she returned to the table, a mug of spiced milk in her hand. Why hadn't Eric heeded her pleas? She'd cried and cried, telling him how she hated it every time he collapsed on the sofa, oblivious to her and the fact that she needed him to be part of her life, and yet he'd continued to drink himself into a stupor. Why hadn't he stopped? Marisa had done everything she could, but it still wasn't enough. Where had she gone wrong?

*"No one can change another person. That's up to the individual and God."* Blake's words echoed through her brain, and on their heels, Marisa heard Eric telling her, *"Thanks to God, I'm sober."* Her hands cupped around the mug, Marisa nodded. That was the answer, the piece of the puzzle she'd been missing for all those years.

She'd been so arrogant, so convinced that she had the answers. The truth was, she couldn't change Eric, no matter what she did, no matter how hard she tried. That simply wasn't in her power. Only God had that power; only God could change a person. Thinking she could do anything other than love Eric had been wrong, the worst kind of pride.

The hostility Marisa had shown Eric had hurt not only him but God himself, for she had broken one of his commandments. She had not honored her father. And through her stubbornness and her anger, she'd hurt Blake, the man who'd shown her how wonderful love could be. If anyone needed to change, it was Marisa.

She folded her hands and bowed her head. "I'm sorry, Lord," she said, tears sliding down her cheeks. "Please forgive me. I know I can't do this alone, but I pray that you'll give me the strength to conquer my anger."

Marisa wasn't certain how long she sat there, the aroma of warm spiced milk wafting through the air, but as she did, she felt a mantle of peace settle over her.

"Thank you, Lord."

———————————— ✳ ————————————

"I'm going to have a new daddy," Fiona announced as she made her way into the kitchen. Though she'd become adept with her crutches, her pace was still slower than normal, the thump of the cast on the floor marking her progress.

Marisa smiled at the striped sock that covered the cast, clashing beautifully with the floral print sock on the uninjured foot. Many things had changed last night, but Fiona was not one of them. "Yes, I know."

"He said I could call him Daddy Drew, even before the wedding." Fiona plunked herself into her chair and grinned. "Isn't that great?"

"It is," Marisa agreed. "Before you know it, you'll get to be a flower girl."

For the first time, Fiona frowned. "Yeah, but Christmas comes first. I'm worried, Aunt Marisa. I don't have a present for Daddy Drew."

"I'm sure your mother will take you shopping."

Fiona shook her head, setting her braids to swinging. "She said she already bought something from both of us. That's not right. I want Daddy Drew to have something special just from me." Fiona's eyes brimmed with tears as she looked up. "Can you help me?"

Marisa hesitated, remembering Lauren's story of Fiona's determination to make penuche for her father one Christmas and what a disaster that had been. "What did you have in mind?"

"Socks. Special socks. Not the kind you can buy here or at Walmart."

As memories of the goat farm flashed through Marisa's brain, she smiled. "I know just the place. As soon as we finish breakfast, you're going to buy Daddy Drew the best socks he's ever owned."

And while they were there, Marisa was going to make a purchase of her own: a certain blue scarf and matching sweater for Eric.

# 32

"This is the coolest thing I ever saw." Fiona stroked the side of the ark, as if she somehow believed the painted hippopotamus peeking through the window was real.

The school grounds, which had been designated as the staging area for the parade, were growing crowded when Drew dropped Fiona off at the curb, but though vehicles queued behind him, he waited until Marisa reached her before he left. It might be six weeks until the wedding, but Daddy Drew was taking his parental responsibilities seriously, and both Lauren and Fiona were flourishing as the result of his love.

Though Fiona had chattered about what seemed like a hundred different things as she and Marisa had walked to the ark, her conversation became narrowly focused when they reached the Rainbow's End float. She oohed and aahed over the ark, unaware that a month ago it had been nothing more than a large wooden box. Eric had worked wonders with it, somehow managing to make it appear that the sides and ends were curved.

"Alice can't believe you're gonna let us ride in it."

Biting back a smile at the girl's enthusiasm, Marisa forced a deadpan tone to her voice. "We needed two porcupines, and I hate to say this, but there's something pretty prickly about you and Alice."

Fiona gasped then giggled. "You're just kidding, Aunt Marisa. I know you."

"And I know you—prickly to the core." She bent her head and pretended to study Fiona's neck. "Aren't those quills I see there?"

"No way!" But Fiona had taken the bait and rubbed her neck to convince herself there was nothing odd on her skin. Fiona was still rubbing her neck when Alice arrived, trailed by her mother.

Susan Kozinski gave Marisa a warm smile. "I can't thank you enough for including Alice in this. It's all she's talked about for the last week. Bert and I are thrilled that we have a reprieve from the 'why won't Santa bring me a puppy?' refrain." Susan's smile widened. "Those animals are a great substitute for a live one."

Marisa wrinkled her nose as she watched the two girls petting the painted animals one last time before they followed Kate to the costuming area.

"I'm beginning to think we created a monster."

"Not at all." Susan shook her head. "You gave everyone another reason to watch the parade. It's good to have a new float, especially one that's as nice as this."

"That's what Kate and Greg thought." The seed of the idea had been planted when they'd attended the Independence Day parade, but it might not have germinated had it not been for Eric. Kate had admitted that he was the one who'd lobbied for it, insisting he could finish the float in time for the Christmas celebrations.

Susan looked around the grounds, her eyes narrowing as she studied a couple other floats. "It seems the rumors are true. I'd heard that some of the others were going to spruce up their floats. They didn't want to be overshadowed by Rainbow's End."

Since she hadn't been to a Dupree parade in eight years, Marisa had no way of knowing which floats had changed, but the word *rumor* triggered a memory. "The rumor I heard is that your son is going to wear swaddling clothes tonight."

A frown was Susan's response. "That had been the plan. Bert and I couldn't say no when the church committee asked us. After all, it's a Dupree tradition that if there's a baby under six months old in town, he or she plays Jesus. We were all set, but Liam's been throwing up since early morning."

"Oh no." No wonder Susan looked slightly harried.

"Doc Santos assures me it's nothing serious, but a sick baby would not make for a very pleasant manger scene. Fortunately, my mother volunteered to stay with Liam so Bert and I can watch Alice's moment of glory."

A wide grin split Susan's face as two familiar figures pranced toward them. "There they are, Dupree's prettiest porcupines."

*Pretty* wasn't the word Marisa would have used. *Odd* or even *bizarre* seemed more appropriate. Like all of the costumes for the Rainbow's End float, the girls' consisted of only enough porcupine to cover their head and shoulders. Below the dark brown head, Fiona's red sweatshirt and jeans were clearly visible, as were the split pant leg that accommodated her now colorfully painted cast and two mismatched socks. Alice's outfit was slightly less jarring, because she wore a navy sweatshirt and socks. Despite—or perhaps because of—their unusual costumes, the girls were hopping up and down in a decidedly unporcupinelike manner.

"Marisa," Kate called from the other side of the ark. "Time to get ready."

Nodding, Marisa bade Susan farewell. "The next time you see me, I'll be masquerading as a dove."

"Have fun."

"I expect we will."

Five minutes later, Marisa was in the float with the others. Kate and Greg were dressed as giraffes, Mom and Eric as elephants. In addition to them and the porcupine girls were Marisa and one of the teenagers who waited tables as the ark's doves. Knowing that the sides of the float would cover most of their bodies, Kate had ordered the half costumes, but now that they were inside, Marisa wondered if that had been a mistake. It was clear that Fiona and Alice wanted to wave at their friends. Unfortunately, if they did, their sweatshirt-clad arms would destroy the illusion.

"You can pretend you're royalty and simply nod," Marisa told the girls.

"But even the queen does that little wave," Fiona whined, giving a surprisingly good imitation of Britain's monarch.

"Not tonight, Queen Fiona. Your subjects don't want to see red arms."

"Okay." It was a grudging acceptance, but with the mercurial change of mood that was so common for her, a second later, Fiona was nudging Alice and giggling.

"We'll have the porcupines and elephants on the left side, doves and giraffes on the right," Kate announced.

Marisa nodded. It was just as well. She wanted—no, she needed—to talk to Eric, but this was neither the time nor the place. They needed privacy and plenty of time. Marisa suspected she would also need a box of Kleenex.

After the parade ended and Fiona was back home with Lauren, Marisa would drive to Rainbow's End. Eric had been busy all day, putting the finishing touches on the float, but once his masterpiece was safely in the garage, there would be time for Marisa to say everything that was in her heart. For now, she would enjoy the parade.

Within minutes, the ark had taken its place in the queue, and the parade had begun. One of the things Marisa had always enjoyed about life in Dupree was the way almost everyone in town participated in community events like the Independence Day and Christmas parades. If residents weren't riding on a float or marching, they lined the streets as spectators, cheering on those who had a more active role.

The high school band marched, followed by the cheer squad, who paused at each intersection to give onlookers a sample of their repertoire. Various organizations sponsored floats. The police chief rode in an antique cruiser, and not to be outdone, the fire department drove its largest engine, with four firefighters ready to give spectators the waves that Fiona and Alice could not.

Though the shopkeepers on Pecan Street did not have a float, Lauren and Samantha planned to stand in front of their stores, serving cookies to paradegoers, while Russ Walker handed out cups of coffee and hot chocolate at the Sit 'n' Sip. The parade created a party-like atmosphere that brought the community together.

Marisa stood next to Kate, laughing at the residents' reactions when they heard the sounds coming from the ark. Though other floats played Christmas music, Greg had insisted that Rainbow's End's float be true to its theme, and so they had a soundtrack of animal sounds.

The donkeys' braying and the elephants' trumpeting made spectators laugh. Or perhaps they were laughing at the fact that this ark defied natural law, and doves were almost as large as giraffes, with porcupines only marginally smaller than elephants. No one seemed to care. What mattered was that Rainbow's End was once again a vital part of the community.

It was the perfect evening for a parade, cool but not cold, clear skies with a half moon, only a light breeze. Fiona and Alice squealed with delight when they passed by friends but somehow remembered to keep their arms at their sides. Marisa smiled. This was an evening both girls would long remember. And so would she. Even though they hadn't spoken, Marisa had given her father a warm smile and had seen first his surprise, then his delight. The best was yet to come.

As the parade made its way at its traditional snail's pace, Marisa sniffed, then sniffed again. It was difficult to be sure, since the mask blocked much of her face, but she thought she smelled wood smoke. Someone must be using their fireplace tonight. Though almost everyone in Dupree came out for the parade, there were always a few—the bedridden and the curmudgeons—who stayed home.

The parade continued, following its traditional route from the park, east on Avenue N, south on Maple past the fire department and the bowling alley, west on H, and then north on Pecan back to the park. Altogether it was less than two miles, but those were two miles of pure excitement for the porcupine girls. Marisa heard their exuberant cries each time the float rounded a corner.

The ark was traveling west on H when Alice's cries of delight faded and she began to scream, her voice filled with panic.

"My house! My house is on fire!"

---

"You didn't need to do this, Blake."

He smiled at the petite woman whose auburn hair bore no trace of silver. Hilary was looking around the dining room of the small restaurant that had the reputation for serving the best steaks in three counties. "It's my pleasure. I consider it a small thank-you for your potato salad and a big thank-you for making my dad so happy. He's a lucky man to have you in his life."

Blake had liked Hilary from the moment he met her. With a ready smile and startling green eyes, she seemed years younger than the sixty-two Dad had told him was her true age. And watching the two of them together had only reinforced Blake's belief that this was the woman his dad was meant to marry.

"I'm the lucky one," Hilary countered. "I never thought I'd find someone like Gus."

Dad laid his hand on Hilary's. "That's enough. Blake doesn't want to spend the evening with two love-struck seniors."

"Actually, I do." It was heartwarming to see such a happy couple. "I want to get to know the lovely lady who's going to be my stepmother." Dad had proposed to Hilary last night, and they'd chosen her ring this morning. That was one reason Blake had insisted on taking them to dinner tonight: he wanted them to have an engagement party.

"There's not much to tell," Hilary said, giving Dad another of those smiles that announced she was as smitten as he.

"You taught school for forty years," Blake told her. "There must be a story or two in there."

There were. They were all laughing at one of Hilary's more amusing anecdotes when Blake felt a chill run down his spine. He blinked, trying to dismiss the feeling that something was terribly wrong, but it only intensified. He closed his eyes for a second, and as he did, Marisa's face flashed before him.

"She needs me."

———— ✳ ————

Marisa raced to the other side of the float and stared, horrified by the billows of smoke coming from the Hickory View apartments. This must have been what she'd smelled before. The north wind, even though it was little more than a light breeze, had carried the majority of the smoke away from town, leaving only a slight odor to waft toward the parade route. That and the fact that almost everyone in town was watching the parade explained why the fire had not been noticed before.

"My brother's there!" Alice shrieked, her voice filled with panic. "Liam's there!"

As Marisa remembered Susan Kozinski saying that her mother was caring for the sick baby, her heart began to pound. Surely Liam's grandmother had gotten him to safety, but if she had, why hadn't she called 911?

Marisa reached into her pocket and pulled out her cell phone. "Hickory View's on fire," she cried when the call went through.

At the same time, she heard Eric shout "Stop!" as he pounded on the truck's back window. Without waiting to see whether the driver heard him, Eric tossed his costume aside and ran to the tailgate, quickly lowering it and jumping off the ark. A second later, he was sprinting down the street. In the distance, the fire sirens began to wail.

Eric couldn't go alone. Marisa knew that. He couldn't stop the fire. Only trained firefighters could. Eric probably thought he could rescue Liam and the grandmother, but he didn't know which apartment was Alice's. Ripping off her costume, Marisa leapt from the float and raced toward Eric.

Marisa ran and ran, the five blocks feeling like five miles. She was more than twenty years younger, and she would have said she was in better shape, but no matter how fast she ran, she could not catch Eric. He raced as if his life depended on it, barreling down the street toward the burning building, his longer legs covering the distance faster than Marisa could.

Her legs ached, and the stitch in her side made her want to stop, but she could not.

Where were the fire engines? The sirens were still blaring, but they sounded no closer. She took another stride, trying to catch her breath as she realized what was happening. The fire truck that had been part of the parade was boxed in on Maple Street, unable to turn around. The other engine was probably unable to leave the station because of the crowds lining the street.

It would take less than a minute for the firemen to clear the road so the engines could move safely, but that might be too long. Memories of the fire chief speaking to her high school class and stressing that every second was critical raced through Marisa's brain.

And still Eric ran. Marisa was less than a block away when she saw him enter the building.

"No!" she screamed as he disappeared into the flames. "No, Daddy, no!"

# 33

I'm sorry, sir, but the last flight has left." The airline representative's voice registered no regret. Not that Blake had expected it. She was doing her job, and whether or not he could reach Marisa made no difference to her. He, on the other hand, was gripping the doorway in an attempt to keep his fear from escalating into panic. Marisa needed him. He knew that. And the fact that he'd been unable to talk to her only deepened his conviction that she was in trouble. That was the reason he was standing in the entry to the restaurant, trying to find a way to get to Texas.

Blake heard the click of keys. "I have one seat left on the early morning flight," the woman said. "Do you want me to reserve that for you?"

There weren't a lot of alternatives. Greg or Drew might have chartered a private plane, but Blake was not comfortable on small aircraft. Give him a 747 any day. "What time will that get me to San Antonio?"

After a second's delay the clerk said, "Ten oh seven, local time."

"All right." Blake recited his credit card number and waited for the confirmation, trying to convince himself that the delay would give him more time to call Marisa and find out his fears had no basis in reality. Worst case, he'd be in Dupree by noon. Marisa would be home from church, probably amused that he'd thought she needed help and that he'd come all that way on a wild goose chase.

Feisty, independent Marisa St. George never needed help. But deep in his heart, Blake didn't believe that. She needed his help, and more than that, she needed God's. Even if nothing was wrong—and Blake's gut told him something was—she needed God to help her with her relationship with her father and the anger that colored so much of her life. Blake began and ended each day with a prayer that Marisa would open her heart to her heavenly Father's healing, but now she needed more. He said a silent prayer that God would give the woman he loved whatever help she needed.

Shivering slightly as the door opened and another couple entered the restaurant, Blake tapped Marisa's number. Perhaps this time the call would go through. Once again he got voice mail. Once again he left no message. He'd keep trying, but if he hadn't reached Marisa by midnight, Blake would arrive on her doorstep and pray that he wasn't too late.

"Is everything all right, son?" his father asked when Blake returned to the table.

"I don't know. I can't reach Marisa."

It was possible she was ignoring his calls, but that didn't jibe with the feeling that something was terribly wrong. Though he had tried to convince himself that it was nothing more than his imagination, Blake had failed. Marisa needed him. No one could tell him otherwise. Perhaps it wasn't rational. Perhaps he should have called Lauren or even Kate to see what they knew, but Blake did not. Whatever was wrong was between him and Marisa and God.

"I hate to do this," Blake said as he spread the napkin on his lap and cut a piece of the steak that had seemed so delicious a few minutes ago. "I hate to desert you, but I'm going to Texas tomorrow morning."

His father and Hilary exchanged a look that said they'd expected this. "Will you be back for Christmas?"

"I don't know."

———— ✳ ————

She was almost there. Marisa took a breath, then choked on the acrid smoke. The building was enveloped in it now, dark billowing clouds that hid the entrances, obscuring the lights that had once shone from the windows. Now the only lights were sparks, shooting in all directions as beams tumbled and flames consumed more of the powder-dry wood. It was the most dangerous thing Marisa had ever seen, and somewhere in that inferno was Eric.

"Dad, where are you?" she screamed as she approached the burning building. "Get out!"

Behind her, the siren wailed then stopped as the fire engine reached the site.

"You need to get away, ma'am. It's not safe," one of the firemen shouted as he leapt from the truck and sprinted to Marisa's side.

Marisa shook her head. "I can't. They're in there."

"Who's in there?" a second firefighter demanded.

"At least three people. My father went in after a baby and a grandmother." Marisa's throat burned, but somehow she managed to force the words out. So much depended on the firemen finding Eric and the others in time.

"Where?"

She pointed to the second of the six entrances. "The first floor apartment on the right is the Kozinskis'." Though she couldn't explain how he'd known that was the place baby Liam and his grandmother would be, Eric had headed unerringly for that doorway.

The first fireman nodded, then began barking commands. The others responded in what seemed as well choreographed as a ballet. As water streamed onto the building and two firemen raced toward the doorway where Eric had disappeared, a crowd began to gather. Some of the townspeople shouted, others remained silent.

A collective gasp went up when the west end of the roof collapsed, sending sparks in every direction.

Marisa took a step backward, fixing her gaze on the burning building. *Keep him safe, dear Lord,* she prayed silently. *Keep them all safe.* It would take a miracle for anyone to have survived the fire, and yet she refused to give up hope.

As the first pair of firemen reached the doorway, two smoke-covered figures stumbled out. The man—Marisa could tell that much even from this distance—was doubled over, while the woman clung to the back of his sweatshirt.

"Daddy!" Her prayer had been answered. Eric was alive. Heedless of the firemen's shouts, Marisa raced toward her father. "What's wrong?" she demanded when she saw he was clutching his mid-section.

Coughing violently, he reached under his sweatshirt and pulled out baby Liam, handing him to the waiting fireman before his legs buckled and he tumbled to the ground.

"No!" Marisa screamed and lurched forward. He couldn't die. Not now. Not without knowing how much she loved him.

One of the bystanders restrained her. "You'll only be in the firemen's way. Trust God."

Marisa did, but that didn't stop her from wanting to be at her father's side. She had to know if he was still alive. Even with all the noise, there was no mistaking the sound of a baby's cry. Marisa gave a silent prayer of thanks. Though it was too soon to know how serious their injuries were, Liam and his grandmother were still alive, thanks to Eric. And then she saw it. It was nothing more than a clenching of his fist, but it was enough to tell Marisa that her father lived. As tears welled in her eyes, she sent another prayer heavenward.

For Marisa, the next few minutes seemed like controlled pande-monium. The firemen continued to fight the blaze, a pair entering each of the apartments to ensure that no one was trapped by the fire or overcome by smoke, while others pumped water onto the building.

Flashing lights and blaring sirens announced the arrival of the EMTs. After what seemed like only seconds of triage, they strapped Eric to a gurney. As one of the paramedics cradled Liam and another helped his grandmother into a police car, Marisa rushed toward them.

"Where are you taking them?" she demanded.

The paramedic who'd helped Liam's grandmother looked at Marisa. "The clinic. Doc Santos is waiting."

Marisa took a deep breath, regretting it the instant she did. The last thing her lungs needed was more smoke-filled air, but she couldn't help rejoicing. The fact that the patients would be treated locally rather than rushed to a trauma center was good news. Another prayer had been answered.

As the ambulance pulled away, Mom arrived with Alice and her parents. Alice was crying, and the three adults looked haggard, as if they'd aged ten years in the last ten minutes.

Sprinting to close the distance, Marisa stretched her arms out to her mother, uncertain who would comfort whom. All she knew was that she needed her mother's embrace.

"How is Eric?" The trembling in Mom's voice told Marisa how frightened she was. When Marisa had worried that Eric might leave again and that her mother would be devastated, she had never envisioned a night like this.

"I don't know. He couldn't talk, and the EMTs weren't answering any questions, but he's alive. That much I know."

Marisa turned to the Kozinskis while she patted Mom's back. "I think Liam's all right. He was crying, and the EMTs didn't look too worried. Your mother was disoriented. I heard her say something about a nap."

Susan began sobbing. "I should never have left Mom with the baby."

Her husband put his arm around her and offered words of comfort, while Alice kept a firm grip on her mother's hand, as if she feared being separated from her.

"Can you walk to the clinic," Marisa asked her mother, "or do you want me to get my car?"

"We'll drive," Bert Kozinski said. He let out a short, mirthless laugh. "If my truck hasn't burned up."

It hadn't. Since the apartment complex had no garages, residents parked on the street or in the lot behind the building. The fact that Bert had had to park a block away meant that his truck was safe and out of the area the police had cordoned off.

When they arrived at the clinic, Doc Santos's receptionist was at the desk. Dressed in her signature uniform of Betty Boop scrubs, she gave no indication that a few minutes ago she'd been one of the spectators at the parade.

"It shouldn't be much longer," she said, offering the adults coffee and Alice a can of soda.

Half an hour later, the doctor emerged from the back of the clinic, trailed by his nurse. During that time, Marisa had done everything she could to encourage the others, all the while battling her own fears. *He has to live*, she told herself. *If his condition had been life-threatening, they'd have airlifted him to San Antonio.* But doubts crept in. Until now. The smile wreathing the doctor's face told the story even before he spoke.

"Everyone's going to be fine. I'm keeping them overnight, but you can visit them."

"Thank you, doctor." *Thank you, God.* Marisa's prayers had been answered.

The Kozinskis ran in the direction the nurse pointed, and Mom started walking toward Eric's room. It was time to go, and yet Marisa held back, unsure of what she was going to say, unwilling to intrude on Mom's time with her husband. They needed time alone. Marisa's turn would come later. That was as it should be. Eric had been a husband before he was a father.

"C'mon, Marisa. He's waiting for us." Mom turned and beckoned to Marisa. When she hesitated, Mom grabbed Marisa's arm. "He's waiting for both of us."

Seconds later as they entered the small room, they found Eric sitting up in the hospital bed. Though he sported three bandages on his face and both hands were wrapped in gauze, his eyes were shining and his lips curved into a grin. He was alive. More than alive. He looked happier than Marisa could ever recall.

"Oh, Eric," Mom cried as she ran the few feet to his bedside and wrapped her arms around him. "I was so worried." Her English deserted her, and she murmured a few sentences of heartfelt Spanish that Marisa doubted her father understood. But there was no mistaking Mom's sincerity when she reverted to English and said, "I don't know what I'd do if I lost you again."

Eric stroked her head, his bandaged hands awkward but his expression tender. "You don't need to worry about that," he said, his voice raspy from the smoke he'd inhaled. "Doc says this old body's got a lot more years in it." Eric winked at Marisa, as if inviting her to join the celebration. "Doc said the baby's going to be fine too."

"Thanks to you." The lump of fear that had lodged in Marisa's throat had dissipated, replaced by a different set of emotions. Relief that Eric was safe mingled with worry about the conversation she needed to have with him. That would happen later. Now she wanted the answer to the question that had puzzled her from the moment she'd seen him disappear into the apartment complex. "How did you know where Liam was?"

Eric gave a little shrug, as if the answer were insignificant. "I fixed Bert's car once. I had to drop off a loaner while we waited for the parts." And though that had to have been close to a decade earlier, he'd remembered.

"You're a hero. You know that, don't you?" Mom asked, patting her husband's hand.

When he started to shake his head, Marisa nodded. "Yes, you are, Dad." The name came out as easily as if she'd been saying it all her life. And she had, deep inside. Marisa smiled at her father, noting the tears that welled in his eyes, tears that were mirrored in her own.

Mom gave her a long look, then rose. "I think I'll see if Doc's got any more coffee," she said as she strode to the door, closing it softly behind her.

"What was that all about?" Dad asked.

"Mother's intuition. She knew I wanted to talk to you." This wasn't the way Marisa had imagined the scene. She'd thought they might sit in the gazebo or even in Rainbow's End's beautiful lodge. Not once had she envisioned a hospital room and her father with bandaged hands and raw vocal chords. Perhaps she should wait until he could speak more easily, but now that she had been given the opportunity, she didn't want to waste it.

Marisa took the seat her mother had vacated and reached for her father's hand. "Mom wasn't the only one who was worried about losing you. When I saw you run into that building, all I could do was pray that I wasn't too late."

He started to speak, but Marisa shook her head, blinking back tears. "Please let me continue. There's so much I want to say. Most of all, I'm sorry for all the unkind things I've said and done to you. I love you, Dad. I didn't think so at the time, but now I know that I never stopped loving you. It's just that I was so afraid of being hurt that I pretended I didn't. I let anger blind me to the love I really felt."

Her father patted her hand, then cleared his throat. "I'm the one who needs forgiveness. You were a child. I was an adult who shirked his responsibilities. I won't try to defend what I did— there is no defense. But I will tell you that once I was sober, my prayer each morning and night was that you and your mother would forgive me and give me a second chance. Will you do that, Marisa?"

"Of course." She nodded as she leaned over and kissed his cheek. "I love you, Dad."

"And I love you." He gave her a hug, then stroked her hair with one of his bandaged hands. "I hear your mother's footsteps. She and I need some time together, and you . . ." He paused and smiled.

"I suggest you go out and do what you do best: find a way to turn this fire into a happy ending."

———— ✶ ————

Marisa stared at what had once been home for twenty-four families. In the bright midmorning sun, it looked worse than it had last night. The tape cordoning off the area only highlighted the piles of sodden mattresses and charred wood. It seemed that Marisa's fears had proven accurate. Nothing could be salvaged.

The families who had once lived here had lost everything: their homes, their personal belongings, their sense of security. Fortunately, as the minister had reminded them this morning, there had been no loss of life other than three goldfish. Hickory View's "no pets" policy had proven a blessing. So too had the parade, which had meant that most of the residents were out of the building.

Though the investigation was still incomplete, it appeared faulty wiring on a string of Christmas tree lights had caused the fire. The county fire marshal had arrived last night for a preliminary walk-through, and he was back now, searching what remained of Hickory View to rule out the possibility of arson.

One by one, the answers were coming. Liam's grandmother had admitted that she'd been tired, and so when the baby had gone to sleep, she'd turned off her hearing aids and had taken a nap. That was the reason she hadn't heard the smoke alarms. Though Susan had told Lauren she might never again trust her mother to babysit, Marisa suspected she would change her mind once the horror of last night faded.

It had been a hectic and yet surprisingly rewarding night. More pleased than she'd thought possible by her father's faith in her, Marisa had volunteered her services to the mayor. Working with him and the town council, she'd helped set up emergency housing in the school gym.

Residents had provided cots, blankets, and food, the basic survival needs, but no one had been able to answer the most critical question: what's next? There were no other apartments in Dupree, and none of the families had the money to purchase a home. Most were un- or underinsured, which meant that replacing their furniture, clothing, and other possessions would be difficult. And Christmas was only a few days away.

Though she had brainstormed with the others, they'd found no easy solutions. The town could hold a fund-raiser, but that took time, and time was one thing Dupree's least fortunate did not have.

———— ✳ ————

"Blake! What are you doing here?" Surprise and wariness crossed Lauren's face as she opened the door. Still clad in her Sunday church clothes, Lauren looked as if she'd slept as little as he had. Perhaps she'd worked late, trying to finish her Christmas orders. Blake had spent the better part of the night at Newark airport, not wanting to risk missing his flight.

"I'm looking for Marisa. She's not answering my calls." Blake had left her a voice mail once he'd made his reservations. There had been no response.

Lauren pursed her lips. "That's because her phone was run over by a fire truck. She's got mine now."

"I tried calling her a gazillion times, because I had this weird feeling, but . . ." Blake stared at Lauren as her words registered. "Did you say fire truck? What happened?"

Blake's confusion must have been evident, because Lauren's face softened. "That's right. You don't know. The Hickory View apartments caught fire during the parade last night. They were completely destroyed."

A shiver ran down Blake's spine. "What time was that?"
"Around 7:30."

Exactly the time he'd sensed that Marisa needed him. And she needed him now. He managed to call a brief thanks to Lauren as he raced back to his car.

Within a minute, Blake approached what used to be the town's apartment complex. His eyes scanned the area, his heart aching at the devastation. There she was, sitting on a bench across the street, staring at the cordoned area.

Blake pulled to the curb, switched off the engine, and sprinted toward Marisa. It was a measure of her concentration that she didn't seem to register his arrival until he called her name.

She turned, and as she did, Blake saw that her eyes were ringed with the same dark circles as Lauren's. But what caught and held his attention was the expression in those beautiful blue eyes. Something had changed—something fundamental—for the anger he'd seen there so often was gone, replaced by something he could only describe as radiance. There was only one possible explanation: Marisa had found the peace that comes from God. If that was true, and he believed it was, Blake's most fervent prayers had been answered.

"Blake!"

As she gave him a smile filled with hope, he opened his arms. A second later, Marisa rushed into them, letting him enfold her in his embrace. "It'll be all right," he crooned as he stroked the back of her head. "Together we'll find the answer."

## 34

Perhaps it was wrong to feel happy when so many of Dupree's residents were homeless, but Marisa couldn't help it. Her heart skipped a beat as she told herself it was true. She was in Blake's arms, and he was looking at her as if the trip to the goat farm and the angry words she'd hurled at him had not taken place. If it hadn't been for the stench of burned wood and smoky ashes, she might have thought she'd gone back in time. But she hadn't. Somehow, the one thing Marisa had thought impossible had happened. Blake had come to her.

"How did you know I needed you?" she asked when she could form a coherent thought.

There was no denying that Marisa needed Blake. Though a huge hole deep inside her had been filled last night when she and her father had been reconciled, an empty space remained in Marisa's heart.

When her brainstorming with the town council had produced no ideas for temporary and longer-term housing, Marisa remembered how she and Blake had worked together to resolve the problem with Rainbow's End's tablecloths. That had been simple compared to this, but Marisa was confident that Blake would have good suggestions. And even if he didn't, having him nearby would boost her spirits. That he was here when they'd parted so badly and that he'd said they would work together seemed like a miracle.

A hint of wonder filled Blake's eyes. "The only explanation I have is that God told me. I was sitting in a restaurant with my dad and Hilary, celebrating their engagement, when I knew you needed me. I tried to call you but got no answer."

Marisa nodded. "I dropped my phone. Something—probably one of the fire trucks—ran over it."

"Lauren told me, but it seems that's the least of your worries. What happened?"

As she recounted the events of the previous evening and her father's role in saving Liam and his grandmother, Marisa's eyes filled with tears. "I've never been so frightened. All I could think was that he might die without knowing how much I love him."

"But he didn't."

"No, he didn't, thanks to God." Marisa brushed away the solitary tear that was making its way down her cheek. Fixing her gaze on Blake, she said softly, "And thanks to God, you're here too. Oh, Blake, I'm sorry for the way I treated you. I wouldn't have blamed you if you never wanted to see me again."

"But I do. We've got a lot to talk about, and we'll do that later. Right now it seems to me you're facing an immediate challenge. Where will all those families live?"

Marisa laid her hand on Blake's cheek, grateful beyond words that he'd accepted her apology so easily. He was right. They would talk later, and that talk would be far different from the one at the goat farm.

"Housing is the question of the day." And one that Marisa believed Blake could help answer. "We set up an emergency shelter in the school gym, but that's not a long-term solution. There are no vacant houses in town, and although we've got more than our share of empty stores, it would take a lot of work to turn them into residences."

When Blake raised an eyebrow, she explained. "I know that because Drew considered buying a couple for his first employees. He said it probably wasn't cost effective to convert them. That's why he wants to extend Maple Street to the north and build some duplexes as well as his computer center there."

"Like an old-fashioned company town?"

Marisa nodded. "Sort of. The problem is, his houses are only a dream at this point."

Blake kept his arm wrapped around Marisa's shoulders as he led her back to the bench. Somehow he'd sensed that her legs were threatening to collapse. Too little sleep and too much stress had turned them into limp noodles.

"Will the owner rebuild Hickory View?"

Marisa shook her head. "That doesn't seem likely. The man who owns it is the former mayor. He's living in Austin now. Fortunately, his son is in Dupree and knows what happened." Marisa gave Blake a mischievous smile. "Remember how I told you I was dreading Hal Lundquist's visit? It turned out to be a blessing." She told him what had happened when Hal had met her father.

"Hal was at the parade," she continued. "When he realized what was going on at Hickory View, he called his dad to see what he should do. Mr. Lundquist claims he's tired of being an absentee landlord." Marisa shrugged. "I suspect he's going to collect the insurance money and then try to sell the land."

"Someone'll buy it."

Blake was more confident than Marisa. Even though the local economy was beginning to improve, Dupree wasn't an ideal investment.

"Maybe, but that doesn't solve the immediate problem. Those families need a place to live now. And who knows what the new owner would build? The rent might be more than they can afford."

Though the morning was surprisingly warm for late December, Marisa shivered, thinking about the winter to come and the now-homeless families.

Blake drew her closer, the warmth of his arms helping to dissipate the chill that had settled over her. "Affordable rent's a good point," he said, "but let's start with the immediate need: temporary housing. I doubt you can get FEMA trailers, but what about RVs? They're already furnished, and folks live in the bigger ones for months on end."

As she pictured some of the RVs she'd seen advertised, Marisa nodded. It was a good idea. It might even be a great idea. As she had hoped, Blake had identified a possibility she and the town council hadn't considered. Only one problem remained, and it was a big one.

"I like the idea, but there's still the issue of money. I doubt very many of the families could afford to buy an RV, new or used. Renting one might even be a stretch. When Lauren and Patrick wanted to take a camping vacation, they said rentals were exorbitant."

Marisa knew the expense of buying or renting RVs would make only a small dent in Greg's charitable foundation, but the town council had decreed that they would ask Greg for financial help only if they could find no alternatives. Everyone felt—and Marisa agreed—that Greg and Kate were already doing so much for Dupree that it would be unfair to ask for more. Still, Marisa suspected Kate and Greg would be unhappy if they couldn't contribute in some way. The question was how.

Blake refused to be discouraged. "I don't know about long-term rentals, but there's always year-end sales. If Texas is anything like Pennsylvania, dealers are eager to reduce inventory. Let's see what we can find."

He looked at the charred remains of Hickory View and frowned. "I think we've got another problem. Assuming we can get RVs, where can they be parked? It obviously can't be here."

Marisa thought for a moment, picturing the few vacant lots in Dupree. The area Drew wanted for his company required substantial grading before it would be usable. Even the park wasn't large enough to accommodate two dozen RVs unless they were practically on top of each other. While that might be acceptable for a brief vacation, it was a less than desirable solution for what could turn into a year's residence. There had to be an answer. Marisa closed her eyes, then grinned as she remembered the tax bill she'd just paid.

"Firefly Valley," she said. "It's flat, and though there are some trees, they're far enough apart that we could park RVs there."

Blake's grin matched hers. "Good idea. Who owns it?"

"That's the best part. It's part of Rainbow's End. Apparently, the first owners thought they might want to expand, so they bought ten acres on the opposite side of the road. Right now, it's just empty land. I'm sure Kate and Greg would let the RVs park there." That would be one way to have them involved in the project without asking them for money.

Blake smiled. "One problem down. Now we need to find some affordable RVs." He pulled out his phone and started to search for local dealers.

"Why don't we go to my office? We'll be more comfortable there." Marisa had come here looking for inspiration, and she'd found it. There was no longer any reason to stare at the ruined building.

As she and Blake entered the Rainbow's End lobby ten minutes later, they found Greg sitting behind the desk.

"You're back." Greg didn't look particularly surprised to see Blake. "I wondered how long you'd be able to stay away."

"Apparently it was long enough that you've found a new job."

Greg shrugged. "Everyone else is in town. Carmen insisted on cooking dinner for the . . ." He paused. "I can't figure out what to call them. Homeless? Victims? That sounds so depressing. Anyway, Carmen cooked, and the rest of the staff went along to help serve. Some of the guests are even helping." Greg frowned. "I've got to tell you, buddy, I wish Kate and I could do something. When I called the mayor to offer a donation, he just brushed me off."

Marisa nodded, suspecting that although the mayor had tried

to be diplomatic, he'd offended Greg. That wasn't the plan. "The town council thinks you've already done more than your share for the town," she explained. "I was there when they said they wanted to try to solve the problem without any more gifts from you. But," Marisa said, giving Blake a conspiratorial smile, "no one said anything about loans."

Greg grinned. "At very low interest rates."

"I was actually thinking about interest-free."

As Marisa explained what she and Blake were planning, she watched Greg's enthusiasm grow. "Of course you can use the land, and since we're so close, we can provide meals—at least for a few weeks until everyone gets settled. And, if you need that other kind of loan, just let me know."

As Greg called Kate to tell her what was happening and Marisa and Blake headed toward her office, Blake started to chuckle. "What do you bet that within two minutes, Kate will decide that the Hickory View people will celebrate Christmas here?"

Marisa glanced at her watch. Ninety-three seconds later, Kate appeared in the doorway to Marisa's office. "We're going to need more Christmas presents, but don't worry, Marisa. I'll take care of that. You and Blake worry about those RVs."

Once Kate had left, Marisa turned to Blake. "Kate and Greg do so much. I hope we don't have to ask them for money."

A curious expression crossed Blake's face, but his words were matter-of-fact as he said, "We won't have to. We'll find a way to make this affordable. First, let's see how much those RVs are going to cost."

Though it was early afternoon on a Sunday, it appeared that RV dealers never closed and that their owners worked on weekends. Marisa said a silent prayer of thanks when she reached the first owner and explained what had happened. "These people have lost everything," she concluded. "I wondered if you'd be able to offer us a discount."

The man's reply left her speechless. "I've got three of last year's model that I haven't been able to sell. You can have them for as long as you need them—no cost. The only thing I ask is that you let me put my dealer sticker on them. Maybe someone in Dupree will want to buy something from me."

Free! It was more than Marisa had dared hope for. Though the news was often filled with so many reports of wars, gun violence, and major thefts that viewers might believe there was no kindness left in the world, this man was proof that people did care about others.

"Mr. McIntyre, I don't know what to say other than thank you. What you've offered is extremely generous, and it'll make a huge difference to three families." Marisa felt tears of joy and relief begin to choke her throat. "Thank you, Mr. McIntyre. Thank you."

When she hung up the phone, she turned to Blake. "Did you hear that, Blake? He's going to lend them to us—free! I can't believe it."

"Why not? God's in the miracle business. It seems to me he's using Mr. McIntyre for this one."

"And all he wanted was a little free advertising." Marisa grinned. "I can do better than that. Will you call the next dealer? I want to write a press release. This is the perfect Christmastime human interest story."

"A modern *Miracle on 34th Street*?" Blake appeared faintly amused by the idea.

"Exactly. We may not have peace on earth, but Mr. McIntyre is doing his part for goodwill toward humankind."

"And with him as an example, the other dealers will want to jump on the same bandwagon."

Marisa nodded. "I hope so."

An hour later, they had promises for all twenty-four RVs, most of which would be delivered today, all of which were being offered free. The dealers had even anticipated a problem Marisa hadn't considered: transportation. When they'd heard what happened, in addition to offering RVs, the owners had volunteered to enlist friends to get those RVs to Dupree.

"You don't need me for a few minutes, do you?" Blake asked when the last RV had been accounted for. "I've got a couple things I need to do."

Marisa shook her head. Though she was curious about those errands and the fact that he wasn't sharing any of the details with her, something in Blake's expression kept her from asking where he was going. It didn't matter. What mattered was that Blake's idea had become reality. The Hickory View families would not be homeless much longer. Marisa turned her attention to getting the publicity the dealers—and Dupree—deserved.

She emailed the press release with the names of the participating dealers to the San Antonio newspapers and TV stations, then began follow-up phone calls. As she'd hoped, the human interest aspect of the story intrigued the editors and news anchors, and within half an hour Marisa had a promise from one of the TV stations to send a news team to record the delivery of the RVs.

She was giving the anchor directions to Firefly Valley when Blake returned. Though his expression remained neutral, Marisa saw a glint of excitement in his eyes. Whatever his mysterious errands were, it appeared they'd been successful.

"Do you need to check in with anyone?" Blake asked when Marisa hung up the phone. He was fingering his cell phone, as if he wanted to make a call, but with no cell coverage at Rainbow's End, that wasn't possible. If he'd made calls while he was gone, he'd either used the pay phone or driven to the top of Ranger Hill to get a signal.

"I was going to call the mayor," she told him. "He'll let the town council know what's happening, and they'll tell the residents."

Blake slid the phone back into his pocket. "Why don't we go in person? I want to see the mayor's face when he hears about the RVs."

So did Marisa, and she wasn't disappointed. The mayor's expression turned from admiration when he heard the idea of providing RVs in Firefly Valley to astonishment at the dealers' generosity.

"This is the best news Dupree has had since Greg and Kate bought Rainbow's End," he said.

"There's only one possible glitch," Marisa said when she explained that Greg had agreed they could park the RVs there for however long it took to find permanent housing and that he'd do what he could to get utility hookups expedited. "I'm not sure how the land is zoned."

As she'd expected, the mayor shrugged. "It doesn't matter. We'll write up a variance if we need to." He tapped his phone to call the head of the town council, asking him to tell the others they were needed at the school. "Let's announce the good news," the mayor said when he hung up the phone.

Blake and Marisa followed the mayor, parking a few yards away from the entrance to the school. Many of the Hickory View children were outside, burning off excess energy in the playground with a few adults supervising, while the other adults remained in the cafeteria, cleaning up after the midday meal. Though Marisa had thought her parents might still be there, one of the women said they'd gone to Lauren's.

Marisa frowned. It was because of her father's suggestion that she'd become involved in the residents' plight. He ought to be here to learn how it was being resolved. She picked up her borrowed cell phone and called Lauren. "Y'all might want to come to the school yard," she told Lauren. "There's going to be an announcement."

When Lauren had agreed that she, Drew, and Fiona would accompany Marisa's parents, Marisa raised her voice to be heard over the chatter. "The mayor wants everyone to come outside." Though she saw lines of worry form between several women's eyes, she didn't want to upstage the mayor. The man liked being the center of attention, especially when delivering good news.

It took longer than Marisa had expected to get everyone assembled, but she wasn't complaining, because by the time they were outside, her parents had arrived. They stood at the far edge of the crowd, one of Dad's bandaged hands resting gently on Mom's shoulder. Lauren and Drew were smiling at Fiona as she made her way to Alice's side. If it weren't for the lingering stench of smoke, this might have been any other Sunday afternoon. But it wasn't. The mismatched and ill-fitting clothes and the strained expressions bore witness to last night's drama.

When the last of the town council members arrived, the mayor picked up his bullhorn. "May I have everyone's attention?" Once the crowd was silent, he smiled. "I'm glad you're all here, because Marisa has something to announce."

# 35

Blake couldn't help smiling at the look of sheer horror on Marisa's face. This was the woman he loved—always ready to help others but unwilling to take the limelight. Once she recovered from the shock, Blake was certain she'd be a good spokesperson for their project. The announcement she was about to deliver would be received with cheers and unmitigated approval.

Blake wished he could be as certain about her reaction to his own announcement. Chances were she'd be uncomfortable, but that wouldn't stop him. He'd prayed about this, and he was confident it was God's will, just as it had been God's will that he come to Rainbow's End. Even the writer's block, which had seemed so terrible, had been a blessing. It was because of it that he'd met Marisa, that he'd changed the direction of his writing, and that soon he'd . . . His thoughts ended abruptly as Marisa gripped his hand, seeking support.

"You'll be fine," he whispered and pushed her toward the mayor.

---

"Me?" Marisa stared at the mayor as he handed her the bullhorn. She wasn't prepared to make a speech. It was one thing to sit around a table with clients and discuss tax returns, quite another to stand up in front of half the town and deliver a speech.

The mayor nodded. "It was your idea, Marisa. Your work. You should get the credit."

"But Blake was a big part of it."

Though she'd hoped he would accept the bullhorn, Blake shook his head. "You can do it," he said softly. "You can do anything you set your mind to."

That made twice in less than twenty-four hours that someone had expressed that level of confidence in her. Buoyed by their faith in her, Marisa took a deep breath, trying to calm the butterflies that had taken up residence in her stomach. She would pretend she was sitting at a conference table, addressing two or three clients. She exhaled slowly. She could do this. She *would* do this.

"I have some good news," Marisa began. When she finished her explanation, there was a round of cheers and applause. Marisa smiled and managed to make eye contact with several of the residents while she answered a few basic questions. When her gaze reached the back of the crowd, her heart lurched at the pride she saw on her father's face. The way he looked, you would have thought Marisa had won the Nobel Peace Prize.

"I don't want you to think this was all my idea," she said when the final round of applause died down. "It was actually Blake who suggested RVs, and he made most of the calls. Let's give Blake Kendall a big hand."

"Thank you," Blake said when the crowd was once more silent. "I'm happy to have been part of today's planning." Marisa noticed that although he did not use the bullhorn, Blake had no trouble being heard. "The RVs will give you a place to live while the new apartments are being built."

New apartments. What was he talking about? Marisa stared at Blake. He shouldn't be promising something that wasn't assured. Andrew Lundquist had already said he had no intention of rebuilding, and even if new buyers emerged, there were no guarantees that they would build another apartment complex. They might decide duplexes or single family houses would be a better investment.

"Blake," Marisa said, putting her hand on his to stop him.

He merely shook his head and continued. "It's too soon to have blueprints," Blake told the audience that was staring at him with a mixture of awe and disbelief, "but I can assure you that the new units will have everything you need. As the first tenants, you'll be able to select the carpeting and the kitchen appliances."

What was going on? Only an hour ago, they were arranging for RVs. Now Blake was promising new apartments.

"Sounds expensive," one of the men called out. "How much is this gonna cost us?"

Indeed. And who was going to build the apartments? It certainly wouldn't be Andrew Lundquist.

Blake slapped his forehead. "I forgot the most important part, didn't I? The rent will be the same as you've been paying."

"You're the one who's gonna rebuild Hickory View?" a woman asked, her voice mirroring the astonishment Marisa felt. Blake was certainly sounding as if this was his project. A dozen questions whirled through Marisa's head, the most important being *why*. Why was Blake doing this?

He shook his head as he addressed the woman who'd asked if he was the developer. "I'm not, but the St. George Building Foundation is."

Marisa's gaze shifted from Blake to her parents. They looked as mystified as she felt. Though the crowd murmured, as if trying to digest what Blake had said, Marisa started to sputter. He had gone too far. First he promised there would be new apartments; now he was claiming that they were going to be built by a non-existent foundation that just happened to have her family's name on it. What was going on?

"Blake," she protested, but once again he ignored her.

Keeping his gaze fixed on the audience, Blake continued to speak. "The decision hasn't been made, but I recommend that the new apartments be called the St. George in honor of all that family has done for Dupree. I haven't been here for a long time, but I've heard about all the kids' bikes and toys that were repaired for little or no cost and the delicious meals that just happened to be delivered when a family needed them. And at least two people owe their lives to a St. George. It seems to me that's a better name than Hickory View."

"Hear, hear!" The man who'd questioned the cost began to cheer.

Mom was staring at Blake as if she couldn't believe what she'd heard, and Dad's face was flushed, but they both looked pleased when the people standing next to them began to hug Mom and shake Dad's hand. Though the questions that raced through her mind had multiplied, Marisa could not argue with the pleasure Blake's suggestion had brought her parents. The years of whispered criticism seemed to be over, replaced by public recognition. All because of Blake.

When the cheering died down, Alice raised her hand as if she were in school. "Hey, mister," she shouted. "Can we have pets?"

As the crowd laughed, Blake nodded seriously. "We might be able to arrange that."

"Yay!" Alice pumped both fists into the air and twirled around, her enthusiasm translating into kinetic energy.

There were a few more questions for Blake to field, then the crowd began to disperse, the adults leaving in small groups and casting looks at Blake as they returned to the school. Their expressions reflected the same incredulity that Marisa felt.

"That was quite an announcement," the mayor said, clapping Blake on the back. "I want to hear all the details."

So did Marisa's parents. That was obvious from their expressions as they approached Blake.

"Sorry, folks," he said with a smile that betrayed not one smidgen of regret. "Marisa and I have a couple things to take care of, including finding spots for twenty-four RVs. We'll see y'all tomorrow."

We. He was acting as if they were in this together, when she was as mystified as the others.

"Talk to me, Blake," Marisa said as he led the way to his car.

"I will," he promised. "Once we get there."

*There* turned out to be Firefly Valley. When he'd parked the car and they'd walked a few yards from the road, Blake turned to Marisa. "Where do you want me to start?"

"How about the beginning? There's no St. George Building Foundation."

"Not yet," Blake agreed. "As soon as I get the paperwork filed, it'll be official."

Marisa stared at him. From the time he'd returned from his mysterious errands, he'd been acting in a very un-Blake manner. "I don't understand."

"You will. The fact is, you're responsible for the foundation. When you started talking about press releases and publicity, I knew what I had to do." Blake reached for her hand and threaded his fingers through hers. His touch was warm and reassuring, and the way he looked at her made Marisa's heart race.

"I should have seen it sooner, but we both know sometimes I need a nudge. You gave me that. Again." Blake's eyes were warm, holding a hint of amusement and something else, something Marisa couldn't quite identify, something that kicked her pulse up another notch.

"While you were on the phone with the newspapers and TV stations, I made a few calls of my own. Those were my errands, and I'm glad to say they were successful. The first was to Andrew Lundquist. As I'd expected from what you said, he was more than happy to sell the land. He called it an albatross."

"So Mr. Lundquist is willing to give you a fire sale—pun intended—on the land. That still doesn't explain how you propose to pay for the construction and for funding subsidized housing. The town can't afford any new taxes."

Blake paused to look at Marisa. "I know. That's where the foundation comes in. It'll be like the one Greg has for Rainbow's End, only in this case it's designed to help people who need a little assistance."

"I understand the concept." Marisa had set up a separate set of accounts for Greg's foundation so he could have a complete picture of its profits and losses and would understand how much he could afford to contribute to Rainbow's End. "What I don't understand is where that money is coming from and why you named the foundation St. George." Greg's foundation carried his name.

Blake gave her a smile. "The second call I made was to my agent. I told him I'd do the talk show circuit the way he's been begging me, so long as everyone knows the money is going to the foundation."

Marisa stared at Blake. She'd been shocked by his announcement of the St. George Building Foundation, but that surprise paled compared to this. Blake on TV?

Before she could say anything, he continued. "From what Jack has told me, the networks would be standing in line to be the first to interview reclusive author Ken Blake. Jack's also expecting a big spike in sales, so I'm planning to contribute those additional royalties to the foundation."

As the blood drained from her face, Marisa leaned against a live oak tree, her fingers gripping the rough bark. "You're going on TV?" she asked, still not believing what she'd heard. "You're going to reveal that you're Ken Blake?"

Blake shrugged. This was the man who'd declared that he would never give up his anonymity. Now he was going to reveal his identity on television so that he could give two dozen Dupree families new homes. If that wasn't a miracle, it was awfully close.

Blake shrugged again. "I'm not planning to tell them my real name, but my face will be on book covers and TV screens. It probably won't take long before people make the connection to Dupree and come here."

His lips curved into an engaging grin. "Some enterprising person who loves books and has a flair for numbers might want to open a bookstore and stock autographed copies." He gave her a piercing look that left no doubt about that person's identity.

Marisa had thought Blake had exhausted his supply of surprises, but he hadn't. "Are you suggesting I run a bookstore?" she asked.

"Why not? The town can use one. Think about the additional tax revenues, not to mention the fact that you can hire a couple employees and further boost the economy."

"But . . ." He was acting as if opening a store was easy.

Blake gave her another smile, this one obviously meant to convince her. "I'm confident you can do anything you set your mind to. Look at all you've done for Rainbow's End—and don't tell me that was in your job description, because the last time I checked, general managers don't make tablecloths and plan variety shows."

"You're going way too fast for me. I'm still grappling with the idea of rebuilding Hickory View."

"The store would be good for Dupree."

"I can't argue with that, but you sound like you're planning to stay here. Are you?" Marisa had never considered that. While it was true that he could write anywhere, she had assumed Blake would want to return to California. Now he was acting like a resident of Dupree.

"I want to, but that depends."

"On what?"

He smiled. "On who. On whom," he corrected himself. "On you." Blake's smile faded, and his expression became serious as he said, "I didn't answer your question about why I'm calling the foundation the St. George Building Foundation. You heard part of the explanation when I talked about naming the new apartment complex after your family, but there's more. I want to honor the woman I love. The full name will be the Marisa St. George Building Foundation."

Marisa stared at him, speechless. In all her dreams of love and happily-ever-after, she'd never expected it to be like this. In the romance novels she'd read, there had been moonlight and roses or at least a romantic setting. Suddenly Firefly Valley felt like the most romantic place in the world.

Blake reached for her hands and captured them in his. "I love you, Marisa," he said, his voice firm and steady, unlike her breath, which was still catching in her throat. "I know we have issues, but I also know that when we're apart I'm miserable."

"I'm miserable too," she said, remembering the weeks of their first estrangement and the days after their visit to the goat farm. "You were right. I needed to put my anger aside and forgive. More importantly, I needed to ask for God's help. I've done that, and he's given it to me."

A light breeze stirred the air while a squirrel scampered by, its cheeks filled with acorns. It was an ordinary day in Firefly Valley for everyone but Marisa. For her, it was the most extraordinary day of her life.

"I know it won't always be easy," she said, hoping Blake would understand, "but I'm going to conquer my anger. I had a counselor in Atlanta who helped me with anger management. Obviously, I can't go there, but she recommended someone in Blytheville that I plan to see."

When Blake nodded, his approval obvious, Marisa managed a small smile. "So many good things have been happening. You came back, I have a father again, and I feel like a new person."

His eyes brimming with love, Blake returned her smile. "Does the new Marisa love me?"

"She does. So very much." More than she had dreamt possible.

Blake tightened his grip on her hands. "Will you marry me?"

For a moment, Marisa thought she was dreaming. So much had happened in such a short time. Just a few hours ago, she'd been staring at the charred remains of Hickory View, wondering what she could do to help the residents. Then Blake had arrived, bringing a plan to provide the victims with better homes than they'd ever had. That would have been wonderful enough, but being here with him, seeing the love in his eyes, made this the best day Marisa could imagine.

And now this. Blake loved her. He loved her enough to give up his anonymity to help her hometown. He loved her enough to marry her despite her problems. All of Marisa's dreams had just come true.

She smiled at him, hoping he would see the love shining from her eyes. "Oh yes, Blake. I will marry you."

Slowly, as if he had all the time in the world, he dropped her hands, then drew her into his arms and lowered his lips to hers. His lips were soft and tender, their touch sending sparks of excitement through her veins. As his arms drew her closer, Marisa reveled in the warmth of his embrace. How had she ever doubted that this was the man God meant for her? Here was Blake, giving her the sweetest of kisses, one that promised love and laughter, hope and happiness.

"Will you share your future with me?" he asked when they broke apart.

There was nothing Marisa wanted more, for she knew that future would be strengthened by their shared faith. "I will."

Blake lowered his head and pressed another kiss on her lips.

"Will you love and cherish our children if God blesses us with them?"

Marisa nodded again, smiling as she pictured a small boy with Blake's features chasing an even younger little girl who had her father's hazel eyes and mischievous grin. "I will."

Her smile widened as she thought of everything that had brought them to this point. Mom had been right that first day when she'd claimed Marisa had met the man she was going to marry.

"I love you, Blake, and I always will." Marisa looked up at him, her smile turning into a grin. "I could spend the rest of the day telling you how much I love you, but I'd rather show you." She puckered her lips for a kiss.

Blake did not disappoint her.

# Author's Letter

Dear Reader,

I hope you enjoyed Marisa and Blake's story and that you're looking forward to spending more time at Rainbow's End, because there's a third Texas Crossroads book.

Did your heart ache when you read about Gillian's accident and the end of her career as a concert pianist? Mine did, which is why I'm giving Gillian a second chance at happiness. When she accepts Kate's offer to spend a few weeks at Rainbow's End, the last thing she expects is to meet a man like TJ Benjamin. From his scruffy appearance to his motorcycle, he's the last man she wants as part of her life. For his part, TJ has no intention of getting involved with any woman, especially a fancy East Coast woman like Gillian.

If you're intrigued, I hope you'll read the teaser chapter at the end of this book. Gillian and TJ's story, On Lone Star Trail, will be available in spring of 2016. And, if you haven't already read the story of how Kate and Greg acquired Rainbow's End, At Bluebonnet Lake is available wherever books are sold.

As those of you who've read Bluebonnet *know*, *I enjoy sharing my favorite recipes, and so I wanted to give you another one. I'll admit it's not a summer staple, but when the temperatures drop, I turn to comfort foods like the vegetarian chili Carmen serves to Rainbow's End's guests.*

---

## *Vegetarian Chili*

Combine and simmer for 15 minutes:

| | |
|---|---|
| 28-oz. | can of tomatoes, undrained |
| 8-oz. | can tomato sauce |
| ½ cup | water |
| 1 tbsp | chili powder (or more, if you prefer a hotter chili) |
| 1 tbsp | dried onion flakes |
| ½ cup | dried cranberries |
| 1 12-oz. package | frozen winter squash, thawed |
| 1 12-oz. | package chopped spinach, thawed |
| 1 15-oz. can | black beans, drained and rinsed thoroughly |
| 1 15-oz. can | corn, drained |

Makes 8 servings. Carmen serves this with cornbread, and so do I.

---

*If you try the chili, please let me know what you think. And, of course, I look forward to hearing your reaction to Marisa and Blake's story. One of my greatest pleasures as a writer is hearing from you.*

*Blessings,*
*Amanda Cabot*

# Acknowledgments

Writing may appear to be a solitary task, and for the most part it is, but writing "the end" is only the beginning. It took a team to turn my raw manuscript into the book you hold in your hands. I am blessed to have not just any team but a truly talented one at Revell. Vicki Crumpton and Kristin Kornoelje are, at least in my mind, the perfect editors—two women who gently point out the flaws in my manuscript and work with me to correct them. Lindsay Davis and Claudia Marsh are tireless in their efforts to find new ways to market and promote my books. Cheryl Van Andel consistently gives me "to die for" covers. And they're only the proverbial tip of the iceberg. In addition to them, there are countless other people, all of whose contributions are essential to making each book the best it can be. I am deeply grateful to each and every one of them.

I would like to extend special thanks to Chief Max Konz of the Bandera, Texas, Volunteer Fire Department. When I was writing the fire scenes, I realized how much I didn't know about firefighting. Fortunately, Chief Konz was willing to take time out of his already busy schedule to answer my questions. I suspect some of them were so basic that he was tempted to laugh, but he was polite enough not to do that. I thank Chief Konz for sharing his time and expertise with me. Any mistakes are mine alone.

Keep reading for a sneak peek
of the next book
in the
TEXAS CROSSROADS
SERIES

On Lone Star Trail

Available
Spring
2016

*Relax.* Gillian Hodge forced her fingers to stop gripping the steering wheel as if it were a lifeline. There was no reason to be so tense. This wasn't her Carnegie Hall debut or the finals of the Brooks competition when so much was riding on the outcome. This was a vacation, for Pete's sake. A week with her best friend and the woman who'd been a surrogate grandmother. She should be filled with anticipation, counting the minutes until she arrived, not wound as tightly as a metronome.

Gillian took a deep breath, exhaling slowly. In, out. In, out. The technique had never failed when she'd used it before performances, and it did not fail now. She could feel her neck and shoulder muscles relaxing as she repeated the slow, even breathing. The tension began to drain, and for the first time since she'd left the freeway, Gillian looked at her surroundings rather than concentrating on the highway.

Kate was right. The Texas Hill Country was particularly beautiful in the spring. It had been lovely when she'd been here for Kate's wedding last September, but the fresh green of spring grasses and leaves and the patches of vividly colored wildflowers turned what had been simply lovely into something spectacular. No wonder Kate kept raving about her new home.

Though it was still difficult to believe that Kate, a dyed-in-the-wool city girl like Gillian, had given up a major promotion and traded a seemingly glamorous life as an advertising executive to run a small resort in the middle of Texas, that was exactly what had happened. Of course, the presence of one particular man had a lot to do with Kate's decision. She had come to Texas almost literally kicking and screaming and had discovered true love.

Gillian's smile faded. Despite her father's seemingly endless advice that marriage was what Gillian needed, love wasn't the reason she was headed toward Rainbow's End. She wasn't looking for love, just a change of scenery and a chance to rest after months of physical therapy had not accomplished their goal. Her dreams had been crushed—literally—leaving her no choice but to build a new life. At this point, Gillian had no idea of what the future would bring other than that concert stages would not be part of it. All she knew was that after six months of concentrating on what she could no longer do, it was time to discover what other talents she had. But before she did that, she wanted time with the people who'd known her before her name ever graced a marquee.

*Breathe in. Breathe out. Focus on the progress you're making, not what you can't do. The scars will fade, and so will the memories.* Brushing aside the memories that had so far refused to fade, Gillian scanned the roadway, smiling when she saw what appeared to be an armor-plated animal lumbering along the shoulder. Who wouldn't smile at an armadillo? They looked like something out of prehistoric times, not the twenty-first century. Though she thought they were supposed to be nocturnal, what did she know? Other than her weekend trip for Kate's wedding, the only parts of Texas Gillian had seen were airports, hotels, and concert halls. There were no armadillos there, other than the stuffed varieties in airport gift shops.

The chuckle that curved her lips upward died as she glanced in the rearview mirror. It couldn't be. Not now. Not here. Gripping the steering wheel so tightly her knuckles whitened, Gillian stared at the approaching vehicle. The bright red motorcycle, the black-clad rider, the black and red helmet were indelibly etched in her memory along with the damage they had wrought.

She bit her lip, trying to tamp down the fear. It couldn't be the same one. *That* motorcycle was almost two thousand miles away. There must be hundreds, perhaps thousands, of men in black leather riding red motorcycles. There was no reason to believe this was the one who had changed her life.

He was going faster now, that horrible red machine eating up the distance between them. Maybe it was the same motorcycle after all. *That* one had been going too fast. Though the police had cited the rider for excessive speed, they'd also claimed the crash was an accident. An accident that would haunt Gillian for the rest of her life.

She slowed the car, wanting the bike to pass her. The sooner it was out of her sight, the better. Dimly, she was aware of clouds blocking the sun. In mere seconds, the day—like her mood—had gone from bright and sunny to ominously dark. It wasn't an omen, a portent, or a warning. It was simply a change of weather. And yet Gillian could not tamp back the sense of foreboding. She flinched as a crack of thunder split the sky and the deluge began. Within seconds, the pavement had gone from dry to wet. And still the motorcycle continued.

He was in the left lane now, getting ready to pass her. Gillian's eyes widened and her heart began to pound. No! Not again! No!

---

He probably shouldn't have detoured. TJ Benjamin frowned as he headed north. Deb would never have done it. She made plans, developed itineraries, and followed them. Deb did not detour, and none of her plans involved a motorcycle or sleeping under the stars. As much as she loved traveling, she also loved her creature comforts. That's why she'd insisted on a Class A motorhome equipped with air-conditioning and a microwave. There was no roughing it for Deb. But Deb wasn't here, and that meant there was no reason not to detour.

TJ gave the throttle another twist. Speed might not be the cure for everything, but it did help clear away melancholy. So did the countryside. He was deep in the heart of his home state on a beautiful early April day. If only he let himself, he could find reasons to smile.

As if on cue, a hawk soared above him, looking for an afternoon snack and making TJ grin as his stomach rumbled. He could use a snack himself, something warm instead of the energy bars that had become a staple of his diet. He'd stop in the next town and see what was available. Meanwhile, he was going to enjoy the detour.

He leaned back and started to relax. Though he'd traveled many of the state's highways, TJ had never explored this part of the Hill Country. The plan had been to continue on US 90 heading west. If he'd followed that plan, he would have reached Big Bend today. Instead, when he'd seen the sign pointing toward Dupree, the town that claimed to be the Heart of the Hills, something had urged him to turn, so here he was, heading north. The old TJ wouldn't have done that. But, like Deb, the old TJ was gone.

So what if he was a day or two late getting to Big Bend? The park wasn't going anywhere. There was no reason to rush. It wasn't as if he had anyone waiting for him or had anything planned after that. Big Bend was the last item on the bucket list. Once he'd seen it, he would . . .

TJ frowned. The problem was that he didn't know how to finish the sentence. His frown turned into a wry smile as he felt a moment of sympathy for his former students with their complaints about open-ended questions. Multiple choice quizzes were definitely easier.

The hawk, more single-minded than TJ, swooped down and landed on the ground, its head diving into a hole. It appeared the hawk had found its prey.

Focusing on the highway in front of him, TJ noticed a light blue sedan in the distance. It had been little more than a speck when he'd seen it from the top of the last hill, but it was much larger now. Judging from the speed with which he was catching it, it must be going less than the speed limit. Probably some tourists looking for the Hill Country's fabled spring wildflowers. If that's what they wanted, they'd come to the right place. Bluebonnets carpeted the meadows, their color providing a vivid contrast to the green hills.

TJ had seen his share of bluebonnets, but these were extra special. Though his stomach was protesting his decision, he pulled off the road and grabbed from his saddlebags the digital SLR that had cost more than a month's pay. As he rotated the polarizing filter to deepen the hue of the flowers, TJ scowled at the realization that a dark cloud was approaching. At this time of year, a cloud like that could mean a thunderstorm, and that was one thing he didn't want to experience. He probably shouldn't have stopped, but the bluebonnets were as enticing as the road itself had been.

While his head told him to skip the pictures, his heart rejoiced at the sight of the deep blue flowers with the white and yellow tips, and he carefully composed the shots. It might be foolish. It wasn't as if he was going to try to sell the photos. That had been Deb's dream, not his, and yet he couldn't deny the pleasure of composing a picture that lifted his spirits and made him happy, if only for a moment.

With the camera once more safely stowed, he climbed onto the bike and headed north, determined to reach Dupree before the rain began. The last sign had said it was only ten miles farther. With a little luck, he could get there and find shelter from the storm that seemed to be gaining on him. The thought had no sooner lodged itself in his brain than the clouds opened and the deluge began.

As raindrops dotted his windshield and slid down his helmet, TJ shook his head. He should have known this would happen. It was just another in the string of bad things that had formed his life for the past eighteen months.

The blue sedan was only a short distance in front of him now, rooster tails rising from its rear tires. TJ hated rooster tails. They weren't a problem in an RV or even in a car, but they did nasty things to a motorcycle, throwing dirty water on the windshield and reducing the already lowered visibility. There was only one solution.

A quick twist of the throttle and he'd accelerated enough to pull into the left lane. It would take no more than a couple seconds to pass the car. Only one person inside, he noticed as he approached the sedan. A woman. And then the only thing TJ noticed was that his bike had begun to hydroplane.

Braking did no good. The bike had a mind of its own, and right now that mind was making it slide. *Please, God*, he prayed as he attempted to keep the bike upright. *Keep me from hitting the car*. Though God hadn't answered his other prayers, this time was different. The bike slid past the car's front fender, then skidded into the guardrail. The next thing TJ knew, he was flying over the handlebars.

——————✳——————

No! No! No! Gillian stared in horror as the motorcycle crashed into the guardrail, catapulting the rider into the air. With memories of another motorcycle on another day flashing before her, she stomped the brakes. Oh, how she hated motorcycles! They were nothing but trouble. Big trouble.

Switching on her emergency flashers, Gillian backed up slowly until she was next to the bike, then shifted the car into park. The rain had stopped as suddenly as it began, but the damage was done. The bike had crashed, and the rider . . . She grabbed her cell phone, frowning at the absence of bars. Kate had joked about the spotty cell service, but this was no joking matter. The rider could be seriously injured, just as she had been.

Forcing the painful thoughts aside, Gillian climbed out of the car and approached the guardrail. Deliberately averting her gaze to avoid looking at the bike, she stared at the rider.

"Are you all right?" Gillian called to the man who was lying motionless on the ground. *Please, Lord, let him be all right*. Though she'd spent more than her share of time in hospitals, she knew nothing about CPR and almost as little about first aid.

She started to climb over the guardrail, but as she did, the motorcyclist stood. *Thank you*, she said silently. The man appeared to be checking various body parts as he shook first one arm then another before repeating the process with his legs. It was only when he extended his left hand a second time and winced as he clenched the fist that Gillian felt herself grow weak. Not him too!

"Just bruises," he announced. His voice was brusque, almost as if he was unaccustomed to talking aloud. Or perhaps it was the effort of pretending he wasn't injured. Gillian was certain that, even if his only injuries were bruises, they were painful ones.

As he pulled the helmet off his head, she saw that his dark brown hair was long enough to be restrained in a ponytail and that he sported a beard that sorely needed trimming. If she'd had to describe him in one word, it would be scruffy. And then she saw his eyes. Almost as dark brown as his hair, they were so filled with sorrow that Gillian felt tears well in hers. Something had hurt this man deeply, and her instincts told her it was not having crashed his bike.

"Are you sure?" she asked, surprised that her voice sounded so calm. Inside she was anything but calm. Just the sight of a red motorcycle was enough to send her into a mild panic, and one with a crumpled front fender brought back memories that still had the power to paralyze her.

"I was going to call 911, but there's no cell service." She held up her phone.

The man shook his head as he bent to inspect his bike. "There's nothing the EMTs can do. They can't fix this." He pointed to the front wheel. The fender had been bent so severely that it had cut the tire. Gillian glanced at the bike. Even if he'd somehow been able to straighten the fender, the man was carrying no spare tires.

"It's not going anywhere," he said, confirming her thought.

Though the sun was once again warming the air, Gillian shivered. She'd come to Texas to relax, to try to forget about motorcycles and the damage they could do, and here she was, only feet from another motorcycle crash.

Instinct urged her to flee, and yet though she wanted nothing to do with motorcycles or the men who rode them, she could not. Even though she owed this man nothing more than a call to the closest repair shop once she got a signal, she couldn't let him stand here waiting for a truck to rescue him. What if his injuries were more serious than he believed and he collapsed? He might still be in shock and unaware of how badly he'd been hurt. Gillian knew that was possible, because the full scope of pain hadn't hit her until she'd been in the ambulance, being rushed to the ER.

"Where were you headed? I'd be glad to take you to the next town." Glad was an exaggeration, but Gillian knew she couldn't abandon this man.

As he straightened, she revised her first impression. He was taller than she'd thought, probably six feet, and though it was hard to tell through the leather, he seemed to be well-muscled.

The man nodded in what seemed like a grudging response to her offer. "The next town's where I was headed. Dupree. The place that advertises itself as the Heart of the Hills."

A frisson of something—apprehension, excitement, Gillian wasn't sure which—made its way down her spine. It was probably a coincidence that he had the same destination. "That's where I'm going too. A friend of mine owns the resort there. Is that where you're staying?"

It wasn't Gillian's imagination that he stiffened. "All I wanted was an afternoon snack. Now it's looking like I'm going to need some repairs. Expensive repairs," he muttered so softly she almost didn't hear him.

As another car drove by, Gillian was tempted to flag it down and ask the driver to take care of the man who seemed as prickly as the cactus that lined the highway. Instead, she forced herself to smile as she said, "I don't know about repairs, but Kate can provide that snack and a nice warm, dry cabin."

"I'm afraid not."

The way he was balking made Gillian suspect that money was an issue. What he didn't know was that it wouldn't be an issue at Rainbow's End. Kate and her husband had a sliding rate scale, and on numerous occasions that scale slid all the way to zero. But it wasn't Gillian's place to tell the stranger that.

"You're wet, you're hurt, and your bike is in even worse shape. Let's get you to Rainbow's End and sort the rest of it out there."

"Are you always so bossy?" The man took a step toward her, his halting gait proof that he'd done more than bruise himself. Gillian wouldn't be surprised if he'd pulled a ligament or suffered one of those deep tissue bruises that some people claimed were worse than broken bones.

"What if I am?" she asked. "It doesn't look as if you've got a lot of alternatives."

"Good point." He stared at his bike for a moment, indecision etched on his face, then limped toward it. Opening one of the saddlebags, he pulled out a backpack and tossed it onto the backseat of Gillian's car, then opened the driver's door for her.

"Thanks, Miss . . ." As he extended his hand for a shake, he let his voice trail off, clearly expecting Gillian to offer her name.

"Hodge," she said. "Gillian Hodge. And you're . . ."

The man's shake was firm, and if he noticed that she winced ever so slightly at the contact, he said nothing. "I'm TJ Benjamin, and as you can see, I'm having a very bad day."

"It could have been worse," she said bluntly. "You could have hurt an innocent bystander."

Dreams have always been an important part of **Amanda Cabot**'s life. For almost as long as she can remember, she dreamt of being an author. Fortunately for the world, her grade-school attempts as a playwright were not successful, and she turned her attention to novels. Her dream of selling a book before her thirtieth birthday came true, and she's been spinning tales ever since. She now has more than thirty novels to her credit under a variety of pen names.

Her books have been finalists for the ACFW Carol Award as well as the Booksellers' Best and have appeared on the CBA bestseller list.

A popular speaker, Amanda is a member of ACFW and a charter member of Romance Writers of America. She married her high school sweetheart, who shares her love of travel and who's driven thousands of miles to help her research her books. After years as Easterners, they fulfilled a longtime dream and are now living in the American West.

# MEET
# Amanda Cabot

## VISIT
# AmandaCabot.com
to learn more about Amanda,
sign up for her newsletter,
and stay connected.

"Crafting characters rich with emotion, Amanda Cabot pens a compelling story of devastation and loss, of healing and second chances. But most of all, of transcending faith."
—Tamera Alexander, bestselling author

"One thing I know to expect when I open an Amanda Cabot novel is heart. She creates characters that tug at my heartstrings, storylines that make my heart smile, and a spiritual lesson that does my heart good."
—**Kim Vogel Sawyer, bestselling author**